KARMA

Sarah Michelle Lynch

For the deep thinkers,
like Freya

KARMA

a

novel

"Even chance meetings are the result of karma... Things in life are fated by our previous lives. That even in the smallest events there's no such thing as coincidence."

Haruki Murakami

Chapter One

The Truth

He's the man of my dreams. Six foot. Cloudy green eyes. Dark brown hair. Divine hands. The best shoulders. Full butt. Cut chest and amazing cock. Sumptuous mouth and dimpled chin, cheekbones you could grate parmesan on. Mediterranean complexion, strong thighs and bulging calves and no hairy toes. What's not to love? There's everything to love. He's wonderful. From his body to his laugh to his soul, his heart and the way he loves me—everything is to die for.

It's been one week since he rode back into my life (literally on a motorcycle) and we haven't spent a second apart since. Even my brother who's newly loved-up himself had to leave the house and go stay with his new girlfriend or he was going to vomit at our displays of affection. Ruben never cares who's looking or where we are. Sometimes he'll bite my nipple over my top in a supermarket. Or we'll be wandering around town and he'll have his hand down the back of my jeans, resting on my bare bottom. It wasn't like this before but that's not to say I'm complaining. I keep telling myself it's just that he's freed from the prison his father created for him—that's why he's publicly mauling me this time around.

I'm watching him do laps of the pool while I sip my morning probiotic smoothie. The dogs Sooty and Sweep are avidly spectating from the pool edge, desperate to join their master but no way brave enough to get wet. In just a week, those dogs have changed their allegiance and given up their hearts to Ruben. Perhaps they're gay dogs. It would figure. Or perhaps just that Ruben is a more attentive pet owner, I don't know. I'm wearing my black and white polka dot bikini and a wide straw hat and to be honest, I'm not going to complain that my dogs love him more than me. He's the reason I'm living this life. He's my reason for even existing. My mind turns back to that night, a week ago, when I'd just had a bad date with a beautiful man called Rafi who drove a Ferrari but didn't know how to seduce a woman like me.

Ruben showed up, the news about Freddie having reached him, obviously. I climbed on the back of his bike without a second thought. We rode out of Nice and down the coast, heading west, and eventually we found a place to stop. It was almost midnight, the insects were humming, and we stood on a clifftop overlooking the shimmering velvet sea, yachts floating on the water, moon high in the sky, the heat of another delirious hot night drifting around us. The ride had been exhilarating but standing looking out at the water was just as life-affirming.

Ruben looked like he had the first time we got together, with his shaggy hair returned and his beard. During his exile he cut off all his hair and bulked up to epic proportions. Now he seemed back to 'normal'. I had dozens and dozens of questions, but none that seemed to really matter. He seemed sad and shocked I'd climbed on his bike, that I still wanted and needed him as much as ever, and he even appeared a little ashamed as he looked at me, eyes twitching at the corners.

"Why have we stopped here?" I asked. "The view is great, but..."

"I, uh, wondered if you wanted... to talk. It's a good spot. Not that I'm looking to be chucked off a cliff tonight. I just wondered... maybe we could clear the air before we decide where to go next."

I tried not to laugh because he sounded so nervous. "Did you kill him?"

"No," he exclaimed.

"So, what were you going to do? Wait forever."

Ruben looked at the floor. "I don't know."

"You do know."

He shook his head, looked up and betrayed resignation, defeat... something else, too.

"I know that I'm here. I'm not seeing anyone. You're not seeing anyone. That's what I know," he said, shrugging, "and it's safe. He's gone. This is just fate, Freya. That's what this is."

The woman he was looking at was no longer twenty-eight and naïve, nor desperately seeking escape or anything like the person I used to be. I'm now thirty-two, rich, more experienced, mellower... myself. Still batshit crazy, beneath, of course. Also, still as sharp as a tack.

"I ought not to forgive you for what you did the last time you were here."

"You don't have to forgive me," he said, seeming cool, "but we could just move past it and find out what we could have right now."

"As you once said, Ruben, I am a special woman. However, I'm not that special. I'm human. I've moved on. I've lived a life while you've been gone. I've suffered, yes. I've mourned so much more than you could ever know. I've clung to stupid fantasies but I've eventually thrown them out like ashes into the sea." I mimicked that motion. "If we were to have anything now, it'd have to be real. Not like it was back then. Scary and crazy and hurtling at a hundred miles an hour. Do you know what I'm saying?"

He flicked one eyebrow up. "Does that mean we're going back to yours or mine?"

"My brother is on a promise. Let's go back to mine."

We climbed onto the bike and I wrapped my arms tight around his waist, the heat of his body exuding through the cotton of his shirt. I had to trust we wouldn't crash because aside from our helmets, he was wearing just a t-shirt and jeans and my only clothing was a thin dress.

We made it back to my house and I walked inside as he followed. Since he was last at the villa, I'd changed a few things but it was largely the same. Four years had passed and, in some way, it felt the same, but in other ways, so different. Who was he now? Because I sure as shit was different to the girl he knew before.

"Do you want a drink?" I asked.

"Please."

"Wine, something cold? Hot? What can I get you?"

"Whatever you're having," he said.

I stood at the open fridge wondering what to drink when I spotted him out of the corner of my eye, transfixed by the view out the back. He was staring at one of the things I'd definitely worked on since he was last here. The garden.

"It's looking good, right?"

"Amazing," he whispered, overawed.

I grabbed the remote so the sliding patio doors opened and he could walk outside and see for himself. It was dark but there are solar lights everywhere so you can still see your way around the garden most nights—especially helpful with two dogs who occasionally get lost when you send them out for a late-night pee.

From the pool area, you take steps down to the lawn and surrounding the lawn is a wide border filled with all kinds of flowers, trees, ornaments and trelliswork burgeoning with life. I pride myself on having created a haven for birds, bees and the occasional reptilian friend. The dogs these days don't go in the borders because of that one time they came upon a little brown snake which had been taking shade beneath a peony tree.

I poured two glasses of Malbec and took them outside, joining him on the lawn, my shoes kicked off by this point.

"Where are the dogs?" he asked.

"They're at the doggie spa. The ladies love them so much, they offered to have them overnight."

"Sweet," he chuckled. "Wasn't because you thought you might get lucky tonight?"

I couldn't help but bark out laughing. "No. I sometimes just don't have anything better to do than have dinner with a good-looking man, that's all. Rafi wasn't my type, trust me. He was just a nice guy to pass the time with. And you never know who these people are friends with. The connections around here are endless."

"And your type is?" he asked.

"Oh, my, god, Ruben," I chuckled throatily. "What the hell happened to you?"

I turned to see his face, lit up by the solar lights, but it was the moon giving me the better outline of him, being that she was still hugging the sky above us. He looked beautiful. Haunted, but the same.

"I've been busy," he said, "but I've not been totally absent. I know you've dated since we, you know..."

"Stalker."

He shrugged his shoulders.

I raised my eyebrows. "So... you haven't?"

He shook his head.

That explained the nerves, then.

"Whyever not?" I shrieked. "Good lord, Ruben."

The thought of Ruben Kitchener going without sex for four years because of me... almost sent me doolally and dropping my knickers already.

He moved towards my redwood arbour, its trellised arch showcasing my pungent, sweet red roses. I naturally moved with him, joining him on the bench, my scarlet dress almost matching the flowers. It wasn't a slutty dress, rather conservative actually, but the criss-cross straps at the back were a little sexy.

I crossed my ankles and stared into my wine, the solar fairy lights behind us on the garden wall lighting the scene.

"What is it you want to say, Ruben?" I sensed he was holding something inside.

"It's been a really tough few years for me, Frey."

"Okay."

He gulped back a large mouthful of wine. "I helped the police wrap up everything regarding my dad and Freddie. That took a few months, even after Freddie was sent down."

"Well, I thought as much."

"And then..."

"Alexia?" I guessed.

He looked at me with the saddest eyes and the most tender smile. "You knew?"

"She wouldn't answer my calls anymore. I knew you'd be together."

He broke down crying. I don't know why, even now. I have no idea why that made him react so out of character.

I took his glass from him and put both of the wines on the small drinks table next to the bench. I wrapped my arms around his shoulders and he pulled me close, gathering me to him, his face pushed deep into my hair. I ran my fingers through his thick mane and soothed him, "It's okay, baby. It's okay."

He got it out of his system, then he wiped his wrist over his eyes and sniffed back tears. I put my hands over his and he looked me in the eye.

"She's okay now, Freya. That's all I want to say about that, okay?"

I licked my lips, my mouth suddenly so dry. "She was ill?"

"I don't want to talk about it just yet," he said, casting his eyes downwards.

"Okay."

After a while, he reached out, tucked my hair behind my ear and gazed at my face. He stroked his fingertips over my cheek and brushed his thumb over my mouth.

"You're so beautiful, Freya. You get more gorgeous every year."

I felt heavy with lust, but also with the weight of it all... what it could mean. It was different this time. It felt like we weren't kids anymore, that this was deeper, had more riding on it... that he'd changed, been bashed about and now needed taking care of, not the other way around.

"You're tired, Ruben."

He looked sad and helpless. "Yes."

I stood up and took his hand, leading him back inside. I pressed the button for the doors to shut and we went into my bedroom and lay on the bed. I held his head to my chest and he relaxed, holding me close. I played with his hair and murmured, "Do you still love me, Ruben?"

"More than ever," he groaned.

"I love you."

He lifted his head off my chest and our noses brushed. "You mean it, Frey?"

"More than ever."

He ran his fingers through my hair and I stared up at his eyes as he studied my throat and chest. He brought his gaze back to me and we locked eyes.

"I could've become anyone while I was gone," he muttered.

"So could I."

"Then how do we know?" he asked.

"There's only one way to find out."

He gave a little grin. "Oh yeah?"

"Make love to me. Tell me everything that way. Let's not talk anymore. Just show me through that and I'll do the same. What do you say?"

He slid one arm beneath me and rested some of his weight on top of me. I lifted one leg and rested my calf on his behind, my foot against the back of his thigh. I put my hands on his face and held his cheeks, still slightly damp from the cool night air we were enjoying outside only moments before. He touched my hair and brushed his nose to mine again. My heart was on fire. The deliciousness of his beauty, the way he made me feel... the story we shared.

"What happened to my hard-knock girl?" he groaned, his chest pushing hard against mine as he breathed in deeply.

"Some man loved me enough that I found a different life. A different me."

I saw his throat move as he gulped. I had no idea what he was waiting for. None whatsoever. He and I were back in each other's arms... after all that time apart... all that pain. What was he waiting for?

I took my hands away from his cheeks and unzipped my dress at the side. I slid down the straps and unclipped my bra. Then I unbuttoned his shirt at the same time as pushing my dress down to my waist. By this point Ruben was starting to sweat and gasp for air. I pushed his shirt down his arms and away. He was slick with sweat in seconds, his skin shiny, glowing, his muscles twitching with anticipation.

I pulled his bare chest to mine and everything I possessed as a woman whooshed down to my core, my body throbbing for him, the centre of my being crying out for him, like I was pure need incarnate.

"This is the truth," I said, licking my lips, "this heat, this fire, our touch, this is the only thing that's honest about it all, Ruben. This."

I held him close and he stared at my mouth, eyes hooded with lust, his bottom lip pinched between his teeth. I'd known some men during our years apart but none had had this effect on me. I'd loved Ruben when he was traumatised and wrecked, when he didn't know what life was, when he didn't know what he was capable of. And now he knew what he was capable of, he didn't want to taint my life with that—but this love is forever. It cannot be matched.

"Do you love me, Freya? Really?"

"Yes."

"Then how could you fuck other men?"

I looked away from him, half tempted to slide out from beneath him and throw him out. After all, he was the one who left me.

"I didn't know if you were coming back," I said, snarling, "and I ought to kick you in the balls for asking that of me."

He took my cheek and made me look at him. "That's the Freya I love."

He covered my mouth with his and there was no warning, no warm-up; he fixed his mouth to mine and gave me a deep, passionate kiss that stirred my soul, deep inside. The type of kiss no other man had ever given me, not even him. We didn't break apart, we became one again, our tongues engaged in battle and reunion at the same time—no other lover having ever given me a truer kiss.

It was like I was floating on the surface of a warm, placid lake, until his kiss took me down into the darkest depths and I had no control of the swirling, careening power of his craving to take me and pull me into him—the core of me drowned by him, flooded, the need to breathe again so powerful but the ache in my belly happy to take more and more of his dominant desire.

Then he pulled back, shocked and delighted. We caught our breaths and I wanted more, but he was too distraught, I could tell.

"I love you more," I groaned.

"Freya," he sighed, face contorting, nearly shaking his head.

"This is the truth," I reminded him, sliding my hands down his back and pushing my body up towards his. I took his hand

16

and placed it on my breast. "Don't you remember, Ruben? Our first time. I thought I would die. I was determined for it not to happen, the same as you are now. Because I knew then exactly what it would mean, like you do now."

"Yes," he said, regret in his eyes.

"There won't be any going back. Ever again."

"Ever?" he asked.

"Ever."

He kissed my mouth, softer this time, gently tugging on my resolve until he had me once more, forfeiting my body and my control. He kissed me so deeply, for so long, I almost became the lake itself—swallowed into it, a symbiote, no longer myself.

Then he slid his tongue along my throat and to my breasts, sucking and licking, manhandling and mauling me. I yanked on his hair and begged for mercy but got none.

It became frenzied, my clit was beating out of control with lust and I screamed when he flicked my skirt up and tossed my legs apart, his tongue on me the moment he hooked his finger under my knickers and tugged them aside.

I cradled him between my thighs and rocked with him as he licked around my clit. I arched up against him and shivered painfully when I came, my walls clamping against nothing, so much that it hurt. He undid the belt on my dress and got it off me, then my knickers. He was on his knees, looking down at me. I fancied I looked pretty much the same except that I now had more muscular thighs from all the cycling up and down hills around Nice. I saw him studying the same sturdy hips and the slightly soft belly he once told me would carry his babies.

He unzipped his jeans and I saw underpants beneath. That was new. He never wore underpants in the past. I covered my mouth with a hand when he got his jeans past his hips and I saw the erection bulging in his black boxer briefs. He tugged his jeans all the way off and threw them away.

He came towards me and I pushed down his underwear and kicked it off, urging him to move into me without any delay. Thankfully he wasn't on the warpath, nor determined to make me suffer, not this time. He wrapped his arms around me and dug his hand underneath my hair, grabbing it and angling my head just so, meaning he could sink his lips into mine and our mouths melted together.

Ruben slid smoothly into me and gasped, then a couple of pumps later, he came shooting into my body and I threw my head back laughing, trying not to but unable to stop myself. He rested his face between my breasts as I laughed the house down. The greatest lover of my life... felled by years of loneliness... our love put on pause.

"Baby, I'm just getting you ready for the night ahead," he growled.

Then he pulled us both up so we were sitting and my god, his lap seemed to me the greatest throne in all the world. I let my arms hang loosely around his shoulders and I kissed his forehead, his little blonde hairs tickling my chin. I kissed between his eyebrows and over his closed lids. I kissed his mouth until he fought back, then I licked his throat, bit into his shoulder, urged him to lean back a little on his hands so I could suck his nipple, flick it with my tongue, bite and kiss it... then the other one. I sucked his earlobe into my mouth, ripped at it a little, and then I groaned when he took hold of my buttocks and started rocking my body over his.

"We will never be apart, ever again," he said, his voice ragged as he licked my breasts and rocked us both wildly. I threw my head back but nodded I was in agreement.

He found that sweet, sweet spot and I moaned his name and my approval with every stab of his thick, delicious stem inside me. He rubbed my clit and I came, his cum firing into me at the same time. It was utter perfection as I drank him in and he shuddered beneath me.

I wrapped my arms tight around his head and rested my cheek against his hair. His arms covered my back and he didn't let go, making me feel clothed in his love.

When we locked eyes again, my whole body ached. I felt my entire being fill with something powerful and racking. He seemed to feel it, too because his jaw was loose and he couldn't catch his breath yet. He pushed my hair over my shoulders and kissed the centre of my chest. Then he hoisted me off his lap and we lay looking at one another, side by side.

"Ruben?"

"Yes, Freya."

"When can we do it again?"

"Whenever you want, my lady. My light."

I pulled him in and kissed him until our mouths became tired and sore. Then he worshipped my body until he'd kissed me everywhere, and when he moved back inside me after that, we never took our eyes off each other.

By the time it was over, the sun was just starting to come up.

RUBEN LEAVES THE POOL entirely naked (all the nakedness another reason Adam fucked off out of here) and leans over me, kissing my mouth.

"Is it over yet?" he asks.

"This is going to be a long three days if you keep asking."

"Then it will be a long few days," he says, grabbing his towel and moving indoors.

Ruben hates me having my period. When we were together before, I didn't have a period during that time. That denotes how much of a short amount of time we spent as lovers in the past. We were friends for two years. Lovers for two minutes. It says everything, really. It says that this time, it has to be for the right reasons, because what we had before wasn't. It was two people inexperienced at love... it was two people dealing with outside factors who so desperately wanted to be together, but didn't think it through.

This time, things have to be different. There's no other way.

Chapter Two

On the Beach

He showers after his naked swim and emerges smelling great, of lime and mint. And something else. My shampoo, again. We've hardly been out and done anything since he got here. He needs to get his own stuff and stop using Adam's shower gel and my hair products. He does smell good but it is weird he smells like my brother.

We have brunch these days. Breakfast never happens. We wake, kiss and cuddle, and (bodily functions allowing) have sex, then he swims while I digest one of my healthy shakes. The secret ingredient—apple cider vinegar—is gross but really works. I haven't had any break-outs or bad periods in ages. It was one of my lovers who got me into shakes when I stayed on his yacht. I say lover but nobody has been my lover except Ruben. It's just better than calling them what they were... stand-ins for the real deal. Shags. Fucks. A man with an appendage. Boyfriend. Fun time. Person with benefits. All that...

I'm sitting on the kitchen counter reading a magazine when he places himself between my thighs. I pretend to ignore him, but man, does he smell good.

He kisses my throat and clavicle and I'm struggling not to become breathless. I've made the pancake mix ready for him to fry but he's more interested in me, evidently.

"Ruben, I'm hungry."

"You're too beautiful, lady love."

"Why do you keep calling me lady?"

"It's what your name means. Lady. Goddess. All the things you are."

He makes me shiver when he strokes my hair behind my ear and kisses my cheek. He's wearing just a pair of stonewash jeans and looks ridiculous. I can tell he spent time outdoors in Portugal because his tan is deep.

"Ruben, why don't you ask Alexia to come out and stay with us?"

He frowns and pulls away, like I've offended him deeply.

"It's not a good idea."

"When are you going to tell me—"

I don't get to say anything else because the front door opens and clangs shut, shattering the moment.

"Please say you're dressed," Adam bellows.

"We're dressed," I tell him, "although, well..."

I'm not really dressed, but I'm also not naked. I'm wearing a camisole, knickers and the thin nightgown Ruben bought me four years ago. I had it in a box and never wore it when we were apart, but now I'm delighted I can wear it and not feel so sad.

Adam enters the room in a pink polo shirt and navy chino shorts.

He and Ruben lock eyes but say nothing to one another. In fact, Ruben grabs the pancake pan and puts it on the stove, heating it up, eyes down.

"Run out of clothes?" I ask him.

KARMA

Adam has blonde hair, brown eyes like mine and matches Ruben pound for pound. Except my brother is perhaps an inch or two taller than Ruben. And almost fifteen years younger.

It feels a bit like the air just got overwrought with hormones and warning signals.

"I can't hold the fort at the gallery any longer, it's too much," he says, hands up, in defeat.

He removes his glossy aviators and puts them down on the tiled kitchen counter.

"Has there been a problem? What happened?" I'm shocked because high summer is a lovely time of year when it's mainly passers-by who pop inside and are happy mainly just to chat and perhaps purchase the odd painting or two. Nothing major.

"I'm going back to Paris," he blurts.

My heart's racing and I glance sideways at Ruben, who's focused on the pancakes, not getting involved. Wow. So, his protectiveness doesn't extend to this, then?

But why would he be leaving...?

"What happened with the girl? What was her name?"

"Athena," he says, "and we broke up. I've been staying in Old Town. It's shite, by the way."

"Fucking stay here, you twat," I yell, "we'll build you something of your own if needs must. For god's sake, Adam. I can't do without you right now. I need you at the gallery otherwise I will have to close. I need this time for me and Ruben. Please."

He inhales a big deep breath. "Fine."

"Not like it hasn't happened to the best of us, buddy," Ruben says, adding his weight to the matter. Though going by the look in Adam's eyes, Ruben's two pennies' worth is very much unwanted.

23

Adam raises his eyebrows. "When I want your opinion, I'll ask."

"Sorry I spoke."

"You didn't see her, *mate*," Adam warns, shaking his head, a nasty look in his eye. "I did. I saw her. She was a fucking stick insect when I got here. Cycling herself to death every day. I fed her back up. So please, keep your opinions to yourself and we'll be good, all right?"

Ruben raises his eyebrows, holds his hands up and carries on cooking.

Adam storms upstairs to his wing of the house in the loft. It's spacious but there is the matter of the sloping roof to contend with. The three bedrooms on the ground floor of the villa are better, but I think he likes feeling he can escape, or something. Maybe reminds him of home.

"He ought to be a little bit more fucking grateful. After all, my money pays his tuition."

I creep up behind Ruben, wrap my arms around his waist and kiss his back. Then unexpectedly, I slide my hand into the crotch of his jeans and grab hold of his balls.

"Behave yourself, Ruben."

God, his junk feels so good. The hair on his pubis is so soft from the shower and his willy feels silky and beautiful, his balls plump and warm.

I remove my hand the second we hear Adam descending from upstairs. He's changed into jeans, vest and flip flops. He has a rolled-up beach towel under his arm containing swimming shorts and snorkelling gear.

"Do you want some pancakes?" I ask, before he leaves without another word.

He stops in his tracks. "I was gonna meet some mates down at the beach. We're off sailing."

"Got two minutes, though. Right?"

He sits on a stool nearby and waits with a sullen expression for Ruben to serve up the first batch. Ruben slides a few onto a plate and I pass it to Adam, who gratefully adds maple syrup and strawberries I prepared earlier. He starts scoffing like an inmate.

"Listen, I know this is going to take some getting used to, but we can set some ground rules. Me and Ruben will behave during daylight hours and if you wanted the house to yourself a night or two, that's fine. We can figure things out."

Adam huffs, like no compromise where Ruben is concerned will ever be enough... purely because he hates the man he believes did me wrong.

"In the autumn, you'll be going back to Paris and there will be a million freshly arrived students for you to take your frustrations out on. But until then, you've gotta earn your keep, Adam. I'll always help out where I can," I insist, trying to sound big-sisterly.

He finishes his pancakes just as I'm lavishing syrup on mine. "Are we done?" he asks.

I move around the counter, grab his chin and make him face me. "Don't take that tone with me, Carter. I wrote the book on sullen behaviour, you know."

We stare at one another but it doesn't take long before he cracks, grinning. I give a chuckle and he wraps his arms around my waist and cuddles me.

"She was gorgeous, Frey," he mourns.

"There'll be others. Or maybe it'll just work out, eventually. Trust me, you've got all the time in the world."

Ruben and I share a look and I can read his thoughts. He thinks Adam better be prepared for a few more knocks to come.

"Go on, go and have fun with your mates."

He stands up and takes a deep breath, looking over at Ruben. "Cheers for the pancakes, mate."

"No worries," Ruben says, in his gruff voice, "just get back in one piece tonight, all right? I'm taking your sister out so we can't be coming to your rescue because we might need rescuing ourselves."

"Understood," Adam laughs.

Once he's gone, the atmosphere of before restored, I glance at Ruben as I cut into my pancake stack. He seems happy with himself. "What are we doing tonight, then?"

"It's a surprise," he says. "Thought we should get out, seeing as though you're... and we're going to become hermits otherwise."

"Great idea," I exclaim. "What should I wear?"

"Something snazzy," he tells me, a conniving glint in his eye.

"All right, then."

I PONDER WHAT TO WEAR until I decide to go with what I feel like wearing, pulling my favourite dress off the rack. It's the one I wore in Paris, when we went there together. Another item that hasn't been worn since, at least outside the house. Sometimes I've worn it indoors, cried while wearing it, or otherwise I've held it like a teddy bear against my chest, stroked the fabric and yearned for him... remembering the night we had when I last had it on. There were some of his shirts, too which I used to wear in private and never washed so his scent wouldn't leave.

So much pain and yet I always knew what we'd shared was more than I ever deserved. I sort of came to accept it—how he disappeared, left me, etc.

When I get downstairs, I'm expecting him to be eagerly awaiting my appearance but he's nowhere in sight.

"Ruben?"

"Out here."

I see the front door is open and I drop my shoes to the floor, slip my feet into them and clack across the tiles towards his voice.

The first thing I see is him, dressed drop-dead in a grey pinstripe suit and white, crisp shirt. He looks divine with a capital D especially because, earlier on, he went out and got his hair cut. It's combed back and gorgeous. He looks so handsome with all the hair out of his face.

"What's this?" I exclaim, when I spot what it is he's standing beside.

"My new ride," he says, "can't have you on the back of my bike all the time."

It's a Ferrari Roma and it's black. It's almost as stunning as him.

I walk around the vehicle and am about to orgasm from just feeling the paintwork, when he slides his hands around my waist from behind and asks, "Do you like it?"

"I love it," I gush, covering his hands with mine and loving how he feels against my back and behind, his breath on my neck. Tonight, I've pinned my hair up because it's time to try out new things, right?

"Good. Shall we go?"

"Aren't you going to say anything about my dress?"

"If I even remark on the dress or look anywhere south of your face, I'm going to force you onto your back and you know it, no matter the consequences."

I throw my head back, snorting with laughter. Ruben whistles and the dogs quit sniffing the bushes out front and head indoors.

"No pooping while we're gone," he shouts, and strangely, they've stopped doing that since he showed up. Perhaps that's the beauty of having a dominant master in the house.

Ruben locks up while I seat myself inside his new toy. My chair feels snug and extremely expensive, hugging my curves fantastically.

He joins me and chuckles to himself, watching me stroke the interior. "We're going to have a lot of fun in this car."

"There's no back seat," I laugh.

"As if that would stop us," he chuckles.

"True."

He starts the engine and it growls, the framework humming, gently vibrating my seat. This car definitely matches its master—not just something pretty to look at, but also has the goods, the style and the follow through.

"You didn't hand over all of your money to me, then?" I say, as he rolls the car towards the gates and presses the button for them to start opening.

"Half," he says, "is that a problem?"

"No problem."

He gave me half? I romanticised the idea that he'd given me everything.

We're about to tear off when I ask, "Ruben?"

"Yes, my lady love."

"Where are we going?"

"It's still a surprise. I know you hate them, but you will have to trust me."

I can't help a smile. "I trust you."

"Let's go then."

As he throttles the vehicle, my heart is left behind and I'm soon covering my mouth, in shock.

"Yeah, I kinda have a few racing hours under my belt."

I can barely breathe as we rocket down the hill, but at the same time, I don't care.

WE CRUISE ALONG THE roads that hug the coast for around half an hour, until we reach a small car park at the top of a cliff.

"Oh god, not again, Ruben," I chuckle.

He has a thing about cliffs, clearly.

"Trust me," he demands, half a laugh spitting out of his throat as we vacate the car. "You'd better lose the shoes, though."

He takes my hand and I notice a large white van parked on the other side of the car park. Should I be worried?

We take a path that begins to lead us down to a private beach and as we get around a little bend, I see what he has planned for tonight.

"Oh, Ruben."

"Well, I know you hate restaurants."

"I do not."

"Well, I know they're very samey to you these days."

"True."

Down on the beach, a little tent has been erected, with fairy lights lighting up the area and a couple of firepits adding to the atmosphere. My feet sink into still-warm sand and as we head downhill, I'm very aware I will be required to walk back up after dinner. Won't that be fun?

"It's amazing," I gasp, once we reach sea level.

"Well, I did promise you a few dates but since last week, all we've done is screw every night... until last night, of course."

He still looks sore and I'm amused, I can't hide it, I am. He's such a baby sometimes. I love it really.

Under the small gazebo, there's a table for two and it has been laid with white bone china and silver dinnerware. There's a bucket of ice and a bottle of something inside. There are two waiters, one a man, one a woman. They seem to be married, I decide, going by the way they are looking at us as we approach, then at one another.

"Is this a thing?" I demand of him.

"No, it's where you pay two chefs enough for them to leave their own restaurant behind for a night."

"You pig."

"Ooh, I know."

The lady greets me in French. "Hello, Freya. I'm Isabella and this is my husband, Pierre. Welcome. Please sit, enjoy your evening. Everything possible has been taken care of. Sit back, relax. You will be happy."

I thank her as Pierre helps me into my chair. They've even erected a little platform for us so that the chairs don't sink into the sand.

"Are you happy?" he asks, after Pierre has poured the wine.

"How did you do this?" I demand, shaking my head.

"You mean when did I do it?"

"Yes."

"Well, there's this thing called an afternoon nap. Apparently, you have one every day. Who knew?"

So, he did all this while I was taking a nap? I notice another tent nearby but this one is cordoned off slightly and not entirely open to the elements like ours is. The kitchen, then?

Pierre is soon back and draping my napkin over my lap while Ruben sees to his own.

He then places a tray of seafood canapes on the table and explains each of them, but I lose track, maybe because everything is being communicated in French. I'm no linguist by any stretch of the imagination, especially when it comes to different dialects. I expect Pierre and Isabella are Parisians going by their deep, clucky way of speaking, or possibly they spoke to Ruben in French on the phone and don't know I'm not a native, nor have I gone full-blown immigrant, yet.

Once Pierre is gone, I lean over the table and point at the squid. "You're having everything with that on."

"Fine by me," he says, filling his mouth with a whole canape.

I put a couple of canapes on my small plate, which is stacked on top of two larger plates, and pick up my tiny little starter cutlery. Ruben pulls a face and realises he is, after all, still expected to uphold decorum, even if we are on a beach with nobody else around.

I eat the ones with prawns, salmon and scallops, but Ruben has the rest. They are all rather delicious and I tear into some warm bread, filling it with butter and waiting for it to melt before I dip up some of the leftover white-wine sauce on my plate. So, maybe a little decorum has gone out of the window.

"Did you plan the menu?" I ask him.

"Nope, we've got four more courses to go, though."

I shoot him a look of shock and he chuckles.

"When I can't fuck, I eat, so it's your fault. And I left the menu to them. I don't know what the fuck we'll be fed. Possibly camel and tortoise, for all I know. Except I expect it'll be good. These people have three Michelin stars."

"NO!"

"YES!"

Pierre's back and clears my top plate, then studies Ruben with crumbs all over his side of the table and chuckles lightly. Ruben has clearly been away from civilisation a while.

Pierre leaves but I know he will be back soon with yet more delicacies. I look over at Ruben and chuckle, "So, you've been eating like a maniac then, have you? Since we last were together. You'd be the size of a house eating like this every day."

He shrugs his shoulders. "That was different. You weren't within reach but unavailable."

I shake my head at him. He reaches across the table for my hand, just as Pierre returns.

"This is a little palate cleanser," he says, "before the starter."

It's a tiny little silver bowl with a wisp of lemon sorbet or something. I lift my spoon to my lips and pull a face, it's so tart and strong. It's cleansing, all right. Wow. That packs a punch.

When I look over at Ruben, he's already finished his and is patting his stomach, ready for more.

"You're a maniac, you know?" I tell him.

"Yep."

I take my time ingesting the sorbet and wonder if Pierre has me on a timer. I'm going to eke this out because I want this meal to go on forever, but I also feel like there should be lots more talking going on.

"I wonder if Adam will be on the rebound tonight."

Ruben smiles knowingly. "He's hopefully having some good old-fashioned male fun and has collapsed in an alleyway already."

"I worry about him," I admit. "I worry he feels alone in the world."

"Nah, he's just jealous," Ruben tells me, "but he'll get over it."

"Of us?"

"Yep."

"It's taken us years, though. I'm not sure he has that patience."

"Most people live never having known what we have. It doesn't happen for everyone, Freya. I am sad to say. But there are other things."

I scoop a tiny bit of lemon sorbet into my mouth and get another hit, sending my taste buds into a riotous frenzy. "I've tried to tell him to be young, have fun, but he's not like that... he wants something meaningful right now and he's not going to be satisfied with anything else."

"God, at twenty-one, I did not know myself," Ruben laughs, shaking his head, "I was an utter mess."

"I can picture it." And damn, I just finished my sorbet and Pierre is rushing over instantly.

What the hell are they in a hurry for? Are they still hoping to be back at their restaurant tonight?

Our sorbet cups gone, Ruben tells me, "I was in a relationship with twelve women and none. I was drinking and puffing all sorts and I was a fucking disaster."

"But because of Fred, right?"

"Partly," he says, "but I think it's in me, too."

"Yeah?"

"Mum's an addict, you know?" he says, out of nowhere.

"I did not know."

"We never got it from Fred. We got it from her. Fred did drink but he could stop, too. His main vices were cigars and women... mostly women. And fried food, maybe. Freddie was a chain smoker and that killed him, but yeah, my mum is an addict and I think she passed that on."

"She doesn't seem like one."

"Pills, mostly, pain meds and stuff. The kind that make you really out of it."

I take a long look at the sea to the side of us, staring out at its seemingly infinite vastness.

"Doesn't mean you're all addictive personalities, just that you were all looking for something to dull the pain."

"Maybe." He stares at the sea, too.

"Did you just stop one day?"

"The first time, I think I did," he confesses. "I woke up, didn't know what the fuck I was doing, and stopped. I met Gia shortly after that. I thought it was everything falling into place, you know? Like people do. They think they've made some good decisions finally so some good is coming their way." Then his expression darkens. "After she was killed, I took to drinking again, but when Laurent was taken, too... I asked myself what he'd want and I knew he'd want me to do better, so I pulled myself together."

"Yeah. Well, addicts don't just stop one day. There's the physical withdrawal for a start, not to mention the psychological attachment. Maybe your mother found it hard to stop taking pills because it was going on for so long and it became her absolute normal. She got so that she didn't know anything else."

"I think so," he agrees, with sad eyes.

"So that's what you've been doing? Helping her get off them."

"Trying," he says, his eye twitching. "She's been in and out of facilities. I feel like he damaged her that badly, it's beyond my capability to repair her. That's the worst thing, when you know you can't do much but try and make them go and get help."

"I understand." I squeeze his hand.

"I've been able to undo a lot of his misdemeanours, but not all. My brother isn't ever coming back and I won't ever truly know why he got to the place he did. My mother can't console herself that she eventually left him and saved herself, because she didn't... it took his death for that to happen. She's working through it, but not very well." He puts his hand over his mouth and looks hopeless.

Pierre arrives with our next dish and explains what it is, how it's been cooked and seasoned. I think this is the fish course: halibut with lots of baby vegetables arranged like a rainbow around the plate.

Ruben tucks into his food, although he still has a little strain in his eyes.

"Baby, you can't save the world," I tell him, and bring my fork to my mouth, the fish literally melting on my tongue. "Shit, this is good."

"Told you so," he laughs.

We eat a bit more, and I'm literally swallowing the most beautiful food in the world, when he says, "I think that's why I fell for you. You're different. Strong. Stronger than anyone else I ever met."

"I don't know about that."

"Would you have put up with a husband like Fred?"

I gesticulate that certainly wouldn't have ever happened. "Nope, no way. Eventually I'd have got free."

"Exactly. And would you have left Adam to defend himself if you knew your dad was starting on him, too?"

We both know the answer to that. "Not a cat in hell's chance I'd have left him if I knew that, but then sometimes abuse goes on behind closed doors. Nobody can ever truly place themselves in another's shoes. We can't always know what they were going through or understand."

"I did leave him, though," Ruben admits, taking a sip of wine.

"He told you to go, Ruben. So, you went. You still don't know for sure he took his life. We're talking about Fred and Freddie here. Either could've had a hand in it. You never saw a note, nobody found one, right?"

"True."

"It's going to haunt you, for sure. That's grief."

"It all seems so..." He puts down his knife and fork and looks forlorn.

"...like you're trapped in it, still?"

"Yes," he says, looking at the table in front of him. "Even after all this time. And Mum talks about him, still. She says 'Fred would've wanted to go here, do this, would've enjoyed a mojito or a cognac by midday at least.' She remembers him fondly, sometimes."

"We can't judge her." I am getting through my dinner much quicker than him this time, because it is bloody delicious.

"But if I was a cunt and we had two boys who were drowning under the weight of knowing their father was a criminal and it could wreck everyone's lives one day, what would you do?"

"Honestly?" I exclaim, nearly laughing.

"Yeah."

"I'm much too self-absorbed to ever be ruled by someone else. I knew the first time I met him, and the second—although, admittedly, the second time the connection didn't click—but I still knew both times I met him that there was something not right. And I only know about the wrong 'uns of this world because I was raised by one."

"You're right." He worries his lip before remembering to eat again.

I'm almost done with my food and look across the table, right into his eyes. "You know what, Rube? How can any of us say we know anything, hmm? Unless we live long enough to learn. I've lived a few lives already. Learnt a lot. But I'm still learning. It's when people stop learning, that's when things become worrying. When they stay the same, never changing, always living in the past. You can't do that. It's not good."

"You are so right," he says. "So right."

"Laurent will always remain that teenager in your mind, your little brother. We don't know what he might have become. Nobody knows. He took drugs from a very early age. By the sounds of it, he wasn't even as badly treated as what you were. He might have been doing it because he could, because he didn't have any self-control, not because he was in pain like you were. But we shan't ever know, and at the same time, we can't draw a line under it either."

37

He finishes his fish at the same time as me and we put down our cutlery at the same time, too. Pierre takes our plates, without a word.

I take Ruben's hands across the table and smile. "I know I can only do so much for Adam because at the end of the day, it will be up to him. He's a good kid, you know. He's not like me at all. He's good. He's his own man. He'll be okay. But I don't want him to settle for mediocre, that's all. But most people do."

"Sad, but true," he mutters.

"Everyone presumes if they get married and settle down, then everything is sorted. But it never is sorted. We always have work to do. If anything, my mother taught me that. She always worked, whether it was as a violinist or around the house or on herself, she worked hard. Maybe she was married to a psycho, but she never gave up hope for her kids, and there's generational cycles we can break, Ruben. It can all change, you know? We can be the change."

He reaches across, strokes my cheek and smiles. "I love you very much, Freya."

"I know." I turn my face, kiss his palm and hold his hand to my cheek again. "Love you, too."

Chapter Three

You Paint?

After the main course, coq au vin, which we ate in thrall, Isabella brings out a sort of platter of desserts served on a large wooden serving board.

"We have to leave for home now," she says, sounding nervous, even resorting to English. "But please, do enjoy the beach. We shall send someone to come for the tents and tables later. Au revoir."

"It was lovely, thank you," I tell her.

"You're so welcome. Enjoy."

She and Pierre carry their portable kitchenware up the hill and Ruben grins as I start to work my way through the miniature desserts. Everything is divine.

"Try this," I tell him, and he slides his fork through a chocolate, gooey mess.

"Wow," he murmurs.

"Not cheesecake, though," I complain.

"Shame," he says, sniggering.

He pours the last of the wine in my glass though we still have some bottles of water on the serving table nearby, not to mention they appear to have left a little canister of coffee behind and plenty of cream, sugar and plastic cups.

I look down at my watch and see it's nearly midnight. "What do we do after this?"

He gestures at the entire beach we have, all to ourselves, looking joyful and a little frolicsome. "We have this beach, this night, why don't we just see what happens?"

"Okay!" He watches me eating and I point my fork at the platter. "Come on, dig in. I can't eat these all to myself."

He pulls a face.

"Okay, maybe I can!" I concede.

He's watching me eating, looking so handsome and beautiful, when he says, "Should we dance?"

"Okay."

He stands, removes his jacket and plays some classical music from his phone. I'm barefoot in the sand while he still has his loafers on. I wrap my arms around his neck and kiss his mouth before we start to sway. It's a kiss I didn't intend on being long but it becomes epic.

He pulls me close and we taste the meal on each other's lips, the wine... the sea air... each other. I love him more than anything. I believe he's my soul mate.

We pull apart and he stares down into my eyes. I want so badly to believe we can make it work this time. Every day we tick off is a miracle to me. There was a time when I didn't think I'd get even one more hour with him, let alone a chance at a real life together.

"Where will we live?" I ask, breathless.

His hair is ruffled by the wind but mine is just about staying in place, pinned to the back of my head.

"Why not here?"

I take a deep breath. "I came here because it was my fantasy. I want our life to be real."

"This is real," he laughs.

"You know what I mean. What will you do here? Wait for me at home all day?"

He cocks his head. "Sounds good to me."

"Ruben, be serious."

"I am being. If you want the fantasy, then fine. You have your gallery. Enjoy it. Maybe you could sell some of my work. I've done some, you know?"

I cover my mouth. "Really?"

"I'll have to get Mother to ship it out, but yeah... it's something I love."

I worry my lip. "Life can't be this easy, Ruben. We don't get everything we want."

He pulls me close and our noses touch. "Freya, karma works both ways, angel. It's about time we got what we're due after everything. Don't you think?"

"But is he really dead, Ruben? How do you know?"

Ruben takes a deep breath. "He's dead, Freya. I promise you. Your cousin buried him. I saw from a distance. She didn't know I was there so I know from how she cried at his graveside after everyone else was gone... Debbie was inconsolable."

"But what if she's like me... duped? And learns different, later down the line."

"No," Ruben insists, shaking his head, "he died. Lung cancer."

He was a terrible chain smoker, for sure.

"Are you absolutely certain nobody is going to come after us...?"

"Nobody," he says, forthright, "I trust he had cancer. I checked his medical records. It was all there. Black and white."

"But you managed it, Ruben."

"No, not really. Freddie would've had to con a dozen people to stage his death. I only conned him and Debbie."

"And me," I whisper.

"To protect you," he answers, "to keep you safe."

"I know."

I push my face into the centre of his chest and he wraps me up tight.

"He was a monster, Freya. Karma took care of him for us, now I will take care of you, I promise."

"Really?"

"Absolutely. I just can't wait to spend the autumn nights curled up together. Make dinners at home. Walk the dogs on empty streets when the tourists are all gone. I'm happy to stay here if you are. I don't have anything pulling me back to the UK."

"Are you sure?" I groan.

"I'm telling you," he assures me.

"Okay. Okay."

"Good. Now, how's about a bit of skinny dipping?"

He unbuttons his collar and cuffs and has his shirt over his head before I can protest against it.

"RUBEN!" I scream, as he starts running towards the water, kicking his shoes off and unbuttoning his trousers on the way.

"Last one in is a rotten..."

I slide my zip down and start running after him. Fucking hell.

The water isn't too bad as we dash in together, but that's probably just because I've got wine inside me. Ruben is entirely naked while I've kept my knickers on. I fly into the water after him and he catches me, scooping me up into his arms. I'm laughing so hard, because I can't believe he got me to do this. It's ridiculous. Eventually his expression changes to serious and I stop laughing, my lungs aching after our escapades. I wrap my legs and arms around him as the water cascades around us.

"I love you," he says, "I always will."

"Me too."

He kisses me, saying so much, mainly that he can't be without me.

"I don't wanna wake up ever again if it's not by your side," I tell him. "It can't be like before. I don't want you to be gone when I need you most. I want to see you every time I open my eyes. Want your arms to be the first thing I feel in the morning and last thing at night. That is literally all I want, Ruben. I don't need anything else. Just promise me."

"Yes, I promise," he says, nodding.

I'm grinning when he kisses me again because he definitely has an erection.

"Ruben..."

"You could just give me a little blowy on the beach?"

"You are so rotten, you know?"

"I know."

WE ARRIVE BACK AT THE villa and aside from the dogs, I'm not sure anyone else is home. The alarm bleeps and I have to put the code in. A new day has dawned and Ruben chuckles as the dogs rush for him. He takes them out back and they do their wees. They're back in bed within moments—still too early for them.

"I wonder if Adam came home last night?"

"Doubt it," he answers, "no evidence he's come in with the munchies."

"Let's just hope he's safe, then."

"Let's go to bed, honey baby."

He leads me to the bedroom and I use the en suite, then crawl into bed naked aside from a pair of bed shorts.

Ruben slings his arm around me and mumbles, "Best date ever."

"Do not disagree."

After skinny dipping, we got dressed and talked on the beach until the sun came up. It was the best night of my life so far.

I roll over, rest my head on his chest and sigh, happy. His skin is cool, his body firm and welcoming.

"Love you."

"Love you more," he says, wrapping the sheet around us.

I didn't give him that blowy on the beach he was asking for. However, once we got back in his car and he was sat there with his suit crumpled, his hair ruffled and a look in his eyes that would make even the toughest of women keel over, of course I gave him my mouth and he took advantage.

Life really couldn't get any better.

WHEN I WAKE, I'M LYING on my front and have this sensation of a large weight on top of my back. I groan and see the clock reading ten a.m. I've managed four and a half hours sleep, then?

"What the hell?" I mumble.

I turn my head and see the black dog, Sooty lying on my backside.

Sweep, the grey French bulldog, is curled up against Ruben's midriff. He's lying on his side and has his arm around the dog.

"Charming," I chuckle quietly.

My dogs are swines, but they won't live forever, so...

I put my head back in the pillow and stare at Ruben as he continues to snore lightly. He's perfectly at ease, happily sharing his bed with canines.

I bet the little buggers have pooed in the kitchen again and have come in here to escape the smell.

I gently roll to my side and Sooty scrambles off me, dazed and yawning. He comes when I pat the bed in front of me and curls into my hips the same as Sweep is doing with Ruben.

I stroke his fur and he nuzzles my hand, then my leg. "I know, it's very difficult being so cute."

Ruben groans and opens one eye. "What time is it?"

"Ten," I mumble.

"Bloody dogs."

"This one thought my arse was a convenient bed."

"Oh, don't we all," Ruben laughs.

I give him a look of disdain. "I think they look guilty, what do you think?"

"Oh, hell, no!" he shouts.

He throws the sheet off and storms across the room, putting on his swimming shorts and skidding out of the door. He goes through the house and I hear his voice echo down the halls.

"FUCKING LITTLE TWATS!"

I laugh the house down. There was Ruben, thinking he'd reformed my dogs, when really it was probably just that they were constipated because of a change in the household dynamic. They were similarly shitting less when Adam first came to stay.

I hear Ruben open the doggy drawer, get out the poop bags, then he's spraying and wiping up, cursing like a trucker and then heading for the bins outside to disown the feculence.

Ruben washes his hands then lands back in the room.

"Dogs, now," he commands, and the two pooches leap off the bed and sit at his feet, tongues hanging out. "Bad dogs! Bad! No poo. No poo. No poo."

They sit looking up at him and before I know it, he's down on his knees and scratching behind their ears.

"I'll start putting the paper down again," I tell Ruben. "It must be a bad habit they picked up elsewhere. Four years and they still haven't grown out of it, though perhaps it's because we did sleep in this morning."

He shakes his head, eyes full of amused fury. "They're so in sync, are you sure they aren't twins, or something?"

"From different lines entirely, I assure you. They were caged together and looked to have become such good friends, I couldn't part them."

"Fucking mutts," he says, grimacing, "fucking little mutts, aren't you?"

They keep wagging their tails and before long, they're both on his lap vying for attention.

"Yeah, yeah, let's go, then."

I grin as they follow after him, the sound of him opening the dog food making them whine with hunger. I wrap the cool sheet around me and close my eyes. Maybe I'll catch just a few more zzzz's...

I'm about to nod off when Ruben presents me with coffee and kisses my hair.

"I'll just be swimming," he says, "and it looks like Adam came in after us. The milk carton was drained, so looks like I'm jogging to the shop after my swim."

"Okay, strange man. You may leave me now. This bed is all mine." He chuckles loudly as I stretch out, glorying in an empty bed all to myself. "And don't jog there with your top off. You know how jealous I get."

His laugh is raucous as he heads outdoors. Then outside the window, I see his silhouette and hear a splash. The French doors of my bedroom are curtained off but open onto my own private terrace which overlooks the pool. I had better water my plants on the terrace actually, they haven't had a drenching in some time.

Anyway, the world can wait. I snuggle into the cool sheets and when the dogs join me, their little snores help me fall back to sleep.

WHEN I NEXT WAKE, THE clock says it's noon and the dogs have their chins on my stomach, one on another side. I look down and they seem shaken. As I listen out, I discern raised voices. Ruben and Adam. Christ, what's going on now?

I slide off the bed and pull on a t-shirt and my dressing gown. I stand behind the door and hear some portion of what is being said down the hall, but not nearly enough. I know if I open my bedroom door now and the dogs shoot off towards the commotion, the men will know I'm listening in. So, I decide to take both dogs under my arms and am soon puffing and panting because they're not puppies anymore.

"Whatever, Adam. Just show your sister a bit more respect."

"As if she cares, mate. She's had plenty of geezers while you've been gone."

"You can't just bring home anyone you like and don't come off like that with me, I know Freya never brought men back here. I'd hedge I'm the first."

Adam has no reply. It's true I have been with other men these past four years—and can count them on less than one hand—but the point is, I always went to their place to screw. My sanctum is my sanctum. Adam knows he should ask if he wants to bring home girls, though I suspect this was in retaliation to him and that other chick splitting up.

"Fine, it won't happen again."

"Good. And mate? I mean. The two of them were hanging. What did you do with them?"

"Just... you know... we smoked some stuff. That's all."

"I see. And did you smoke it indoors, here?"

"Uh... no... we, um... it was on Victor's boat... everyone was doing it."

"And if everyone was kissing my butt, would you do that, as well?"

I have to press my lips together. It sounds like Adam doesn't know what to say.

"Tell me you were careful, at least?"

"Always," Adam assures him.

"And what about that other girl?"

"Ah, she couldn't have wanted me that bad. Kept texting her ex. What you gonna do?"

"Hopefully Freya won't discover what you did or mark my words, you won't sit for a week. And she especially won't take any shit when it comes to drugs, mate."

"I know," he groans.

"Take it from someone who's been there and done that, none of that is ever gonna do you any good at all."

"Yeah, so what do you do to get out of your own head?"

Ruben sighs. "Find a purpose. I could've totally gone fucking mental when my brother died but I didn't. I found a purpose. I decided to help other people. And besides having an occupation, I take care of my body, eat well and drink good wine. And I found a good woman. But trust me, Freya is rare. She was very hard to find. So, while you're searching, best to have your eyes open or you might not spot her. And fucking hell, painting has helped me, too."

"*You* paint?"

"Do *I* paint?" Ruben barks. "You'll see in a couple of days. My mum is bringing them over on my private plane."

"Wow. Does Freya know?"

"No, I want it to be a surprise."

"Okay, and are you any good?"

"Are you?" Ruben challenges Adam.

"Nah, I'm okay. But I'm gonna be an animator, so it doesn't matter that much."

News to me... maybe he decided art school was a really good way to meet women. Or he's branched out as he's gone along.

Anyway...

"True artists don't say 'Nah, I'm okay,' Adam, they say, 'I'm fucking gonna die with a brush in my hand because it's my goddamn life.'"

"That works?" he asks, sounding astonished.

Ruben laughs the house down while Adam chuckles.

"I wouldn't know, mate. When I was your age it seemed enough that I could kick a ball about. But times change, you know?"

I hasten back down the hallway as their conversation tails off. I breathe a sigh of relief and smile a little. It feels as though the guys have finally found a bit of common ground, which is good, because I couldn't lose either one of them, not now.

Chapter Four

Abso-Goddamn-Lutely

I try to pretend I didn't overhear their conversation, but as we're all lounging by the pool after lunch, it becomes pretty clear to the other two there's something on my mind.

"What's in your thoughts?" Ruben asks, as he tears himself away from reading a book on paint colours. He stole it from my shelf. How else is a girl to teach herself?

"It's Sunday. I'm just in shutdown. Leave me be."

The guys look at one another as I sip from my ice tea. They're probably imagining it's hormones. It isn't. It's my brain.

Why is he bringing Alexia over now? When he said just a few days ago he couldn't talk about her yet. Unless he's going to deal with her himself, not invite her here to the house and just pretend someone else brought over his precious work from Portugal.

I suppose I should be happy that the two most important people in my life appear to finally be getting on all right. That alone should have me content for once. Adam is very much my brother in that he's wary of unknowns, judges people quickly and doesn't like outsiders. If he's decided to give Ruben a chance, that's a big deal. He doesn't trust easily.

"Have you seen who Arsenal have just signed?" Adam gasps, staring at his phone.

"Don't fucking say it," Ruben exclaims. "Thought it was just rumours."

"Nah, check if you don't believe me."

I throw my hands up. "Oh my god. Men!"

I charge away from the loungers and shake my head as their laughter peels out behind me. I don't mind their banter really, I just needed an excuse to escape the pool area just then.

I lock myself in the en suite and sit on the loo, dial Alexia and wait for her to answer. I haven't seen her since Ruben's fake funeral... but we have spoken on the phone, occasionally. Without her, I wouldn't have known where to set up my gallery.

"*Olá?*" she answers.

"It's me, Alexia. How are you?"

"Freya," she gushes, "how are things?"

"Very good. How are you?"

"So-so."

"Your son thinks I don't know that you're coming in a few days."

Alexia laughs, that haughty snicker synonymous with her. "Oh, I see."

"Are you sure you should travel? He says you've been unwell."

"I have, but I'll be okay. The flight is very short. It'll be just me and my bodyguard and monsieur's work."

"Is it any good?" I whisper, almost afraid to ask.

"It is magnificent," she boasts, laughing. "But whatever you do, do not tell him I told you so."

"Okay," I chuckle.

"How are you, my love? Really?" she says, her gentle tone soothing.

"Ecstatic, knackered, elated, emotional... everything."

"I understand."

"He's not the same, Alexia."

"I know."

"He's... burdened."

"Partly my fault... partly... the weight of it all."

"What he did."

"Yes. He's going to need a lot of tending."

Here was me thinking I was the one who needed that.

I tell her all about the meal last night, how we ate on the beach, how I felt sure men didn't organise such evenings unless they intended to propose. I tell her we talked until sunrise... about my scholarship programme, my brother, the artists I've helped, the networks I've established... friends I have. She mostly listens and throws in the odd, "Ah, yes, hmm, uh-huh, oh yes, I see," as I ramble on.

"You're lucky, Freya. Most people would reunite after such a long time apart and discover they have absolutely nothing in common anymore. That their feelings have gone. That they don't recognise one another."

"I know," I murmur.

"Anyway, I'll be there the day after tomorrow. Tuesday. Pretend to be surprised."

"I'll try."

"Goodbye, dear girl. Be well."

"See you, Alexia."

She hangs up. I would never hang up on her because she's the elder and it would feel disrespectful.

Leaving the bathroom, I head for the kitchen and open the fridge. There's still some tarte left so I cut myself a slice and head to the living area in my bikini, my body sticking to the white leather corner group as I switch on the TV.

Ruben finds me watching trash TV and laughs. "I think she's gone mad."

I finish my tarte and put the plate on the coffee table. He thinks that's his cue to move in and slobber all over me. I wrestle his head to my lap and he lies on his back, looking up at me as I play with his thick hair.

"What's up, baby?" he asks, the tone of his voice changed, so he sounds worried.

I look down into his eyes and smile. "I'm still thinking about last night. It was pretty special."

I lean down and kiss his mouth, then stroke my fingers over his lips. He's a little sweaty from having been outside in the sun and what I wouldn't give to roll around in bed all evening with him later on. But I don't do that when I'm on. It's a crying shame that the day I'll get my body back, his mother will be arriving. Perhaps we could send Adam and Alexia out for an hour or two on an expedition of some sort. I think Adam will like her as much as I do and will be pleased to speak to an actual living artist who's sold thousands of pounds worth of canvas.

He's still staring at me, curious, so I tell him, "It's hard for me too when we can't, you know..."

He brightens instantly. "Ah."

"We need a night, very soon, just me and you. No dogs. No big kids. No interruptions. Just you, me, a hot date and an empty room at the end of it."

Ruben looks up at me, flush with delight. "You're so beautiful, Freya."

His gaze does however leave my face and head to my tits for quite a few seconds, so I jab him in the ribs.

"Arsehole."

"Good arsehole, though?"

"Haven't tried yours out yet, have we?"

He laughs a little, but then his face becomes blank. He sits up, pulls me across his lap and holds my body to his. He rests his cheek against my chest and stares out of the windows.

"What is in your thoughts?" I ask.

"Nothing except how I love the way your heart beats."

So, I sit still, stroke his hair, hold his body and sigh. If this is what he needs, he can have it.

THE NEXT MORNING, I wake to the sound of him showering. Before his recent return, I'd have been straight out of bed upon waking, but while he's here I know I don't have anything to worry about because Ruben always takes the dogs out, feeds them and sends them back to bed. It must be his biological clock ticking—a yearning to have something regular, fixed, a routine... family. He loves to be awake first and to take care of things before I'm up. Though perhaps he's always been an early riser. I hate not to wake up next to him and he knows that, but he is an early bird and I'm a lazy slob enjoying a few lie-ins while I can.

I creep into the bathroom and he doesn't look over his shoulder, appearing not to have heard me come in. I remove my knickers and use the toilet, shutting the lid but not flushing. He still has his back to me and is enjoying the rainfall shower, scrubbing his muscular body and letting the water revive him. He must have already had a swim, perhaps a run, too. I'll make him a big omelette for breakfast with goat's cheese, shallots and spinach, his favourite.

I open the cubicle door and he spins around, delighted when he finds it's me.

"Hmm, Freya," he groans, as I press my body to his back and run my hands over his abs and chest. He feels tense and taut, obviously having exercised already, yet his skin has that same quality as suede leather. The water slides through his silken body hair and he just feels... divine.

"Good morning, my love."

The centre of his back is thick yet elegant. I push my nose to his skin and breathe in the heat of him and the scent of his newly acquired sandalwood wash. It's incredibly tempting to slide my hand down and feel whether he's hard or soft, both just as glorious as the other. I want to feel him so badly.

He turns in my arms and his gaze is potent and pleading. I wrap my arms around his neck and he kisses me softly, then as I part my lips, he slips his tongue inside my mouth and we slot together, absolutely perfect. I hold him around his waist and back while he grips my shoulders and pulls me so close, I can feel he's hard.

He kisses my cheeks and my throat, my head falling back. My stomach is groaning with lust, my clit beating for him. I want his body to reassure me, pleasure me... but mostly, to silence me.

"Maybe we could... it's almost nothing now," I whisper, as he holds my breast in his hand and tangles his fingers in my hair.

He slides both his hands down to my bum cheeks and turns me so that I'm backed up against the wall. He shuts the shower off and pushes me against the tiles. I wrap one leg around his hips and he leans down a little, biting my lip as he finds he easily slips inside my body.

"Ruben," I gasp, clinging to his hair.

"Are you okay?" he asks, his voice deep and rough.

"Be gentle, baby." I mean emotionally, more than physically.

He rubs my breast and we rock back and forth against one another, my skin on fire, the steam of the room unbearable. He slides his tongue along my throat and I almost lose my shit. Things get worse when he grabs my buttock and holds me steady so he can press himself deep inside me.

It feels exquisite and my belly craves him, even like this... especially like this.

"I love you so desperately, Freya," he groans, touching his mouth to mine. "I love you more than any man has ever loved a woman."

I bury my face in his shoulder and cry out as I convulse and tremble, coming around his beautiful, gorgeous cock. I love every part of him. I cannot imagine a world without him in it. Not now. Not when I know what he did for me... what it cost... how he tried to save the world for me.

He withdraws gently and his milky cream drips down the insides of my legs. He pulls me close and embraces me tightly, kissing me passionately until my belly is a powder keg of need once more.

Ruben eventually pulls away, starts to wash himself and me, careful to touch me gently and with tenderness. He doesn't know I want him again and I'm too afraid to tell him I do. Also, it seems too greedy, perhaps over-confident. He wraps me in a fluffy towel as we leave the shower and I have to have a few minutes to myself. When I get back in the bedroom, he's waiting on the bed and I climb onto his body, wrap my arms around him and lie, listening to the beat of his heart.

"I needed to do that," he says.

"I needed it, too."

"In the past when we were in the dreaded friendzone, I could always tell when you were on your period. You'd chew your lip a lot more and get snappy. Also, you'd flush at the littlest dirty comment."

I giggle into his chest. "I'm terrible when I'm not getting any."

"It was difficult for me then to not give you what you need. Now it's nigh impossible."

I rub my cheek against his chest and tug him towards my body. "I just need your embrace, Ruben. Honestly. Your arms are everything. When you hold me, it's better than anything."

Our bodies entwine and he kisses my forehead, holding me close.

"The years apart... almost killed me, Freya," he moans, and starts to cry.

I hold him tight and kiss his chest. "I know, baby. I love you so much."

His sorrow breaks my heart and I let him have his moment to show me how much it hurts to have been away all this time.

"I've not been on the pill and I'm not going back on it, Ruben," I blurt, out of the blue.

"What are you saying?" he asks, catching his breath.

"I'm not going back on it. I don't like it and I never did and I don't care if I fall pregnant with your baby. I want to start living. I'm not going to wait, Ruben. Do you hear me? We're not putting our future on hold, not for a second longer."

He pulls my face to his and kisses me hard on the mouth, staring into my eyes, his nose squidged to mine.

"What are you saying, Frey?" he demands, unsure but inquisitive.

"We can't look back, Ruben. Ever again. We have to move forwards." He looks hopeful, a spark of light in his eyes again. "I know it's hard and it is going to be for a while yet, but I am not hanging around a second longer. We're not conventional, we never have been. It might be too soon to be trying for a family, but I don't fucking care. I want to start, don't you?"

He squeezes me tight and growls, "Abso-goddamn-lutely."

"Okay, then."

Chapter Five

His Soul

Tuesday arrives and Ruben wakes me with coffee, tells me we're going out today and to put on something nice and professional—we have a date at the gallery and Adam's already there, waiting for us. I pretend like I don't know anything and do as he says, acting intrigued. I shower and straighten my hair because for events, that's what I would normally do. When Ruben comes into the bathroom and finds my hair long and arrow-straight, he gives me that look where his mouth doesn't know whether to smile or pout and his eyes like what he sees. I don't think I've ever worn it like this before for him. On dates, I would've always have had it wavy or tied up. I think it's good to pull it straight and to one side to achieve maximum impact at times like this. From my closet, I pick out my patent-black slip-ons and a rust-coloured satin jumpsuit with a wrap top half, belt and cropped trousers. It's professional and covers everything but it's still sexy because I've got long legs and the material is glorious. Ruben appraises me in the entrance hall as we're about to leave and asks, "Where did you pick that up?"

"Online, darling," I tell him. "I'm usually a size ten for future reference. Excerpt in certain shops that do not appreciate hips or a bust."

He cracks a wink and an appreciative grin. "You look understatedly hot."

"I know."

I don't tell him he looks savage in a pair of cropped coral trousers and a crisp white shirt with the cuffs rolled to mid-forearm, three buttons left open at the top. He could wear any colour of the rainbow with that tan. And his footwear is super sexy, too. Brown leather slip-ons like mine, crocodile effect. Elegant. In London, we used to dress much differently, I think to myself, almost laughing.

He drives me down in the Ferrari and attempts to park outside my gallery where there's normally just a Fiat 500 or two. It tickles me as Ruben tries to sneak his car into the little spot, gives up, then flies back up the street until returning to discover no better spots are available and he'll just have to go where he can. I expect he'll be telling me my gallery needs a car park one of these days, though I usually walk the mile between the villa and here quite happily.

As we leave the car, I notice there's some commotion inside the gallery. The *fermé* sign is up but there are wooden crates dotted around the usually empty floor space.

"Ooh, you've been colluding," I say laughing, as we walk indoors to discover there's been a new delivery. "And it's jolly good we're not open today."

"And we have a visitor," Ruben warns me.

Adam crosses the space and comes into view, in his navy chino shorts, espadrilles and a white polo shirt, tucked in. He's followed closely by Alexia, dressed wildly artistic, a burnt-orange outfit swirling around her. She's wearing beaded sandals, her long, black hair is pulled tight into a ponytail (her hair's even longer than mine), and she's more tanned than Ruben. Her pink manicure and matching pedicure tell me she's not entirely lost to her sadness. She's getting back to herself (I really hope).

"Oh my god, Alexia," I cry, pretending to be surprised.

"Freya," she exclaims, and we dash for one another.

I can't believe it's been four years since we last saw one another. It feels like I saw her last week or last month because she looks the same, feels the same and sounds the same.

"You look sensational," she says, pulling back to survey me. "The Riviera suits you. Prettier than ever."

"Oh, no. Look at you. Come on!" I touch her fancy clobber and she flaps her hand at me.

When you look closer, you realise she's actually wearing incredibly cute cotton balloon trousers and a smock over the top. The crepe material is divine. Everything suits her tall, thin frame to perfection. She could wear a bin bag and look good. If I wore that, I'd look frumpy and fatter than I am. Must be the artist in her, living off cigarettes and odds and ends.

"Has my son been taking care of you?" Alexia asks, finding him over my shoulder.

"Absolutely, he has."

Ruben moves forward and gives his mother a kiss on the cheek, a sad look behind his eyes as he quickly hugs her. "Hello, Mum."

"You're very handsome today, darling."

"Thank you."

"So, what's going on?" I ask, butting in.

"Well..." Alexia begins, just as Adam arrives in the room with a crowbar and starts jacking open one of the crates. Some are much bigger than others.

"Wow," is all we hear from Adam as he gets a look inside, removing oodles of packing material. "Come and see, Freya."

"Are these yours, Alexia?"

"No." She shakes her head. "All Ruben's. All his."

I see he has his arms folded, trying to appear cool when he's anything but. I can tell he's nervous to hear what I think.

I walk over to where Adam is, just as he's getting the sides of the crate down. Then, we see a huge, ornately carved hunk of what is probably mango wood, maybe cedar.

"Wood sculpture, wow. I thought there would be paintings," I mumble, and only Adam hears me, eyebrows raised.

"This pyrography is really in fashion at the moment." Adam points to the scene Ruben has scorched into the wood. It is exquisite... but I don't know why... I was expecting paintings.

I stand akimbo, then turn and look at him. "Aren't you a painter, Ruben? I thought that's what you were into."

"I am, but I've also... found something else. Perhaps you need to check out the whole thing?"

Adam cracks open the crate so there's just the base left and takes the sides away so I can get a better look. So, okay. When you look at it from the other side, it's a sculpture of an eagle and her chicks. But on the other side, there's the picture Ruben has burnt into the flat side of the wood. It's a scene of humans around a camp fire, sat in a circle. It truly looks like a painting, but it's...

"It's so different, the carving... did you do that?" I ask, surprised he has the skill.

"I took a course," Ruben explains. "It's therapeutic. Why don't you check out the other pieces?"

I know how to sell paintings. I know what's marketable in that arena. However, wood carvings and pyrography... I would not have a clue. Do they auction, or do they go to furniture shops? I don't know why I'm surprised and taken aback. Maybe it feels a bit as if I don't really know him. I know I don't actually need to sell his pieces, do I? We could just keep these at the house if he wants. He doesn't need to sell. We have money. However, something tells me he wants to sell his work. Or why else would he have set this up?

When Adam cracks open the next crate, there are sections, and I don't know why, but my heart breathes a sigh of relief.

"Okay, then," Adam says, chuckling to himself.

My brother grabs a pair of cotton gloves and looks at Ruben. "Any breakables?"

Ruben taps his fist against his mouth. "My heart?"

Adam takes a breath and looks at me, raises his eyebrows and goes for it, sliding one of the next items up and out of the crate. He removes all the bubble wrap and corrugated cardboard and holds up a large wooden canvas so he can see it but none of the rest of us can. Adam studies it, then shakes his head.

"What is it? Is it shit?" Ruben blurts.

"Son, please," Alexia demands, half-chuckling.

Adam walks to one of the easels erected at the back of the gallery and sets up the piece so we can view it properly.

Adam stands back and stares.

I stare, too.

"Oh god," I whisper.

I charge across the room and put my hand on Adam's forearm, seeing what he sees.

Adam is still transfixed, saying nothing.

It's a picture of me, laid in bed asleep, curled up on my side. I'm covered by a thin sheet. My hair is fanned out around me. It's not a painting, though. It's pyrography. A picture burned into a huge slab of beautiful wood. It's exquisite and could be a photo.

"Did you do this from memory?" I mutter, tears in the corners of my eyes.

"Yes, baby."

It reminds me of when we were in Florence together. It was warmer there and we didn't sleep beneath a duvet or blankets. I get a shiver down my spine.

"It's so lifelike," Adam says, chuckling, "it's beautiful. And lord knows she has a ton of admirers who'd pay thousands for this."

Ruben wraps his arms around my waist from behind. "There are many more. Some aren't of you."

The heat of his body caresses my back and I take a deep breath. "You're gifted, Ruben."

"Doing this kept me alive," he says, breathless. "There's a lot more back at the farmhouse in Portugal. My mother just brought a taster."

"Exquisite," Adam repeats, absent-minded as he continues to stare at the outline of his sister's naked body—although I'm fairly sure it's just the artistry he's referring to.

"What are you intending?" I mumble, turning my face and bending my neck so I can give him a peck on the jaw.

"I don't know yet," he sighs, "I just wanted you to see them. I hope there's something here, don't you think? A story."

"I thought I hated you before, mate," Adam exclaims, turning and walking back to the crate, "but I think I'm about to hate you even more."

He grabs another wooden canvas out of the crate and brings it over, setting this one up, too. This time we have an etching of someone I saw only once before but definitely recognise.

It's Laurent, Ruben's brother, who died when he was only a teenager. The likeness is unmistakable.

"Is this you?" Adam asks. "Your football days?"

"It's Laurent," I hastily correct Adam. "When he was going up to Cambridge."

"Oh, okay," Adam says, realising who I mean.

I turn and wrap my arms around Ruben's neck, hugging him silently. A million tears balance on the edge of my lashes. The likeness is just as accurate as the one of me. Ruben can obviously draw from memory. He doesn't even need a photograph. Unless the one of me asleep in bed did originate from a photograph...

But still, this one of Laurent looks so natural, like he was either caught unawares by the camera or this is a real snapshot straight out of Ruben's imagination.

"You should organise an exhibition, no?" Alexia says, suddenly arriving at our side. "There are even better ones, trust me."

"I'm on it," Adam gasps, heading back to the crate.

Once Adam is out of earshot, I pull my face out of Ruben's shoulder and take his hands, standing in front of him. He looks relieved, maybe a little terrified still.

I turn my head and look at his mother, who appears righteously defiant. "He can't put his name to these, Alexia. He's been in the shadows for a reason."

"He can't," she murmurs, "but god doesn't bestow talent just so it can remain hidden. And you can exhibit under an assumed name."

Adam puts his latest find on the last available easel and I spin to see what's next. The sight almost makes me crumble.

There's Alexia, unmistakable, her robes around her. She's in a storm, appears as though she's being attacked by the elements. She's small, a crouched bud. The tiny details of the expression on her face are heart-breaking.

"Fuck," Adam says, "I've been waiting to see something like this all my life."

I almost want to run from the room because it's too much. He's...

He defies reason.

RUBEN DRIVES ME BACK to the house and I'm unable to speak because of the emotion caught in my throat, plus the fact I'm horny as heck.

We pull onto the driveway and I'm about to get out, when he tugs on my hand and I turn to look at him, trying to figure him out.

"When we get inside, you know I'm gonna fuck you, right?"

"Yes," I answer softly.

"You could've just gone to Canada, Freya. I would've joined you there. That was my hope for you. That you'd get there, safely, then I would show up. It'd be beautiful and we'd live happily ever after."

I sense he's got something else to add because he looks worried about how I am going to react. I turn my body to face forward, stare through the windscreen at the front door and fold my arms.

"I thought you'd get the message, somehow. Don't ask me how. I thought you would somehow guess I was alive and was willing you to go there. Didn't you guess, at all?"

I shake my head. "Never crossed my mind. Don't know why."

"And then you didn't go. And I couldn't meet you."

"I suppose I didn't expect my boyfriend of two weeks to fake his own death. I don't know. Maybe it was too outlandish and sadistic to cross my mind."

I'm shaken and he can tell, his sharp intake of breath and the way he's jangling his keys letting me know he feels just as uncomfortable about all this as I do.

"Maybe life has a funny way of working out, Freya. Because you didn't go to Canada, I managed to get Freddie in prison. And then I went to Portugal and did a lot of work on myself, including finding my artistic side. Today I needed you to see what I did with my time. For me it's obvious how you spent your days, but I wanted to show you how I spent mine. I wanted to prove to you, I didn't go lightly. I *had* to go. Even from prison, Freddie could've forced someone's hand. But now he's dead, all the secrets he kept are, too. He doesn't have any power over anyone anymore."

Of course, it crossed my mind dozens if not hundreds of times that if I'd just done what he asked and gone to Canada... we could've already been married and had kids by now. Lived already, instead of existing these past four years... wishing and praying and hoping.

"You're right, about Freddie," I murmur, "and you were right about Adam and me reconnecting with him. And I wouldn't have got the gallery where it is if it wasn't for our separation, although I like to think people do buy art in the wilds of Canada, just that they probably don't pay quite the same big bucks for it." I hear him snigger. "And we're here, now, and I'm ready to fuck... and you're dredging up the past again which I said not to do. And yeah, I'm happy you've found your happy place and you're exploiting it. I think one of the reasons we fell in love is that we're the same, you and I. We share this love of art, but more than that, too. I don't need to see your soul represented in art, I know your soul already because it's a part of me." I turn in my chair and see he's biting his lip, studying me furtively. "I love you. I don't know why you think you even need to impress me anymore. I love you. Nothing could ever change that. Not distance or separation or even death. We're only truly whole when we're together. You and me make one, Ruben. Don't we?" He nods that we do, his eyes shiny. "We didn't know that night, at Freddie's wedding, not consciously, but definitely there was something deep. We made a connection. We understood one another so quickly. There's no breaking that, Rubes. We're the same, do you hear me? Only you could understand me, only I could understand you. And now I don't want to talk anymore. You know what I want, don't you?"

"Yes," he growls.

"And no more of this, baby?"

"No," he assures me.

"I love your work, Ruben. I love it. I'm already wet because that's how much I love it."

"Say another word and I'll have you right here."

"This car isn't going to allow for that, Ruben."

"Then I'll take you on the bonnet."

"When the gates have gaps and people often walk right past on the street?"

"Yeah." He looks deadly serious, chest heaving.

"Inside, you wretch. Or I won't let you inside me. And even though Adam isn't due back until later, he has friends around here and I don't want them reporting back to him that his sister is an exhibitionist whore."

"A whore, no. An exhibitionist? We can always make one of you."

I leave the vehicle at lightning speed and race to the front door with my keys ready. I'm letting myself into the house just as he's slamming the car door behind him and locking it. I race across the hallway to key in the alarm code and then he's inside too, the door slamming behind him, his chest heaving up and down and his head bowed like it's too heavy to hold up, eyes peering at me from beneath dark lids.

He barrels towards me just as I'm kicking off my shoes and we crash together, him picking me up and me wrapping my arms around his head and welcoming his rampant tongue into my mouth all at once.

The state of my stomach... my core is throbbing with need. I have a heart in my groin, it feels like, pulsing blood at an alarming rate and my empty pussy might convulse at any moment. His hands are fixed on my bum, gripping me harshly, his tongue a tornado of mixed emotions in my mouth. Passionate one moment, savage the next... always desperate. Never apologetic. He can't be. Not with his love. We're too strong to ever really say sorry. We forgive because we have to, because we only exist together. We can't waste a second more. Tomorrow isn't promised. Not even today is.

He carries me directly to the bedroom and sits himself on the edge of the bed. He's unbuttoning his trousers as I tackle my belt and unwrap my jumpsuit, letting it fall off my body. I step out of it and leap onto his lap just as he's got his cock out. God, it's amazing. I put my hand around him, feel the heat of his erection, the solidity... he's so hard. The dark skin covering his cock is shot through with bulging blood vessels and I can't wait a second longer.

I shuffle forwards at the same time as he reaches around the back of me, tugs my thong to the side and exposes my folds to his big, beautiful penis. I point him at my entrance and hover, then put my arms around his neck and stare into his eyes, sliding down the length of him until I'm almost bursting.

He stares up at me, his green eyes smudgy, like a forest blighted by grey, hazy rainfall. He's the most beautiful man alive, and I know I would say that being biased and all, but he actually is. Not because I'm ordinary in comparison. Just that he's one in a billion. Not just a red-hot lover and physically glorious and highly artistic, intelligent and passionate, but he's just... so delicate and vulnerable and beautifully insecure, beneath all that. His heart is wonderful. He can hold so much inside his heart and yet he still goes on. He's a lion. He's my warrior man.

Ruben slides his hands up and down my back as I tear open the few remaining buttons on his shirt. I move in even closer until our fronts are touching and our noses are pushed together. I'm full of him and I know as soon as I start moving, my orgasm is going to tear the roof off this house and render me incapable of savouring these moments of reflection.

He sweeps his hands around the front of me until he's got my breasts in his hands, cupping them and then grasping them tight. I love the way he touches me. Only he could touch me like this. Everyone else feels crass, wrong, dirty.

KARMA

He kisses my throat until lifting my tit and going to my nipple instead. I almost, almost convulse, tipping my head back and begging him with my cries to stop. I start swinging my hips towards his and grab his hair between my fingers. I cling on for dear life as the guts of my soul clutch him, shuddering around him over and over, until I can't see anymore.

"Ah, god, Ruben," I cry, rocking aggressively into his groin, his cock responding to me, getting bigger and fitting even more snugly inside the dripping cage of my desire, his love trapped inside me now.

"Ah, Christ, Freya," he groans, pressing his face between my breasts and taking his hands to my rear again, his touch encouraging me not to hold back.

I pull his head into my chest and my hair flicks about as I bounce with no coordination or rhythm at all, needing all the pent-up anguish out of me with any friction I can manage while I'm feeling like this... crazy and knowing it will wrench me when it comes.

Ruben slobbers on my throat, licking and sucking, his saliva frothing everywhere. It's manic and animalistic. He grabs my arse even firmer and bangs me up and down on him until I'm a shivering mess, screaming and crying with the most bittersweet pleasure, my face pressed into his hair as I tremble from head to toe. It only ever feels right with him. I only feel whole with him. With anyone else, it doesn't quite fit. With him, it's like we're not even two beings; we're entirely one and he belongs inside me, just like this, because I couldn't come harder or for longer or take anyone deeper than I can take him, because he's made to be inside me. With me. Only in these precious moments does anything make sense; do any of the pieces of the puzzle fall into place.

"Uh, no, no, no, uh, god, no," I complain, because I didn't want it to be over.

His face is buried in my chest, our bodies sweaty and hot, his scent earthy and overpowering. I push the shirt off his back and he kicks the trousers away he never fully got off.

I wrap myself around him and he slides us up the bed, his cock still buried inside me.

By the time we're entwined, he naturally slips out of me and we hold one another close. I know as soon as he's recovered, we'll be doing it again. Being apart isn't good for either of us because when we're together again like this, it's a drug we can't get enough of and everything else goes out of the window while we top up our stores.

He pushes me onto my back and pulls my knickers down my legs, staring at my skin. He touches my body with his fingertips, caressing and appreciating my womanly form. He sucks my nipple gently and kisses across my chest until finding my other breast. He moves on top and I'm suddenly full of him again. I lie back and groan, arms above my head, willing him to do as he pleases.

"Freya," he says, his chest rumbling.

My eyes fly open. "Yes?"

"I need you to be present, always, I need your arms as much as you need mine."

I wrap my arms around him, clutch my legs around his back and give him my lips.

KARMA

He makes love to me and I'm swallowed, down into the bottomless cavern of the pleasure only he can give, lost to everything but the deep, endless depths of his soul... his kiss.

Chapter Six

Salt and Pepper

I suck in a breath of warm, sea air. It's lovely as ever down here. Ruben puts his hand on my knee under the table, sat next to me at my favourite restaurant on the beach, my brother and Alexia sat opposite us.

"A toast," Ruben proposes, "to having everyone together."

Alexia manages a sad smile, catching my eye, and I determine her thinking.

She's definitely not sure everyone is together. There's Laurent and Fred for a start, gone a long time now, but still part of her family.

Plus, there's my mum and dad.

Well, just my mum, I suppose. Adam gives me a look and I know he's thinking the same thing. In fact, Alexia and our mother Delphine would get on swimmingly. It's a shame she's not here.

"To us," I offer, and we clink glasses and savour the Portuguese wine Alexia ordered. It is actually divine. A sauvignon blanc like no other.

My body is still humming from our lovemaking earlier, but at the same time, there's still some unsettledness inside me. I think perhaps it's the looks Ruben and his mother are giving one another.

It doesn't matter how hot we are together, or how much we love one another, I can't help but still notice anything that seems wrong or out of place. It's odd that she has refused to stay at the villa with us. Now I know Alexia is her own woman and has a dozen friends in the area, one of which she decided to stay with instead of with us, but we would have made her very comfortable at the villa and she could have spent even more quality time with her son and future daughter-in-law... because that's what I expect will happen. Well, I know it will.

Even this dinner tonight seems a bit of an effort for her.

There's the look she keeps shooting Ruben, but she also keeps fidgeting. I wonder if she is in recovery or something... perhaps doesn't want us to pick up on things...

Adam leans forward on his elbows and looks at Ruben. "So, mate. What's the deal with the art? Got any idea what you're gonna do?"

This will be as much news to me as anyone else because between making love all day, we haven't had time to discuss what he has decided.

"I do have a few pieces I'd be happy to part with," Ruben says, "but only if Freya wants to exhibit and sell them for me, because I want to remain anonymous. Guess I'll have to figure out a co-dename or nom de plume type thing."

Adam doesn't seem convinced. "You're not gonna put your name to them, really?"

"Don't need to, do I?"

"You'd get more for 'em." Adam shrugs. "And as we know, the story of the artist is behind 90% of every sale."

I pout my lips because I can see where this is going. Butting in, I suggest, "I could organise a preview and see what the vibe is. Nothing to lose. The pieces of me naked will remain for our own private collection." I watch as Adam's face falls. "And the rest, we'll see what demand is like. I'm not going to make Ruben do anything he doesn't want to."

"Missed opportunity," Alexia says, sniffing.

"Couldn't agree more," Adam concurs.

I slide my hand into Ruben's beneath the table and he squeezes my fingers.

"I'm not looking for attention, just for these to have a happy home. We don't want Debbie finding out I'm alive and kicking."

"She may already know," Alexia chuckles. "Freya isn't exactly unknown down here, you know? It won't have escaped people's notice she's recently been hanging out with someone new. This is the South of France. Your father and Freddie used to come and hang out in Monte Carlo all the time. There will be people in the area who know the story."

"Debbie's too thick to do anything, trust me," Adam scoffs. "Last I heard, she was working in Morrison's again and going out with a car washer. Come off it, ma'am. Absolutely no way."

"Interesting," says Alexia, in her posh accent, which is a little of this, a little of that, and a lot Portugal when she is relaxed, which she sure isn't at the moment. "So why the fuss, Ruben? Who else are you running from?"

"Where do I start?" Ruben says. "Do you think I managed what I did alone, hmm?"

"You mean, killing your own father and half-brother?"

They glare at one another across the table while Adam and I feel like we're caught in the crossfire.

"Ruben didn't kill anyone, Alexia," I remind her. "Ruben was the only one brave enough to do what a dozen others couldn't."

I want to include her in that, but going by the way she's shooting daggers at me, I'd say she knows exactly what I'm insinuating. She could've stopped Fred years ago, but didn't.

Ruben removes his hand from mine and grabs the salt and pepper. He creates a pile of salt and then draws a ring around it with the pepper.

"The salt represents the victims, including Debbie, who he got up the duff. Do you remember that, Mum? And he and Freddie and their gangsters are the pepper, hemming everyone in, including you and me, Mum. I'm sorry if I had to get dirty trying to get through the pepper, but that's what I had to do. And my life will never be the same again because I tried to do the right thing."

She stands, shoves her napkin on the table and shakes her head. She's so angry, she can't even form words. We watch in shock as she leaves the table, heads out of the restaurant tent and waves for a cab.

Ruben takes a deep breath and sighs. "Sorry you had to see that. But that's what I've been up against."

The entrées are brought over and the server sees the napkin on Alexia's side of the table, worried what to do.

"She had to go home sick," Adam says, "but I'll have two, not to worry."

"Ah, okay," says the waitress, putting two in Adam's hands. He inelegantly scrapes Alexia's pâté onto his plate and Ruben and I can only watch on, wincing.

"Can you cancel the lady's main course," I gesture, smiling at the waitress.

"No problem."

KARMA

The waitress leaves and Ruben tips back the rest of his wine, then pours himself some more. I'm only glad my brother is trustworthy and knows the whole story already or we could be here all night trying to fill him in and/or pay him off. I had to tell him ages ago because it was the only way to explain to him my strange moods, my withdrawal from the world... my occasional bouts of depression. I can see why Adam was sceptical of Ruben when he first got back, and I can also see things from Alexia's point of view, as well.

"She still can't admit who he really was?" I pose the question to Ruben.

"Nope." He digs into his steak tartare and I remind myself to make him clean his teeth before bed tonight.

"You didn't kill anyone, did you?" Adam asks, his mouth full of green leaves, melba toast covered in balsamic vinegar and duck pâté. I really must educate my uncouth, endearingly boyish little brother one of these days.

"Didn't kill a soul," Ruben says. "Just told the truth. But believe me, the truth is heavier than a sledgehammer and deadlier than any weapon out there. My mother has problems admitting who he was and what he did. She's developed a sort of fond, nostalgic way of coping with it, I suppose. Totally forgotten her younger son would probably still be alive if not for his father."

"It's fucked up," Adam says.

I say nothing, wishing I could simplify my own response like that.

I feel sorry for Alexia, I can't help it. Ruben shouldn't have made his half-brother so angry. Ruben should've gone to the police, told them what he knew about his father...

Unless, of course... the police had been bought, all along. The night of Laurent's graduation party from Eton (which became a brawl), someone on the force had been paid off and Fred wriggled out of going down to the police station for the night like everyone else caught up in it. He got away with the things he did because he knew people who could be bought. How high up the corruption went, I don't know, but why would Ruben have done the things he did unless he was terrified of reprisals? Like what happened to his ex, Gia.

Speaking of... "Does your mother know about Gia?"

Ruben seems uncertain. "I think my mother is the reason Gia got shot. My father feared if the two ever met, my mother would discover the truth about Freddie because I'd been pretty open and honest about all that with Gia. It might have been the one sin he knew she wouldn't forgive. The lovechild, a living product of infidelity. One you can't turn a blind eye to." He screws up his face. "Yeah, my mother would at first have tried to explain it away with tales about his hard upbringing, his violent father, his lack of a role model... but she would've found it difficult to stay, if my father had brought Freddie into their lives."

"So, really, your father trying to protect Alexia accounts for some of the worst things he ever did? Deep down, she knows that. No bad upbringing can account for a madman simply trying to disguise his infidelities."

Adam laughs as he continues to stuff his face, dribbling balsamic vinegar everywhere.

"In a nutshell, yeah," Ruben says. "He was just bad, but for her, admitting that seems impossible. In Portugal, I had the housekeeper's cottage and she had the main house. We wouldn't speak unless absolutely necessary and she didn't want to hear what I had to say. I think the only reason she came here with the art was so she could see you, Freya and get my stuff out of the barn. She tells me she already has everything else ready to go. I just have to let her know."

"She wants you to suffer like she has." I offer my slant. "She wants the truth to come out. You're still alive. All that."

"She wants something... I don't know what. She wants me to fall, it feels like. I can't help feeling that behind her pretence of being proud of me, she wants me to fall."

Adam grunts, throws back some wine and tells us, "Welcome to mine and Freya's world. They're only happy when you're failing, otherwise it makes them feel bad."

"I don't know..." I've been half-heartedly eating my fishcake starter and no longer have the stomach for it, setting my implements down. "I truly think there's more we don't know. I always thought so. More than meets the eye with Alexia. She and I emailed over the years, you know?" I bump my shoulder to Ruben and he looks shocked.

"She never fucking said," he exclaims.

"She never, ever mentioned you," I tell him, and that part he isn't shocked about, "but I sensed that was because she knew it would hurt. But the other stuff she would write about... how much she missed London, her work... the house she'd had to sell to pay off Fred's debts. It seemed to me like she was either bitter or winsome, I could never tell. And she was always very jokey when it came to asking me about my work, like I was having a bash at it and shouldn't be too hard on myself if it didn't work out... and always quiet when I'd describe my successes."

Adam uses his napkin and rubs his stomach after eating half a pound of pâté. "I told you. They don't want us to prove them wrong. Do you know, Ruben? Our mother is a classically trained violinist who studied in Prague and could've been a really big name. Then she got ill and our dad convinced her to knock it down a notch, never to achieve her full potential. She gave him two artistic kids. Neither of us is a waste of space like him and he didn't like that. But she forgives him, all the damn time."

"Mindfuck," Ruben mutters, his steak tartare demolished. Even after a little argument with his mother, it seems he still has a big appetite. Then I remember what we were doing all afternoon.

The waitress takes away our plates (mine with a bit left on it, although Ruben snaffled some over my shoulder) and we're left with just the wine again. Adam pours himself some and offers me a bit more, but I decline. Ruben has what's left in the bottle and I pour Alexia's leftovers into the cobbles beneath the table.

"There's really only one explanation," I tell the pair, cradling my wineglass, "our fathers were control freaks. And when our mothers got ill, instead of going through it with them which they couldn't do because they were both cowards, they fought for ways to gain control over what was completely outside of their control. Because that's the truth of mental health, right?"

Adam and Ruben nod, both seeming more sombre.

"Trying to control what is impossible to control—that is, Alexia's response to things he did and nobody forced him to do—that got people killed. Nothing else. And Dad's nastiness" – I stare at Adam – "that's what stunted Mum's talent and potentially ours, too, if we'd have let him. I have an innate appreciation of art but I'm not artistic. I always had a business brain. But if I'd have listened to him, I'd be packing bags in Morrison's too and going out with a car washer, because I wouldn't have known I could do any better for myself. Not listening to them is the best way, I reckon. It should be taught in schools that you look at what your parents do and go the opposite way, because otherwise you're likely to get stuck in the same cycle."

Our main meals are brought out, Ruben orders another bottle of wine, and the evening becomes our opportunity to tell one another about the things we can't believe happened to us growing up... and the ways in which nothing seems to change for some people. We talk shit until the restaurant is closing.

And then we stumble home, plastered.

I WAKE BURIED BENEATH a pile of limbs. As I come to, I realise it's just Ruben's arms, but they feel like ten arms. My head is pounding and I groan. He has an arm slung around my neck and one around my chest.

"Ruben, you're too heavy," I moan.

"I'm incapable of moving."

"You drank less than six glasses of wine!"

"And I fucked you four times right before that. Not a good idea," he says, wincing as I press the button for the shutters to come up.

Through the voiles, we see Adam doing laps of the pool and Ruben groans, "Fucking twenty-year olds."

I roll over and chuckle in his ear, "Poor baby."

Resting my head on his shoulder, I inhale deeply the smell of his neck and stroke my hand across his chest. He puts his arms around me and kisses my hair. It takes us a while to get ourselves together.

"I'm exhausted," I groan, "but it feels like we slept for years."

"Me too."

Exhausted though we are, lying here like this feels nice. No rush to go anywhere, or do anything. Adam isn't opening the gallery today because we still have all the pieces to organise. I think we'll store them for the time being, until I've had enough time to think about the best way forward.

"That was rough last night," I say, pausing, "with Alexia, I mean."

We might have talked shit over dinner and drank wine while chewing the fat like boisterous, over-ambitious teenagers, but in the morning things always look different.

"I think, to be honest, she just wanted to check up on you," he groans, putting one of his hands under his head to prop himself up.

"What're you going to do to me? Recruit me for your new cult?"

"I don't know," he says, his throat croaky.

I lift myself over him and look into his eyes. He looks tired and sleepy but so handsome, his dark hair ruffled, eyes like slits, mouth puffy and swollen. I lean down and kiss his mouth softly, then tuck my head under his chin and cuddle into him. He gives me a sated growl.

"Does she trust you so little?" I ask, sighing.

"She's definitely got a bee in her bonnet about me releasing that work in my own name."

"Because she wants you to have the fame she never had?"

"I already had that, as a footballer. Believe me, I know I'm not a genius. I have skill, but if I'd never been a footballer, I would've sold a few bits on Etsy now and again and happily taught art history or something."

I take a deep breath, lie on my side and puff up the pillows underneath my head so I can look down into his eyes as he lies there flat on his back. He would've broken a thousand hearts as an art history professor.

"Ruben, you have more than skill. There's a talent there you don't see because you can't. You're too close to it. I have people sending me stuff all the damn time. Trust me, I know when I see something that is raw and from the soul of the artist. Your work is."

Ruben folds his arms and huffs. "So why does she still hate me so much?"

"I think it's more that she loves you too much. Maybe if you release your work and the danger gets bad again, you'll have to return to Portugal to hide and take care of her."

"Nah," he snaps, "Freya, I don't buy it. She can't let it go, any of it."

"Maybe seeing me and you happy together is tough for her?"

He shakes his head, biting his lip. "I don't know."

"She doesn't hate you, Ruben. I don't want you to lose your mother, okay? Trust me. I know what it's like and it sucks big style."

Ruben turns and puts his hand around my neck, bringing me closer so he can kiss my forehead.

"I won't lose her. It was probably just her medication making her bitchy last night. Her moods get majorly affected."

"Medication for what?"

"For coming off the other medication, I presume," he groans.

I take a deep breath. "Baby, just try to see her again before she goes. You'll regret it otherwise."

"I will."

I bite my nail and shake my head, not convinced of the whole way she was. "You know, Alexia could have anyone. How old is she?"

"Fifty-four," he says.

"Even Adam was looking at her, didn't you notice? He probably stroked one out over her this morning."

Ruben turns to me, eyebrow raised and grunts. "I sometimes forget what a filthy, wanton sex goddess you are, but that was just gross."

I roll quickly on top of him. "You sometimes forget? We can't have that."

I kiss him for about twenty seconds before he cries, "Freya, my cock is still sore."

I laugh against his mouth and complain, "Oh, god. I see then."

We play fight until we end up spooning, him behind me, gripping my breasts and his mouth pressed into my neck.

"Hasn't she had any gentleman callers?" I ask him.

"I wouldn't know. We practically lived apart."

"I remember you saying. I think she just needs a mature man, someone to show her it can be different."

"I think it must be difficult to get over an abusive relationship," he says, "always willing them to get better, but they never actually do. She will always be wondering if he would've got better, eventually, even though there was little to no chance it would've ever happened. Not when he got to almost seventy and hadn't changed his ways. I think she wouldn't trust a normal man. She'd feel like there was something wrong because he wasn't sneaking around. The way my dad was became her normal."

"Yuck. And it's repulsive that he got Debbie into bed."

"I know."

"And she was crying at Freddie's graveside?"

"You know the type... some kind of sick loyalty. Or maybe even crying for the man she really loved... Fred. Pretending it was Freddie she was really sad about, but method acting sort of thing. Who will ever know?"

"We could go and ask her," I laugh.

"Never," he exclaims.

He's right.

"Let's get away for a bit," he says, "get the dogs taken care of. Leave Adam in charge, or something. Let's just go. I need some headspace. It feels like we need neutral ground, what do you say?"

"Where?" I ask.

"Leave that to me."

"Okay."

"Yeah?"

"Yeah."

"Good. Great."

He leaps out of bed and into the shower. While he's gone, I locate my phone and dial Alexia.

"Hello," she answers, sounding surly.

"How are you this morning?"

"Amazing," she boasts.

"Then what was that all about, Alexia?" I ask, keeping my voice down. "Last night."

She sighs loudly down the line. "I don't know, I snapped."

"You could have anyone, you know? Find a good man. Someone who will really love you. Even my brother was a little intrigued by you."

"Oh, god," she says, sounding so tired, "I've had youngsters chasing me for years. What is it about pre-menopausal women to these little pricks?"

"And you've never been tempted?"

"What's the biggest age difference you've had?"

"Erm, I don't know. Maybe twenty years."

"Older, of course."

"Uh-huh," I laugh.

"See, acceptable. Me and a man thirty years my junior, not acceptable. Yet all the men my age want a twenty-five-year-old bimbo who will suck cock and not talk back."

I laugh down the line, covering my eyes with my hands. "Alexia, Ruben does want you to be happy, you know?"

"I know," she resigns herself. "I fear I'm incapable."

"Be brave, if you haven't kissed a lot of frogs yet, you're not even a little way to finding your prince."

"Well, there was one guy," she admits.

"Oh yes?"

"He's my childhood sweetheart. When he learnt I was back in Portugal and living alone, he started dropping flowers on my doorstep every day."

"That is so sweet," I gush, my heart clenching.

"I can't, Freya. Fred did love me. It would feel a betrayal."

"What, even now?"

"He had demons."

"He didn't love you enough, Alexia. It's simple."

"What about Ruben? Do you think he loves you enough?"

"I do," I whisper, sensing something about her tone. "Unless you know to the contrary?"

"I know nothing," she says, snapping her mouth shut. "I must go. Tell Ruben I will be at the café in Old Town until twelve, then I leave for Portugal. Okay?"

"I'll tell him."

Ruben comes back into the room just as I'm about to hang up.

"And Freya, promise me you will always take care of you."

"I will."

"Okay, bye."

She gets off the line and my heart is racing.

"Was that her?" he asks, looking terrified.

"She says she'll be at the café in Old Town until twelve."

"Oh, okay."

He starts getting dressed and I don't know if she was shit stirring just then or genuinely trying to warn me about Ruben being like his father.

Well, all I know is that two weeks ago was when we got together for real... and he's been nowhere but inside my arms since then.

So, fuck you, Alexia.

She's a complex woman and I forgive her, but from now on, I will remember to be careful.

After all, she was married to that bastard all that time. Who's to say he didn't rub off on her? Who's to say Fred wasn't more scared of her than she was of him?

Sometimes, the whole truth eludes us, doesn't it?

Chapter Seven

Hidden Threats

Ruben goes off on his own to meet his mum for lunch or brunch, who knows, taking a cab there instead of risking his car in Old Town! Or maybe he knows he will need alcohol to get through it—whatever they need to get off their chests.

While he's out, I jump in my electric car and head to the gallery to catch up with Adam who I just missed this morning.

"Didn't know you were popping down," he says, welcoming me as I walk indoors.

He's at his tall desk, laptop open, his arse perched on the edge of a stool.

He's wearing stonewash today and a pink linen shirt. That's why the aircon is on, then. Looking lovely comes at a price. July in Nice doesn't require much more than flip flops and a bikini.

"Ruben left to wave his mother off, so I wanted to get another look at what he brought in yesterday without him peering over my shoulder."

Adam's silvery laugh fills the air. "Have at it. There's some music festival going on in town today. I think we'll be quiet so if you need help, I'll happily close."

"I'll happily have you stay right here so I can take a look on my own."

He salutes me. "Yes, sir!"

I walk away laughing.

I punch in the code for the door to the back room and let myself inside. The room is always kept at a cool fifteen degrees Celsius and there's no natural light in here. I flick the lights on and the racks and shelves come to life.

I rub my hand on the back of my neck and try to work out the tension in my spine. It's not working. There's something about Alexia I don't trust. Which is odd. Because I trusted her before. When I thought Ruben was dead, I trusted her. Even when I found out he wasn't dead and that she'd known all along he wasn't dead, I still trusted her because I recognised the impossible position she'd been put in. After witnessing how she was with him the other night, and now forcing me to question his fidelity, I am super unsure what I am meant to believe.

Over the years, she gave me free advice which did prove useful. However, we really only ever communicated over email after a certain point. Now I've seen her in person again, behaving like that, I have to wonder how genuine she is. Did she keep in touch just so she could report back to Ruben about the goings on in my life? And why did they hole up together in Portugal? Ruben could have travelled anywhere, done anything, but he decided to stay with her. Maybe because parts of Portugal are remote, sparsely populated and Alexia would know the places foreign people never visit—thus keeping Ruben safe.

I was honest with Ruben about my love life during our separation, but was he honest? In four years, how could a man so sexual not have had sex with anyone? Look how he was last week, when he couldn't get in my knickers for just a few days.

Unless Alexia was actually trying to tell me something...

Maybe he started up something with someone out in Portugal, not expecting Freddie to die so young, then he dumped her the moment he knew Freddie was dead. Came running back to me, omitted the truth about being with someone out in Portugal...

I take a deep breath because we've been here before. I once ran off because I couldn't handle the uncertainties, the newness of everything... his odd, clingy, domineering behaviour... and I ran. I kept running until I felt so silly, I didn't do it anymore. This time, I won't run. I shall stay. I shall see this out. Find out all the truths I can about Ruben's choices, his motives... the years we spent apart and what he was really doing all that time. Speaking of...

I locate the pieces Alexia brought in yesterday. Adam has left them in the work area, where we usually look at paintings or sculpture across a huge wooden desk we can spread out on to evaluate things that have come in.

There's the eagle sculpture which is the only sculpture she brought over, but apparently there are other similar pieces back in Portugal. I do like this sculpture but I think these are highly niche and only a certain type of client would buy a wooden sculpture, perhaps someone who wants to buy out the whole lot, no matter what the collection contains—or someone with a log cabin in Canada or the Alps.

I lift the cloth off the first wooden pyrography canvas and find myself staring at Alexia, surprisingly. It is stunning and would be the centrepiece of the entire collection, I would hazard. I find the next one, the picture of Laurent. It's haunting and again, very well done. Then there's the three pictures of me. The first one is the one with me asleep. There's also another where

I'm sleeping but this one pictures me in a huge armchair, my head turned to the side, arms wrapped around my legs. It looks as though I was crying and fell asleep racked with pain. I wonder what night this was. I don't remember. Perhaps this one he did from his imagination and nothing else. The last picture finds me barefoot on a cobblestone street, wearing just a thin silk slip down to my ankles. My boobs and hips are filling the slip and this piece is a little more than erotic—no underwear beneath the slip. The rain is falling all around me, I have my arms raised to the skies, my face too. My hair is clumped and damp, I'm wearing a smile and it looks as though I'm carefree. This one is definitely interpretational. I can't imagine myself ever doing this. Not in the middle of the street.

If Ruben was spending all his time out in Portugal making art that resembles my image, then I hardly think any woman would have been happy to spend time with a man so obsessed with someone else.

But what did he say yesterday? He wanted me to know he hadn't been idle during his time in Portugal, and that he hadn't forgotten about me. Was that guilt talking? Did he burn my image into wood during the night, only once his substitute lover was asleep?

Or did he really save himself for me all these years?

I truly don't know.

I slide his artwork back inside its protective covers and switch off the lights, heading back out to where Adam is browsing the internet, turning when he hears the door click shut behind me.

"See all you wanted to?" he asks, winking.

"Think so. What did you think, honestly?"

He turns to me, arms folded. "I'd kill to make anything that good."

"Hmm." I mirror him, folding my arms.

"Not convinced?"

"I love what he's done, just not my image in them."

"What? You don't find that a turn-on? Most women would."

I shrug my shoulders. "Did he intend that, or does he want to sell them for money? What do you think?"

He rolls his eyes. He knows whatever he says will add to my already blatant paranoia.

"He's an arrogant git, but you saw yesterday... he was nervous for your reaction."

"Yes." I still have my arms folded, chewing my lip. "Was that just the artist's curse, though?"

"He doesn't need money, does he?" Adam reminds me, eyes narrowing.

"Don't think so."

"So, he just wanted you to see what he can do?" Adam wonders, pouting. "He does love you, it's obvious."

"Then what about what happened with Alexia, what do you make of that?"

"Honestly?" he asks, scratching his chin.

"Yep, please. Tell me."

He stands, walks towards me and cups my elbows. "She's just jealous, sis. Honestly."

I throw my hands up and Adam chuckles, grabbing me and pulling me in for a quick hug.

"Ruben mentioned about you taking a break. I think it would be good for you. When did you last have a holiday? And don't say you're on perpetual holiday out here. You still need a break away from this city."

"Trying to get the house all to yourself?"

"Maybe," he guffaws.

"I could do with going away, it has to be said, but he just got here. It feels already like he's running away." I inhale deeply, trying to centre myself.

"The gallery is quiet and will be through August. You worked right through the spring which is our busiest time. Come on, you taking a proper rest is well overdue."

"You're right, but I will still think about it."

I'm about to exit when I turn around. "Sure everything is under control?"

"Sure," he says, brightly. "I've got that dinner tonight, remember? With that artist. I'll tell you all about it later."

"Won't wait up."

I leave the gallery, jumping back into my car. Before I drive off, I have to breathe for a moment. There's something about that picture of me barefoot on a cobbled street, dancing in the rain. That's not me. Maybe it's who Ruben wants me to be, but he has to know, that isn't me. He can't wish me to change. I am who I am. Unlike the girl in his pictures, I won't have the wool—or a veil—pulled over my eyes. I go through life with my eyes wide open. He should know that by now. I know some artists like to imagine their muses in fantastical ways, but it has me feeling unsettled. I decide to drive myself somewhere for lunch, have an hour to myself and some time to breathe.

KARMA

IT'S JUST GONE TWO o'clock when I pull up at the villa. Ruben's Ferrari is still blocking the garage and I grumble to myself. It was annoying earlier when I had to reverse all the way out of the drive because I couldn't turn the car around, what with his sports car parked so domineeringly across the whole bloody driveway. It is becoming clear I bought this house for me and it doesn't quite fit as many people and vehicles as are living here now. He comes rushing out of the house when he sees me arrive, holding his phone and bleating, "Where's your bloody phone? I've been calling for ages."

I dip into my handbag, pulling it out. I have a dozen missed calls. "I always switch it to silent if I'm in a restaurant. It's not polite and besides, I've only been gone an hour or two. I went to the gallery and then treated myself to lunch at Caro's café. She and I hadn't caught up in ages. It was nice."

He looks at me like I'm insane, throws his arms up and huffs, "I was worried sick."

"Don't be so ridiculous."

I push past him and into the house. The dogs are waiting to be scooped up and I carry one under each arm, taking them to the sofa for cuddles. They pick up on tension and seem unnerved by Ruben.

The door slams shut.

"Can you leave a note next time?"

"Why?" I laugh.

"So I know where you are."

"Ah, so you can come and snoop on me."

"No, so I bloody know you're safe."

"Same thing," I mutter under my breath.

"It's not much, you just let me know where you're going and what time you'll be back."

I leave the dogs on the couch and head to the fridge for chilled water, filling a glass.

"So, where have you been today? How long were you there? What was said and how come you're in such a foul mood, hmm?" I turn and stare at him as I gulp my water. I'm instantly refreshed, more than can be said of him.

"We met at 1882 and had coffee and croissant outside under the awning. I walked her back to her friend's apartment and made sure she got into a cab with her luggage. She's taking a commercial flight back because she says my money stinks."

I try not to burst out laughing, chin to my chest, but I can't stop myself.

"Anyway, we might need the plane if you agree to come away. What do you think?"

"Where?" I ask.

"Well, I have some business in Paris. We could start there, then decide where to go next."

"What business?" I ask, trying my hardest not to sound suspicious or overly intrigued.

"It's a secret," he says, "but you'll find out eventually."

"And why would your mother make a suggestion to me earlier that you might be unfaithful, just like your father? Why would she say that, Ruben?" It wasn't the first time she said the two were alike—I remember her once telling me they had a lot more in common than Ruben would ever admit.

I've put him on the spot and it's clear he doesn't know what the bloody hell to say in response. He shakes his head eventually, like he shouldn't be surprised.

"What did she say?" he asks, scratching his scalp.

"I said she should find some male company. She could still have a big love, it isn't over for her, she could find someone, yet. She kept telling me Fred was it, blah di blah, and then she cast shade on you, like I should question your fidelity. As though all men do it, it's to be expected, like that's how she justified Fred's philandering with much younger women."

Ruben throws his hands up and asks gruffly, "Why didn't you tell me before I left this morning?"

"Because aren't these the ravings of a madwoman? Someone who refuses to admit what Fred was really like, who he really was, what her life used to be. She's in denial about everything."

Ruben comes to the sofa, takes Sweep in his arms and cuddles the little mutt, perhaps fearing he won't get any sympathy off me.

"She's out of order and she's wrong. All I did was employ a model for my art. Sometimes artists can't do it all from memory. I employed someone who had the same figure as you. We didn't fuck. She was never naked but Mum's imagination must have jumped there."

That makes sense, sort of.

"In four years, you really didn't fuck anyone?" I search his eyes for answers, but he looks blank.

"Nope."

"Why?"

He shakes his head. "Don't you believe me?"

"The thing is, she immediately knew she'd said the wrong thing. It doesn't add up, Ruben."

"We talked about this last night. Laughed about it." He laughs nervously. "Maybe she wants me to take care of her for the rest of her life, hates that I've come here to be with you, and is just trying to drive a wedge between us."

I notice he's wearing expensive slacks, brown leather sandals and a white, short sleeve shirt. He still cares what she thinks, doesn't he? He even combed his hair. He's also arguing this too strongly, like a man who knows he needs to defend himself—because there's guilt, somewhere.

"She talks as if she puts up with you. The other night. Me and Adam were both there. She talked about you with us there as though she tolerates you only because you're her blood, no other reason."

"I told you, she's on a lot of meds. She gets maudlin in the evening."

I take a deep breath and stare at my lap. "If there's something you're not telling me, now is the time to tell me, Ruben. If you're hiding something, I will find out eventually. That's who I am. I didn't run a hotel without knowing how to dig into people's psyches."

I feel his eyes on me, but I don't give him mine. I want his words, for once. His truth.

"I told you, Freya. She's an ill woman. She was married to *him*. You, me and Adam discussed all this last night."

I lift my eyes to his and catch him off guard. "So, there wasn't some village girl you were romancing? Some substitute to keep you sane?"

"No," he barks.

"A girl, someone, I don't know... maybe not the model... just someone. Maybe you thought it would never be safe for us again, maybe you thought I'd moved on, so should you... maybe you weren't even thinking, you were just so lonely... maybe..."

"NO!" he shouts loudly, making the dogs bark. They stand either side of me on the sofa, threatening Ruben. I pull them into my sides and hush them. "There was no one, I swear. No one. There wasn't time. If I wasn't cleaning up London, I was cleaning up her messes. I told you. She's ill. I've employed a nurse to look after her. That's why she wouldn't stay with us. She doesn't want outsiders to know she needs a nurse. She didn't want me to leave the farmhouse. She wants me to be there, all the time. I can't be, not anymore. It's not fair, Freya. What do I owe her? I don't owe her my life. I didn't wreck things for her. She and Fred did that all by themselves. I deserve a life, don't I?"

"Yes," I murmur.

"Then can we please leave this and move on?"

I hold the dogs close and take a deep breath. "I want to have lunch with Adam tomorrow, to make sure he can handle everything. We need to talk through some things. I will also need to talk with the dog walker, see if she can fit them in again and maybe do extra walks. Adam won't look after them, you know that."

"Whatever you need. So, can I arrange for the plane to take us tomorrow night?"

"Arrange away." I leave the sofa and the dogs are hot on my heels. "Now I'm taking a nap and I'm taking it alone. It's been an exhausting couple of days. I mean it, Ruben."

"Fine, I'll... be productive somehow."

"Good."

I slam the door on the bedroom and the dogs madly lick my hands as we all lie together on the bed.

I didn't know I needed permission to take myself out to lunch. I love taking myself out to lunch. Is he going to be like that anytime I need some time to myself? He tried to suffocate me before and it didn't work. Is he going to be just as bad this time?

Or is he worried a threat still exists? Hidden, but still there...

Chapter Eight

In the Gutter

I wake to the smell of cooking. Spices. Maybe rice? I don't know what the heck time it is but I have slept good. The dogs aren't even with me anymore. They must have sloped off earlier to bother Ruben for food and the toilet.

I'm sweaty from sleeping through the day in a blouse and skirt so I skip straight to the en suite, peel off my clothes and jump right into the shower. The cool rainfall revives me instantly as I stand under it and do nothing but let the water cascade over my hair and down my back. It feels so fucking good. I really needed that siesta. Last night we were drinking and yesterday afternoon we were screwing like bunnies. It all caught up with me, I suppose.

I towel off and rough dry my hair, finding an ankle-length kaftan in the closet that I often throw on when it's too hot and I'm too lazy to assemble a proper outfit.

"God, something smells good," I moan, spotting the huge sauté pan bubbling with food. Either the pan was hiding at the back of a cupboard or he went out and bought it today.

He's sitting on a stool staring at his laptop screen and seems surprised to see me. He shuts the lid and turns to look at me.

"Just had a shower?"

"Needed waking up."

His eyes travel from my neck downwards and don't leave my thigh when he spots the slit in my kaftan.

I grab water from the fridge and down a glass in one. "What's cooking?"

"Paella," he says, pronouncing it with a heavy accent.

"Paella, you mean?" I use the English version.

"No, I mean paella, that's how you properly pronounce it."

It sounds like *pie-ay-sha* when he says it.

"Okay. Sounds good."

"It will be. Would you like wine?"

"Yes, please."

I walk through the sliding doors and out onto the patio, relaxing back on a lounger. He joins me outside, still wearing slacks and a white shirt, now marred by the odd splash of tomato. He hands me a glass of wine and sits on the lounger next to mine. He has his legs spread, hands clasped together between them, barefoot. I'm barely wearing anything and my hair is still damp.

"Do you feel better after a rest?"

"Much better, thank you."

I look out at the pool and the dogs, running off their last bit of energy on the lawn before they sleep for the next twelve hours. It's dusk and the sky is pink and violet. It's beautiful.

"Freya?"

I turn and find him looking desirous. "Yep?"

"You do believe me, don't you? There was nobody else."

I lick my lips. "What about Gia?"

He looks puzzled. "Come again."

"Gia. Weren't you two engaged? Or about to be engaged. I can't remember now." I look at him, looking frantic, like he knows I'm zeroing in on him. "My point is, I know I'm not the only woman you've ever loved, Ruben. You're that guy who wants marriage and kids. You're the guy who can't be alone. I'm not like that and we both know it. I'm happy alone. I know what it's like to be with a hundred different people and still feel alone, so alone is where I've been and I'm used to it. Thing is, now that I don't have to work for my supper, I only want the real deal. If this is it, then great, I'm in. But only if it's worth me giving up parts of myself. Whereas, you don't have to give yourself up. You're a man, you can do as you please as all men do. It's different for you. You can't be alone. You hate being alone. Even fake partnership is better than loneliness for you. I'm the opposite. I don't do fake, not since several years ago. You ought to know that by now."

He doesn't have anything to say. His chest is moving up and down and his facial muscles are fixed in place.

"Freddie told me you were tying her up every night. He said Fred had videos. He said you liked to eat her ass. Did tying her up every night wear her down? Is that why she cheated? She was tired of you. Or was it just that she couldn't handle the truth about your family?"

Ruben bows his head, stares at his bare feet and sighs. "Why are you doing this, Frey?"

"Answer me."

"How am I supposed to know why she cheated? She died before I could find out."

"What about Portugal, Ruben? Who was she? How long? What did you do to her? Tie her up, too? Why won't you tie me up, hmm? What's wrong with me?"

"Freya," he growls, "just the other night, we were saying this is the only true thing, me and you, you and me. I meant every word. Didn't you? This is the truth. The only truth. Me and you."

"Answer me straight, Ruben. Was there someone out in Portugal? Why would Alexia put this seed of doubt inside my mind? Unless there really is something here to be doubtful of. Because if she doesn't even want to take your plane, then she most certainly doesn't want to take your help."

He inhales sharply and I can't meet his eye as he lifts his head and searches my face. I feel his gaze on me, seeking sympathy... something.

"I never thought I'd see you again, Freya. I thought... I thought... I was keeping you safe."

I feel like I've been pulverised. "You lied to me?"

He doesn't respond.

"Get out of my house," I demand, but when he doesn't move or react, I yell, "NOW!" I don't sound myself, my tone of voice unnatural—only he evokes this seething side of me.

The air leaves his body. "It's technically *our* house."

"Get out. Go. I don't want to see you again. Go."

"You don't mean that."

"I can forgive a lot. Hell, I had to forgive myself, didn't I? But you lied to me last week and this week and you'll probably do it next week, if I let you. Get out."

"You don't want me to go, Freya."

"I actually do. I don't need you. I proved that, didn't I? I made a life for myself without you. You left me. You went. I begged you not to go and you did. There are a million different ways we could have handled Fred together but you chose the way that kept me out of it. Was I pleased you were alive? Yes. But can I get over what you did? No. You made me believe you were dead. I can't ever, ever forget that. Now, I want you to go,

Ruben. GO!" I scream, throwing my wine and watching as the glass smashes, red liquid cascading across the paving slabs.

He dashes away and I hear the front door slam, the Ferrari engine rev up and the tyres screech away.

How could he do this to me?

How?

I'M STILL AWAKE AT two in the morning. I haven't wanted to text Adam to come take care of me because I'm not going to be that clingy sister who stops him living his life. Nor a substitute mum checking up on him all the damn time.

It might be my indulgent afternoon nap or maybe even that the adrenalin still hasn't left my veins since I yelled at him earlier. I'm up watching TV in bed, some film I haven't really taken in since the opening credits. It's just noise to dull the mess inside my head.

How could he lie to me?

I know.

Oh, I know.

I definitely know.

He knew if I knew about him having had 'a relationship' during our time apart, I wouldn't want him. I'd brand him duplicitous. Capricious. Thinking with his cock. Not in love with me, like I have been with him all these years. All these things. True things. I would tell him he's a lying, cheating, rotten arsehole and that even if he didn't expect Freddie to die, he should've still kept our flame alive, somehow. Fuck a few life models, yeah. Not almost take one to wife... because the looks Alexia was giving him... oh, she knew, she knew...

He hurt a woman out in Portugal when he came chasing back here to be with me. He did. He broke someone's heart. Oh, I know it. I do. I absolutely know it.

He never forgot what I was like, did he? That's why he wasn't going to tell me. Even though he knew, Freya Carter, the bloodhound of truths, would find out eventually. Perhaps that's why he got Alexia over... because he was too chicken to tell me himself.

Rotten...

I hear a noise. A car engine. Then the front door being opened.

There's Adam's voice.

I turn the TV down and hear Ruben laughing and Adam wincing.

"What the fuck?" I whisper to myself.

Adam didn't drive tonight. I never let him drive my car. Was that Ruben's car?

What the hell has happened?

I stay still until I hear a tap on the door.

Well, fuck him. He's not getting in here tonight.

"Freya, are you up?" Adam whispers.

I switch off the TV and pretend I've been asleep when I open the door, yawning. "What's up?"

"Can I come in?"

I quickly open the door and close it, but I can hear Ruben drunk snoring in the living room, even from so far away down a long corridor.

"What the fuck happened?" I ask.

"I just drove home your boyfriend," he says, smiling like he'd rather have done anything else tonight. "And no, the chance to drive a Ferrari wasn't worth it."

110

"How the fuck did he find you?"

Adam throws his head back, the veins in his forehead and temples bulging. "I have no idea. I was having drinks in Old Town at that place with the outdoor burners and he shows up. Destroys my meeting. Tells the artist he got the job so could fuck off. Then I'm taken to bar after bar, listening as he laughs, then cries, then laughs, then drinks more shots. He didn't make any sense. Eventually, I got a couple of security guys to carry him to the car. He passed out. He's still passed out. On your couch. Good luck with that cleaning bill."

Adam's about to storm out of the room when I stop him, my hand on his arm. "He didn't tell you anything?"

"He was babbling on about you not trusting him, his life being a mess, not being able to do right for doing wrong and myriad rambling thoughts strung together with candyfloss."

I shake my head. "I don't trust him, Adam." My tears start to fall.

"You were happy up until he got back. He has come and fucked you up again, hasn't he?"

I nod my head he's right.

"I have to sleep, Freya. We'll deal with him in the morning. Don't worry, I gave him a pillow. He won't choke on his vomit."

He leaves the room and though I can't bear the thought of leaving Ruben alone for the night, I know I have to. I can't take care of him... not when he doesn't take care of me.

I WAKE AND CHECK THE clock. It's eight a.m. That's good, considering. I got five hours sleep. Amazing, really. I guess I was exhausted by the time I did shut my eyes. I lie still for a few minutes. The house seems to be in silence. The sheets are twisted around my legs and my vest and short shorts even appear to have become victims of my unsettled bedtime activity. The nightmares must have been bad, because I can't remember them.

Then the silence is shattered. I hear him vomiting in the bathroom down the corridor. I never heard him being sick before, but it sounds like a moose being strangled. The noise must have woken me.

I lurch out of bed because the dogs are what probably woke him... needing the loo.

The dogs are indeed waiting by the sliding patio doors and panting for escape. They bolt down the bottom of the garden, poo and wee immediately, then chase back when they hear me splashing fresh water into their bowls and shaking their bag of food. Once I've been down and picked up the poo, the morning dew on the grass soaking my feet, I chase back indoors in case one of the local nutcases has their drone flying around and catches me like this, barely dressed.

Back indoors, I discover the dogs still munching and getting tired from all the food in their bellies. They will slide back to their bed soon and have their next big sleep.

I check the couch and the carpet. No vomit. He made it to the bathroom before all that happened, then. Got to give him that.

I switch the coffee machine on because Adam will be up in an hour and prefers stewed coffee. Besides, he will need it as he's opening the gallery at ten... even after last night's adventure. No matter what my brother gets up to the night before work, he is reliable and always shows up the next day, it has to be said. I expect part of his dedication is that he loves it.

KARMA

I run a glass under the tap before pressing it to the fridge dispenser to fill it with water and ice. Then I grab the aspirin because he's going to have one major headache.

I arrive in the bathroom to find him hugging the seat. Since he arrived back in my life, he's made this toilet his. He does all his business in here and is incredibly shy about sharing a toilet with me. I don't know why. Perhaps it's a thing men have. They need their private loo for time alone pooing while also scrolling on their phones. We're lucky Adam can use the attic en suite which has a tiny shower cubicle, vanity and loo.

"You're such a fucking idiot, Ruben," I groan.

He turns his head, eyes bloodshot, mouth swollen and dirty. He rolls some loo paper off and wipes his mouth, staring at me in shock. Like I shouldn't be helping him. Either that, or he's still so drunk he can't actually tell it's me and is only semi-conscious.

I spot his clothes in the sink and start to wonder...

When I walk over, he blubs, "No, Freya! No!"

I see his shirt was used to catch the sick earlier. He stripped once he got here. Lovely.

I throw his clothes into the bathtub and grab the showerhead, spraying off most of the chunks. Lord knows what he actually ate yesterday. The paella he made went in the fridge in a big plastic box, because I didn't have the stomach for it after he stormed off. I bet it would have been good, too. It smelt good.

I wring out his clothes and wrap them in a towel, heading out of the bathroom to the laundry room to deal with his mess. I check the washing labels and even though his trousers are dry clean only, I have a cycle for that on my magic washing machine.

I traipse back to the bathroom and he's not budged an inch. I grab his glass of water off the bathroom cabinet and offer him it, alongside some aspirin.

It's then he begins to cry. He curls up on the bathroom floor, clutching the mat beneath him, crying. What am I supposed to do?

"This is what you reduce yourself to, Ruben. Because you lock me out."

He continues crying and I leave the room, shaking my head.

What am I supposed to do? Not be me?

He ruined my life.

He did.

I can admit that now.

He ruined it.

I was happy. Working at the Claremont Estate hotel. Running it, even.

I could've taken my CV and gone anywhere else. Anywhere in the world.

I was happy as a hotel manageress. Content. I took pride in my job. It kept me sane. Balanced. Made me hungry every day for a new challenge.

Then he had to sweep into my life, didn't he?

Freya Carter's name became associated with his and I was dirt, suddenly.

He gave me more money than one woman could ever spend in a lifetime, but what does any of it mean? Without him. What does any of it mean?

I love my gallery. Love the life I have here.

But there's something about being rich. It makes everything seem pointless. There's nothing to chase anymore. Nothing that's worth busting your balls for. It's all just a bit of a pastime.

Pointless.

I was happy once. Truly. In my world. Before him.

Then he came and fucked me up. Like all men do. They fuck us up. Oh, they go on about how we get under their skin, but they fuck us up, too. They make us give up so much of ourselves so they can *feel* because they can't feel anything unless they've got a woman beside them.

None of it means anything... without him.

I pour myself coffee and Adam walks into the room rubbing his head, groaning.

"Was that him spewing?" he asks, taking the coffee I'm offering.

"Don't ask."

"Twat," he mumbles, walking off with his eyes barely open.

He grabs his sunglasses off the counter and takes a slurp of coffee before diving into the pool, then wearing the glasses as he does breaststroke. It's not even sunny today.

Perhaps swimming is the secret to staying sane?

I head back down to the bathroom and Ruben has fallen asleep on the floor, on his stomach, snoring into the bath mat.

What am I going to do with him?

I go into my bedroom, pull on a tracksuit and finish my coffee.

I grab the dog leads from the drawer and holler at Adam, "Just taking out the dogs. Don't go before saying goodbye. Won't be long."

I head out and even though it's cloudy, it's a humid morning. The dogs pad along a bit, then want to sniff, then want to walk again. Lazy buggers. It feels like there might be a thunderstorm later on. Maybe, it'll be bad enough we wouldn't have been able to fly tonight, anyway?

We make it to the boulangerie and the dogs wait outside, some passers-by tickling their chins as they wait dutifully, lying on their bellies. I order and come out with a couple of bags of stuff under my arm. The dogs must know something I don't because on the way back, even though the walk is only ten minutes long, they pull me practically all the way home. As I'm putting my key in the door, the first splashes of rain hit the driveway and I notice one of the windows on the Ferrari is still open.

Adam is making himself a sandwich in the kitchen as I walk in.

"Where are the keys to his car? The window is down and it's about to pour."

"I threw them somewhere," Adam mumbles, "over there."

I search the couch area and find them on the carpet.

Dashing outside, I get in the vehicle, press the button for the window to roll up and exit just as quickly. It's pouring by the time I have to dash from the car to the front porch. The flowerpots are drenched the same as I am by the time I get indoors again. The dogs look up at me smugly from their bed by the door.

"Turds," I curse.

I grab one of my brown paper bags and hand it to Adam. "Some savoury flan for your lunch. Take it."

"Oh, thanks."

I know how he loves it.

I grab my own bag and begin making light work of a couple of chocolate croissant.

"Are you going to be all right?" he asks.

"Sure, lemme just eat this and I'll drive you to work."

"Why can't I just take your car? I did get Ruben home safe. I am a good driver."

I shake my head. "Fine. Fine."

He kisses my cheek on the way out. "We're not having lunch anymore, then?"

"Not today, kid. But don't be late tonight. Okay? Promise?"

"Be home at six. See ya."

He takes my white Tesla with the same glee a young man would once have taken a Ferrari. I guess times are changing. I just don't want him to bust that thing up. It takes practise to drive it!

After I'm done with my breakfast and I've poured myself a second cup, I head to the study and sit behind my desk. I'm loading up my Mac when I hear, "Freya... Freya...!"

I head down the hallway and he's groaning in the bathroom.

"Need bed," he moans.

"Roll onto your back, Ruben. Come on. Don't expect me to carry your sorry carcass."

He rolls over and sees my face, bursting into tears again. I shake my head and put his arms around my neck, but he grabs me like he's trying to hug me.

"Up we get, come on, up we come, use them muscles... come on."

I get him up and he stumbles to the next room along, the guest bedroom, which I made up the other day just in case Alexia did stay. It has some lovely silk linens on the bed and fresh roses in a vase. Never mind.

I untuck the sheets at the same time as shouldering his weight. He tosses himself into bed and rolls onto his back inelegantly. He still has a bit of sick on his chin. I grab a tissue, spit on it and wipe his face.

"All clean now, baby boy," I laugh.

His chin wobbles and he blurts, "You've got no fucking idea, Freya. None."

Tears fall down his cheeks and his eyes look cold. Hateful.

"And whose fault is that, eh? Get some sleep, you muppet. Be ready to enlighten me when you wake. Or you won't get another chance. I'll have Adam toss you into the gutter. Don't think he won't. He's younger and fitter than you. And he never lied to me."

I turn and walk out of the room.

Chapter Nine

Last Chance

It's approaching six and I can't wait for Adam to get home. I've been in the study all day, making plans... and I don't want to be derailed by anybody, but...

I have a call to make.

"Freya?" she answers.

"I wanted to check you got home okay?"

"Yes."

"And what about the admirer?"

"We had dinner last night. It was actually nice."

"I'm glad to hear that."

"You are?"

"Yes. Well, I just wanted to say your son probably isn't going to talk to you ever again. And even you shouldn't die alone, Alexia."

Silence, then she clears her throat. "He told you, then."

"He hasn't told me everything, but he will."

"He's weak, like his father. They're all weak, Freya."

I take a deep breath and try not to choke on her fake female loyalty. "What were you hoping to achieve, Alexia. Hmm? For me to break down and toss him out, send him back to you?"

There's nothing from her for several long moments, but I can hear her tapping her nails against her teeth—her nervous tick.

"Freya, if Freddie hadn't died in prison, Ruben would've married the girl he was spending his nights with here. Maybe he doesn't love her like he loves you, but for god sake Freya, he needs to learn to do the right thing. Not one decision he made was right and you and me both know it. Don't we? Why didn't he just take you somewhere, anywhere, all those years ago? Away. Far, far away. He had the money. He could've done it."

"He tried to," I plead his case, suddenly defensive of him. "He tried to tell me he wasn't dead. I didn't see it. He sent me tickets, another identity... I was to go somewhere remote. I didn't listen to the messages he was sending. I ignored them. Like the self-inflicting bitch I am. Because we both have that in common, don't we, Alexia? So don't fucking berate me if I'm making the same mistakes as you. At least my eyes are wide open. At least I don't need medication to hold me together—"

"You don't know anything about what I went through—"

"No, because you and your kin are so fond of keeping people in the dark, aren't you?"

"I knew you were trouble, the moment I met you. 'Goddamn girl,' I told Fred. 'Goddamn girl is going to screw us over.' I knew it."

"Oh my god," I cry, disgusted, "you were in on it."

"You, with your ideals, Freya. Your work ethic. Ugh, you revolt me. I knew you'd be trouble. Knew you were turning him to the other side, I knew it."

"He was never, ever like you or Fred, neither was Laurent. You just didn't see it. You're not the only one good at lying," I scoff, clucking my tongue. "And when I didn't leave with my new identity, deciding I wasn't afraid of Freddie's wrath, do you know what? Ruben was emboldened. I didn't change him. I just gave him the strength to be who he really is. That's when he decided to go after Freddie, too. And don't pretend you're sorry about Freddie. You'd have put a bullet in that guy's head if you could have."

"What does any of it matter now? You got what you wanted. You got his money. I'm left living like a hermit out here, not drawing attention to myself, and you got exactly what you wanted."

I shake my head, vying not to say what is on the tip of my tongue. It's more like she got what she wanted. She got out of a bad marriage and gets to blame her destitution on everybody else... because of course she's not in charge of her own existence. She got so wrapped up in the gangster life, she can't remember any other way of being.

She was on the books. Just like any other employee. A kept woman. The price: her morals.

"And Gia?" I ask, almost snarling. "What do you know about Gia?"

She breathes heavily down the line a few times before she pushes words out of her mouth.

"You know exactly what happened to Gia," she fires back. "You know."

"I know she got shot."

"She wasn't an art student, Freya. Come on. How ridiculous that Ruben, drinking with his teammates and singing *la Marseillaise*, happens to be approached by a French student? An artist no less. *She* came onto him. She knew exactly how to seduce him. She wasn't a student. Nor an artiste. She wasn't heading to a class the day she got shot. She was off to meet her handler. She was undercover. Don't you understand how big my Fred was? Don't you? And how dim-witted my son was until he met you? Well, good luck to you, young lady. Good luck—"

Sensing she's about to hang up on me, I interrupt her, demanding, "WAIT! WAIT!"

"For what?" she says, gasping for air.

"I was there."

"Where?"

"I was working at the Beaumont, the night of Laurent's finishing party. The Beaumont is down the road from Eton. I was there. I was managing the hotel all those years ago."

She starts puffing down the line. "What do *you* know?" She sounds grave.

"There was a brawl. Didn't Laurent come home ruffled that night?"

"The police brought him home," she says, sounding weak. "He told me it was because he was walking the street and they offered him a lift."

"Fred was arrested along with Freddie and the non-biological father. Freddie let the cat out of the bag that night. He was jealous, in a rage, couldn't stand how decent Laurent was. What a future he had ahead of him. Freddie's father and Fred brawled and the lads got caught up in it. I had a major clean-up operation to deal with the next day."

"So, what?" she mouths off.

"Laurent knew and Fred made him keep his mouth shut. The son you thought was yours, the young man you thought was untainted, even he wasn't untouched. Keeping secrets killed him, Alexia. So don't you dare come at Ruben, ever again, with that bullshit about Fred not deserving what he got. And no, I wasn't the genius behind the operation. Ruben's charity was a front for his agency, to bring the drugs ring down. He fooled you. Even you, Alexia. The cleverest people don't have to show their hand; they are clever because they keep back that little bit of themselves you might never see coming. Ruben learnt that from you, you know? When I first met you, I wouldn't have known the truth. Not even I figured it out. You played your part. Played it so well. Even if Fred didn't have people covering his tracks, he might still have managed it just because his wife seemed so put together and oblivious, therefore, how could a man such as he get a woman like you unless he was decent? The perfect ruse. The perfect set-up, am I right? He knew if he stayed married to you, he could uphold this veneer of having got his money righteously. But you inadvertently taught Ruben how to defeat Fred with these deceptions on top of deceptions you're so fond of. And you're just as much a victim of your husband as everyone else. Ruben didn't want to destroy you, that's why he didn't allow you to believe he was dead, because he knew you couldn't take any more pain. But he also knew he couldn't trust you with his other secrets. The ones that mattered. If it were up to you, even now, you'd have Fred back in a heartbeat, wouldn't you?"

Her voice comes down the line, a weak, croaky sound... "Yes."

"Laurent died because Fred wanted a fantasy. The same fantasy you're clinging to. The rich gangster lifestyle you led all those years. And you have no idea what it cost, do you?"

I hear her sobbing. "Tell me."

"He got it all because of Ruben. He blackmailed Ruben for start-up money. The big leagues awaited him after that. He probably already had people bought. Owning a cab company, with his network, he could have used the secrets of the less faithful husbands and wives working high up in government and the police and blackmailed them to look the other way."

"Blackmailed my Ruben? Rubbish," she shrieks.

"You wouldn't take it if I told you what really went on, suffice it to say, Ruben and I knew the very first night we met that we had an affinity... something like sordid history. Well, I expect you can guess mine if you don't already know."

"Tell me, goddammit," she cries.

"Fred watched Ruben having sex with older women, said he would get more women for him if he agreed to give Fred his first million. He was barely out of puberty, Alexia and I think we know what Fred's sick pleasure was, don't we? He couldn't fuck women, they didn't do anything for him, he could only get hard for young girls. So, if he could watch his own son doing more mature women, well... I think living vicariously is the term, right? So, please, tell me again how much you loved your goddamn saint of a husband."

"Rot in hell," she shouts, then I hear a crash, the line going dead shortly after.

I push my chair back and gasp, throw my phone onto my desk and stare at it like that didn't just happen. My heart is going so fast and I didn't mean to say all that but it's the truth and she refuses to face the dirty reality of her dead, sick bastard of a husband. She riled me into revealing everything. God... everything!

I stand up, hands on the edge of the white wood, in shock.

"You stuck up for me," he says from behind me, his presence a surprise.

I turn and stare at him, wearing nothing but his boxers, arms folded and hip pushed against the doorframe.

"You heard all that?"

"She was loud at certain points."

I shake my head slowly, side to side. "She was bloody in on it, all the way."

"Now you know," he says, eyes pinched at the corners. "Escaping that, Freya. Do you know what that's like?"

"No," I whisper.

"Going against the two people who raised you. Do you know what that's like? Both parents fucked me over. I thought she would get better. I truly thought she and I had made progress lately. Then she sees you and the green-eyed monster reveals its true colours. She never wanted me to escape. Jealous of her own son for managing it. You don't know what I've been through, Freya."

"So maybe it's time I did, eh?"

He looks at the floor. "If you think you're ready."

"The truth I can handle, lies I can't. Anything but lies. Lies are the devil's work."

"Fair enough, I'll get dressed."

He starts walking down the corridor and I shout after him, "Did you know about Gia?"

"Not until just now."

I peer around the door, but he doesn't look upset.

"You're not surprised?"

"Nope," he says. "Just the tip of the iceberg."

BY THE TIME RUBEN EMERGES, washed and dressed, Adam and I are sitting at the breakfast bar eating leftover paella. I point to the pan and gesture to Ruben, "It's still good and there's plenty."

He seems a bit put out that things have been taken out of his control and that Adam is here with us, too. Well, I asked him to be.

"I'll catch you up, Ruben," I say, as he starts eating his food.

He and Adam are parked on the other side of the bar to me. The dogs are camped out beneath our feet, waiting to see what drops from up on high. My brother and Ruben don't have the best table manners when dining at home.

Thankfully, the rains of this morning are gone and the evening is pleasant and fresh, a little sunshine brightening things up, a bit of breeze blowing in through the sliding doors.

"Adam is going to keep the gallery going for the next few weeks, but after that, he will shut everything up so I can sell it. I've arranged everything. A lady I know will arrange the sale."

Ruben's jaw drops. He didn't see this coming.

"If you do decide to sell your art, some friends of mine will start to spread a rumour that the pyrography was done by someone well-known but shy, therefore the rich clients on my list will want it just because of the intrigue. Otherwise, we can just put the pieces in storage. Adam will take care of everything and any stock artwork unsold before closure will be sold with the gallery or online if needs must."

"Why, Freya?" Ruben asks, agog.

"Adam's going back to Paris soon for school. And I don't trust anyone else to run my gallery. And I'm about to embark on a trip that I'm fairly sure I won't be coming back from."

Ruben's face burns red, and I see he's fearing the worst.

"Adam is set up nicely. He has his gallery experience and plenty of contacts. He will be fine. He will be able to contact us if anything untoward happens."

"*Us?*" Ruben almost chokes, eyes wide. "So, there is an us?"

"You have one last chance, Ruben. One last chance."

My lover gulps.

"You better believe her, Ruben. Trust me. She's given blokes one last chance before and cut it down to half a chance before they even realised. And you'd be lucky to be getting half a chance, to be fair."

Adam smirks, eating his food with a cocky look in his eyes. I've said he can have my electric car... but only if he pays me back eventually.

"I just bought the Ferrari," Ruben groans. "What about... I haven't had time... I haven't..."

"Haven't what?" I demand, eyebrows raised, my expression daring him to challenge me.

"I'll have a friend store it," Ruben answers. "No worries."

Everyone continues eating for a little while. Adam's the first to finish, asking, "Where are you going? Are you going to tell us?"

"No, little brother. That's for me to know and for Ruben to find out." Ruben and Adam look at one another, afraid to say a word more. Ruben looks utterly flummoxed. "I can say this, though. Ruben needs to become a real artist and so far, he hasn't fulfilled his potential. I'm going to take him where he can become who he was meant to be. A certain person, I suspect, was holding him back. If you ask me, I'd be inclined to sell all but Laurent, keep him in my locker here at the villa. And the eagle, I'd send that one back to Portugal. She needs to live with herself and be reminded of what she lost."

Adam gulps down terror. "I'm not going to ask. Just write it all down for me. I'm going for a lie down." He puts his plate in the sink and dashes away upstairs, without so much as checking the fridge for dessert.

"You knew it was her?" he chuckles, staring at me with an astounded look in his eyes.

"Come on? The campfire. It all makes sense now. On the surface, the sacred mother. Indelible because she created life. She can kill and devour whatever she likes without persecution, she can say she's doing it for her chicks; a higher purpose; an untouchable, fantastical emblem of goodness. The eagle, on the surface, suggests fabled symbolism; eagles are powerful omens. Honourable, protective, they represent strength, vitality, the all-seeing eye. Like Alexia's. Her all-seeing eye saw everything but she chose a double life, chose to turn a blind eye to what she didn't like. Beneath the surface, she wasn't brave or magisterial, powerful or spiritual, she was just surviving. The eagle who's given up hunting waits for the men to leave the campfire and she takes the scraps back to her chicks. In this case, the scraps are what she and Fred gave of themselves to you and Laurent. Their vanity, greed and deception got them where they were and they convinced themselves it was to give you and Laurent better lives. But truly, if you and he had walked off into the woods and lived wild, you would've had better lives. Without them. Criminals justify their own cause by whatever means necessary."

Ruben puts his hands together and shudders. "You got all that? How did you get that?"

I take my plate and put it in the sink. "Sometimes I don't know how I know things, I just do." I stand at the sink, staring through the window at the garden outside, running the water just to wash these few plates. "Like the pictures of me. They're who you want me to be. But I'm not that woman you portray.

That's your rose-tinted view. The woman I am isn't a romantic. How can I be when I'm utterly incorruptible?"

"I have work in Portugal," he sighs, remorseful. "She will destroy it unless we go and pick it up."

"And what are these other pieces?"

"Just... more..."

"Me?"

"Yes," he sighs.

"Then they're not the real me. The real me you've seen ten per cent of. Four years ago, we were together barely two weeks. It was like a runaway train. We'd had plenty of conversations down the pub before we became lovers, I know that, but how much of our true selves had we given up before the night we first made love, hmm?"

"None," he admits, "there's still so much, even now."

"Let her burn it all. Or sell it so she can show off. Who cares? The best is yet to come."

Ruben comes up behind me, places his plate on the side and puts his hand on my waist.

"Where are we going?" he whispers into my hair.

"You'll find out."

"When are we going?"

"Saturday morning," I tell him. "And we're flying premium. You may as well put that stupid plane in storage, too. Or sell it. We'll leave the villa vacant once Adam's back up in Paris. It's quiet here in the autumn anyway. We'll see how we feel about everything in time."

"And the dogs?" he asks.

"Adam is driving them to Paris. He has a lovely apartment there and I'm giving him a small allowance for looking after them which means he won't have to do bar work anymore. Anyway, something tells me they will enjoy prancing the streets and Adam will enjoy the attention from girls. They will be fine and if they get too much, he will take them to the nearest airport and they will be posted out to us."

"And you're really not going to tell me where we're going?"

"Nope, but you'll need clothes. You can't travel naked."

He laughs and groans in my ear, "I need to kiss and hold you, Freya. Please. I cleaned my teeth. I'm sorry. Please."

I shake my head, finish the dishes and grab the towel to dry my hands. "I'm not ready."

"Please. Just let me hold you."

"I'm not ready. We'll talk later. For now, I need to work in the study. And you need to put your own affairs in order."

I hear him swallow hard. "I'll get started."

"Shut it down, Ruben. I mean it. Shut it down for good."

"I thought that's what you meant."

I turn and look into his eyes. "I'm in charge now. You'll shut it down, Ruben."

He nods labouredly. "I will."

"No, don't say you will and then you don't because you still have fears and doubts. Shut it down. Where we're going, you won't need them anymore."

He takes a deep breath and rubs his forehead. "I'll shut it down."

His little investigative team... I know they're still out there. I've seen him sneak around corners when his phone lights up.

"Good. I'll know if you haven't."

I sneak past him and head towards the study.

No more lies... he has to learn a new way of being.

It'll be hard. After all, Alexia and Fred built their empire on lies. Their marriage only survived because Fred spouted such good lies, and Alexia, well, she chose to believe them. Either that, or she found the truth so disturbing, she was glad of a good lie. Ruben had a front-row seat to the desperately sad and inauthentic relationship his parents shared. It was a hugely abusive and one-sided dynamic. Can't he see that?

Will Ruben learn to be honest with me? Will he realise that I'm not glass, I won't shatter like she did, if he tells me the truth?

He will have to realise I won't model our relationship on theirs. If anything, the next time he lies, he has to know that I'll be gone. There won't even be a conversation.

I'll just leave without saying goodbye.

However, if he can be honest about everything, finally, maybe we'll make progress. He might even begin to heal.

Chapter Ten

That Other Dimension

Adam and I are sitting on the terrace at ten o'clock the same evening, drinking wine. The solar lights look pretty and it's a warm night, considering there was so much rain this morning. The insects are humming and, in the distance, you can hear the hustle and bustle of summer nightlife.

"He took it well," Adam sniggers.

"He has no choice."

"True."

"Are you going to be all right?" I turn to him.

He pulls a tight smile. "I know I said last week I was ready to give up my position at the gallery, but now I'm not so sure. It's grown on me. It was just because of Athena I was wanting to get out of here."

"I understood that, but... this is for the best. Believe me. You've got some amazing experience under your belt already. I've given you all the tools you'll need. And I'll always be just a phone call away."

"Yeah, send me a postcard when you get there. Wherever *it* is."

"I will."

We sit in silence a little longer. Then it's obvious Ruben is standing behind us in the doorway. Not only does his body cast a large shadow on the patio, the dogs are growling slightly as he stands near their bed. They still haven't forgiven him for hurting their mistress. And there was me a few days ago, thinking they'd forgotten their loyalties.

"You'll look after my pups, won't you, Adam?"

"They don't need much, do they? Food, a few walks, a bit of company. I often throw dinner parties and stuff. They will be the talk. And besides, one of my neighbours has two schnauzers. I know if I'm ever stuck, she will offer to walk them alongside hers."

"Okay, but if things get tricky, just call me."

"I will."

"And don't neglect your studies. Promise me?"

"I won't."

"And if you do go back to the UK after university, take them with you."

Adam turns and stares at me. "How long are you planning to be away for?"

I try to hide my emotion but even in the dark, with only the moon, the terrace lamps and the solar lights enabling us to see one another, he can see I'm upset.

"You just need a pet passport. And sell the car if you do go back to the UK."

"A couple of hours ago, you were saying..." He doesn't spell out what it is he's really thinking, but I sense it anyway.

"Have the car, Adam. It's yours. Sell it and use the money to start up somewhere. This is your last year coming up. By spring, you'll be done. You can do whatever you want after that. Trust me, I trained a few dozen people in my lifetime and hardly anyone I ever taught picked up things as quickly as you. I know you can do anything, I really mean that. Have your own gallery one day. Or sell your own art. You know how to do it now. I've given you everything I can. It's your choice what you do with what you've learnt."

Adam looks over his shoulder at Ruben, but I bet Ruben is unreadable. Going by his shadow, he looks to have his arms folded and his eyes fixed on something in the distance.

"They're still after him, aren't they?" Adam demands.

I reach out for his hand and squeeze it. "Adam, listen to me. I will always be here for you. Always. I promise. But now you have to grow up a little bit. Just a little. If you travel, take the dogs with you, or leave them with someone you trust until you get back. Whatever it takes. Don't give them up because I'll be back for them, I promise you."

"You're not telling me something," he says, tears in his eyes.

I turn and look at Ruben, who's unreadable and detached from the discussion. He's not wanting to get involved.

"I'm a big girl, Adam. I can take care of myself. You know that."

"We'll talk more tomorrow." He takes his glass of wine inside and upstairs to bed.

Once we know he's gone, Ruben walks the few yards to where I am and plonks his arse on the first step leading down to the pool area. He sits staring at the night sky.

"We'll get bitten to buggery sitting out here," I murmur.

"I just want to know where I stand," he says softly. "Last night, I was out getting sloshed, drowning my sorrows, now we're going away? But not on my plane, which is safer by the way. No. We have to do it all your way."

"Yep."

He turns and scratches his head. "Have you lost your mind?"

I have to laugh, so I do. I laugh and laugh. It's all ridiculous.

"Why don't you tell me her name? How you met."

He turns his body slightly sideways and I can just see his face in profile as he speaks.

"You don't want to know any of that. It's irrelevant. I broke it off. It's done."

"Okay. We'll come back to that. Tell me about Gia. Did you know she was playing you?"

His face contorts. "No, I thought it was real. I really did. She was so different... and for once, I knew for certain it wasn't someone *he* was trying to set me up with."

"Your dad often tried to set you up?"

"Dozens of times," he admits. "A different guise every time, but same kind of woman. That's why I moved to France. Thought I'd get away."

I sip some of my wine. "I'm going to speak now and you're going to tell me if I'm wrong, only after I've spoken. Okay?" He nods he agrees. "Four years ago, you knew as soon as you got together with me, shit would hit the fan. Fred would realise who you'd been meeting in secret. I've been back to that pub, you see. Every time I'm in London, I go back there, have a drink and think of better times. One time, I decided to try the back exit. I nearly didn't find my way out." He looks impressed. "It was like pressing the nuclear button, exposing your feelings for me. Those two weeks we were together, you were pushing and pushing for someone to make a move. You took me to their door and they did nothing. You even orchestrated a dumb little fake engagement dinner to see if your mother or father would hear about it and act, didn't you?"

He says nothing, but doesn't disagree.

"The thought of them doing to me what they did to Gia drove you mad, didn't it?"

"Yes," he spits.

"They weren't making a move, so you went ahead and moved first, handing Freddie a grenade to take out Fred with. Before thinking things through."

"You don't know what it felt like, Freya. Not knowing when they would strike... if they would strike. I truly never knew about Gia being undercover. I didn't."

"They might have left us alone for all you know." I throw my hands up, annoyed that we're here again... but needing to run through it, anyway.

"That's all well and good now, but I didn't know that then. Besides, killing Fred meant one less scumbag on the street and Freddie deserved what he got. Deserved to know his wife and kids weren't even his. That's how Fred got people, you know? He made you think all the stuff you had gained in the world was your own, but it never was. It was all his. He'd just allowed you to have a life on loan. On his authority. That's how it would've been between me and you, eventually. He'd have used something against us, I don't know what, but he would've destroyed us."

I shiver and shake though it's not cold, trying to wrap my head around everything. The moon moves across the sky before I speak again.

"Who was the Portuguese girl?"

He doesn't answer right away. There's a lot of fidgeting and faffing with his clothes.

"It was last year," he starts. "I was in Nice. Incognito. Sometimes, I just had to see you, even if from afar. And I saw you on a date. Dining on some guy's yacht. You looked happy. You absolutely radiated it. I didn't stick around long enough to see what happened next. But I knew you looked happy."

I cover my mouth to hide my chattering teeth.

"My mum's maid had been coming onto me for months, years actually, and one evening things happened. And kept happening. But I was numb, Freya. I wasn't in love with her. It was like Fiona. Less than Fiona, actually. It was just... nothing."

I hold my jaw in place, staring down at the floor. I don't want to react.

"The woman got it in her head... I don't know... that I would make things official. I thought, like everyone else, she'd determined I was just a shell of a man and not good for anything but the basics, you know?" He rubs his forehead. "And when the news about Freddie broke, it was the perfect excuse to flee. To make her see what I'd been saying all along... that it was just sex, at least for me. I never came inside her. It would always be in a condom or, well, you know, not inside her. It wasn't anything, I swear, and the only reason I didn't say was because I didn't want to frighten you off. In the way I'd done before, like the night you fled to the airport, remember? And I thought when I saw you that night on a date that you looked happy. I was glad for you. I decided it was time for me to stop pining. To let you go because it would be best, all round. You seemed really... much better off without me. But I swear, for me, nothing ever has or ever will come close to what we have. I've never loved anybody in the way I love you. I mean that with every fibre of my being. But I know that it isn't easy being with me. And I thought... I just... I gave up. That's what I did. I gave up hope. And I hated myself. But if you'd have been me that night, seeing you from a distance as I did, looking so happy, you would've left yourself alone to get on with life, too. You'd have done the same. It was nice seeing you like that. Like I was seeing a different version of you."

I put my head in my hands and bite my lip. He got it all wrong.

He comes towards me, kneels by my side and wraps his arms around me.

"I am so sorry, Freya. I love you. You ought to know that. I love you. I've never loved anyone else, not truly, not in the way I love you. I only didn't tell you because I was scared. I cannot lose you, not again. Please."

I cry against his shoulder for reasons I can't spell out immediately. All I know is that, if I did look happy, it was because I was trying to be. But I was really just acting.

"Hey, hey, please, baby. Don't cry," he soothes, rubbing my back.

I cry some more.

When I've caught my breath, which I eventually do, I wipe my eyes and stare at him through bleary vision.

"In the four years we were apart, I was never happy, Ruben. I pretended to be. For Adam's sake so he didn't worry about me. For the sake of the gallery so people didn't think they were doing business with an actual crazy person. Which I am, by the way." He laughs sadly. "The guys I dated were just a means to an end. Connections. Sometimes conquests. They were all nice guys, though. It's always been easy for me to pick out the bad apples having been reared by the biggest of them all." He looks so sad about that. "But not one of the flashy, yacht-owning, week-end-bag dragging Euro elite was you. Not even close. Half of me has been missing all these years, like I was hollow inside. I've felt rudderless, totally lost on more occasions than I can count. I've fallen in and out of depressions. I've hid them from Adam, from myself, even. In the winters I shut up the villa like nobody's here, take myself to my bedroom and hibernate until he comes back from university in the spring. In warmer weather I would bury myself in work and go on stupid little dates out, like the one you saw me on. I'd get dressed up, convince myself I was better, things were going to get good again. And come morning, I'd wake, accept the superfood brunch and a free facial. I'd leave and come back here. And I'd be myself again. The escapism into their world is nice, you know? For a few hours. But I never fully got onboard. I was passing through their master suites and their double showers and their saunas and spas. Nothing I've ever known has been as true as what you and me have."

"Do you mean that?" he asks, tucking his fingers into my hair.

"Yes, it makes me feel sick to admit it, but it's true. I'm sick with you but sicker without you."

He presses his lips together, a mixture of elation and amusement in his eyes. "That's the nicest thing anyone ever said to me."

I reach out and stroke my fingers through his dark beard. "I liked it when you were clean-shaven that once."

"Why?" he asks, his eyes glinting.

"I felt like there was more of you to kiss. And I do love your beard, but when you brushed your smooth mouth over my pussy, it felt wonderful."

He takes my hands and kisses them, holding them between his, showing me his devotion.

"That was the rawest night I ever had, inside your bedroom down the hall. Four years ago, now. I felt like a prisoner on release. I was living in hell, truly."

"I sensed that." I stroke one hand through his hair. "You were desperate."

"I didn't know what the future held, but I knew I needed to keep you safe. That's my one job Freya and I don't mean to ever stop doing my job."

I shake my head, look up at the stars and pray he never has to leave me again in order to keep me safe.

"Will you shave it off, then?"

"Maybe once we're good and lost in South America."

I flick my eyes in his direction. "How did you—"

"Freya, come on. It's me. Please," he asks, reminding me he has resources.

"You just won't stop?"

"Keeping you safe? Never."

I wrap my arms around his neck and he pulls me to my feet, kissing me almost the moment we're both standing. He drags my body into his and we let the love we share drown us, draw us into her mythical bosom and plunge us into that hidden dimension we escape into whenever it's just us and the world has fucked off for a minute or two. He tugs my legs around him and we walk indoors. He slides the doors shut and locks them, then carries me to the bedroom.

On the bed, he peels off my shorts and knickers, licks along the length of my slit and almost makes me come with the first swipe of his tongue across my clit. I drag my t-shirt off over my head and rub my breasts, watching him watching me, the look in his eyes dirty and grateful. Holding me open with his hands, he relentlessly tastes me until I'm *hee-hawing* and rocking my hips towards him, the tender way in which I'm brought to orgasm making me throw my head back and arch off the bed, my hands digging into his scalp as I come, pouring with sweat and drenched between my thighs.

Then he's naked, his shorts and shirt gone. He brings his body to me, so hot, sweaty and virile. I need him so much. When he puts his arms around me, I gulp and he kisses me deeply, so many apologies within his kiss and his fervent hold on me. He surprises me by pushing into me when I'm least expecting him to and I yank my mouth off his to scream.

Ruben ejaculates after a few lunges, then reassures in his ragged, tortured tone of voice, "Just getting you ready, sweet love."

He makes love to me, his body moving slowly, deliberately, carefully. His hips rock with no haste and he kisses me with his chapped lips, his bruised tongue, until I'm gripping his buttocks and demanding he sort out the shiver in my endlessly aching legs.

I'm dying again in no time and the quiver inside me turns to jolting electricity, my pelvis locking tight, his cock squeezed so hard, he's definitely never getting out ever again. I dig my teeth into his shoulder and catch my breath, holding on while he takes his own pleasure.

He rolls over and pulls me on top, kissing my shoulder tenderly, the act so intimate and enthralling, my aftershocks are enhanced. He plays with my hair and strokes my skin. He whispers he loves me, over and over, my spirit tingling every time he does.

Ruben's arms are solid around me as we lie in bed, watching the moon continue to travel.

"You were so drunk, baby."

"I'm not proud of myself. I was out of my mind."

"Adam brought you home."

"I know. He's a good lad."

"If nothing else, our time apart gave me Adam. I can't be sorry about that. You were right. He needed me and I needed him. You were right."

"I hope there will be other occasions when you're able to admit I was right."

I laugh and playfully kick him in the shin. He tugs me even deeper into his embrace and I love every second of having him close and warm and alive.

"Sleep, my love," he says, "I'll be right here, all night."

"I love you," I whisper.

"Love you so much more."

Chapter Eleven

Missing Piece

The morning arrives and the sheets are warm but not hot. That's how I know he's already up. He's nearly always the first to wake, rise, get on with a new day. He's not a slave to anyone or anything, even sleep. The more I think about what he achieved by taking down Fred and Freddie—especially if Alexia was intimately complicit—I know I will never understand the strength that must have taken. There will always be just a little bit of him I can't get to. Not that he would deliberately make himself off-limits to me, but Ruben has a dark inner self he guards closely. If anyone might understand that darkness, it's me, but he still won't subject me to his secret demons. If he could carry both our worries he would, but he can't, so he'll carry his own—protecting me always. That's why he lies, that's why he kept me in the dark about the Portuguese girl, because he didn't want to hurt me. I'd rather not have known, true. However, what if that girl ever came looking for him in the future? How would that feel? To learn, much later down the line, he'd fucked a girl during our separation and never told me about it. It's better I know now. He can't hide all of his sins.

I realise he's in the bathroom when I hear him pull the plug on the sink. He never uses the sink. What's going on? He spits into the sink. Never fills the sink. Unless...

Just the thought of it...

Has he...?

Breath catches in my throat.

I'm praying he has.

When he opens the bathroom door and stands there with just a towel wrapped around his waist, I'm floored. He sees me watching and doesn't move. I slowly slide out of bed and head towards him.

Wrapping my arms around his bare shoulders, I touch my nose to his.

"You shaved."

"You asked."

I don't know why I feel so emotional, but I do. His bare jaw, smooth mouth, chin and cheeks...

He looks ten times more handsome without the beard. He's devastating. It reminds me...

The last time we made love, when he didn't have a beard—the only time—was when I saw him six months after he allegedly died and we had *that night*. That one night to end all nights. That amazing night I've dreamt and dreamt about. Memories of that night kept me going.

I stare at his mouth and he slides his hands up and down my back, pulling me closer. Our mouths meet and I close my eyes, feeling the same kiss, just... more naked. No barrier. Nothing between us. Our kisses are always savage, but like this, there's more to feel of him. Perhaps there's more to feel of me without his beard getting in the way. I allow myself to kiss his mouth, around his mouth, holding his chin steady so I can explore the new landscape. I sound so greedy, moaning and groaning, desperate for him.

He puts his hands under my thighs and lifts me, my calves gripping his backside as I wrap my legs around his waist. He pushes me against a wall and I drag my hands through his hair. My core is throbbing with desire as we kiss deeply. He has his tongue inside my mouth, kissing me like he needs to possess me, devour me. I haven't even cleaned my teeth yet. We're not breaking contact as we become engrossed. I can't get enough of the taste of him.

He drops his towel and I'm sure he's about to penetrate me, when he pulls back.

"I have an idea," he says, eyes wild and hair sticking out in all directions.

He carries me into the bathroom, grabbing his razor on the way. I'm wondering what the hell, when he sets the shower running and pushes me under the spray, locking us both inside the cubicle.

"Soap up your pussy," he says. "Get her ready."

My eyes widen. "You're not bringing that thing near me."

I grab it out of his hand for inspection as the water begins to beat down on me. It's not a cutthroat razor but rather one of those stainless steel, heavy razors with a knurled handle and feels like it probably cost a lot of money, with a very sharp blade designed to give the closest of shaves.

"When did you get this?" I ask, my stomach full of butterflies, my libido on pause.

"Had it years. Used to use it on my chest. I did shave my face once upon a time, too."

I lift my eyes to his. "Before you were trying to be someone you aren't?"

He shrugs and hands me the soap, still determined to do what he wants with me.

"If you cut me, Ruben..." I warn, breathing in deeply.

I step out of the direction of the spray and Ruben turns the knob so the shower relaxes and there's more of a trickle. He takes to his knees and puts his hand between my thighs, pushing my legs apart. I rest one hand on his head for balance while I'm stood like this.

"Stay still," he asks.

"Yes, sir."

He looks up at me, challenging me to disobey, all the while amused and aroused... his cock still a bit chunky.

He's careful to work away at the little bit of hair down there. It's not exactly Desperate Dan but I'm not utterly bare, either. He cleans the razor every now and again, holding it under the shower. Once he's on the last little fiddly bits, he holds my right thigh up in his left hand and stretches me open, working carefully around my lips. He does the same on the other side. The concentration in his eyes as he works reminds me of someone painting a picture, focusing so hard, they almost forget someone might be watching them work.

"Go wash yourself," he says, so I do.

I step under the spray, lather my hair up and grin as he watches me carry out my full routine. I know he meant for me just to wash the soap off myself down there... but it's a woman's right to make him wait.

I have my back to him as I'm washing out the shampoo, my head flung back, moaning as I shower. I grab my loofah and bodywash next and turn to see him standing with his arms crossed, one eyebrow raised and a not-so-subtle erection dancing against his navel.

"Did you not mean for me to fully shower, darling?" I ask, scrubbing across my breasts, stomach, then down my legs.

"Turn around when you're scrubbing yourself," he demands.

I do as he requests and bend over, scrubbing my shins with my bottom pointed in his direction. I grab the intimate wash next and turn to see him stroking himself a bit.

"How does it feel?" he asks.

"I'm getting to it."

I wash my bottom first because it's another minute he has to stand there watching me while I clean up—another minute he's thinking about what he wants to do with his new toy.

I put my hands under the spray, the bottle under my armpit, thoroughly washing my fingers before I take the next step. He's staring as I squeeze a bit of the intimate wash into my hands, then slowly lather it up between my palms and fingers. The shower spray has been at half strength this whole time, so the routine is taking twice as long... at least.

I slide one lathered hand down my lower belly until reaching my mound. It feels like silk and I bet he knows it. He was watching as he was unmasking me. The same as he unmasked himself earlier. Smooth skin he made.

I wash my folds and there's not a hair left. It's completely silken and perfect. Not one nick. Not one little graze. I grab the plastic jug off the shelf, fill it with water and pour it between my legs, washing everything away. I make sure my boobs are soap free, jiggling them under the spray.

One last thing...

I take my face wash and feel rejuvenated as the charcoal ingredients wash away the grime of last night. Switching the shower off, I wring my hair out, watching him still standing there with his folded arms, wolfish expression and massive erection.

"You don't know what to do with me?" I ask, challenging him to act... or not.

Whatever he wants.

"I could probably do whatever I liked."

I watch his mouth, the full, blood-red lips. He's too beautiful. I watch him fighting not to smile, the little twitch in the corner tugging at something deep in my belly, butterflies making me light-headed. God, he's never having a beard, ever again. Every little quirk of his mouth is on display...

When he licks his lips, that's when I crack. I launch across the cubicle and we slam together. He pulls me close and we kiss exactly like before, two people crazy and inebriated on kisses, never getting enough of one another. He tears himself away to kiss my neck and I groan so loudly, it sounds like I'm in pain.

He sucks my nipple into his mouth, kneads my bud, then tenderly kisses it.

"Oh god, Ruben," I moan.

He lowers to the floor, chucks my thigh over his shoulder and covers my pussy with his mouth, sucking me whole. It takes a couple of flicks of his tongue against my clit to make me come and after that, I'm a constant, gasping mess, shrieking as he tongues, tastes and devours me.

He pulls away and I can barely stand it when he brushes his finger over my sensitive folds. There's no way he's getting inside me, not when I'm exquisitely throbbing, having just endured one orgasm after another. When he presses his mouth to my mound and groans, I know he really enjoyed that. I want to really enjoy him, too.

He takes to his feet and kisses my mouth. I stroke my hand over his face and murmur, "Are you mine, Ruben?"

"You could whore me out to a million women and I'd still be yours."

I grimace and he regrets his words. "That's not going to happen. I hate that you've been with anyone else."

His mouth twitches with disgust. "Not as much as I hate that you have."

"Want to bet?"

"Why do you think I went looking for companionship? I was wretched and jealous. It was the worst moment of my entire life, seeing you with someone else."

I wrap my hand around his cock and whisper against his ear, "If I ever saw you with another woman, I'd murder her and then castrate you."

Breath catches in the back of his throat. I stroke him carefully, his skin damp from the steam, the head of his penis wet.

"Let's make a pact, shall we?" he asks, swallowing hard.

"Go on..."

"Even if one of us dies tomorrow, let's promise never to be with anyone else again."

I breathe in deeply. "That's not fair."

"Why?" he asks, unhappy even though I'm stroking him.

"I'm least likely to die. Your pact is in your favour. You get to haunt me if you go first. And I never asked to love you. I never asked to love a man whose..."

He's perplexed that he's upset me. To be fair, I'm annoyed at myself that I'm having a reaction to something that he can't be serious about... can he?

"Whose past is so fucked up?" He has a go at finishing the sentence for me.

"Whose life is more at risk than my own."

His jaw stretches, side to side.

"You're wrong, Freya. *They* knew that without you, I'd be susceptible. I could be coerced to become like them, a creature of the dark, if not for you. When a man doesn't have anything good to live for, he can happily dwell in the dark. Like Freddie. He was only ever with money-hungry whores and his father's mistress. He was Debbie's husband on paper only. A custodian of his father's whore, nothing more. My father loved my mother but decided if he couldn't find it in him to fuck her anymore, he could buy her the sort of lifestyle nobody else could give her. His sickness was needing young girls, but my mother had her own sickness, in being unable to give him up though deep down she must've known about his predilection. She also knew about the crooked things he did but justified it somehow in her head. The romance was dead, maybe wealth was a bit of a soother, a consolation prize. Their fragile, fake marriage was barely held together. Meeting you, seeing how in love we were—are—must have been a shock. My mother must have known as soon as she met you, you weren't the same as her or the other women in their world. If you were in my mother's league, you'd have married a rich fuck a decade before and never made hotel management. But you enjoyed your work, the satisfaction of going home after a hard day and feeling like you'd accomplished something. You're real. It's the reason I love you. Because you try. You're a fighter."

"Like you," I murmur, "you're a fighter. Fought your way out. We both did."

I plant a kiss on his lips and he stares at my body, devouring me with his gaze. We're two oddities who didn't belong in the families we grew up in. We only feel like we belong when we're together.

"I did what I did to protect you, Freya. Maybe they killed Gia because she was an undercover detective, or maybe they killed her because she could have potentially turned me to become good. Because let me tell you something, darling. The man I used to be before Laurent died was an animal. Grief wreaks havoc, reduces you. The man I was, undiluted, full of hate and aggression and wrath, you never would've loved him. You would've despised him. If we'd met ten years ago, you'd have taken one look at me and ran a mile. You'd have known right away I was a prick of epic proportions."

I look at him, still holding his cock, and raise one eyebrow. "How apt."

"I wouldn't be standing here, like I am now, dying to break you open but somehow reining myself in. I wouldn't be in love with you. I'd hate you. Hate you for being so beautiful and perfect. I didn't want anyone or anything that I cared about. The artist became a footballer because it catered to my need for an outlet for my aggression. Because I didn't care about it in the same way I care about my art, to the point where I almost wanted to crawl into a hole the other day when I first showed you my stuff."

I stroke him up and down. He's fully hard again. He holds his hands over my breasts and bites his bottom lip. He's adorable, sexy and boyish with no beard.

"Let me show you how bad I can be," I whisper, taking to my knees.

He puts his hands against the sides of the shower cubicle and moans as I lick his cock. He's been dying to come for the past forty-five minutes. I grab the intimate wash, coat my fingers in it and stroke them over his pucker.

"Did you wash and did you...?"

His lip curls. "Go for it."

I stroke his anus until he opens and push my fingers inside him. I'm barely sucking his cock but he's rock hard and trembling from head to toe. The inside of his body is red hot and he's tensing continually. The veins in his groin are throbbing and he's in some sort of trance. He's getting close when I remove my mouth and my fingers. He's clinging to the wall. I decide to stroke his balls a bit and stare at the dark shaft dragging his big pink balls upwards.

"I've got you by the balls, my love," I chuckle, stroking their heft, "I could make you do or say whatever I wanted."

He can barely speak, I can tell. His head is whipping about on his shoulders and he's trying not to think about how much he wants to come. I wrap my hand around his shaft and squeeze gently.

"What do you want to know?" he asks, almost aggrieved. "What do you want from me?"

I consider it a moment.

Then I jack him off, pumping him a few times before he spurts a little, dribbling down the side of his cock. Not enough friction to give him a full-blown orgasm.

He grumbles, a complaint on the tip of his tongue.

"I want to know what it feels like to fuck me, what your body feels like," I ask him, licking the tip of his manhood, tasting his salt. "I want to know what I do to you. What it's like to be aroused by the woman you love."

I stroke my hands over the perfect, tight swells of his buttocks, kissing his stomach at the same time. I love him more than anything. I'm obsessed with him. I've never loved anyone else. Not even family. Maybe my mother. Adam, too. But I've never loved a single other person in the way I love Ruben. I never even had a best friend. There was no girl I went to school with who I stayed in touch with. Nothing of the sort.

His hands are combing through my damp hair and his eyes still aren't quite open when he mumbles, "It's like this feeling, like if I don't get you in my arms, it'll hurt. For almost two years, after we'd meet at the pub, I'd go home feeling sick. With desire. I'd have this tight feeling, right here" – he points at his stomach – "and it wouldn't go away. If I thought about you naked, I'd get this ache in my hips and groin. Deeper than arousal, though. Combined with the tight feeling in my stomach, it'd feel like pain. Like, I don't know, the male equivalent of that yearning women say they get in their womb. I'd take my cock in my hand and tremble all over to thoughts of you. The sickness wouldn't go away. I'd go to Fiona and try to pretend she was you but it didn't work. Her hair didn't smell right, she didn't feel right. I'd only call her if it got so bad, I didn't think I would even be able to open my eyes unless I got it out of my system."

I slide my mouth over his cock and suck him deep into my throat, at the same time sliding my fingers back into his bottom and locating his prostate. I stroke it until he's exploding into my mouth, the sounds he's making echoing around the shower and driving me insane. I've never heard him sound so raw... so unleashed, yet tormented, captured. I show him the cum on my tongue and he growls as he watches me swallow it back. I never swallowed anyone else. Maybe one day I'll tell him what I did do when I was an escort... but not yet.

I switch the shower off and we clamber out. I towel down his weary body and mine a little, too. We head for the bed and lie together, catching our breath.

"When we make love, my breasts feel heavy, like stones. When you kiss them it's ten times more sensitive than normal. But even so, I want to feel your touch. When I'm aroused it feels like my womb is a giant ball of fire. My muscles contract, sometimes before you've even entered me. My clit feels almost too sensitive, that sometimes when you touch it, even with your tongue, I have to fight the impulse to push you away. And when you're finally inside me, I don't know, I can't even breathe sometimes. I wish you could know what it's like because it's utterly consuming and it feels like I'm complete. It feels like... it feels real." I wrap my arms around his neck and push my nose to his. He looks wrought and shocked. "I think I fell for you the first time we met at the pub. You were so different to me, or so it seemed." He presses his lips together, trying not to get emotional. "You had this wild hair, this carefree attitude, I loved you that night and every night since. And the day I thought you'd died, my stomach left. I had no appetite for much after that. It was an ache, like a full body ache actually, but something... memories... conversations... I'd sometimes long for the nights. I could lie in bed, re-running times we'd had together, going over them again and again. Inside my head, we could still be together, and I longed for the nights."

"Freya," he begs, sounding weak.

"Nothing will ever measure up, Ruben. Even if you died to-morrow. Or in twenty years. Or fifty. Nothing else, nobody else, will ever measure up. We were meant to be together. It was in-stant. It didn't brew over time. If it hadn't been for your fucking family, we would've got married within months if not weeks of meeting, wouldn't we?"

He nods his head, tears streaking down his cheeks. "Weeks? No, days."

I laugh, my eyes wet, too. "We'd have three kids already. Two girls and a boy. They'd be bilingual, of course. We'd live in Switzerland. You'd have a studio you paint in. I'd be a full-time mum with a little house down the road I run, for the holiday crowd. We'd put the rent money in an account for the kids' uni-versity fund."

He chuckles, biting his lip.

"Instead, I've become this" – I point at myself – "an art deal-er. Gallery owner type. I felt so unglamorous when I first moved here. I didn't belong and I knew it, but I made myself belong. Used your money to make it appear that I do, even when I don't. It's a role I play so I can vacate myself. So I can pretend what hap-pened to me didn't. Or maybe it's just what the younger version of me thought was the pinnacle, you know? The thing all girls as-pire to be... a millionaire living on the Riviera."

Ruben kisses my neck, wraps himself around me and begs me not to keep talking.

"And then you, my love. You're this broken wreck, mis-shapen, tortured inside. The art can't get out like it could in the fantasy, because breaking down walls isn't as easy for you as it was for the guy who escaped with me half a decade ago. But this is who we are and we still love one another. And no matter what happens" – I take his cheek and bring his eyes back to mine – "we take what time we have and we don't waste a single second and we don't ever, ever regret what went before. Because we can't, Ruben. That has to be rule number one. No regrets. No looking back." He takes a shaky breath and nods he agrees. "Rule number two: we love hard and we love true. And rule number three: we survive for each other, do what we must. We won't be apart, ever again. I won't have it, do you hear me?"

Ruben breaks down, buries his head in my chest and begs, "Forgive me, Freya, forgive me?"

"I need your love, Ruben. I swear, that is all I need. If I have your love, honesty, respect and loyalty, I don't need anything else. I swear. No fucked-up bullshit. No fantasies. Just you. The real you. Like this. It's all I need."

Ruben nods his head, the look in his eye like he's broken but relieved. He kisses me deeply, holds me close and moves on top of me. We make love, naked and vulnerable, wide open to one another. His kisses are much gentler and full of longing. He no longer looks at me like I'm his victim, but like I'm his saviour, his partner, the other half of his soul... the missing piece, finally re-covered.

Chapter Twelve

Too Hard on Him?

I venture to the kitchen a little later, dressed in a robe with a towel wrapped around my head. I'm surprised to discover Adam lounging in the living room. Ruben and I have been rolling around the bed all morning, thinking he'd be out, but he's not. I feel myself turning a light shade of pink, when Adam starts speaking in a serious tone of voice and doesn't give me time to dwell on my embarrassment.

"Erm, so, I've been thinking," he says.

"That's why you're not at the gallery this morning?"

"I asked Lorena to open for us today. She'll call if anything big comes her way."

Lorena being my occasional assistant who has keys to the gallery but doesn't know anything about prices, showing people around... all that. All she knows is about my social media, organising events and answering emails on my behalf. I pay her well for the few hours she works, and I definitely pay her more than I pay Adam, who mostly sits on his ass all day long surfing the internet or scribbling down ideas.

"You should've asked me first," I scold him.

Adam folds his lips inside his mouth. "I know, but this is important. It couldn't wait."

I busy myself around the kitchen, pouring coffee for Ruben and myself, warming pastries under the grill.

"I'm thinking I'll defer a year," he says, breath catching in his throat. "So that I can run this place for you. While you're away. You won't be gone longer than a year, right?"

Truthfully, I don't have an answer to that question. I don't know if we'll fall in love with some other place while we're away and decide to stay there. Or, one of us could get run over by a bus in South America (lots of buses down there) and the other might decide to slip off the face of the earth. Nobody goes through life and ever sticks a hundred per cent to the plan. If they do, then they're probably not living.

"I wouldn't have thought we'd be gone longer than a year, but it'd be just easier for me to sell the gallery, Adam. Even if I leave you in charge, I'll be away thinking about things... wondering if you're all right. If I sell, it's not my responsibility anymore. Otherwise, it still is, even if I'm halfway around the world."

He chews his lip, dressed in just a white t-shirt, his usual chino shorts and leather sandals. The girls in this area seem to love him. Perhaps I should let him have this.

"I know it's big, okay, I know that" – he holds his hands up – "but you know I can do this. And it seems such a shame to give up everything you've worked for, just like that. You'd be throwing away contacts, potential leads, I don't know... future business. Not to mention Ruben has a guaranteed space to sell his stuff if he ever does produce more."

I take a deep breath because it's clear this is what he wants, but is it what I want? I take my coffee to the breakfast counter and he joins me, parking himself opposite. I stare into his brown eyes, the same as mine. Adam reminds me so much of Dad sometimes, I have to blink a lot to get rid of the feeling that Dad and Adam have morphed into one. Adam has the same height, build and colouring as Dad. His hair is very yellow like Dad's, whereas mine is more dirty-blonde with thick brown streaks running through. Mum is a brunette and I guess I got half and half.

My mother isn't a remarkable looking woman. She has small features. A tiny body. Neat, petite. Unassuming. Sometimes, I used to wonder, did Dad hate me because I was so different? I'm tall, like Adam, strong, too, not a thing like Mum, really. Except for the brown streaks. The same small mouth, which on my tall body seems too small. But my mother is beautiful in her own way, could be more so if she just expressed herself a bit. I see why she chose my father, though. He would've been as handsome as Adam or Ruben, once upon a time, before the drinking gave him a pot belly, a perpetual set of shiny cheeks and a thinning hairline.

"I *really* don't know, Adam."

Ruben enters the room fully dressed. He's got errands to run because we're leaving, tomorrow.

Joining us at the breakfast bar and taking up his pastry and coffee, Ruben looks between the two of us.

"What's going on?" he asks, sensing there's something we're debating.

"Adam wants to stay on, to look after the gallery."

Adam nods, lips pursed, sure of his decision. "I'd defer my studies for a year."

Ruben takes a deep breath, eyes Adam with a puzzled look and swishes coffee around his mouth before revealing his take on it. "Wouldn't that be risking your studies? Trust me, once

I'd made the decision to do football instead of school, I knew it would be really hard to go back."

"It's a risk I'm willing to take," Adam states, "because I just know I'm not gonna get this sort of experience anywhere else. It's invaluable. I mean, I might not do as good a job as Freya, but I can keep the place alive. And I've been making connections. There are a few artists I want to work with and it'd be an edge over my classmates, real experience. And I can always email you if I get anything big come up, but Lorena could help with stuff."

I turn to Ruben to gauge his response but he's entirely unreadable, shredding a croissant with his teeth. He's not enthusiastic, but he's not a downer on it, either.

"It's up to Freya," Ruben murmurs, sensing I'm waiting for him to say something. "It's her gallery. It's up to her."

"I just don't know if I can go away and truly relax if I'm wondering what's going on here," I admit, giving Adam my best concerned look. "It'd be a loose end. And my preference would be for you to finish school first, enter the world of work later. We can always start a new gallery. Anytime. Ruben's right, if you leave now, it'll be harder to go back."

Adam looks upset, like we're snubbing him. "I see. You just don't trust me."

"She didn't say that," Ruben warns, not raising his voice, but speaking concisely enough that Adam realises he's not in charge here—I am.

"It's a beautiful concept, Adam. But I'm ten years older than you. I've been around. I can spot a con artist when I meet one. I know how to wine and dine people. How to network. It's much too much for a young man to take on. I wouldn't ask this of you. Besides, I've studied intensively while I've been doing this job.

And part of the reason we're going away is so I can broaden my learning. Your repertoire can never get too big, Adam. Ruben's right. Your education comes first. I wouldn't have been successful at this unless I'd studied and learnt a bit about the art world, first."

Adam starts shaking his head. "So, you read a few books on art? Big whoop."

I look at Ruben whose nostrils flare as he takes a deep breath. I don't have to justify myself and I won't. Yes, I've read a lot of books and been to a lot of Europe's weird and wonderful libraries, galleries and museums, but I've also walked the streets, met a ton of different artists, asked them about their concepts and how they learnt to paint or draw or sculpt. Who taught them? Or were they self-taught?

"There's six weeks of summer left, Adam. Finish the summer out like we planned, then please go back to school and get your degree. Trust me, next year when you graduate, you'll thank me. I promise you."

I take my plate and cup to the sink and leave them there. Behind me, I hear Adam's stool screech as he moves back and takes to his feet. In the window, I see a partial reflection that must be his. His fists are clenched in front of him.

"You just don't trust me," he repeats.

I could say much in response. That I barely trust anyone. Ruben was the first person I ever truly trusted and even so, he tested that trust on occasion. Anyway, it's not that I don't trust Adam. It's that I'm too worldly. I don't want loose ends. I want for my brother to finish his degree and become something legitimate, not just my helper. He needs to go his own way. In life, we all do. That's the only way we ever truly learn—not by hanging onto someone else's coattails.

"Why can't you admit it?" he persists, and when I turn, he's got his arms folded and seems annoyed as hell.

"Admit, what?" I challenge him.

"You don't trust me."

"It doesn't work with me, Adam."

He shakes his head. "I don't know what you're talking about."

"We're done here, mate. Okay? My word is final. You'll go back to Paris in September."

I leave the room and head around the corner, but just before I leave the area completely, I listen out as Adam seems to scoff at Ruben.

"You could've helped out there, mate."

"Trouble is, *pal*," Ruben growls, "she doesn't need any help. Freya's the boss of that gallery."

"Don't I know it."

"You'd do well to remember that. She didn't get where she is because of dumb luck."

"No, she got here because of your dollar," Adam laughs, haughtily.

"Any cunt can take some money and set up a gallery," Ruben warns, "but it takes someone with actual talent and people skills, not to mention a brain for finance, to make it work and not become a money pit. Freya knows what she's talking about and I hope to god that one day you have even a tenth of the brains she has. Because if you do, you'll be all right in the world, but right now you're coming across as a stupid knob who can't take it that his madcap scheme has been thwarted. Now get the fuck to that gallery and tell Lorena to clock off. Goodbye."

"Whatever," Adam shrills, then leaves the house, slamming the door as he goes.

I tiptoe into the kitchen once the front gate shuts and Ruben turns and sees me.

"Hear all that?" he asks.

"Yep."

"Little scrote," Ruben chuckles. "Reminds me of someone I used to know."

"Oh, yeah?" I wrap my arms around him from behind and kiss his hair. He smells divine, of cucumber and mint, woodland and spice.

"Full of it, thinks he knows it all, thinks the world will make it happen if he's given just half a chance, all that. Deluded by notions of greatness."

"Laurent," I guess.

"I'd give a million quid just to have one more argument with him. He never really understood what it took for me to make it."

"Buns of steel?" I chuckle.

"Ruthless determination. Not dreams. Not wide-eyed fantasies. Pure and utter brutality."

"You shouldered it for him, like I'd shoulder Adam."

"Exactly." He turns and gives me a kiss, wild-haired and beautiful. "I love you."

"I know."

AFTER RUBEN LEAVES the house to make his errands, I set up my suitcases in the closet and start throwing things inside. I don't exactly know what to take, so I decide to take everything I like—the rest can be given to charity, if Adam's feeling in the mood, once we're gone.

I start to wonder if I was too harsh on him. He's my little brother and he means well, but I was quite quick to dismiss him and he had valid reasons for wanting to stay on. The experience he'd gain... and not letting my hard work fade to nothing. Plus, we don't have anything to lose with the gallery. It's true what I said this morning: the only thing that concerns me is Adam giving up university too soon... not finishing... then losing his way. Like I did. Yes, I clawed my way back through sheer determination and hard work, but I don't want that for him. I want Adam to get a degree, have something like a foundation to build up from. Something that can never be taken away from him. He doesn't yet understand the perils of the real world, the people out there who'd rather take than ever give... the freeloaders, the con artists... the fakes. He doesn't know about any of that. He's still childish, living in his own bubble. He decided to follow his heart and do an art degree, in the process losing Dad's respect, and it's left Adam on his own. He must feel like I'm abandoning him. Right when he needs me most. The last year of his studies... when he needs me most... and I'm leaving him.

Adam is young, though. Resilient. The older you get, the harder it is to adapt.

That's why I'm yanking Ruben and myself away from here. From everything. We have to go somewhere different for a little while, see if what we have is true and that we're not just two broken pieces trying to fit together. For once, we need to be allowed to be a couple in love, rather than a pair always having to run or conspire or hide secrets from each other. We need a break. This will be a good test. An adventure, but also a chance to discover if we can make it together in foreign places.

My cases are almost full and I'm wondering if Ruben has spare luggage space, when I'm bothered by something... a memory.

Ruben said Alexia used to take Laurent and him away on holiday as kids, just the three of them, and when they'd go, they'd stay in humble digs, go off the beaten track, seek authentic experiences and see the world from the perspective of ordinary people, not the privileged.

Yet Alexia claims... she said on the call the other night... she always knew about Fred. She knew about me being a problem for Fred. I don't understand the woman. Either she's unbelievably contradictory in character, or there was a time when she used to appreciate the simpler things of life... and then all that changed, one day. Perhaps the holidays she took her boys on were a secret. Meant for nobody else to know about. The mob boss wife still has a reputation to uphold, even now. But with me? Why? She has no reason to lie to me now; those days are long gone. Unless she wasn't lying for my benefit, but someone else's. Why would she desire to pull the wool over my eyes? Unless she's genuinely ill and confused. Doesn't know whether she's coming or going.

Or... Alexia never lied, but Ruben did. The line about their humble holidays together was a little thing to put me off the scent. When we were in Florence, we stayed in a nice little apartment but it was rather lacking the grandeur of the hotel we'd stayed in, not many days before we headed there, when we were in Paris. In the capital city of France, we'd enjoyed luxury, oh so much luxury at one of the city's top hotels.

Ruben planned it all. What took place in Florence, he'd planned it all.

He must have employed a fake cop to inform me of his 'death'. The cop whose line was that he'd contacted Alexia and she'd given him an address in Florence, said the humble apartment was where Ruben would stay, if he were ever in Florence. A haunt from the past.

In the middle of the night, when I got that strange phone call from Alexia telling me to return to the UK immediately—no explanation as to why, just to come—it's clear to me now that Ruben staged the whole thing. We stayed in that apartment because it was in a building that was rather empty. Most occupants weren't there, they only came home for weekends or holidays. It wasn't exclusive, fancy, didn't have a concierge or staff on hand for me to get help from 24/7. As I screamed and wailed through the night, a sobbing, manic mess, nobody in the building would've heard me. Had we stayed someplace fancy, other guests might have heard my wails and complained. Authorities might have been called. The ruse would have been ruined.

It wasn't a great apartment. I distinctly remember the cob-webbed cupboards... the slightly crispy sheets as I washed and dried them... the odd damp smell in some of the cups and glasses. Alexia had been given her instructions to contact me. She'd been briefed. I was the only one in the dark. She'd been put in a difficult position, I imagine. Freddie caused Fred's death so she wanted retribution. I expect she resented Ruben but also was looking forward to escaping to Portugal with him... finally getting her son all to herself.

I'd been brainwashed by Ruben's story about the eccentric holidays they took as kids, the bohemian mother who wanted to show them real life. I was bought hook, line and sinker. He's that clever. Four years ago, I was as much a part of the plot as everyone else—the plot to kill Fred, expose Freddie and destroy the Kitchener dynasty. Ruben used me to make it happen. I was a pawn. He made me the ultimate accessory. My reactions guaranteed the integrity of his so-called death and convinced Freddie he no longer had anything to worry about. I was used.

The dynasty lives on... doesn't it? In Ruben. Who finds it easier to lie than tell the truth.

And this is why we need to go. Be transposed. Because unless I get Ruben somewhere he's never been—an alien environment where he can no longer make up stories, bring me into some plot or drag me into another strange fantasy—I don't think I'll ever find out who he truly is.

I don't think even he knows who he is.

Leaving for another continent might be our only chance to make this work.

I have to try and save him from himself.

I'M STILL PACKING WHEN Ruben arrives home, hollering, "Freya, you here?"

"Closet!"

I'm sitting on the carpeted floor, deciding which knickers to throw out, when he crouches behind me, wraps his arms around me and inhales my hair, deeply.

"My baby's back," I groan.

He slides his hands across my boobs. "Oh, god. You're not wearing a bra."

"It's summer. I hardly ever wear a bra in summer."

"But not even a bikini?"

His body is hot, pressed against my back. All I'm wearing is one of my kaftans and nothing else. I'm travelling tomorrow. I have my travelling outfit picked out. I'm packing everything else. The kaftan can easily be left behind or rolled up and shoved in my case last-minute. You could say I'm packing everything I like and nothing I wouldn't miss. I'm packing as if I'm never coming back... or... whatever.

He digs his hand beneath the material of the plunging neckline and scissors his fingers either side of my left nipple.

"Where did you go?" I whisper, tipping my head back against his shoulder and turning so I can look up into his eyes.

He's wearing a haunted look. Sexy. Incredibly horny.

"I sold the Ferrari. I couldn't stand to think of it sitting in storage. I lost a few grand but got a good price."

"Okay." I gulp, staring at his eyes, more grass-green than sludgy green beneath the bright spotlights of the closet.

"I missed you," he groans, even though he was barely gone three hours.

"I missed you, too."

He covers my mouth with his and his lips glide smoothly across mine, pushing my mouth open so he can taste me and drive me insane with his tongue. We turn towards one another and he ends up falling on his back, flat on the carpet, a pile of knickers beneath his head. I land on top of him and kiss him back, biting his mouth, licking his tongue and under his top lip. I suction my mouth to his and he lifts my kaftan, his hands grabbing my rear and squeezing.

I'm roasting hot and sit up, straddling him, reaching for the hem of my kaftan and removing it. He swallows hard when he stares at my naked body, which he had carnally earlier this morning, but evidently, still wants more of.

"I love you," I groan.

He gets his t-shirt off quickly and tosses it away. Sitting up, he pulls me close and kisses my breasts, groaning. He licks my throat and wraps my curls around his hands, yanking my hair gently. He loses himself in kissing and licking, while all I can think about is needing him inside me.

I shift back a little, unbuckle his belt, rake down his zipper and smooth my hand along his shaft. Ruben groans and continues sucking my nipples, driving me ever more insane. I yank his shorts out of the way and press him against my wetness, sliding down onto him smoothly. I'm so wet. It rarely ever hurts with Ruben. I'm always ready for him.

Ruben grips my shoulders and groans as I rock carefully over him. I'm still sensitive from this morning. I'm bare and everything is so heightened like this. I bite my lip and ride him leisurely, my hands gripping the back of his neck. He's still sucking my nipples, licking my throat, kissing my shoulders and breastbone.

"Oh, god, Ruben," I groan.

Once again, he proves how powerful he is—just one hand of his against my bum helping me to rock more consistently along his length—enough that I begin to feel a build-up inside my pussy of pure, ecstatic pleasure.

"Yes, Ruben!"

He digs his hand underneath my hair, brings my face to his and kisses me deeply as we fuck. I can't hold it in any longer and I grip his hair and make peculiar faces at him as I stare into his eyes, groaning, my core wrapping around his cock, gripping and milking him, the pressure unleashed inside me immense. Ruben grins wildly, and towards the end of my display, he bites his bottom lip and lets go of his own pleasure, his unmistakable heat shooting inside of me.

I feel so happy in the aftermath. Carefree and desired and sexy. He slides his hands all over my back and rubs my bum, groaning even as he shrinks inside my body. I bite his ear and whisper into it, "My love."

"You're so beautiful, Freya. I'm always so hard for you."

"Oh god, baby."

I fling my arms around his neck and hold him tight. He grips my body in his arms and even though we're sweating and it's a claustrophobic space, I need to feel his body next to mine and his arms hugging me remorselessly.

He has his face buried in my hair but I hear him when he says, "I love you so much, it hurts. It physically fucking wrecks me, every time. I love you so fucking much, Freya. I can't lose you, ever again."

"Never again," I whisper, and I begin kissing his face, all over. "Never, ever."

He kisses me and they are messy, fraught, desperate, unhinged kisses... two people who desperately love and desire one another.

"Third shower of the day?" I ask, breaking our kiss so I can breathe.

"Fuck, no. I need a lie down. I'm broken."

I throw my head back laughing. "Enjoy a little rest, baby."

While he heads to bed for a siesta, I head to the bathroom to stand under the spray for twenty seconds, careful not to get my hair wet. I walk around drying off before slipping back into my kaftan.

I catch his eyes as I'm walking back through the bedroom. He isn't asleep yet. He's watching me as I pass through. He looks tired, but alert.

"Was I harsh on him?" I ask Ruben. "Might he be scared I'm abandoning him?"

Ruben shakes his head. "He thinks he can be you, Freya. But he can't. Nobody can."

"You're right."

Nobody can.

My experiences shaped me.

And I wouldn't wish them on anyone else.

Chapter Thirteen

Not a Pushover

I'm getting ready for bed in the en suite bathroom, the bundle of nerves in my stomach down to one of two things—or perhaps even, both.

Adam didn't come home for dinner tonight. In the past (before Ruben showed up), we had an agreement that he would always call if he couldn't make it home for dinner. No such call this evening. It's approaching eleven at night and he's not returned... and we're travelling halfway around the world tomorrow. And he's not here.

Today, I packed all mine and Ruben's clothes into six or seven large suitcases. I'm selling the gallery. At the end of the season, Adam will hand over the keys to an estate agent and it'll be put in their hands. The villa will remain empty over the winter months but my cleaner will pop in now and again, just to check everything is safe and the place hasn't been disturbed.

I pay for Adam's university fees and he gets a decent wage for his summer job at the gallery—he's going to be fine financially—and actually, he's being a bit of a brat not coming home the night before Ruben and I are due to go away, for who knows how long. I'm not sure I can get on a plane tomorrow unless we've resolved things. Unless we can cheerfully bid adieu, see you later, au revoir... until next time.

I'm leaving behind dozens of acquaintances. People who make my coffee, my dinner, help me pick out dresses in their stores... clients whose houses I've filled with artwork.

But no real friends. I'm leaving behind no real friends.

Ruben is my only true friend in the world. He might be the only one I ever open up to. Sure, I told Adam about things that happened in my life, but it's different with Ruben. It's equal. We can be naked with one another. That's how it should be between lovers, partners and best friends. Adam is my much-younger brother and he doesn't know everything.

I finish my nightly ritual—putting on cream—and tuck my jars away in my make-up bag. I'll pack that last thing tomorrow morning.

Ruben's waiting in bed when I get to the bedroom. I untie my silk robe, leave it on the chaise and dive into bed next to him wearing a tiny silk slip. He wraps himself around me from behind, his arms a miracle—yet that gut-churning feeling is still there.

"I tried calling him and got no answer," Ruben says. "Left a stern voicemail. He might be home soon, you never know."

"Or he might be screwing some bird to make himself feel better."

"This isn't on you, Freya. You've given him so much. He doesn't know how lucky he is."

It doesn't matter what Ruben says, the sick feeling in my gut won't budge. I feel...

Like I ought to give Adam a shot at it.

But that's my heart talking.

KARMA

My head says he's much too young and inexperienced to run a gallery for an entire year while I'm abroad. It'd be at the expense of his studies, and I...

I can't sanction that.

"I feel absolutely wretched. Why is he doing this to me? He knows we're leaving tomorrow. He knows that."

Ruben's chest pushes against my back as he breathes heavily. "He's a kid, Freya. This is what kids do. You've made the right decision, you know. He needs to focus on his studies and we need to get some distance. I think we both need some new inspiration."

"That's very true." I've been bombarded by the French art scene for so long... it's time for a change.

"Please, don't let him upset you, Frey."

"I'm trying not to. It'd be much nicer... if he'd just... at least text... call... show up to give me a hug. We leave at midday, how do we know he'll be back before then?"

"We don't, but if he isn't, then we'll assume he's not serious about the gallery. Maybe it can't be left in his care."

"Oh, god," I groan, because that's another thing.

If he's *that* pissed off with me, can he be trusted to run it for even just a few weeks?

"Freya," he soothes, pulling me over to face him. "I will sort it all out in the morning. Please, just don't be upset."

"I can't help it!" I bury my face in his chest and try not to cry.

"What's the worst that could happen? He screws some rando tonight. Nothing new about that. He comes back tail between his legs in the morning, or he shoots back off to Paris to finish his studies and refuses to run the gallery any longer. Either way, it's just a gallery and it's just money, Freya. He's not stupid, he'll be all right."

"You promise?"

"He's twenty-one. He can do a lot of things legally. He's a proper adult. He can take care of himself. He's not your responsibility. He's a man."

"I know." I press my nose into his chest and sigh. "It's just... he's so... and if I could just leave knowing there'll be someone, but he's not on speaking terms with the 'rents and there's his mates. They're just... idiots."

"Freya, he can still call you. Loads of kids his age study abroad and only have contact with their family over the phone."

"Ruben," I growl, "it's not that easy! Will you just desist?"

I roll the other way, right to the edge of the bed. I can't help feeling cut up about all of this, it's just the way it is. I was the one who chose to go abroad, I know that, and this is all at my behest. But Ruben doesn't always understand that as a woman, we have feelings we can't switch off. That's how it is. We make choices and we know we have to stick to them, but we also have feelings. That's life.

It's unfair that everything a woman feels goes right to her stomach. When that happens, you can't ignore the feeling. Maybe it's because the womb is so near the stomach and it's highly sensitive, but when a woman feels something in her stomach—like sorrow or pain or even happiness—it cannot be ignored. My gut feeling has been right so often and I regretted the times I ignored it. I feel like I'm going to regret it if I don't give Adam this chance to run the gallery.

There are risks whatever I decide to do.

That's when we hear the front door slam shut. I turn over instantly and look at Ruben. He rolls his eyes and folds his arms, knowing I can't stop myself.

I fly out of bed, grab my robe, and storm down the corridor of the villa. He's standing with the fridge door open, drinking juice out of the bottle, the fridge lights illuminating his silhouette as I stand behind him, seething.

"You didn't call, Adam."

He jumps with surprise, like he expected me to be in bed, not up and about.

He worries his lip and shrugs off whatever feeling he just had. "I thought you'd be busy packing."

He finishes drinking from the bottle, then returns it to the fridge.

He slowly turns around, arms hanging low, head bowed. "I went for drinks with a mate tonight, big deal."

"We're leaving tomorrow. I made dinner."

"Sorry," he says, stroppy, shrugging.

"This isn't fair, Adam. I've done a lot for you. This isn't fair."

He sniffs and takes a few deep breaths, his face in shadow, but I can still see his annoyance. The only light in the room now he's shut the fridge is the moon streaming in through the window.

"I'll tell you what isn't fair, Freya. You made me think you'd always be here for me, and now he's back, well..." His mouth does that thing Dad's used to, when he was so mad, his lips wobbled. "Now, you're off. Just like that. And not two or three nights ago I brought him home stinking drunk. You were done with him. And now, god, you're just off. Like that." He clicks his fingers. "It

179

suddenly doesn't matter about me anymore. Sod what he's done, the pain he's caused you, nothing else matters but him, does it?"

"Tell me how to fix this," I beg, trembling, "tell me. I can't be on bad terms with you, Adam."

He walks forward, puts his hands around my shoulders and levels with me. "Let me have the gallery to take care of. Then at least when it goes tits up, you've got something to come back to."

I swallow hard. Is he trying to emotionally blackmail me, or is he making perfect sense?

"I might fuck it up, Freya. I know that. I know, all right? But I've watched you and I can't go far wrong if I just do as you've done, and anyway, as long as it's owned by you, people will still trust me to do business with." He's pleading, his eyes serious. "I honestly do not give a fuck about finishing my degree this year or next or the year after. I don't, Freya. I like art, I do. I love it. I love painting, drawing... all that. But if I have to become like him" – he points to where Ruben is, at the other side of the house, lying in bed – "to become a great artist, then no thanks. If I have to be *that* fucked-up to produce the stuff he does, no thank you. You've said it yourself, life is long, people change careers, change their minds, change their direction. If I fuck this up, we both know you can come back and fix it, don't we? You show up and it's all fixed again. But what about if you've sold it all and you come back and he's gone and you've got nothing again, like before? Absolutely nothing."

He's challenging me to tell him he's wrong, even though I agree with him in part.

"If the figures at the end of the summer are good, then you can keep the place on," I offer, but in a warning tone of voice. "If they're not, we close and sell. You go back to Paris and do whatever you want with your degree afterwards, okay?"

Adam breathes a sigh of relief. "Thank you."

I hold my finger up and point at him. "If you fuck this up, it won't be me you'll be answering to. You don't know about the people Ruben knows. If you so much as move a decimal point in the wrong direction, it won't go unnoticed, do you hear me?"

He salutes me. "Aye, aye, captain."

I grab his jaw firmly and bring his eyes to mine. "I'm not kidding, Adam. Ruben is dangerous and knows dangerous people. If you fuck up, he will have you seen to. Trust me. That's why I'm taking him away, why we have to leave. You don't know how fucking screwed up he is." I keep my voice down. "He's lived on the edge for almost a decade now. He needs to find another way to live. He needs to find a life where he's not constantly scared of his own shadow. If you think the El Chapo of London got caught by some freak of luck, you're gravely mistaken."

Adam's eyes widen. "That was Ruben?"

I push my finger over his mouth. "Ruben is a killer, Adam. But he's not a monster. The monsters made him who he is. I need to unmake him, undo what they did to him. Do you understand? That's why I'm taking him away. I'm going to save him. And we'll be coming back with lots of art. So, I don't want any fucking nonsense, no bad rep attached to my name, you got me? I want to be able to sell again."

Adam gulps, takes a deep breath. "Straight down the line. By the way, I was drinking with Lourde Jameson tonight. He's agreed to show at the gallery."

"REALLY?" I almost scream.

"Yeah, I went to his lock-up. You'd have been so impressed. Ruben must know something we don't because his stuff is on wood panel, too. Not pyrography but resin. It's already got interest as far as New York."

I swing my arms around his neck, elated at first, then sad.

We've been a great duo, but now it's over... for the time being.

"I'll miss you," I whisper.

"I know."

I pull back and slap him playfully. "Pig."

"I won't let you down," he assures me.

"You better not."

He trudges upstairs to bed while I prepare myself to tell Ruben the news.

When I get there he's still awake, propped up in bed. "You're letting him stay on."

"If he can prove continual sales, if not, he's out."

I remove my robe and slide back into bed. Ruben cuddles me, his naked, hot body soothing mine instantly. The sick feeling in my stomach has somewhat settled, but having him close by will help the rest subside.

"I'm not a pushover," I tell him.

"Never said you were."

"I warned him he has to be good; it has to work."

"And he will, or else he'll face me."

"Oh, he knows it. Either way, it's just money, like you said..."

Ruben pushes up my silk slip and kisses my stomach. "Either way."

I groan beneath his touch and finally, the stomach ache's gone.

Chapter Fourteen

Rio de Janeiro

We arrived in Rio three days ago. Walking through the airport, Ruben was accosted by a barrage of fans wanting everything signing, from shirts and caps to breasts and trainers. Ruben was visibly shook and I had no idea it would be like that. He signed a few things but eventually, airport security pushed back the crowds and we were able to get away with our luggage. He said nothing except, "Even after all these years..." I guess when you have a jawline that's unmistakable, a bit like David Beckham's, you're screwed. Especially when you recently shaved. Even more especially when you decide to visit a football-mad nation like Brazil. Anyway, he was thankful that I'd thought to pre-book a hire car. Once we'd jumped in the SUV, our luggage filling the back, we sped away up into the hills and nobody seemed to follow. Once we arrived at our rented villa nestled in a quiet spot on the border of the Santa Teresa neighbourhood, I met the owner on the steps and took possession of the keys while handing over our deposit in cash. Ruben only emerged from the blacked-out SUV once we were safely inside the gates of the villa.

So, it's been three days now and there hasn't been a single paparazzo hanging around outside. I went out in the car to buy groceries, and when I came back, Ruben had shaved his head. *Back to being incognito*, I thought.

He's been withdrawn ever since we arrived. He sits in the window staring at the world outside, watching... waiting... for something. He becomes ever more like that thug who made love to me in Nice, when he visited me for one last night and to say goodbye... and it never really was goodbye. He's returning to that thug, more and more, day by day. I can tell. Except the frantic lovemaking part. He hasn't wanted that since we got here. He must be wound tight.

All I can think is that someone on our flight—perhaps an air steward—tipped off the fans or something. Otherwise, how did those people find out Ruben was going to be passing through the airport? Unless, they're just always there.

Today, I'm making the most of the sunshine. We left behind the height of summer in the South of France, but here it is low season. The past three days it was overcast and seventeen Celsius at best. Today it's twenty-four and sunny. We're only staying for a month (at least that's how long the villa is ours), but we could stay longer if we wanted. Come November and December, it will be sweltering here.

Ruben emerges from the house and joins me by the pool. He's wearing shorts and t-shirt, looks awkward and sort of vulnerable and exposed, his face clean shaven and his crew cut revealing all the little white bits of his face and neck that the sun couldn't quite catch before.

Back in France, he would swim every day, but this is the first time he's actually left the interior of the villa since we got here. It's been a bit of an arse getting used to the time difference and all, but I know that's not what's wrong with his head. And he doesn't want me to know. I've seen this look in his eye before—the night he told me Fred was dead and that he'd arranged it—and I know what it means.

He doesn't want to be pushed on the details.

"Why aren't you topless?" he asks.

Of all the questions... "Should I be?" I laugh.

"It's private here. People would need a long lens."

"They would, would they?"

He sighs, as though disturbed I'm not topless.

I'm like...

Of course, we skinny-dipped that night of the romantic meal... and I would sunbathe topless at the beach sometimes in France, if I knew Adam was nowhere in the borough. I never bathed nude around my own pool in Nice because my neighbours were too close by... and I thought I might scare the dogs.

"It's not your fault, you know?" he says.

"Yes, I know."

"It's my shit... I'm dealing with it."

"I'm letting you deal with it." I still have my head buried in a fashion magazine, enjoying the rays on my skin. The infinity pool needed cleaning earlier so I did that, but I may as well have not bothered. I don't think he's getting in... and I don't like the chlorine.

He sighs, exasperated, because he doesn't want to be like this, but he is... and I'm accepting him. Why does that make him feel bad, I wonder? Does he think he needs to be perfect for me?

"I should've known but it's been so long and I didn't think—"

I look up quickly, regarding him. "You're scared that the gangsters who believed you dead might not anymore?"

"Correct."

"Did you check the papers?"

"No, but I have people checking them for me."

I shake my head, disappointed. "Ruben..."

"I can't get rid of them. They keep us safe, Freya."

"And will there ever be a day we're truly safe and can let them go?"

He shakes his head. "I don't think so."

I gulp, even more aggrieved than I already was. I'm not going to show him I am, but he'll know anyway...

"Why did you bring me here?" he asks.

"You know why."

He suppresses a laugh, looks away and rubs his nose.

"To paint," he mutters.

"To create," I correct him.

He worries his lip and I laugh.

"Look, if it'll make you feel any better, I'll go topless. But I'm not really bothered about a few white bits. I'm mostly sitting out here for the view. Isn't it magnificent?"

Beyond the infinity pool, you can see all the way down to the beach at the edge of the city. At night all the lights of the bars, restaurants and hotels make the place look like a constellation of stars and it feels like we're at the edge of the world, or maybe the beginning of it. I don't know. I've sat on a chair with a glass of red the past few nights, just staring at it all, the whole lot of it waiting out there for us.

While he's remained inside... hiding... scared.

"I won't be able to go anywhere," he says.

"Yes, you will. Just wear shades and a hat. Besides, if we visit the museums and stuff, we'll blend in."

Ruben covers his mouth with a hand, shaking his head.

"What?" I snipe.

"Blend in? As if *we* could ever blend in."

I shrug and go back to my magazine.

"Well, I'm happy here," I mutter, "it's a change of scenery and all."

My phone pings and I pick it up immediately; I've been scared the past few days that there will be a fire at the gallery, or at the villa... or the dogs will get loose... or something.

Adam has sent me a picture of the pooches asleep on his bed, with the caption: *Think they hate being without you.*

I smile to myself and let Ruben see. It's a weight off my mind. Ruben smiles a little but hands the phone back, still with that foreboding look in his eyes.

"We could go to this beach I read about tomorrow, if you like," I suggest. "It's a bit of a drive but it'll sure be picturesque, oh, and... it's a naked beach."

His eyebrows lift. "Naked beach?" He's definitely interested.

"Grumari Beach is off the beaten track, a bit more scenic, and yes there's an area where nudity is allowed."

He nods his head, trying to keep his cool. "Yeah, okay."

"I'll make a picnic. We can spend the day. Perhaps admire the nature reserves nearby."

Ruben gets up from the lounger he's been sat on the edge of and holds out his hand.

"Freya, come with me."

I put my magazine on the ground and he takes my hand, yanking me off the lounger.

I'm pulled into his arms and he stares down into my eyes. This close up, I'm finally able to see into the chaos inside his mind. Ruben kisses me so ardently, I'm not allowed to breathe for at least thirty seconds as he dominates my mouth.

He lifts me up and I wrap my legs around him. His hair feels strange, familiar, but odd. I only had him that one night with shorn hair. The dozens of other nights we've spent together, I've had a massive crop to grab hold of and tug. Today under my fingers is a silky-soft crew cut and the curvature of his cranium. It's very sexy, even though I can't grab his thick mane like I normally would.

He starts walking me indoors but before we've even got there, he's tugged down my bikini cups and is sucking first one nipple, then the other, out in the open air. It's been three (maybe four days) without his arms or cock and I'm dying of need.

He slides the door shut behind us and stalks across the living area, passing down the corridor for the bedrooms until reaching our room. I might have picked this holiday let because the layout is very similar to our place back in Nice; the only big difference is that this villa doesn't have all the tech and mod cons I installed back home. He's still sucking my breasts as he throws me down on the bed beneath his body, quickly untying the drawstring on his shorts as I begin untying my bikini knickers.

Ruben's kisses are sumptuous as he lines himself up, stroking the tip of his penis through my folds, finding out if I'm wet and ready, open and desirous.

His eyes widen when he pushes into me just a little, holding back, his gaze loving and also greedy. He tips his hips all the way and my pelvis rocks up towards his, my body bowing at his command.

"I love you," he groans.

"I love you more."

His rampant kisses mirror his fast fucking. I don't have time to breathe or think or even cry out as I'm kissed, fucked and held in place for his cock to fit inside me, as deeply as possible.

I'm blinking and almost choking when he growls against my ear and throbs inside me, filling me with his seed. Was my response just then an orgasm? Or was it pain? It could have been either. I know he's not done with me because of the look in his eye. He's neither tired nor satisfied.

Is this the man I fell in love with? More deeply than ever before? That guy, the thug... that night... when he was so raw, so exposed and open... I could hardly bear it and neither could he.

"What's that look in your eye?" he groans.

I can hardly find my words, but after sucking forward some saliva, I manage to speak. "It was that night... when you had hair like this and you were shaven and your shoulders were huge... and I fell even more deeply. As deeply as a human can. To the point where you were in me, in my atoms, my molecules... I was so out of myself, it was almost as if we'd fully exchanged and we were one. That was the real you that night, wasn't it? Unhinged and depraved, barbaric and a monster. You fucked me until I cried and you didn't say sorry."

He bows his head, chin to his chest, looking away.

"Yes," he mumbles.

"I want that man," I groan. "I want him. I want him, always."

Ruben lies on top of me so he's almost crushing me, but not quite. He buries his face in my hair and groans, clinging to me, needing me. I grab hold of his t-shirt and yank it up until he lets me help him get it off. Then I untie my bikini top and kick his shorts down.

We're naked again.

He lifts himself slightly, touches his hands to my cheeks and stares into my eyes. I run my fingers down his body, over his glutes and down to his thighs. He hasn't slipped out of me. We've been as one even though he came ages ago and has gone soft.

"I'm so scared of losing you, Freya."

I nod and lean up, touching my lips to his. "I know."

"My chest feels... it feels..." The corners of his eyes wrinkle. "It feels..."

"I know," I whisper, feeling the same way. "Like you're finally alive."

Like everything inside my chest is only working because he's here and he loves me. That before, all my functions were perfunctory and pointless, but with him everything is heightened and makes sense and love exists, finally.

"You're mine," he whispers against my mouth, "and I'm yours."

"Yes," I murmur, stroking his face.

"My instinct to protect you goes above all else, Freya," he tells me, shaking, "it's my entire reason for being. It's my job to protect you. My duty. My role. I will do whatever it takes to keep you safe, even if it means going over your head, do you understand me?"

My lips wobbles but I nod that I agree.

"No crying, baby, no crying," he murmurs, then he kisses me softly, urging me to kiss him back, to partake. I wrap my arms tight around him and let him sweep me up all over again, the deliciousness of the slowly swelling heat inside me electric.

Ruben kisses every inch of my face and rocks tenderly inside me, keeping his gaze on me, my chest heavy and sensitive against his firm, taut pecs. He wraps his fingers around mine and kisses my fingertips.

"Ruben?" I ask, as he's mesmerised by my hands.

"Yes, lady mine."

"I want my animal again."

His eyes dart to mine and he bares his teeth. "We have all the time in the world, my love. Lie back. I'm enjoying myself."

He kisses my fingertips until I'm a sizzling heap of flesh, desperate to watch his muscular body fuck me and not continue with this sedentary phase.

I push him up and sit in his lap, impatient. He growls, wraps his arms around me and jiggles his head between my breasts. I rock over his cock until he's hitting the right spot... and I come so hard, my thighs shake around him until they're numb.

He bites my bottom lip and growls, "You're a wild woman. You just couldn't wait."

I know from that look in his eye, he didn't get his then and he's still got a lot more to give.

I catch my breath, push my nose to his and ask, "What do you like best about my body?"

"I hardly know how to answer. Everything."

"I want to know," I persist.

"What about my body?"

"Your mouth," I reveal, eagerly, no hesitation. "Your mouth. Now you. Your turn. What do you like best?"

He appears shocked and surprised. "My mouth?"

"Yes, your mouth."

"Why?" he demands.

"Everything," I almost shout, annoyed he's delaying.

I know he has so much more to give.

"Freya," he demands again, this time with a warning look.

I swipe my thumb across his bottom lip, staring at his deeply sensual mouth. The fat bottom lip. The colour... plum, at least in this light. His tongue is greedy and thick, long. His top lip is deeply accented with a prominent bow. Everything.

"It's the most beautiful mouth," I murmur, "and the things you do... the words you speak... the kisses you give freely... the way you lick me, suck me... I could orgasm just staring at your mouth. It's sickening how in love with you I am."

I catch sight of him looking at me and his chest is heaving, up and down, up and down. His cock is even moving a little inside me... he's rocked by my words.

"I can come inside you, feel like I'm home, have my cock squeezed between your muscles and have your juice coat me, so you'd think your pussy would be my favourite thing, but it isn't." I'm almost breathless and he hasn't even really got started, I don't think. "Your breasts are utterly beautiful. Perfect. They're the most beautiful breasts I've ever seen. Your chocolate eyes... I drown in them, every time. Your sweet little mouth... I get hard just looking at your mouth. Your sensual curves and raspy voice. Your long legs. God, your legs." He rubs his hands up and down my legs. "Your big, beautiful, complex heart. Your soul. Your mind. Your overall beauty... overwhelms me, Freya. I think I love you as much as it's possible to love someone, and then the next day, I wake up loving you more." I hold him tight in my arms and feel myself frowning deeply... his words overwhelming. He puts his hands in my hair and strokes his fingers through the tangled waves. "When I first knew I was in love with you, I would've done anything—and I mean anything—to smell your hair or touch it or have you accidentally brush your hair across my hand or something. I would smile thinking of your hair. I still absolutely adore it," he chuckles, "and I think, for me, it just says so much about you. Your strength. Your vitality and beauty and wildness. Your hair drives me insane, Freya. When you fiddle with it, tie it up, let it down... I wake up and I spend five minutes every morning trying to guess how you're going to wear your hair that day. I'm obsessed with it. I'm utterly in love with it. I'm mad for you, and so, yes, your hair is my favourite thing... because this wild mane... it's proof of the wild soul beneath the mask. The face you show to the world... that isn't the real you. This hair is your one way of expression and god, fuck, I love it, so much. It drives me wild."

I grab his jaw and kiss him deeply, shoving my tongue in his mouth, holding nothing back. He knows who I am. He's the only man who's ever known me and loved me for all I am.

I throw my head back and he kisses my throat, then my chest, my breasts.

"Ruben, I love you."

"God, baby," he moans.

I know what I want before I've even signalled it and I think he knows, too. I slip off his cock and he's gasping, wondering if it might be happening.

I turn around and get on the bed, holding my bottom open for him. He shuffles into place, asks, "You sure, Frey?"

"Like before, remember? Like before."

I open for him and he slides his wet cock inside my bottom, the walls closing around him almost to the point where his circulation must be cut off. He waits as I breathe and relax, then within a few strides, I've become wetter and he's easing into me, over and over.

He fucks me in long strokes, grunting and cursing. He wraps my hair around his fist and fucks me until I'm arching and warning, "I'm coming, Ruben!"

The pain of release is soon gone as he slips out. I groan because I wanted to keep coming with him inside me, but when I see him behind me, jerking off, I realise what it is he wants.

I find my own extended pleasure by rubbing my clit and he groans louder and louder, as I lie flat on my belly and he spreads my hair out across my back.

"Oh, fuck, fuck..." He comes in my hair, all across my back, spurting up and down. His hand is on my shoulder, squeezing hard, his release intense.

I feel the bed shudder as he collapses into the mattress beside me. I can barely move. I also don't know if it's safe to.

"My hair... my beautiful hair."

"God, I needed that," he groans. "I've fantasised about that... so many times. God, Frey. You drive me to these things. I need more. I always need more."

"And I need a shower, so you had better let me know when it's safe to move."

He laughs loudly and it makes me smile... a lot.

He takes my hair in his hands and holds it in a big bun at the nape of my neck.

"Let's move, shall we?"

I climb off the bed slowly while he's got my hair and we edge our way to the bathroom. I step into the shower and gladly brook the cold spray as it warms through. Ruben steps in beside me and helps me wash my hair, lathering it with shampoo.

He takes the showerhead off the wall and directs water to my armpits, my breasts, my private places and my face, cleaning me up, then making sure all the shampoo and other matter is all out of my hair. He barely cleans himself, except for spraying his pits and cock, his face and shoulders. We're about to get out when he pins me to the tiled wall and spreads open my thighs, lifting me up, hands beneath my knees.

"I can't stop," he growls.

I don't want him to.

Chapter Fifteen

A Woman's Love

I wake cursing because it's dusk and I've slept too long. I probably won't sleep tonight now. I'm in bed alone but I remember having sex in the shower, coming so hard my vocal cords hurt... and then him towel-drying my hair and tucking me into bed.

"Ruben?" I groan, but he doesn't answer. "Ruben?" I raise my voice.

Disoriented, it takes me a while to recognise I'm in Brazil... not France.

He arrives in the doorway wiping his hands on a rag, paint spots on his white t-shirt. If he still had all that hair on his head, he'd no doubt look dishevelled... his eyes appear tired.

I leave the bed and chase into his arms. He drops the rag and wraps me in his embrace. I push my face into his neck and moan, needing him close. His arms cover my back and he buries his face in my hair, half-laughing, half-groaning.

He picks me up and carries me to bed, sitting his arse on the edge of the mattress, with me draped across his lap sideways.

"I lied," I mumble, stroking my fingers across his forehead as he holds me and stares at my face.

"Oh, yes?"

"Your mouth isn't the best thing. Well, sexually it is..."

He appears a hell of a lot shyer than earlier, maybe because he's struggling not to gaze at my breasts.

"Is there a point to your point?" he asks, leaning in and kissing my neck, just below my ear.

"Your arms are the best thing. They make me feel safe."

He ceases what he's doing and tugs me close, places a little kiss on my mouth and murmurs, "I'd starved you for three days. You were sex mad earlier. It's all right."

I laugh and he laughs. We're laughing for ages, in the end, egging each other on.

Then there's silence and serious looks.

"You were absent for three days, Ruben. The lights were on, but nobody was home."

He nods in agreement. The past evenings, he was either not hungry or pushing food around his plate. The rest of the time, he was stewing.

"I forget sometimes that was once my life. It's hard when it's presented to you like that."

"You mean, you forget you were a footballer?" I find that hard to believe.

"Imagine, and I don't mean to sound nasty, but imagine you got a big reminder of what it was you used to do." I frown at him, then he continues, "People asking for your autograph, because you used to be their favourite escort?"

I shake my head. "It's not the same thing, love."

I stroke the satin-soft hair at the back of his head, so irresistible.

"How is it not the same?" he says. "I was prostituted out by my father. In a way. It's the same thing."

I clear my throat and press my lips together, looking up at the ceiling. "You're ashamed of the career you had?"

"Yes," he admits.

"Why?"

"Because I got there off of... you know... doing his bidding."

"But those people love you, Ruben. Your football career gave others a lot of joy, and even if you feel like the person you were then isn't who you are now, you ought not to be ashamed of the game you played. Football must have been something you loved—"

With that, he bursts into tears and I'm sad, watching him fall apart. I don't know what to do except hold him as he cries into my hair and holds onto my body.

"Baby, it's okay," I soothe, "it's okay."

He lets it go and I wait until he's found enough relief from letting it all out.

He pulls his head out of my hair and I hold his cheek, kiss his mouth and let him know I love him.

"I'm not ashamed of what I used to do, Ruben."

He gulps, staring at me. He presses his lips together, keeping whatever it is he wants to say reined in.

"What I mean is that sometimes I would sit and talk with the clients a while. Sometimes we wouldn't even... you know." Ruben looks uncomfortable as I talk. "There was a gay footballer, actually. You might have known of him."

"Archie Robinson?" Ruben asks.

"Yes," I giggle. "It started out his mate bought him a birthday gift... he hadn't had any action in a while sort of thing... but Archie kept coming back. It helped him just to be able to talk."

"It's the worst kept secret among all the players, of course," Ruben laughs, "but that's football for you. It's all about the image. And that's what I'm saying. None of that was ever, ever really me. It's all a role I played, Freya. You're owned. You're not your own man. When Laurent died, I did lose all joy for it. Because part of it was that I'd promised Laurent I would make it, for him. That I'd get to the premier, all that, so he could see me. But it meant nothing without him and truly, I was glad to be rid of it. It wasn't who I really am."

"I know, you're an artist," I whisper, "but don't worry, I won't tell anyone."

He manages a smile and I smile back.

"You're not ashamed of it, then?" he asks, needing me to go back to that, it seems.

"I was. I was terrified of you finding out. But now... years have passed..." I stroke my hand across his cheek, over his forehead, then his mouth. "It got nasty towards the end. I don't think I ever told you."

"No, but I found out..."

"Ah, yes, your *connections*."

He looks irrepressibly unimpressed, just thinking about it. "I wanted to know there wasn't someone out there I needed to murder."

I can't help but let go a laugh. He looks stern in comparison.

"I got paid for having sex," I remind him, "and I like sex. And it got that I knew the men well, and it became... it felt... routine. I don't know. Then there was this one guy who couldn't get it up and it just broke me, I don't know... it really... it made me wonder a lot."

Ruben gulps and I lift myself off his lap, fetch my nightgown and pull it on. Then as I walk into the kitchen and start pulling out pans from the cupboards, he sits at the bar on a stool and watches me as I begin to cook. I can tell he's waiting... patiently.

"I know now that I was doing all that because I had this void, inside me." I boil the kettle, make a stock and set it aside. Then I grab garlic, onion and chicken, a bunch of spices and a bag of paella rice. I'll add the frozen peas and seafood last. "I told myself I was seeking love. The type I'd never found at home. Maybe not even love. I don't know. Perhaps... it was..."

"Purpose?" he asks.

"Nah," I sigh. "I was seeking..." My face contorts because I have to admit it. "I wanted punishment. To have everything he'd ever said about me confirmed. For my parents to show up, scoop me up, tell me off... get attention, I don't know. To see the look in his eyes when he realised, he'd made me, turned me into that, and it was all his fault. And I wanted to be punished. I worked at that hotel... just as you said... to punish myself. Knew I could get out but didn't. And I screwed men I didn't care for... didn't really want... because I was frightened history would repeat itself. I'd get my hopes up some fella might want me for his own, then he'd turn around like my first boyfriend and screw me over, and I'd be left with no self-esteem whatsoever... all over again."

I look up briefly from my chopping board and catch Ruben looking uncomfortable.

"But that's all behind you now, Frey? Isn't it?"

"Yes, because of you."

The look on his face is so cute, embarrassed and shy.

"What we have, it has wiped the slate clean, Ruben. Nothing that went before matters anymore. Because everything led to this. And yeah, was it shitty sometimes? Of course. Did I hit rock bottom because I'd convinced myself what I was doing wasn't shady, then realised it was, and suddenly couldn't ignore that? Yes. But if I never took the path I had, you and I wouldn't have met. I wouldn't have been working at the Claremont and witnessed the brawl that night. And even though I was lying back and thinking of England so to speak, was I hurting anyone? No. Only myself. I was lost. I was so lost. Probably how you felt when you were playing football. But it's not a part of your life you should shelf, otherwise situations like the other day are going to hurt. Rather, wouldn't it be better to accept that was part of your life and not necessarily embrace it, but just... move on from it? Laurent knew you as the footballer. He looked up to you, worshipped you. Even if that's not who you are now, just embrace that you were once that guy. Once. Not that you've disassociated completely. You're not a whole other person. Just... that guy... he was once you."

I watch out of the corner of my eye as he throws his hands up. I'm frying the onions, garlic and spices and he says, "This is how I coped. I properly disassociated. I didn't grieve, Freya. I just... got on with my plan to avenge him. I became someone else."

I lift my eyes and give him a small smile. "That's why we're here, Ruben. To discover who you really are. What do you say?"

He throws his hands up again, looking anxious but willing. "We can try. I'll try."

"Good enough for me, baby. Now, crack open the red, will you?"

KARMA

AFTER DINNER, WE SIT outside staring at the lights of the city so far below us. We have wine and he asks, "Should you be drinking?"

"Why not?"

"Well, you know..."

"I ovulated a couple of days ago. The opportunity passed."

He looks downhearted. "Oh."

"We have time. I don't want to make it happen if you're not ready. I want the time we make a baby to be really special."

He reaches for my hand. "Me too."

We're sitting around a little table with two chairs pushed together. He squeezes my fingers, kisses them and settles back in his chair, as though relieved to discover I'm not planning to be one of those mothers who drinks while gestating.

"How many kids do you want, Ruben?" I murmur, sipping my wine.

"I don't know. Two?"

"Two's good." I've always dreamed of twins... over and done with in one go.

He plays with my hair. "Do you want to get married?"

"Not immediately. When it's right."

"I agree," he says.

"Thank god." I don't say it, but I'm grateful he doesn't plan on cornering me like he did last time. "I hope they have your eyes."

"Why?" he asks.

"I have my father's."

"His eyes are dead eyes," he tells me surely. "Your eyes are beautiful."

"Your eyes are more beautiful." I lean across and he grins as I kiss his forehead.

"They're my father's eyes," he groans.

"But you have your mother's soul in them. It offsets the evil."

"I don't know," he laughs.

"It's tricky for her, perhaps we should give her more leeway."

"Yeah," he says, staring at the sky.

"She could've been someone so much different if she hadn't met him."

"I don't know," he says, "I think they were two peas in a pod. They wanted stuff and she turned a blind eye while he did what he had to in order to get it."

"Would it make you happy if you went back to being poor, unknown and a nobody?"

"No," he chuckles. "Like you said, you get used to things."

"True. So, you gave me half your money? Why?"

He turns, takes my hand and kisses it, searching my eyes. "Don't you know?"

"No."

"It's what you do when you face being put away. I didn't know... but the possibility was there."

I give him a strange smile. "I see."

"My dad did it with Mum," he explains quickly. "He put half the assets in her name, should something go wrong, so at least one of them would still have something left. Trouble is when Dad died, Mum had to sell the Mayfair house because that was in his name and he had a load of debts to settle. People he owed money to. He should've put that in her name but people still would've wanted their pound of flesh. She really did love that house." Ruben talks with a fluidity I find reassuring; hopefully it means everything he did was for a very good reason.

"Fred had debts? Really?" That seems difficult to believe; the man was a fucking mob boss.

Ruben wears a disgusted expression. "I don't know if I ever mentioned he'd been diagnosed with bowel cancer around the time Laurent went up to Cambridge."

I scratch my head, trying to think back. "It would explain why I didn't recognise him when you introduced me at their house... he'd aged quite a lot because of it?"

Ruben answers with his expression that Fred probably had aged because of the cancer, though he never took all that much notice. "When he was having treatment, my mother struggled to keep on top of things in his absence. They had some kind of hiccup, I don't know. Anyway, it resulted in debts my father was still trying to pay off even up to his death. His assets like the house, cars, some shares, insurance policies and things like that, all got eaten up paying off his debts. My mother owns a couple of properties in Europe she checks up on now and again, as well as the place in Portugal of course, and other commodities like paintings and jewellery, all locked up in Switzerland... maybe alongside some petty cash she wouldn't want me to know about."

"So, you didn't get a cent from him?"

"Nah, wasn't expecting to." He pretends like he has no feelings about it, but perhaps part of him used to wish he'd had a father who cared enough to leave him his favourite paperweight or a rare whisky collection or a cricket bat that held memories. Instead, Ruben had to initiate his own father's demise and likely incurred his mother's wrath as a result. He didn't so much as get a donation made in his name from his father's last will and testament. I expect Fred thought he'd recovered from cancer so would have plenty of time yet to settle his debts and fly high again one day, that he'd live for a while longer yet... but all that went to cock.

"And Freddie? How was he so wealthy? If Fred was practically penniless."

Ruben wears a dark look which I interpret as hatred for the man who potentially killed Laurent, but mostly never apologised for who he was. "Oh, he'd used that period of my father's illness to make a few inroads of his own."

"Really? When I spoke one on one with Freddie, he said he and Fred had patched things up."

"HA!" Ruben barks, disturbed and amused, all at once. "Wanna know my take?"

"Yes, of course," I exclaim, on the edge of my seat.

"Freddie was quite a fanciful person, by all accounts. After all, he was easily convinced Debbie was mad for him, wasn't he?"

I pull a face that shows I'm loath to even think about that. "Gross."

"And he kept his product beneath his own fucking house."

"Idiot."

"Quite," Ruben agrees, sounding a little like Sherlock Holmes on the case, though very much upholding a subjective opinion on the matter. "Whatever this hiccup was that occurred while Dad was having chemo—and the only reason I found out there was even a hiccup is because when I asked Mum why she'd had to sell the mansion, she said Fred had debts from when he was having chemo and they lost money... Anyway, back to Freddie. I think the hiccup involved pissing off one of their suppliers. Something went wrong. I don't know. Anyway, Freddie stepped in, took a large portion of my father's business off him. My father wouldn't have forgiven that. I knew him. He easily forgave me and Laurent for fucking around, for frittering money and things like that. He expected us to fuck up and he bailed us out... but betrayal, my father wouldn't have got over that easily. First, it was the debacle at Laurent's party where Freddie told practically everyone that he and Laurent were half-brothers. Because of that my father cut him off."

I'm really surprised and he sees how much I am. "That was never how Freddie told it to me. He said he and Fred had remained in touch but never made a big deal of it, that he was still in line for the throne, he said. That he'd been groomed to follow in Fred's footsteps since he was twelve. Freddie was adamant they were keeping their shared business interests on the downlow so Alexia didn't find out."

"That's fantasy," Ruben semi-growls. "Absolute fantasy. He was just trying to cover his tracks. Pretend that he hadn't ordered my assassination. Freddie knew Dad would never have legitimised him. Fred's fantasy was to have me take over. It was always going to be me. He knew Laurent wasn't cut out for it. But me? He thought I'd be perfect for the job with my reputation as a topflight footballer, not to mention he knew I had an edge. It was his dream that I would take over. He saw in me himself." Ruben looks frustrated I ever believed Freddie could have taken Fred's place. "If I'd have said to Mum, 'Okay, I accept my responsibilities now Dad's gone,' do you think anyone would've favoured him over me? That they would've looked between us and picked the younger, more imbecilic version? No way, Freya. He didn't just hate that I was Dad's firstborn—that we know of—he hated it that people loved me so much more than they fucking loved him. He hated how close me and Laurent were. I think he even hated that I didn't have a degree and he could've got ten and a string of PhDs and it still wouldn't have put him ahead of me in Fred's eyes. There was a lot unsavoury about my father but ultimately, he did want what was best for my mother and he would've thought I was best to take care of her after he was gone. He never would've reinstated Freddie after what he did at Laurent's party. And I have no doubt, absolutely none, that he apportioned blame on Freddie for Laurent's death, too. Fred was a bastard but his bastard kid was shoddy as heck. I can tell you for a certainty my mum would've never accepted Freddie for all these reasons and more, therefore Fred never would've rocked the boat any more than it already had been in sidelining me and picking Freddie as his heir. Freddie wanted me dead because of the name I bear. Simple as that."

I sigh and ponder that for a bit, tapping my lip with my index finger. "That all makes sense actually." Ruben sounds so passionate about it all; it's almost as though he still needs reassurance that Fred loved him more. Even after everything, I think it would wreck him to know Fred loved Freddie the most.

"Debbie was my father's revenge against Freddie," he continues, in an attempt to convince himself as much as me, I decide. "I'm damned sure of it. Freddie was absolutely desperate to regain my father's favour. He would've done anything. Even if Fred had told him that the girl was pregnant and as a favour to him, could he just marry the bint and be done, he would've done. But Fred no doubt dressed it up, made Freddie believe it was love, that this girl was really into him... and then..." He gurns as he thinks back. What an awful man he was.

Fred never showed up for Freddie's wedding; he'd already ensured the damage was plentiful.

"What did Debbie see in Fred, seriously?"

"Some women love power. Look at my mother. She would never admit it, but she loved the arrogance... the cocksureness. He was more than twice her age when they married."

I absolutely know it could be true, but I also have my doubts. "He would've struggled fertility wise after chemo, surely?"

"It's the dates, Freya. You can't argue the dates on her medical records. She fell pregnant before she even started dating Freddie."

I make a face like I'm close to spewing. "What if they weren't Fred's kids? Or even Freddie's?"

"My dad was a twin," he says, looking up at me sadly. "His twin died in his teens, killed in a motorbike accident. Twins run in my father's family."

"An identical twin?"

"Non-identical," he answers, speaking softly. "But they were close."

"Must have fucked him up."

"That's maybe the only thing I could have sympathised with him on." The weight of his words and the look in his eyes are not lost on me.

He looks deep in thought for a while, then says suddenly, "What was their nickname for him after he got caught... what was it?"

"London's El Chapo," I confirm.

"When Freddie was arrested, everything they owned was taken, obviously. Debbie was destitute." He doesn't appear to have any emotion about that. "But I got some money to her. She believes Fred left it for a rainy day. Truth is, she was just a problem my father needed to solve... and he dumped her on an unsuspecting, desperate little naïve scrote like Freddie. My father didn't give a fuck about her... or those kids. But best she never learns it was me who helped out... I did it for the kids' sake, not hers. You understand?"

I must look shocked because he nods his head to confirm he's not lying. I'm actually trying to wrap my head around how emotionless he looks in this moment. Did he give her that money to ease his conscience? Or truly for the kids? He seems... so cold about it all.

"Is Debbie your only charity case? Or have there been others?"

Ruben works out the stress in his neck, rubbing his nape. "There are probably many more victims out there. Women he used and abused. Half siblings I'll never know about." He stares into the distance and takes a shuddery breath. "I didn't really go looking for the victims, during our time apart, I mean. The bad guys were easy to find, though."

He looks cocky, keeping me in suspense.

"You didn't just spend your time painting?"

"Nah." He purses his lips and suddenly leaves the table, shouting over his shoulder. "Wait a moment."

He heads indoors but comes back a few minutes later, handing me a scrapbook.

I open it up and discover several dozen newspaper clippings, all articles detailing big crooks that got caught. Not just drug lords. Paedophiles. Traffickers. Pimps. Fraudsters. Launderers.

Joey the Great.

"Amazing what you can do as an independent," he says, looking proud but unforgiving. "Whenever there was money involved in taking someone down, I'd donate it to charity. On an unrelated note, I did send money to your mother but she never cashed the cheque. As far as I know, she stays with him."

"I heard that, too." I bite my nails, wondering if my mother has some misguided loyalty to Dad... or maybe she really believes he needs her. I don't know. "Thank you for trying, Ruben."

"Sometimes that's all we can do."

I put his scrapbook on the table, leave my chair and drape myself across his lap, resting my head against his shoulder.

"I love you, Ruben."

"I love you infinitely more."

"You always have to go one better."

"Well, it's true. There's so much to love about you."

I peck his mouth. "Ruben?"

"Yes, my darling."

"Do not underestimate me or my love. It might be your undoing."

He looks at me strangely. "If you say so."

"I do. A woman's love... it's truly endless. Please, believe me."

"I want to," he whispers.

I hide my face against his shoulder and try to slow my beating heart. Ruben is still haunted by what he had to do in order to keep me safe, I can tell.

On the one hand, no matter what he'd done or who he'd hurt, Fred was still his father and if Ruben had been allowed to choose, he would've chosen to be a loyal son and not kill Fred.

On the other hand, he'd already had one girlfriend die at his father's hands; he didn't want another going the same way.

Ruben always knew I would never accept that lifestyle. He picked me.

He played Fred and Freddie off against one another... and nobody won.

Not even Ruben and I.

I fear Ruben's greatest challenge, even now, is in trying to continually distance himself from Fred. There must be parts of him he recognises he got from his father. He donated money and helped catch the bad guys to ease his conscience. I know he was no saint before we met, but I worry he has so much to make up for, he'll never be able to live a normal life—he'll always be trying to make up for the bad deeds with 'good' ones.

Did Fred and Alexia have to make a concerted effort to become embroiled in crime, or was it as natural as breathing and they never stopped to think about the consequences? Do some of us end up in situations of our own making, or do we gradually get so swallowed up by the adventure, we forget we ever lived humbly, once upon a time? How did Bonnie and Clyde get started? Did they never see any wrong in what they were doing? Do some people enable the evil in others, so that it doesn't even feel like evil anymore, but some kind of shared passion that seems to them to be entirely acceptable when understood entirely between two people?

Did Ruben justify his actions by telling himself it was for the greater good, or did he secretly rejoice in his father's ashes and even more so in Freddie's?

Because that's what bosses do, right?

They stay ahead of the competition.

KARMA

Scariest version: maybe the evil takes you so swiftly without you knowing, then eats you whole before you've even seen it coming.

Chapter Sixteen

Life's a Beach

I hate to wake without him but I've begun to accept that he's not a comfortable sleeper and I do love my sleep. So, if I wake and he's not here, like this morning, it's not because he decided to leave me, just that he had to get up and start his day. I lie in bed recalling yesterday's shower sex, grinning at the memory, also reminded why my thighs ache and my back hurts. When I hear whistling coming from the direction of the kitchen, I begin to get my hopes up and grab my dressing gown, knotting it around my waist.

He's cooking pancakes in just a pair of tiny shorts and my jaw almost unlocks from its usual position.

"Good morning," he says, cheerful.

"Morning."

He catches me staring at him. It's not particularly hot this morning and the aircon is in working order, so there's another reason why he looks red, sweaty and ripped.

"What?" he asks, after a while, cocky as they come.

"Did you go out like that?" I gasp, watching his pecs dance as he flips the pancakes and stacks them on a serving plate.

"There's a bunch of weights in the basement," he laughs, "but if this is too much for you..." He gestures at his body. "I'll take it to the streets and train with rocks if you like."

I scowl and he turns off the gas, goes into the fridge and removes the blueberries and maple syrup. We sit at the breakfast bar and I try not to stare but he likes that I'm staring and the cheeky look in his eye isn't helping.

"Shall I be mum?" he asks.

"Sure."

He pours me coffee, stacks a few pancakes on a plate for me, scatters berries on top and drizzles syrup all over.

When I watch him stack at least six, thick, American-style pancakes for himself, my mouth completely ajar this time, he barks with laughter.

"Hey, you want me to be that beast again, this is what I've got to eat."

I hold my hands up. "Not complaining. Not saying anything."

If I were to say anything, it would be a command for him to lie on the floor exactly as he is in this moment and to let me lick every square inch of him clean.

But we have to make the most of our days here. It can't all be that... and I still have an achy back... so some time spent not fucking today will do me good.

I need to think of something to take my mind off sex.

"I had a thought..." I cut out pieces of my pancake stack, like it's a tiered cake, triangular bites going straight down the hatch. He's eating but he's listening. "If I'd got married at some point during these past few years, what would you have done?"

His head drops into his shoulders and he stares, gone out. "Don't tell me you did."

I throw my head back. "Don't be silly. I'm saying, you know, what if I had? And it was real? Let's say Freddie died in prison,

216

but you found out I was married to someone else... nothing could be done, right?"

Ruben gulps, puts down his knife and fork and picks up his coffee cup. He stares out of the window, his tongue working around his teeth, throat moving as he swallows.

"This is entirely hypothetical?" he asks, and I nod. "Not a trick question?"

"No," I giggle.

He perseveres, trying to humour me. "Well, if you were truly happy, such as if you were married and maybe had kids and were living on a yacht or in a castle or... I don't know... you'd bought a hotel to run or something, like you said you were going to... I'd have had to leave you be, wouldn't I?"

"But would you?" I persist, picking up my fork and stabbing a couple of blueberries.

He looks down at his plate and cuts one pancake in half, then folds over that half and stuffs it into his mouth all at once. He's chomping and staring into the distance, leaving me hanging.

"I'd have had to let you be, wouldn't I? If I could see you were truly happy." He gives me a look like that's the best answer, right?

I have to hold in a smile. "You wouldn't have been tempted to drop by anyway, check on my happiness levels and challenge them, maybe?"

He smiles like he knows he's going to fall into a trap if he's not careful. He finishes his pancake mountain before I've even got halfway through my much smaller portion.

"We're not dealing with that situation, are we Freya? I'm thankful. That's all I know. Neither of us fell in love with anyone else, did we?"

"No," I accept, with a gulp.

"So maybe what we have is rare."

"Or we're both as fucked as the other. We're a pair." Just hopefully not the same as Fred and Alexia.

"Maybe," he exclaims, flinging his hands in the air. "Or maybe this is karma, putting things back into place. The things that are meant to be... will always be. Don't you think?"

I try to catch up with him and finish my breakfast. I want to join him in the shower and enjoy long, tender kisses under the spray.

"It's a lot for me to get used to again. I'd barely got used to it before and then you were taken from me... and it's going to take some getting used to again."

He stares, confused. "What do you mean?"

"The truth is, Ruben. If you knew me at all, you'd know marriage and kids wouldn't work for me. Not with anyone. Except you. Being with someone properly, like this, it never ever would've been my choice."

He shakes his head. "You don't know that. If Freddie had lived another few years, you don't know what might have happened in your life. Someone you could fall in love with might have come along."

"No," I tell him, shaking my head, absolutely sure I wouldn't have. "Trust me, nobody would've come along. They're all too stupid or too privileged, too spoilt or too selfish in bed. They're too vain or they've got all these silly things they want to harp on about all the time."

"And your point is Freya? Because there has to be a point?" he demands, holding his coffee cup in the air like I'm stopping him from enjoying it.

"This time, if you go, I go, Ruben."

He sucks in air and covers his mouth, then puts down his coffee cup and sighs.

"Freya..."

"No, I mean it. If something happens... or someone... you have to swear to me, right here, right now... we'll deal with it together. Because although karma might have helped us by killing off Freddie, you were the one who chose to keep me in the dark. And if I'm to go even one step further with you, as each day we grow closer and closer, you have to promise you'll take me with you next time. Because I swear, if you left without me again, I'd not survive it twice. It'd be much worse. You don't know what I have to fight against every single day to stay with you. My demons. My doubts. My fears. Myself. Death, I can face. Death does not scare me, Ruben. What does is the thought of you being out there, alone, my heart trampled again by your absence. The thought that everything I set aside to be with you was for nothing."

"Freya..." He rubs his hands over his crew cut, frustrated.

"Swear to me."

He looks at me sadly, his usually generous mouth a tight line, shaking his head.

"There will never be another, I swear it. So, if you leave, just know that you'd be reducing me to a life of perpetual loneliness and despair. There's only ever been one person for me, Ruben. That's you. And I will live and die by your side. That's all there is to it. For someone as harsh and as cruel as I am, believe me, you recognise the real thing when you meet it. What we have is that. I know that another version of us doesn't exist out there. This is it. I would never settle for any less. I could never have fallen in love again!" I make wild hand gestures, like I know what I'm saying to be so bloody true. "I mean, we fell in love when neither of us wanted to, when everything was against us and you had this dark cloud hanging over you. It's obvious to me you are the only man in existence I could ever really love. It doesn't matter if we get a year or two or twenty or forty together, let's just make sure the time we do have is well spent."

He pinches the bridge of his nose and closes his eyes, his hands shaking. He shoves back his stool and strides away to the window, avoiding my eye. I'm afraid he's going to leave again and never come back. That I'm pushing him away rather than pulling him closer. He warned me he'd protect me above all else... but he doesn't see that us being apart is consigning me to death anyway. I'd rather live with the risk than survive half a life—never knowing what might have been.

Then he comes stalking back to me, pulls me off my stool and throws me up into his arms. I wrap my legs around him as he buries his head in my hair and curses indecipherably at the universe for making this our reality.

We hold one another tight and he pulls his head out of my hair, kissing me furiously, his tears wetting my face.

"I'll never leave you," he groans, kissing me until I'm crying, too.

OUR DRIVE TO THE BEACH is pleasant and reviving. I love days like this... when nothing is set in stone and the day lies ahead, there's no timetable. Anything could happen and it feels as though nothing is standing in the way of our happiness. He appears to relax during the hour-long drive out of the built-up city, his shades hiding his eyes, his demeanour in the driving seat nothing but chilled. The car eventually takes us through some of the most spectacular scenery I have ever seen... the land protected, and I can see why. The lush green vegetation is almost spellbinding. I feel like we're venturing into uncharted territory... stepping onto someone else's land... getting a window into the true beauty of this place, which people here don't want us to know about, lest it end up spoilt, too.

"Wow," I breathe, as we get closer to Praia de Grumari.

Wide, white sands stretch along the coast, dominated on one side by perfectly cerulean seas, and on the other by green, green trees for as far as the eye can see.

"You chose well, girl," he says.

We find a parking spot on the main road. "You don't really want to go to the nudist beach?"

"I'm not that bothered."

"Leave all the valuables," he chuckles.

We exit the car carrying beach towels and a couple of folded chairs we pinched from the basement back at the villa. Once we get down to the beach, the breeze hits me all of a sudden and I feel like I'm out of body. It's a different smell to any I've encountered before. Light and fragrant, not severe or bitterly salty, but perfumed and subtle. I pull off my kaftan, set up my chair and start applying cream. Ruben throws off his shirt and runs straight for the water.

"Are you coming in?" he yells.

"I'm going to get hot and sweaty first."

It's a truly lovely twenty-one degrees today but this afternoon there may be showers and I want to sit in the sun for as long as possible. I won't tan because I'm wearing factor sixty and my skin never tans but rather burns. Anyway, I only want to feel the heat in my skin and bones.

Ruben sprints into the water and dives in, the essence of aquatic, disappearing into the surf. He emerges, head popping up, victorious... waving at me. I wave back and pray he'll be careful.

He swims off, looking like a boy, recharged. There were a lot of salty tears this morning so maybe the swell of the sea will be enough of a reminder that in the grand scheme of things, we're insignificant really. Perhaps all the bad in the world that could be done to us has been done already and now it's our time for some of the good.

I sit back and open a paperback, sighing. A wide hat will protect me from the rays.

The beach isn't heavily populated down here but there are some families, and even though I'd love to go topless, it might not be best or in good taste to whip off my top. I get back into my book and feel lulled into some kind of relaxed trance.

When I start to feel the heat in my legs, I decide to hit my beach towel and let the sun seep into my back instead. That's when a mountain of man appears beside me, dripping with spray. It hits me all over and I scream, yelling at him to step away. He laughs and shakes his arms even harder, his cold droplets a shock to my cooking skin

"Fuck, I forgot how good it is to venture into the ocean," he cries, exultant. "I hadn't swum like that in so long."

He takes the towel beside me, rests back on his elbows and grins from ear to ear, letting the sun seep into his skin and dry him off.

"You ought to still put on cream," I warn.

"Don't be silly."

There's no point in arguing with him. One time back in Nice, he threatened to smother himself in cooking oil while I lounged on the patio, topping up my factor sixty. He wasn't entirely joking, I know that.

"You wouldn't have gone to the beach back home," I remind him. "I mean, not like this, in public. You only took me there once the sun had gone down."

It wasn't just Nice's harsh pebble beach. It was the crowds... and in places like Cannes, famous for its imported golden sand... the possibility of bumping into people from a world he used to inhabit.

"True," he admits.

"See, my evil plan to unshackle you worked. Here, we don't have to hide, Ruben."

"For now," he whispers. "For now, Freya."

I turn and he looks serious. "What's that look?"

"I want you to know, there are people who still wish me dead. That's all I'll say."

"But none as pernicious as Freddie?"

"Nope."

I sniff, tipping my head back. "If I could handle him, I can handle the rest."

Ruben reaches out to touch my back, smoothing out the kinks in my spine.

"Are you sure you don't want to drive to the beach around the other side and bathe nude?" he asks, tipping me a walloping wink.

"Do *you* want to spy on other people naked or something?" I burst out laughing.

"I just know you want me to be naked in public," he growls, truly amused.

"It's nice and all, but I wouldn't want other people to have to see your cock. Nor would I remove my pants for anyone but you. Tits, fine, but my bald lady patch... nope."

Ruben bites his lip. "There's a woman further down this beach who's topless."

I shake my head. "You pervert."

"Go on," he groans.

"You go on."

"All right, then."

He leans over, unties my bikini top and slides it out from underneath me. I'm not completely naked up top, not when I'm lying on my front, but the whole thing leaves me a little shocked in that he did it so quickly—I didn't have time to protest.

I turn my head and look right at him. He's nibbling his bottom lip and his cheeky expression is egging me on to react.

I decide to do everything but react.

I roll over, take out the cream and smother my breasts. There isn't anyone near us within fifty metres but that doesn't stop Ruben checking around, all the time I'm rubbing my tits with sun lotion. Then I lie back and let the sun hit my breasts as I continue to read.

"Freya," he growls.

"Yes, darling?"

"Cover them back up."

"Yes, darling."

I'm wearing a smarmy grin as he helps me tie the bikini at the back.

I expect you never really know how you feel about something... until it happens. Like for instance, your future wife's breasts on display, out in public.

I read for a while but can feel him stewing on his feelings and why he reacted like that.

"Ruben, baby?"

"Yes," he answers, still with that tone.

"Pull the stick out of your arse and cuddle me."

He drags me onto his towel with him and removes his glasses. Within a few moments of us kissing and cuddling, he's all right again.

He doesn't say anything as he bindles up some of our clothes to make a cushion so we can watch the surf together, still cuddled up. I know what he's feeling and it makes me so happy to know I still have this effect on him.

It's one thing going topless at home in your own backyard, quite another on a public beach where you can't act on the feelings evoked. If it's not de rigueur to have sex on the beach, then he can't be looking at my naked breasts in public... especially when they're so obviously still bitten from yesterday's athletic sex.

Going by what I can feel in his shorts as we lie here together, the sight of me with little grazes on my breasts turns him on terribly... and makes him even more possessive.

My dominant lover.

I will make him come out to play again, like the night I tried to flee from him at the airport. Mark my words. Patience is all it'll take.

Chapter Seventeen

Just One Day

On the way home, we stop at a supermarket and I dash into the store on my own while Ruben waits behind in the SUV, cap and glasses on. The car is even parked in a dark corner of the lot. I still don't know much Portuguese even though Ruben is fluent, which would be ever so helpful about now. I'm looking for things for dinner and maybe for breakfast, too. We had a picnic for lunch at the beach, some fruit and nuts, a bit of cheese and crackers, nothing much, just nibbles to tide us over, so I know Ruben will be starving for dinner.

The rental house we're in has some of the basics in the cupboards. Spices and tinned vegetables and bags of rice, things like that. I walk around with a small trolley, throwing things in. Fish and chicken and any fresh veg I think he'll like. I really miss the French patisserie so I pick up a bag of croissants and a jar of jam, which will have to do as sufficient replacement. I noticed we were running low on eggs so I grab some of those.

I'm marvelling at all the weird and wonderful jars of things—every kind of food you could imagine has been pickled—when I turn a corner and find myself down an aisle that cannot be classified and has all kinds of weird things on the shelves. There's everything you didn't know you needed like bathroom accessories, cookie cutters and crafty bits. And these supermarkets are half the size of the ones in France but with twice the produce and this array of bizarre goods.

I spot some men's pants and giggle. He still doesn't much like underwear, has an aversion for some reason. I reach out and touch these hideous looking things when I'm surprised the material is so soft. I pull a pair off the rack and discover they're pure cotton. They're the old-fashioned variety, bright white with a ruched elasticated waistband and the buttons going up the front. I pick out four pairs and dump them in the trolley. They feel nice and they're white. There's something about Ruben when he wears a white shirt or shorts. He looks like a fallen angel newly arrived back down to earth. Man, I really am lost to him.

I throw in all sorts of random goodies once I get down the sweetie aisle, then grab two bottles of Malbec and I'm out of here, heading for the tills. The lady rings through my goodies and gives a wry smile when she puts through the underpants. Either she likes them or thinks they're cheap and ugly. Hell, even if he only wears these to paint in, as long as he wears them at all, I don't care.

She announces the total in Portuguese, but even with my bad understanding, I still recognise the bill is high. The price screen is so dull, though and I can't tell how much it is for certain. Wondering if I'm mistaken, I query her with my eyes and hope she speaks English.

"Sorry, how much?" I ask, sure she just asked me for hundreds of Brazilian real.

Her eyes brighten and she turns the screen of her till towards me. That's a lot. I'm no expert, but when she pulls out one of the pairs of pants and shows me the tag, I see how I racked up such a bill.

"My, my, my."

She starts taking them back and saying something along the lines of refunding me.

However, I take out my card and take them back. "No, no, no, *por favor*."

"It's no problem," she insists.

"No, no, no, it's okay, please."

"Okay?" she submits.

"Absolutely."

I pay and take another look at the underpants. Wow, that's like... thirty euros a pair?

"*Obrigada*," I announce, after she hands me my receipt.

I get outside the store and take one more look at the underpants before I foist them on Ruben back at the car. How are these things so expensive? I can't see a label or anything.

Weird!

I dump the bags on the back seat and he kisses me hello. "Okay? You were in there a while."

I reach over into the back and pull out a pair of pants from one of the bags. "I got you these. What do you think?"

His face takes on a strange expression, a mixture of disgust and confusion. "Erm... okay. They were pricey!"

Man, you can't take the cockney out of the boy when it comes to dollar.

"I didn't realise... just thought they felt nice when I spotted them on the peg."

He's trying not to laugh, turning them around to get a good look. "They're not designer or anything."

"I got you four pairs!" I burst out laughing and he shakes his head, utterly bemused.

"They're actually all right," he shrugs, "feel nice and don't look like they'd be tight. I hate constrictive stuff."

"Yeah? They're all right?" I'm saved, saved!

"Yeah, they'll do." He tosses them onto the back seat and starts the engine. "Just tell me you got food."

"Oh, I got lots of protein stuff."

"Ah, good." We get back on the highway and he gives me a wink. "Freya?"

"Yes, baby."

"You do know why they were so expensive, don't you?"

I'm shaking my head, at a loss. "Were they sewn by monks and that's their only income?"

Ruben smothers a laugh. "No!"

"Oh, god. What, then?"

I hate myself!

I shouldn't have bloody bothered!

"It's a supermarket, honey. Nobody here buys clothes from the supermarket. Not unless they just got out of jail or are in a hurry to leave town or they soiled themselves on the way home. Or did something on the way home they shouldn't have."

I turn and gawp at him. "I just... I don't know... just thought..."

"Hey, baby. It doesn't matter," he snickers.

"I thought your butt would look cute in them."

We laugh the rest of the way home.

WE'RE DASHING INTO the house soon enough, bags and towels and all sorts under our arms as we try to avoid the on-slaught of rain, only a few splashes hitting my hair as we sprint.

Ruben heads straight for the shower to wash off the itchy salt and sand from his swim in the sea earlier. Meanwhile I stand and watch from behind the French doors as the rain falls in sheets, nearly all the water in the pool out back displaced—or that's how it looks—as the heavens roar down. The scene earlier, with Ruben's arms around me as we stared out at the waves, seems entirely distant and almost unreal. Like it didn't happen. A day of two halves, they call it. Or something like that. I don't know why but rain like this reminds me of home. Of the times I'd lock myself away in my bedroom, listening to the chimney rattling as the wind and rain battered our old house. Thinking of all that makes me melancholy beyond anything. Maybe that's really why I moved to the South of France—because it wasn't like home at all. Not the weather, the people, or any of that. It's pretentious there, true. If you don't have a roll of notes in your back pocket or a wallet full of black, gold and platinum cards... you're out. And that's not me. But it was a wonderful escape while it lasted.

I'm emptying the shopping bags when Ruben emerges from the bedroom wearing just a towel.

"Leave that and come to bed," he asks gently, wrapping his hand around my wrist.

"Later," I murmur. "Let me get the food in the fridge."

He stands close by watching as I put the food away. I handle the underpants carefully, trying not to grin. "These will need washing."

"Oh, good god," he groans. "You mean, I'll actually have to wear them."

"'Fraid so."

I de-tag them and take them to the laundry room, put in half a brick and set the machine going on a delicate wash. I almost burst out laughing.

I return to the kitchen and he's still there, hanging about. I hate it when he's standing around like this. He's looming. Too big and tall and I can feel his gaze on me. I know he's waiting. It's incessant sometimes, the way he is in my presence... and I can't get away from him.

"Your mood has changed," he groans, as he drinks orange juice out of the bottle.

"I like the rain, just not the memories it evokes," I explain, as I begin stacking magazines and books, plumping cushions around the living area and whatnot. I spot the beach towels in the bag he left by the front door and grab those, taking them to the laundry room for later.

When I emerge this time, he's leaning back against the fridge, arms folded, his gaze like laser beams, hot against my back as I fill the kettle and make myself a cup of tea.

"I need to get in here." I move towards him, signalling I want milk.

He steps aside, a grin in his eyes, as I grab the milk. Once I've got a splash out of the bottle, I hand it to him and he puts it back. When I head over to the seating area, he follows and I wish he would go... down into the basement... or to the studio upstairs. When I was looking for rental houses in this neck of Rio, this was the only one with privacy I could find that also had a studio space for him to make his art inside. And getting all the supplies he'd need delivered here was another task that wasn't easy.

I suppose this is why couples so often call holidays 'make or break' because you literally have to be around one another all the time; and you're either going to be happy about that or not—unable to escape each other's peccadilloes, quirks and tantrums. Either you love that person enough to see past everything, or you don't.

Does he love me enough?

Happy isn't something I am at this precise moment. I've gone into myself again. I can feel the waves of self-hate threatening to bubble up inside me, my diaphragm under stress, my hands fighting not to clench. This hasn't happened in a while, it has to be said. Normally I know when they're coming, but today, I've been so unaware, because he's been with me this whole time.

"You know," I whisper, because talking might be the only thing that'll slow my racing heart, "when you were gone, I would have this window of time every day, set aside, just for you."

He purses his lips and that dark blush appears across his cheekbones. I love and hate it when he looks like this. He's moveable, I know that, but I don't want him to be. A part of me wants him to be an animal. Unthinking. Uncaring. Take me and then throw me away. And he's not. He's much, much more.

"I'd have things lined up throughout the day. Meetings. Visits to other galleries. Lunch with artists. Dinners with fellow dealers. Drinks with an acquaintance. But in the back of my mind, I'd be living with this gut-wrenching feeling that something wasn't right and the only way I could turn that off was to tell myself no matter what happened that day or how bad I felt, I could always, always go home. Just be with the dogs. Alone. And I could lie out by the pool and just daydream, about you. I could close my eyes and you'd be there; I could rewind conversations. I'd imagine your arms fastened around me. Recall the times we'd been friends, and the times after. When we first made love, for instance. The most special night of my entire life. That evening you were crazy and acting strange and I was trying everything to bat you off, but instead, you took me somewhere new and I learnt what love was, for the first time in my life, I learnt about love."

He leaves the armchair he's been sitting in and comes and sits next to me, taking my hand.

"My love, why do you always have to break yourself open like this?" he says, sounding slightly annoyed, if anything.

"Maybe it's a female thing. Maybe I need to know you're as cut open as I am."

Ruben takes my hand and puts it on his heart. "I'm cut wide open, Freya."

I look up and into his wide eyes; he's so sure of what he's saying. "Freya, I'm spilling blood everywhere, all the time. Maybe I don't show it, but I'm cut wide open to you. I don't want to hurt anymore, either. I don't want to suffer."

"I don't know why I feel like this! I should be the happiest woman alive!" I cover my face with my hands, disgusted I'm so weak... so full of self-loathing.

I hate that I continually get this feeling in my stomach that something is so dreadfully wrong... when there's nothing wrong! He's here. We're safe. Nobody knows where we are. It's just us and I know he loves me, completely. But this horrendous feeling that something bad will happen... it gnaws at me, a bit at a time, until the rain falls and the memories hit and I'm broken open again, forced to recall how unworthy I was of happiness before he overturned all of that and made me think, maybe, just maybe, I am after all due a bit of peace.

"Shh, angel, shh," he murmurs, puts his arms around me and pulls my face to his chest.

Frustrated with myself, I take some deep breaths and let the warmth of him and his earthy, musky scent envelop me.

"I just want to know what it's like to live one day where I don't wonder when the next bad thing is going to happen. Just one day. One day when I might believe everything is going to be all right and everything is fixed. One day of total and utter ignorance, Ruben. Just one."

He runs his fingers through my hair and kisses my forehead. "I want to give you that one day. Maybe more than just one. Just hang in there, honey. We'll get there."

I rub my cheek against his chest and sigh. "Do you promise?"

"I promise you, my sweet thing. I promise."

"Okay," I accept.

"Now, why don't I tuck you in bed? A nap might make it better."

"That's a nice idea. What about dinner?"

"I'll cook tonight. Relax, princess."

"Okay."

Chapter Eighteen

Last Words?

I know I slept deeply because when I wake, I feel groggy and yuck. I roll out of bed, notice the clock is reading eight in the evening, and look outside the windows to see the rain has stopped. I think the smell of food must have woken me. It smells like curry... maybe fish curry. My stomach groans and I head to the bathroom, stand under the shower for a minute with my hair pinned up and let the water hit my back to revive me, shaking myself alive.

I swill my mouth out with mouthwash and grab a clean dress from the closet, pulling it on over my naked body. Just a frilly, flowery dress with sleeves and to the knee. Nothing special, just something I'd usually throw on.

"You're awake. I wondered if I'd be eating alone," he says, when he sees me heading towards him.

He's stirring the pot and checking his timer. I walk up behind him, wrap my arms around his waist and kiss his back, over his t-shirt. He's wearing sweats and feels tall, strong and safe.

"Fish curry?" I spy, over his shoulder.

"Yes. You up for it?"

"Definitely."

Something beeps and he gestures. "Go sit down."

I'm surprised to notice he's set the table on the terrace, beneath the canopy. It may have rained like hell earlier, but it's warm and fragrant again outside as I take my place. He's lit a candle, placed some flowers from the garden in a vase and laid out cutlery. Since we got here, some nights we've taken to eating meals out of cartons with chopsticks or a lone fork.

He brings dinner over and pours the wine.

"Cheers," he says.

I smile because the food looks really good. He's used the sweet potatoes to make thick wedges and the curry is full of herbs and spices, plus the various pieces of fish and seafood I picked up today.

"This looks amazing, Ruben. I'm starving."

"Dig in."

I start to eat and nod my approval. Just the right amount of heat, not too mild or murderously hot, plus the sauce is thick and not runny.

"You do know that I love it that you can not only paint, but cook *and* switch on the dishwasher, too."

He laughs until he's red-faced. "Here was me thinking I was only good for one thing!"

"What? Switching on the dishwasher?" I stick my tongue out and he shakes his head, grinning.

He starts putting his food away, his appetite bigger than his libido, currently—as it should be. We were out all day. He swam, drove us out of the city... and back. Did weights this morning. Perhaps did some painting while I was sleeping. And now he's feasting after a hard day's work, looking after me.

"Once upon a time, I was only good at one thing, I'll admit." He takes a bit of wine, cleaning his palette, readying himself for more. I give him a look like I'm completely oblivious as to what it is he's on about. "Oh, come on! Don't make me spit it out."

"Oh, I doubt you ever spat it out, Ruben."

A little chuckle tickles the back of his throat and he cuts his wedges up before eating with just a fork in his right hand.

"You know what I'm saying, don't you?" He continues to press me.

"Erm, am I to assume you mean that you were once only good at football?"

"I was only good at fucking, Freya," he growls. "But yes, football, too. But that's different. That was a job. I'm talking about in the relationship department. I was only good at fucking."

I drink a bit of the Malbec and watch him get annoyed with himself. When there's just two of you, these tête-à-têtes are all you have to entertain.

"Oh, so... you think you're good at fucking? Interesting." I hold my fork up and study it, pretending to be interested in it more than him. "I see."

"Freya," he demands, and I gaze at him instead. "Will you let me know when to take off the seat belt because the whiplash from your mood swings is ruthless?"

I shrug and eat more of his delicious curry, which seems to have coconut in it... but I'm not sure. There's a lot of chilli, too. And maybe... I don't know... something else.

Something sweet.

Tastes like... hmm... mango?

I'm still not sure.

"Are you seriously suggesting I'm no good at it?" he demands, after a while of watching me ponder over the food.

"Are we still on that? I'm trying to figure out your secret ingredients," I laugh, throwing him an amused expression.

"Ginger, garlic, curry powder, lemongrass, brown sugar and coconut."

I prod the food playfully. "Ah, must be the brown sugar, but it tastes like mango or something, too?"

"I didn't have limes so I mashed up some mango and threw that in. Happy now?"

I can see that me rebuffing him earlier has left him wound up. I expect when he wasn't playing ball, he was playing with his balls. It's just all about the balls with this guy.

"You're giving me that look, Frey."

I shoot him a frown. "Don't know what you're talking about."

He's finished most of his dinner and wants to finish me now, too. I can tell.

"That look, like you're thinking about sex."

"I am not. I'm thinking about balls, if you must know."

"BALLS?" he shouts.

"Yes, balls. Footballs. Plain old balls. That's all."

He stares at me, exasperated. He shovels the rest of his dinner and stalks off to the kitchen. I watch him through the open patio doors as he pulls things out of the fridge. I've polished off my dinner by the time he gets back, carrying two small plates.

I put my dinnerplate to one side and he hands me dessert. He sets down his own dessert plate at his side of the table and then takes my dinnerplate into the kitchen, hopping back within seconds.

"What's this?" I ask, staring down at what he seems to have made himself.

"Well, I know you said you struggled to find cheesecake in the shop, so I made one. I had to go out and get some of the ingredients. I couldn't get everything in the recipe, so I improvised."

I take a bite and grin. "He's not just good at playing with balls, he's good at making puddings, too!"

He laughs a cheerful laugh I adore. It's a chocolate cheesecake and he's drizzled extra chocolate sauce on top along with a scattering of raspberries. Whatever he made this with, he's cleverly disguised it.

"You went out, then?" I ask, surprised.

"Just to the convenience store along the road."

"Seriously?" I'm impressed he was brave enough.

"It was fine, the guy had Arsenal all over his back wall. Never played for them."

"Ah, I see."

I finish my dessert, the chocolate definitely hiding all manner of sins. Was it quark he made this with? Hey, I'm not complaining. He's scraping the remnants off his plate when I put my hands together and stare across the table at him.

"What?" he asks, puzzled.

"You seriously think you're good at fucking?"

He slams down his spoon and warns, "You'd better watch what you say next."

I bite my top lip and try not to smile or laugh. I keep my eyes level with his and force my eyebrows to stay put, too. He thinks I'm trying to goad him to throw me over his shoulder. It's a little more than that, actually.

"What about I fight you for it?" Now I can't stop my eyebrows; they're practically dancing up there.

"Fight me for what?" he exclaims.

"The accolade of best fucker."

"Freya, come on." He gestures at himself that there could be no better fucker than him.

"I'm just saying, it's something men say. Cliché. The 'you only want me for one thing' line. It's so overdone."

He gives me a seriously unimpressed grimace. "I don't get you."

"Those women weren't with you because you were good at fucking, Ruben. They were with you for your money."

He shakes his head, annoyed. "You're actually telling me I'm no good at fucking?"

"I'm telling you I made you good at fucking, Ruben. I'm telling you that you wanted to fuck me thoroughly. Tell me you wanted that with the others."

He looks at me and I know without him saying what it is he's thinking. He's had enough headfucks for one day. He doesn't need anymore. Well, tough.

"I *was* good at fucking, Freya. Trust me. Even before you." He's now wearing the most aghast expression—it's probably the worst insult imaginable to suggest Ruben is no good at that one thing he felt he could always fall back on.

"I'm not going to repeat Meg Ryan's chant, but how do you know for sure?" I'm dying to fall about laughing, but somehow, I'm keeping a straight face.

He's looking at me like I'm a bloody alien. "You said earlier, our first night was the best sex of your life. The best night of your life. The best... you said!"

He's awfully defensive, even has his back up. A woman daring to question a man on the one thing he thinks he's always been good at... because of course, all men are automatically good at sex. It's their birthright, after all. To procreate. Their macho brains scream they must be good at it. It's just biology. They have to think they're good at it, or they won't try it because of the fear of failure—and then the population dies out.

Is it the one thing he's held up as his fallback all these years... that if all else fails, well, at least he's good at fucking? He could make a career of that, perhaps. Is this what all men think? That if they're good at fucking, they don't need to try hard at anything else? I know he's trying hard tonight, but is that only because I threw him over earlier? And I've forced him to woo me some other way? With curry and pudding.

"Are you saying you gave your best before that night?" I ask, staring down my nose at him.

He slowly shakes his head. He's going fucking insane inside there, I know it.

"The truth is, Ruben. Certain partners bring out the best in us. Sometimes, a pairing, just works. But I swear to god, I'm the better fucker. I'll prove it to you."

He's shaking his head, fists gripping the table edge, mouth pulled into a straight line. If he had less pride, he'd be screaming, *How could you do this to me?*

However, I see the reality cross his eyes and recognition hit. Even if I do prove to him that I'm the better fucker, at least it's likely he'll be getting fucked all the same!

"You're on," he growls, throwing down his napkin and taking our plates away. "I'll meet you in the bedroom in ten minutes! And I'm not doing the dishwasher," he hollers, as he rushes into the bathroom.

I can hardly breathe from trying not to laugh as I fill up the dishwasher.

He was right, earlier. That power nap brought me right back to myself.

FIFTEEN MINUTES GO by. I make him wait. Then I saunter down the corridor and find him on the bed with his game face on.

And wearing a pair of white boxers.

I press my lips tight together, but I have to look away or I'll never, ever stop laughing.

"What's up, honey? Something the matter?" he goads, trying to pry a reaction from me.

I take a deep breath—think of big green bogies, the ones that get stuck right at the back of your nostrils—and compose myself to face him.

Trouble is, he looks fucking gorgeous.

"You're not where I want you."

"Oh?" he asks, sounding happy, carefree—cocky.

"Follow me," I ask, leaving the room, matching his cool... if not beating it.

I have him stand in the middle of the living room and I walk around him. My, his butt does look good in these things. It's a butt you can grab. Dig your nails in. Slap about a bit, even. Not a girl's butt, though. Nope. It's rock solid. I see the front of him and he's... slightly visible.

Fuck, he has the greatest cock. All I need do is slip one of the buttons open and eventually, the harder he gets, he'll pop out.

Yummy.

"Tempted to give in?" he encourages. "Let me have my wicked, wicked way and prove I am who I say I am."

"Oh, I know you are who you say you are, Ruben. But I'm much better at sparring than you, hence I'm the greater fucker."

His head reels back and he's burned, again.

Ha.

"Right, so, I think we'll have you on one of the chairs. Yes. Here."

I grab a dining chair, lug it across the floor and put it in the centre of the seating area, smack bang in the middle between the two opposing sofas and the armchair.

He sits himself down on the chair, thinking all is well, but little does he know. It's good that there's a rug beneath the chair, that means it won't slide around.

"Do you like surprises, Ruben?"

He shakes his head. "I hate surprises."

"Me too. Hate them."

He grins and my heart skips a bit. God, I'm madly in love with this bastard.

"Well, I've got a surprise for you, my darling. Nonetheless."

He tries to hide his fear. He hates not being in control. That's why he doesn't like surprises.

My reason is much different... I don't like that a surprise is meant to evoke an emotional reaction. I don't like being caught unawares. I like to know beforehand. Because I hate to not be in charge of my emotions.

So, okay... maybe I am slightly controlling. About my feelings.

Yep.

"When I did that thing I used to do," I begin, and he nods as though he thinks he knows where this might be going, "I was known for a particular specialty. Would you like to discover that specialty?"

His shoulders jump up, but he plays down his reaction. "Maybe. I don't know. I suppose there's only one way to find out."

I head to the kitchen, not finding what I'm looking for. "Stay where you are, mister."

I head for the laundry room next, finding some intriguing items indeed. Beneath the laundry sink are some tools and bits of equipment for doing the gardening.

"Would you shut your eyes, my love?" I yell through.

"Yes, my love."

"Are they shut?"

"Yes," he insists.

I peek my head out and spot he does in fact have his eyes closed. Just in case he's got them slightly open, I hold what I'm carrying behind my back.

"Do you consent?" I ask him.

"To what?"

"To let me do what I want with you."

"As long as it doesn't involve pain."

"Why not?" I grunt, sounding almost insulted (but not really).

"Anything but pain," he repeats.

"Okay, agreed. Now, you consent to anything but pain?"

"Yes, anything... but pain."

"Okay, hands behind your back."

KARMA

He does as he's told and I snap a cable tie around his wrists, tightening it. Like me, the gardener here must use them for the roses in the garden out back—as I do at home in France.

I walk around to the front of him and spot he's slightly chubby in his boxers, but not erect. He does get off on being in charge, I know that. But we can test the theory.

"You know, I think I could have had you that very first night. At Freddie's wedding." I tap my teeth, keeping him in suspense. "I think I could've dragged you into the vestry and we would've had the most blisteringly hot sex of our lives, bibles breaking beneath us, the sacred cloth soiled, tables broken and chair legs bent out of shape as we fucked all over the place. What do you think?"

I notice a slight quiver to his chin as he tries to speak, but stops himself.

"I think if, the first time we met at the pub and I said to you, 'Ruben, I want your hot, thick dick pressed up deep inside my wet cunt, fucking me until I scream and cry,' you'd have taken me back to yours and screwed me until dawn. I'd have been walking funny for days after that."

Ruben's face turns red and he can't hide how I affect him. He's now straining those boxer shorts... and there's a little tiny patch of moisture. God, he's amazing.

"Do you agree I showed more restraint? Do you?" I demand, daring him to defy me.

"I don't know..." He puffs and pants.

"If I'd said take me, you would have, wouldn't you? You wouldn't have been able to stop yourself."

"No, you're right. I wanted you that first night. Even when I was meant to be there fucking up *his* wedding. I would've happily left it all behind. Forgotten all of it... to be with you. But I couldn't."

"I felt there was something, so I steered us straight. Steered us right. And we became friends. We were—"

"We were never friends," he growls, interrupting, "it was a delay. You delayed what was inevitable."

"And did you not come harder than you ever had in your entire life, the night we first made love and you filled me until I could barely breathe?"

He moves his jaw side to side, like it's uncomfortable for him to talk. He shakes his head, unable to communicate all the thoughts and feelings careering around his brain.

"You wanted me, I wanted you, but there was this thing... lurking in the background. You knew you couldn't choose a woman for yourself without Fred's approval."

He shakes his head, ready to argue that it wasn't like that. "I made a lot of bad choices in my younger years, but when I chose to avenge Laurent, I never saw that as one of them... until you. I had it in my mind that I was chasing justice, but I wasn't. I was chasing destruction. My own. Theirs. Ours. You're not the only one who tried to destroy something good before it destroyed them."

There's the truth.

That's the absolute truth of what we are.

"We're the same then, Ruben. That's why we love as we do. We're the same. Except for one thing."

"What?" he asks, almost strangled.

Despite this tough talk, he still rages in his boxer shorts.

"A woman's protective instinct is a hundred times stronger than a man's."

He looks worried.

Then, he looks scared.

Nay, terrified.

"What you did to me in Florence was abhorrent and evil. And I am pissed with you. I am *pissed*, Ruben. I'm going to be pissed about it for a long, long time. I can pretend, oh, I'm good at that... the actress... that's what I'm good at. Pretending to be this character or that... but beneath it all, I'm going to be pissed and I'm going to be angry about it for a very fucking long time."

My mouth snaps shut and my harsh breathing is the only sound in the room as I catch my breath and he stares, dumb-struck.

I'm still angry.

I'm happy he's back.

But beneath that, I am still boiling with fury that he left me.

When that's not what was meant to be.

It's always been me and him. Him and me.

Always.

Since that first evening we met.

We couldn't turn back after that.

Neither of us could admit it, but it was there...

Fate.

She'd decided we were meant to be.

"What are you going to do to me?" he asks, his tone cold and even.

I stand in front of him, put my hands on his bare shoulders and lean down to kiss his mouth softly. He stares up at me, con-founded.

"Be quiet, Ruben. That will help."

I pull out the other cable ties I brought along and fasten his ankles to the chair legs. He makes a noise that sounds like a complaint, but when I whip my head up, he puts on a straight face.

"What was that, fucker?"

"I didn't say a thing."

Once he's secured, I go into the bedroom and change into a racy red balconette and matching lace thong. I pull a sleep mask out of my bedside drawer and one of my scarves from the dresser.

In the living room, I fix his blindfold in place, but only after he's got a really good look at what I'm wearing.

"Last words?" I ask.

"I'm the best fucker," he growls.

I'm laughing my head off as I tie the gag around his head.

Chapter Nineteen

The Teacher

"When I was an escort, I charged a thousand pounds an hour..." His speech, sight and ability to move his hands have all been taken away, so he can't communicate a response. But his eyebrows do lift—his forehead rises—and he sits absolutely still. "Ten thousand for the night. There were a couple of rich blokes, you know... who'd regularly book me for the full night once a month. They did so because they understood what they'd be getting... how it was worth it for them. I was living between hotels. I wanted for nothing. I was nineteen fucking years old and I thought I was so grown up. It truly did feel like life couldn't get better."

I notice a little frown develop in his forehead.

"Joey the Great discovered I had a very particular skill through a couple of fellow working girls I got friendly with... and I didn't realise it at the time, but of course one of my clients turning unexpectedly violent on me seems obvious now. Joey had three days prior offered me a chance to stay in one of his mansions and be waited on hand and foot... be protected, feel safe, keep my existing clientele... he'd just take ten per cent, he told me, but I'd turned him down. After this violent episode—the client came off worse, by the way, but it shocked me, reminded me what I was capable of, like my father—I was scared. I went to

Joey and said yes. He had to have set it up. I didn't see that then, not immediately. He must have leveraged something on my private client and forced him to become violent somehow. Scaring me senseless."

Ruben grunts through the gag, shaking his shoulders, like he wants out.

"Amazing what's so clear with hindsight, hmm? It went from ten per cent to twenty-five very quickly... and when I, well, reacted as you imagine a volatile person such as myself would... he tossed me into one of his housing blocks and into a shoddy bedsit. I had money but he took my cards from me. He started paying me in cash and I knew how it would look, going into the decent places and always paying in cash. I didn't have ID because he took that, too."

Ruben slumps slightly in his chair.

"It was the beginning of the end of my career in that field: the day I trusted him. The clients he brought me weren't as straightforward. I hadn't been able to vet them like the others. I preferred the base ones. To them, I was just a thing, something through which they could reassure themselves they were still men. Those were easy. They provided oblivion. The ones he brought me were complicated but paid more."

Ruben grunts again, aggravated he can't reply... can't comfort me.

I told myself ages ago I'd never tell him any of this stuff... but it's just coming out of me, maybe because he can't interrupt and he can't see my face as I tell it... maybe it's just time.

"There was this one guy Joey introduced me to. I was warned this guy was weird... and not in a sexual way. He had major problems with intimacy, but, as I said before, I had a skill... for figuring people out, if you like. He'd book me for four or five hours and only a few minutes of that would be spent fucking. The rest of the time, he'd need real encouragement... counselling, almost. He was the CEO of some big company, but you would never have known. He didn't wear designer clothes. His hair was messy. He didn't smell or anything, but he wasn't... what's the word? Sharp. At first glance it looked like he could've just been anyone. And when he came to me, he was just this guy with an issue. Couldn't find it in himself to love a woman. And it took him a really long time to even feel comfortable with me."

Ruben sighs loudly and I study him, noticing he's relaxed slightly, in listening mode. He's given into it.

"I'd started to like this guy, I'll admit. Did I ever forget for a single second I was on the clock and being paid? No. For some reason, even though I liked him, I never could forget money was being exchanged. He was weird and he had all these phobias about germs and people in general... and he only ate certain foods. He'd tell me about his strange routines and it was obvious he was a genius, probably from a rich background, so it was never diagnosed because when you're rich, there can't be anything wrong with you."

Ruben snorts.

"He was good-looking, I'm not going to lie. He didn't have a clue what he was doing so I would help things along, but I was starting to have orgasms and I hadn't had a real one in so long."

He goes back to frowning.

"We tried everything that last night to get him hard. I did things, disgusting things, prostrated myself like I was in a porn movie... but nothing worked, and I'd started to like him, and I thought he really liked me because he'd told me all about his life and he would even sometimes want to cuddle. But when I suggested to him that I thought he liked me, and that all we needed to do was have a bit more patience, he denied he thought anything of me. He started crying, admitted he was unable to love anyone, or anything. That it all meant nothing to him. That he was glad he couldn't get it up, in a way, because he'd started to see I was a good girl and he knew he shouldn't have been doing the things he had been with me. Then he admitted he'd fucked a load of women, like in the thousands, abused his power at work and used his wealth to get what he wanted... but that it had always got complicated because he couldn't feel anything... so that's why he'd started coming to me."

Ruben coughs a bit behind the gag and I watch as a tear falls from beneath the blindfold. Just one blob of liquid falling from his eyes leaves me gutted. I wouldn't be able to speak in this moment if I had to see his eyes while I confess the intimate truth.

"It was exactly like it was with my first boyfriend, Oliver. I realised I'd become irrelevant. That's when I threw him out, the CEO guy. He begged me to let him come back another time, just to talk and be friends, but I said I would tell Joey he was always asking too much. And nobody dared cross Joey."

Ruben wants to say something, mumbling against the gag. I stroke his neck and watch his jaw move.

"Did I go home and wonder if he was just some repressed nerd? Did I wonder if he'd started to care about me and that's why he couldn't get hard?" Ruben nods, like he was just thinking the same thing. "The thing is, when he was talking, I knew he really didn't feel anything for me. I was just a thing, literally. I was an echo chamber. I wasn't paid to disagree or to challenge him. I was just a living thing he could talk to instead of a wall. He could talk to me and not be alone, but I wasn't anything more than a paid employee, like everyone else in his life..."

I take a deep breath, the memory of how I felt that night, all too vivid.

"It'd be simplifying it to say I tried to take my own life that night. I knew the amount of pills could potentially kill me, but I also knew I'd probably survive if one of the girls found me in time... and I knew my parents would get the call. I didn't know any other way of getting back home and at the same time, I was prepared for it to all be over, too. If I did die, maybe it was meant to be. It was your proverbial cry for help. I was twenty years old, Ruben. A child really."

He shakes his body against the chair, trying to get free. I wipe away the tears that have dripped down his face and are now clinging to his jaw, urging him to calm down.

"At the time, you feel like you know it all, that you're so grown up. I look back now and can recognise all those men knew they were fucking a young girl and didn't think twice. Emptying their wallets supplanted their guilt, I suppose. They were look-ing for something, not necessarily easy, but something... some-thing they couldn't get elsewhere. Being able to pay for it and leave must have felt like joy to them because they got what they wanted and didn't have to invest themselves in anyone or any-thing. I didn't understand that at the time, though. I thought I was so clever, and so beautiful, all these men getting big and hard for me. But it was all a fucking mess. I'd forgotten who I was and what I wanted. I'd taken a vacation from myself, I suppose."

Ruben cranes his neck back, tired and emotionally fraught. He'd not be tied up if it was his choice—he'd be free to comfort and protect me—stop me talking and instead just hold me.

"The guy killed himself five years later. It was in the news." I shut my eyes and remember that day... at the hotel... when I saw the headline. One of the hotel guests had been carrying a paper under their arm and had put it on the desk when they took out their card to pay. I nearly passed out. He'd made front-page news. I open my eyes and Ruben looks short on breath, as shocked as I was at the time. "I wondered if his struggle to live had rubbed off on me. Maybe that's why I did what I did. But it wasn't entirely that. When I went back home, it was like I'd pressed the button for a circuit break. Somebody else took over after my cry for help. I became emotionless. I became lesser, I reduced myself to a girl staying out of people's way and hunkering down. It was a good thing I left Joey's world, got back into school... excelled, made myself irreplaceable at the hotel... because that meant I wasn't like that guy. I was mediocre and nothing special and quiet and not seeking attention. But seeing the article, in black and white, as I read it later on at home after buying a copy for myself... it was like I was right back in that room with him. Clinically depressed, unable to feel anything, and all this other stuff had sprung up because the depression was never treated... and I expect he didn't feel anything when he did it, either."

Ruben's face is scrunched up in confusion and annoyance.

"For you, when Laurent died, you said another version of yourself came to life. I felt that exact same thing when I left behind my escort days. Except I went from entertaining chaos to shunning in; from the dramatic to the boring; from the dangerous to the safe. I completely dissociated, the way you have from football, but when I went to counselling for depression and anxiety after you left me behind, I had to face up to it all. I spoke to someone about everything and I realised it was all a lesson. It was all a rebuilding. It just took time."

Ruben looks resigned, head bowed, nodding to himself.

"So, why are you trussed up like this, then... you may be thinking. Why am I subjecting you to all this while you're completely immobile?"

He responds with a series of unintelligible grunts and muffled exclamations.

"I'll leave you here for a few minutes to think about it."

I leave the room to a series of murmurings echoing behind me.

I RETURN TO THE LIVING area half an hour later. He hears me approach and lifts his head, moving his ears so he may better detect where I've come from, where I'm going to stop. I see from his sore wrists and ankles that he must have tried to get free, but quickly gave up, knowing he'd sustain an injury otherwise. I wonder if he allowed the solitude to softly sweep over him... his brainwaves to calm. Or if, beneath the cool exterior, he is boiling.

"Sorry, I just had to file my nails," I lie.

He slowly shakes his head.

The chair doesn't seem comfortable for him anymore.

"If I remove your blindfold, will you behave?"

He nods fast.

"Do you mean it?"

He nods even faster.

I stroke my hand under his chin first before slowly lifting the covering. He blinks fast until he's regained his vision. I can see in his eyes, he's feeling a lot of different emotions. Firstly, he seeks out my eyes to check I'm okay.

He sees I'm okay.

Then his eyes travel downwards until landing on what I've changed into. Outfit number two. Got to keep them on their toes. So to speak...

A black lace bodysuit. Crotchless (he doesn't know that yet). It has frilly cap sleeves and a thong back, plus see-through mesh detailing across the midriff that is extraordinarily flattering. I bought this a long while ago to fit beneath a black dress when I was interested in seducing an artist. This ended up consigned to the bottom of my wardrobe when I realised I couldn't face it... and that he'd show with me anyway. It was two years after Ruben left before I slept with anyone else.

His eyes are bulging and I do a little spin so he can get the full effect of the cut-out panels at the back and my delicate thong.

He's tenting his delightful white boxers in no time. And I was torn between this and my long-line bustier... I think this has done the trick.

I straddle his lap and wrap my arms around his neck. The cotton of his boxers is pressing against my naked crotch and he pants when he realises this.

"You love me, boy?" I ask, stroking my hands over his face.

He blinks furiously, the colour in his cheeks rising. I smooth my hands down his cheeks and across his shoulders, admiring his body.

"You thought I meant fucking this, didn't you?" I point down at his cock. His eyes betray fear. I shake my head slowly and point to his head. "Nope, baby. Nope. This."

I back away off his lap but his eyes are on my crotch, trying to catch sight of something, but unfortunately, my legs are closed again and everything falls back into place.

His chest is heaving as I back away. I walk to the table where I left the wine and pour myself a little glass. I tiptoe around the room, knowing his eyes are on me the entire time.

"I know how you feel, you know." I stand at the window, staring out at the view down below. The ever-comforting, familiar sight of Rio at night... lit up like a Christmas tree. "You're desperate to be free. Men always want to fix a woman's problems. Can't take it when we cry or get upset. You want to get up and hold me, don't you?"

I don't even turn my head. I hear from his grumbles that I'm right. It makes me chuckle a little.

"That same way you feel right now... that's how I felt when you left. I couldn't help you. Couldn't save you. I felt utterly powerless, like you didn't trust me and you'd given up on us."

A lot more grumbling from him follows...

"You'll argue over and over that you did it to protect me, but you were hiding at a rural Portuguese farmhouse for the past few years, Ruben. Who'd you think was gonna get you there?"

I hear nothing so I turn and look at him. His head is bowed. I'm going to lose his interest if I'm not careful so I put my glass on the table and return to his lap. He once again feels how exposed I am and responds, tipping his head back and groaning.

I push my breasts to his chest, lean my weight on him slightly and rest my forehead against his, looking right into his eyes. He looks petrified and exhilarated, all at once. I slide my toes up his calves and he seems to mellow, allowing himself to be transported, taken in and devoured by this moment.

I open the buttons on his boxers and his erection slowly breaks free, pointing right at my belly.

"You're going to suffer, Ruben."

He blinks twice. I think he knows.

I firstly kiss his eyelids, then reach down to lick his nipples, his shoulders and his throat. He urges me to recognise his cock is ready and waiting, lifting his hips up towards me. I can hardly avoid him, being he's so big and hard and hot, plus the scent of him is driving me wild.

"They say prostitutes are the bottom rung of actresses but that's false, Ruben. We can be a dozen different characters on the same night. We pretend to be whatever they want or need. The girlfriend. The naughty step-daughter. The bad mistress. The full-blown mummy experience. Which do you want, Ruben?"

He shakes his head, gulping—he doesn't know.

"Shall we show you which experience I was known for?"

His pecs twitch as he nods.

I let down the gag and he wets his lips before growling, "Which were you?"

"Guess."

"Mistress," he groans.

"I was the teacher." I lick my lips before kissing his mouth furiously, until neither one of us can breathe.

When I'm sure he's dying of lust, I break our kiss and glare at him, holding his chin in my hand and lifting his head back so he has to look up at me.

"Do you think you deserve to be freed?"

"Yes," he says, sounding choked.

"What'll you do when you're freed?"

"I don't know," he says, shaking, "I don't know."

KARMA

"Let's find out then."

I walk slowly towards the kitchen, retrieve the scissors and come back. I snap one ankle free, looking up at him, his expression one of anticipation... relief beyond anything. I could really mess with him and not get the other ties... leave him waiting again... but I love him too much. He bites his lip as he waits for me to release his second ankle and the snapping sound is such a relief for him, he exhales loudly.

Standing behind him, I can see his chest heaving up and down, his cock still erect and poking out of his boxer shorts. I lean down and whisper against his ear, "How much do you love me?"

"Too much," he groans.

"You might unlove me if I refuse to snip these off, right?" I taunt him, stroking his bound wrists behind his back.

"I could never unlove you, but I could get even angrier."

"Calm down, baby. I barely did a thing."

"Barely did a thing?" he chuckles, sounding so masculine. "You make a confession like that, which I've been waiting all these years for, and then you come out dressed like that... oh, god... you really don't know me at all."

"Don't I?" I bite his earlobe and snip the tie open at the same time.

He's on his feet in seconds but he's got a dead leg and stumbles, rubbing it.

"For fuck's sake!" he cries, as he watches me chase off towards the bedroom.

I hear him stomping after me, limping around. "You will behave, Freya! You'll BEHAVE!"

"Oh, I'll behave all right... when hell freezes over!"

I make it to the bedroom and throw the door shut, locking it. I run and jump at the bed, collapsing into it so hard, I almost break the legs. I'm laughing my head off, a rush of excitement and adrenalin taking over, when he tries the door and growls, "Freya, don't make me break it down!"

"Break it down, you wretch!"

He fucking breaks it down. It blasts, rather comically, out of the doorframe and slams to the floor with a crash. He steps over the door with his cock tucked back in his boxers but still hard. He grabs the front of his underwear and rips away the entire garment, the sound of shredding material frightening me much more than the door crashing open. He throws the pieces to the floor and grunts as he stares at me, lying frigid on the bed.

He stomps towards me, launches himself onto the bed and pins me down. He forces my legs open, slides up into me with one swift, savage move, and whispers, "Bad girl."

The fullness of him between my thighs seizes me, renders me mute, grabs all my attention, and I lie still as he bangs his hips against me, shoving me into the bed. He pounds me until I'm screaming his name and pouring with sweat, my legs suffering the electricity of my desire—his grunts in my ear, his hands like ton weights keeping me fastened down as he breaks me, like I broke him.

He gives me a moment to recover from such an eviscerating orgasm, but I know he's far from done.

"Is this what you wanted?" he asks, withdrawing slowly and then filling me, just as ruthlessly as before—until I'm stuffed. He kisses my throat, nips my nipple over my bra and mutters a complaint of some sort. "You wanted me wound up, didn't you?"

"Yes," I breathe.

"Well, you got what you wanted. You got your man good and angry and no way ready to let up."

A laugh escapes my chest but gets trapped in my throat so that I sound ridiculously amused. I'm still catching my breath—not sure what the fuck just happened.

When he deigns to kiss my mouth, finally, we catch each other's eye.

"You needed teaching a lesson," I growl.

"You said you're not a mistress," he fires back, eyes goading me.

"You said you're not a monster."

His eyes blaze with anguish and he pins me down harder. "Don't take me there, Freya!"

"Why? Scared you'll like it."

I'm traumatised by what happens next...

He withdraws too sharply, flips me over and pulls my thong to the side, entering me all at once. From this angle, it's too deep. Criminally intrusive.

"RUBEN!"

He slaps my arse and warns, "Don't you complain now!"

He rams at me until I'm fighting the urge with every atom of my being... but I can't fight anymore. Each stroke inside me is ruthless and touches a subterranean place, my belly aching, drawing him in deeper and deeper despite the pain.

I can barely breathe as I come this time, the pleasure bittersweet and agonising... the endorphin and serotonin release the exact thing I was looking for earlier... when I was overcome with memories of the past and couldn't breathe for feeling like I might never truly escape all that.

I fall flat on my stomach, reduced to nothing, all my energy depleted.

I could so easily...

But, no... he has other ideas.

He unhooks the fastenings of the bodysuit at the back, starts stripping it off my body, pulling it down and off. His hands are rough from painting and when they touch my sore bottom, it hurts.

He kisses his way down my back, into my crack and between my buttocks until he's licking my pucker. He lifts one of my legs to one side and slips his tongue away from where I want it and into my other, overly used hole.

"No, Ruben! PLEASE!"

He holds me down, his hands pushing on my back, meaning all I can do is squirm while he thrusts his tongue up into my vagina.

"NO! RUBEN!"

He continues and it's too abrasive, but the more he works me open, the more I can't deny him and I begin moaning, lifting my butt up towards him and riding his tongue.

The excruciating orgasm I'm dealt brings tears to my eyes and I break down, my insides fully exhausted, my internal organs yearning for relief.

My chin wobbles and I decide to ride it, let it go and cry.

Ugly cry.

The whole atmosphere changes and I find myself drawn into his arms, my hands covering my face, my front against his side. He kisses my hair and I feel the weight of everything bubble up from inside of me, a physical manifestation of the release of it all... the sadness, the veneer I had to put on, the strength I had to don, day in, day out... without him by my side. It all comes pouring out of me—the pain I've held in at the centre of myself, all this time.

Only he could help me get rid of it.

Only him.

It would have been bound so tight within me if he hadn't come back... and I never would've loved again. Only Ruben has the power to unlock me.

He holds me through it—my ugly crying, my despair, my disbelief he's actually back, that we might have a chance—the thought of actually being happy petrifying but also scarily within reach.

"It's about so much more than fucking, Freya. I'd rather be in your heart and mind than any other part of you. I love everything about you. Everything. You know that, don't you?"

"Yes," I whisper, meek and frail sounding. "I needed you tonight. I needed you to see, that sometimes, I just need to not think for a minute. To not care about a thing else. The only person who's ever been able to set me free is you."

He kisses my mouth softly, then my cheeks, my eyelids, my forehead. He returns to my mouth and kisses me passionately, roughly, his stubble almost as painful as my cunt is right now.

He becomes ever more passionate, leaning down and kissing my breasts, his hands caressing my bum and thighs, his mouth coming back to my throat.

"You didn't come—"

"It doesn't matter," he says, even though I can tell he's urgent.

He's kissing me like a fraught lover, reunited after months apart.

"Lie back," I urge him, "arms above your head. I like to see your muscles... and your deep, sexy armpits."

He groans and does as I say. I reach out and stroke his cock, watching as his eyes flutter shut. I feel the heft of his balls and recognise he's more than ready.

I stroke him tenderly, though with my hand wrapped securely around him, it doesn't take long for him to begin groaning. I feel the blood surge into him even more as he gets close, and when he's almost there, I slow my movements and lean over and kiss him, keeping him on edge.

He grows impatient when I kiss his throat, working my tongue down his chest until landing on his nipple, my tongue swirling and flicking against it. He almost moves his arms to do something—maybe to encourage me to go for it—but I remind him, "Arms where they are, lover."

I slacken my grip around his cock and tease him. He throws his head back against the pillow and air gets caught in his throat. He's desperate to come, but he's not there... he's trying to focus on it... but I'm not pulling him hard enough.

I get a wicked idea and slide my tongue along his abdomen until reaching his magnificent cock. I slide my lips over his erection and suck, hard, swirling my tongue around him and flicking at the eye of his penis. I use my hand and jack him off viciously, my fingers gripping him in a vice.

His eruption of cum hits the inside of my cheek and I remove my mouth because it's going to keep coming, and it does—it flies against my breasts and throat. His sexy cries echo around the room and drive me to worship him, stroking him until he's utterly spent, his cock entirely rigid and pulsing endlessly.

Once he's done, I lick him clean, kiss him gently. Every inch of him. But especially his sore, tired tip, still throbbing.

I climb up on top of him and lay my weight completely on top of him, curling myself up into his embrace. He wraps his arms around me like he'll never let go.

"That may have just been the most bone-achingly ridiculous orgasm of my life."

"Do you concede?"

"Of course, I fucking concede," he says, and we both laugh.

Every day we get closer. We become more bonded. The flim-flam is non-existent, always really was between us two. Even when we were fucking other people, we were still fucking each other with the looks that passed between us—the signals we'd send one another, about how we wanted to fuck one another, though we could never really admit it.

"You're the only man I've ever loved, Ruben. I'll never love again, I swear it. I could have been happy with a job that kept me interested, a few hobbies, a few friends, but nothing interested me less than being in a relationship. Except with you. You broke down my barriers. And when I decided it was you, there was no going back. It took what happened for me to stop running. And now they'd have to pry my cold, dead hands off you. I'm going nowhere."

When I look up and into his eyes, I see he's weeping. I hold him close, kiss away his tears and stroke my fingers over his shorn hair. I push my nose to his and absorb his hot, tormented breath as it leaves him.

"I want to marry you, Ruben. I want to be your wife. I want to call you husband." My chest burns with love for him and to speak the words makes me come out in goosepimples, all over my body. I shed a tear and suck my bottom lip into my mouth.

He searches my eyes, seeking a lie, but seeing none—he replies, "The ring is already being made."

I fly at him, kiss him wildly, hardly able to cope... all that tension earlier replaced with something new and entirely foreign...

A feeling unknown until I met him.

A feeling I never knew could be so good.

Happiness.

Chapter Twenty

Only Heaven

J ust when I thought things couldn't get any better, I wake up trapped beneath his arms, his stubble brushing against my shoulder, our legs tangled together.

I groan and he follows suit.

"I slept so well."

"Me too, baby," he murmurs.

I stroke my hands over his forearms and sigh, locked inside his warmth and sturdiness.

"I love you so much, bubba."

He kisses my neck. "Love you more."

I roll over in his arms to face him and stroke my fingers over his face. He's still sleepy and looks like a dream, squinty-eyed and relaxed. I kiss his mouth softly, once, then twice and he sighs, scooping me towards him so that I'm brought tight into his chest.

Was this the first night in a long time that he actually slept?

He plays with my hair as I close my eyes, inhaling the scent of him and holding his body, trying to archive all of these things I'm feeling: love, gratitude... hope. I dare not dream of more than him. He'll be the only thing I ever want or need.

"Would you pose for me today?" he asks softly, brushing his mouth against my hair.

"I... I dunno."

"Or, I could take a picture and work from that, but... I think it might be different if you pose for me."

I lift my eyes to his and search his face. He looks bright and hopeful. How can I shoot him down?

"I was hoping for us to go out today, visit some museums. Explore. Do some shopping. Why don't you come with? I could pose tonight?"

"No," he snaps, almost sullenly, "the light. We need the light."

Why do I suddenly feel like last night unlocked something in him? And now I'm not going to be able to get out of this. Because whatever inspiration he has, it has to find a way out. I know what artists are like and when the mood takes, nothing will stop them.

"If I pose just for this morning, will you come out this afternoon?"

He narrows his eyes and stares at me, hard, seeming unwilling to negotiate. I move in, kiss him tenderly, then slip my tongue in his mouth and remind him who's in charge here. When I pull away, his eyes are swimming in desire and love.

"A couple of hours this morning, then you come out with me, mister."

"That won't be enough time to complete anything. You'll pose for me tomorrow, too? And if I need any more time..."

"You can have my time," I reassure him, kissing his cheek. "And my cuddles."

I rest my cheek in the centre of his chest and sigh as he locks me inside his arms, his fingers gripping me as though holding on for dear life.

KARMA

I SPEND A COUPLE OF hours lying on a chaise longue in the studio, dressed in a white bedsheet and nothing else, the fabric draped around me like a Grecian robe. Then, we get washed and dressed and head out.

We leave in the car, even though we're not going far.

"Am I really not allowed to see it?" I ask, as he drives us into the neighbouring Santa Teresa district.

"Only when it's done. It can't have viewers until it's done. And it might not be done for ages. Tomorrow we'll have to get the sheet right again."

He took a photo of me so we can recapture the same pose and look tomorrow. He'd have happily kept painting all day, but we've been here in Brazil for days now and I actually want to start seeing some of it, properly.

We stop on a street somewhere and he parks the car. I'm wondering what's going on when he remarks under his breath, "They're somewhere around here."

I follow him as he navigates using the directions on his phone. We traipse around a few streets and before long, find ourselves staring up at the Selaron Steps.

Selaron, a Chilean artist, decorated over 200 steps with tiles, ceramics and whatever else he could get his hands on. As we stand looking up at the staircase before us, I get giddy.

"I've always wanted to see this. Should we walk up? Are we allowed?"

"It's gaudy as fuck and so South American," he remarks, gazing with an artist's eye.

How one man could do all this... even when people were making fun of him. He turned something bland and ordinary into something colourful, remarkable and fun.

It just proves that sometimes you have to ignore the doubters and do what's in your heart... because what you leave behind might become a monument. It might outlive the doubters by centuries.

There are some other tourists hanging about and a few residents bustling through, none of whom clock Ruben as anyone of significance. He's clean-shaven and shorn of head, though that is starting to grow back, but he's wearing a Panama hat and round black sunglasses, making him look more like an artist than ever a footballer. He's also wearing a loud shirt and fancy slacks like a proper native. I hope for his sake he doesn't get found out today.

"Shall we?" he asks.

"We shall," I reply, and we begin ascending the blue, green and yellow staircase, taking note of every detail as we go.

I expect this is as interesting for Ruben as it is for me, being that this is a part of his heritage.

For me, it's just a wonderfully different culture I'm eager to find out all about.

THE DAY IS EASILY SPENT wandering the neighbourhood. We made plans this morning to visit the big art museums, but Santa Teresa is so vibrant and a day here can be happily used up just looking at all the street art.

I quietly watch Ruben as he takes it all in. We even find a food cart for lunch that is so Brazilian, you can't help but smile.

We also stumble upon a place for him to grab some extra art supplies—and he talks to the cashier like they're long-lost cousins. Though I understand very little, I can tell by his expressions as he speaks Portuguese that he feels at home here and finds the people jovial and personable—as long as they're not asking about football.

I walk into a store and pick up some artsy jewellery and a pashmina while Ruben steps into a shop a few doors down for water. I end up buying a few silly trinkets like a 'Christ the Redeemer' metal keyring and a towel with the Brazilian flag.

When he catches up with me, he peers into my bag and chuckles. "I can't leave you for five minutes. Oh, nice necklaces, though."

"Good, yes?" They have colourful beads, but some even have feathers. A bit wild for my taste, but I still like them.

"Come on, I saw a place," he says, dragging me off by the hand to another shop along the way.

We walk into a store with fancy dresses. Not your hand-stitched, monk-made type garments. No. These were definitely made somewhere fancier.

"Why don't you get yourself something new?" he asks, and stands back, waiting for me to approach the rails.

The shop assistant sees us, bids hello and asks if we need help. Ruben fires off something about me looking for a dress for dinner... and the lady replies we're sure to find something in her shop, then leaves us to it.

I have a whole wardrobe back at the crib, full of Parisian fashion, and he brings me here.

However, it doesn't take long before I spot something I might like.

A black, lightweight dress with multiple straps criss-crossing at the deep, open back, plus a plunging cowl-neck. It's what people call a naked dress, I think. I'm sure you wouldn't wear underwear, beneath. I look at the tag and he yanks if off me before I've had time to figure out the price.

"Right size, is it?" he asks, and I'm left in shock as he heads straight to the till with it.

I guess he wants to get me the naked dress. As the lady rings it in and tells Ruben I will look sensational in this dress, I find an ornate fan on one of the display tables and add that to the purchase—one of those with black lace trim, plus thick embroidery on the handle. Gorgeous.

The woman talks so fast to Ruben, I hear nothing at all, but when they animatedly agree on something, I ask, "What is it?"

She snaps her eyes to me and grins. "Oh, I say to him, this is like that one the lady wears on James Bond. You know? *Casino Royale*," she says, showing off her English skills. "The lady going out with the bad guy, I mean. Except you're not going out with a bad guy... and this isn't a dress for an English rose... but still, when in Rio, hmm?"

I'm blushing furiously by the time she's holding up the bag by the handles, ready for us to take it away. Ruben thanks the lady profusely and when we get outside the shop, he says, "It was definitely a compliment."

"She was saying this is a slutty dress."

"Isn't it?" he exclaims, laughing.

I'm dragged off again, but this time we head down the hill and find ourselves back at the car.

"Are we going out for dinner then?" I ask, as we set off back to the house.

"I think so," he chuckles, a glint in his eye. "Just as soon as you've changed into that dress."

IN THE BATH, I HAVE time to reflect on the day. On the countless art studios we passed and the little galleries we looked in on. It almost felt like we could've been in Montmartre, not only because of the artistic vibe, but there were the cobbled streets and that air of... something peaceful, something calm. A lot of up-and-coming new talent is everywhere and it is inspiring. I can tell Ruben was thinking about what he might do next... in which direction he may go. Hopefully he doesn't suffer from awful self-doubt and actually feels imbued seeing what other people can do... because perhaps he can do it, too.

I truly don't know if I picked the dress up off the rack because it was the only one there I liked... or if it's because, out here in Rio, I'm freer. I certainly wouldn't wear anything so revealing usually. I haven't even tried it on yet but I know it's going to fit because it's one of those occasions where you see something and just know... that dress was made for me.

"How's it going in here?" he asks, strolling into the room.

He stands in front of the mirror with his back to me, sprays on some cologne and checks his teeth.

He's wearing a tailored white shirt, tucked into fitted black jeans.

His butt fills those jeans perfectly.

"Hungry, are we?" I ask, and he spins around.

God. Fuck. Does he look beautiful. Legs that go on forever, tight waist, big naked flipper feet and goliath shoulders hugging his pristine, long-sleeve shirt.

"Ruben, you know I don't like it when you go out like that."

"Like what, princess?"

"Like sex on legs. And I'm not your princess, I'm your queen."

He slides across the room and leans down to kiss my lips as I rest my arms on the edge of the tub.

"Queens need to be dressed before they leave the house and I see no dressing getting done at this present moment," he warns, kissing me again, only briefly. "And I will not get a second look standing next to you."

"I'm soaking my tired legs, we walked all day."

"I'm hungry and horny. Don't keep me waiting too long," he says, eyebrows raised.

I take a deep breath and lie back. I don't have to wash my hair this evening because I washed it this morning, therefore I can soak a bit longer. I'm not going to put on a lot of make-up... and there's not a lot I need to do except pull on The Dress.

Let him wait.

WHEN I EMERGE FROM the bedroom, I find him sitting on the arm of the sofa, legs spread, hands together between them. He's been staring at the floor, patiently waiting for me to get ready. I see he's pulled on a pair of brown suede loafers, sockless, just a bit of ankle on show. His broad, masculine chest also catches my eye, three buttons on his shirt undone. He looks divine.

Ruben looks up when he hears me drop my shoes to the floor and slip my feet into them. He gives a throaty chuckle, purses his lips and shakes his head.

"Fuck...ing...hell," he groans.

KARMA

"Are we eating or what, mate? I'm starved."

He tries to pursue me but I hold my arms out. "Ruben, no, no! I'm not having you mess me up."

"Just a little kiss before we go out. Just a little one, I promise," he begs. "I'm hungrier than a man on death row. Just a little kiss before we go out to eat."

"Fine, a little kiss."

I wrap my arms around his shoulders and he puts his hands on my exposed back. I like it when I'm in heels because there's barely any height difference between us. He's wearing the biggest grin and I realise why, when he pushes his crotch against mine.

"You look absolutely ravishing. I can't wait to make you my wife." He stares at my mouth, then lowers his lips, pressing them softly to mine... lingering sensually.

"There's too much boob on show," I complain. "It's too much for dinner."

"Who cares? Nobody here knows us."

I wipe lipstick off his mouth and wink. "Nobody here knows me. They know you. And one day, even more people will know you when you release your art."

"We'll see." He rolls his eyes, trying not to think about that. I watch doubt enter his mind, then he brushes it off.

"Where are you taking me, anyway?"

"We're going to a *churrascaria*," he tells me, "and I hope that dress is stretchy. I'll be letting out a few belt notches later."

"It had better not be some grubby little hole, not dressed like this."

"Oh ye of little faith."

He grabs the keys and we leave the house.

DOWN IN RIO PROPER, we enter a modern restaurant with fancy lighting and high ceilings, a mixture of booth seating and tables. Ruben has his hand around mine and strides into the place like he owns it. We're met by the person seating everyone who looks at Ruben with surprise.

"Ah, Mr Kitchener... we didn't..."

"You do have a spare table, don't you?" he asks, rather presumptive.

"Mr Kitchener, of course," the young guy says, totally in awe of his special guest tonight. "Private or..."

"Private," Ruben insists. "Sorry we didn't book, but I didn't want to get everyone excited."

It seems everyone in this country knows English, but I still feel a bit uncomfortable not being able to speak much Portuguese. It's the accent, I think. I try to add a French one and end up getting it all wrong. Some days, I honestly don't know what language I'm thinking in. I don't know how Ruben speaks several languages fluently. How does he do it? For all I know, he knows Swahili too. I wouldn't say it was impossible.

We're seated at the back where the booths have little screens. It's not entirely private, but it's better than a window seat... or at the bar. There's been many a time in Nice when I've been sat at the bar or in the window, the waiter thinking a pretty girl like me might entice more people in, when I'd much rather have always been given a dingy corner and an endless supply of red wine as I read my book.

"Champagne, Mr Kitchener? Anything—on the house," we're told.

KARMA

I know from the look on the waiter's face, Ruben has most certainly dined here before. Perhaps years ago now, but he's more than just a famous footballer in here. He's a previous guest. I wonder if he has a place on the wall behind the bar, where all the famous people's pictures are in frames.

"My fiancée doesn't want special treatment, she hates that. Tonight, we're just two people in love, requiring as much privacy as possible."

While once I would've shirked away from being called fiancée, tonight I couldn't be more delighted that he thinks of me that way.

The waiter speaks very quickly in Portuguese and Ruben nods a lot, appearing a little moody and a bit macho, if anything, then all I hear is, "*Aprecio isso.*"

In a matter of seconds, an army of waiters arrive and the whole of the private area is cordoned off with a huge screen and nobody else can get in down here.

"Oh, for fuck's sake," I mumble, and Ruben laughs.

"Jorge just told me we will be bombarded otherwise. I trust him."

I shake my head, giggling. "You were a footballer bloody yonks ago. It's ridiculous, Ruben."

Jorge returns with a bottle of Malbec, which Ruben must have at some point told Jorge is my favourite... but... no, Jorge can't have been told. And Malbec is only my favourite because Ruben got me onto it. So... they even remember what wine he likes?

Jorge pours wine for us and dashes away quickly.

"You lived in Rio at some point?" I ask him, shaking my head. "Why, oh why, didn't you tell me?"

"I didn't live here," he retaliates. "I was here for the World Cup, many years ago now. But this was my favourite place to eat. They obviously remember me. And I remembered them. They looked after me when interest was fever pitch and my coaches wouldn't let me eat anything but fish and lentils."

I look down at the table, utterly relieved. "You should've mentioned you'd visited before."

"It was a military operation just to come out for dinner here. Believe me, there wasn't much I did besides play. I only escaped the pen a couple of times. Three at the most."

I try not to look affected, but I can't help biting the insides of my cheeks. It wasn't just that we arrived at the airport into a football-mad nation and he got spotted...

It's obvious now that the last time Ruben stepped into this city—Portuguese-speaking, handsome as hell, a skilled player and a smooth talker—he made an impression.

That means he's bound to have fucked women here, too—unless that was another thing strictly off the menu. Reserving energy and all that. I prefer to believe he was a good boy when he last visited.

"Do you hear from your old friends?" I murmur. "The gorgeous black guy... a physio, wasn't he? And your school friend Aaron? And the England captain? What was he called?"

"Jamie Friars," he says, "who stole the job that should've been mine."

I chuckle knowingly. "Do go on."

"Nothing to tell," he says, shaking his head. "If I hadn't quit, I would've been up for captain, simple as that. It was a no brainer. I was a player with skill and a single-minded determination to win. I was raised to fear losing with every ounce of me."

I feel like he's about to say more, when Jorge returns holding a couple of metal platters with several compartments. He presents us with everything salad-wise, all freshly dressed with either vinaigrette or herbs. There are also condiments—possibly of the tongue-burning variety—and little mozzarella balls, rice wrapped in vine leaves, corn, pickles, tiny potatoes lathered in oil, croutons, plus a few other little weird and wonderful things I'm not sure of.

"*Obrigado*," I tell Jorge, "looks fantastic."

Next up, a man with a hunk of beef on a large skewer arrives. He rests a wooden tray on the edge of our table and angles the skewer over it so he can cut the meat right in front of us.

"*Por favor*," Ruben tells the man, and our server shaves off the most tender beef I've seen in my entire life. Ruben catches it before it falls.

Ruben looks at me and I nod. "Me too, please."

The server leaves and Ruben flips a card at the end of our table to red. "They'll come back in a bit. Let's enjoy this first."

We spoon everything onto our plates. Little bites of all the flavours of the land, sea and tree.

"So, you were saying," I murmur, as he tucks into his beef steak and groans with pure joy. "About being captain?"

He nods his head, gesturing he's just got to swallow what he's eating first. "I haven't spoken to any of the lads since we left London. I got a new number."

I watch him swallow back some wine, then he tucks into his steak again, lathering it in some kind of jalapeno sauce or something. The heat doesn't seem to bother him.

I'm happy having the steak with a bit of salad and nothing else. It's flavoursome all on its own.

"Not even Anthony?"

Ruben shakes his fork at me. "I knew you had a crush on him."

"Who wouldn't? I bet even you did."

Ruben laughs loudly. "No, but he had one on me. Didn't he give himself away? Can't you remember how off he was after we announced our engagement?"

"I think I was more interested in Jessie's reaction."

Ruben becomes pale at the mention of Jessie, who was friends with Ruben's fuck buddy, Fiona.

"Her and Aaron split around the same time we left for Florence. No doubt she discovered he was cheating after you tipped her off."

I shrug my shoulders. "I did nothing but shed light on what he was already doing."

"I haven't heard anything from Aaron. Not even via Mum. His mother and mine were friends once. I'm sure they probably still have one another's emails."

We continue eating for a while and almost the moment I'm out of wine, Jorge is on the case, topping me up. I don't know how he knew... maybe he's got a hiding spot from which to watch us.

"And Jamie? What is he doing now? Do you know?"

"I read somewhere he's married, three kids. Stopped playing due to a reoccurring injury. He's a pundit now. Crazy he and I once were covering for each other, you know? How things change."

"And Anthony? He never tried to contact you... through Alexia or otherwise?"

Ruben ponders for a moment, looking back. "I think he always deep down hoped I was gay. In denial sort of thing. After all, I was useless at holding down a relationship. Maybe when he saw us together, he saw it was finally right."

I flip the card over and within moments, someone arrives with a great hunk of pork and I'm salivating. Ruben takes some, too even though he was served more steak than me and is still on with it. I flip the card over again to red, though the waiter quickly returns with a huge pineapple on a spit, stinking of cinnamon.

"Oh, go on then," I smile, and I'm thoroughly famished all over again, smelling the pork and pineapple together.

"Did you ever really have a friend before me, then?" I ask, allowing the smells to overpower me for a moment or two before I dive in and break the spell.

"Laurent, maybe," he says, blinking, "but he wasn't my equal. He was my junior. I couldn't ever have put upon him. So, no. I suppose my closest friend was Aaron. He knew about Dad and all of it. He'd stay over at ours sometimes. His mum and mine got on, but if she'd have ever known about the stuff my dad was really into, she'd have never let Aaron stay over. And for Aaron it was a bit of an education. A novelty, really. He had the safety net, knowing he could go back home to his mother and leave me with my reality. It didn't affect him."

I finally feed myself the pork which melts in the mouth and alongside the beyond-tender pineapple tastes absolutely delicious.

"Wow," I tell him, grinning.

"I know, right?" he agrees, his eyes dancing with joy, happy to see me being well fed.

"Do you think Jessie found someone else? What about Fiona?"

He gesticulates nonchalantly with his fork. "I never cared to look in on them since I left the UK."

"So, you haven't stepped on British soil since?"

"Not once," he tells me without hesitation, and for some reason, I believe him. "It was only important for Freddie to believe I was dead. It was all for him. Nobody else was told except you. It was just simpler not to go back home. Not to incriminate or implicate or, you know... spoil the lie."

"Maybe it was worse for people like Aaron and Jamie and Anthony. You disappeared without a trace. They didn't know a thing."

Ruben sighs from the bottom of his stomach. "Aaron was a bastard, but that was obvious, right?"

I nod I agree.

"Jamie... Jamie was one of those guys, you know? He would've been a bit pissed off. But he'd have got over it. I could probably walk into pub and pull up a stool next to his and he wouldn't hold a grudge or anything. He'd be too proud of his wife and kids and his life. He'd recall the good old days but I know, deep down, he was always gonna land on his feet. One of the normal ones."

"I see," I murmur, skewering my meat and fruit. God, it's delicious.

"Anthony needed to move on... and Aaron, yeah, fuck. I try not to think about it. We'd known each other since we were seven or eight. And he must've figured out it was one of us who grassed him up. But yeah, he was a bastard, so I try not to feel guilty."

284

Ruben looks remorseful, deep down. He and Aaron would once have been the closest of friends. Perhaps their friendship disintegrated over the years... but breaking off from one another must hurt less if there's an actual goodbye ceremony of some sorts, rather than the disappearing act Ruben pulled.

"I didn't leave anyone behind," I admit, speaking coldly. "Adam, maybe. He'd have been okay without me. I only went back for him because you suggested I should. And I never made friends at the hotel. I was always the outcast. I learned not to trust anyone after what happened with Joey. The girls I was friends with back then sold me out because they were jealous, simple as that."

"It's a terrifying world out there," he whispers. "But London is London. There's nowhere else like it. The people are as hard as nails. You've got to fight for everything."

"That's why I left, I was done." I look back on all that now like it wasn't even really me. "I had nothing to stay for. I'd always planned to leave for France, so I did."

He smiles, pleased I got away and left. "You thrived."

"Your money helped."

He shakes his head, vehement about something. "You'd have been okay if not. I know you would have. You'd have had a whole chain of hotels by now. I know it."

"So, you left me the money to ease your guilt?"

He doesn't deny it, but doesn't admit to it, either. "I said, didn't I? It was an insurance policy. I didn't know what might happen."

I suppose I should be thankful he trusted me that much—to give me all that money.

I flip the card over and this time it's chicken marinated in some gloopy sauce.

"Yes please!" I exclaim—chicken being my favourite.

I'm lulled into a whole new level of food heaven... and all Ruben can do is watch and grin.

Chapter Twenty-One

Further Inside

Ruben and I leave the restaurant a couple of hours later to be greeted by a veritable street party, people dancing and singing, a band playing in someone's doorway. The crowds are so thick, nobody so much as gives us a glance.

Ruben takes my waist and dances me in the street. I wrap my arms around him and let him practically carry my weight as we sway and jiggle about, the music's fast rhythm sending the revellers into a frenzy.

"Is it like this every night?" I cry in his ear.

"Every night," he tells me.

This place gives me hope that some societies do place love and joy above all else. Art, music, theatre and nature... children, dancing, the freedom to express... and passion for life itself.

Ruben kisses me without a hint of shame, almost sweeping me right off my feet, his insistent lips reminding me who's the physically stronger of us. My heart is thundering in my chest when he laughs and scoops me up against him, asking, "Who's your man, baby?"

"You are, dirty fucker."

"Yeah, I am."

We get lost in the moment, the world spinning around us at a million knots in every colour of the rainbow. Some people are full-on samba dancing, some are gyrating at one another so hard, they're practically fucking... and others are just drinking cocktails and laughing with friends on the periphery, like this scene is entirely normal and there couldn't be a better time to discuss world peace or the opening of a new art exhibition.

Eventually, Ruben drags me away and I'm hoping he's taking me back to the car because these shoes are killing me and I'm sloshed from all the wine and frenetic dancing.

He takes me down a quiet alleyway, pushes me against the wall and squats in front of me. His eyes dare me to object, to push him off, but I'm as caught up as he is and I can't see beyond his face... and it's such a pretty face... all I want is him.

He swiftly hikes up my skirt and pushes his face firmly between my legs.

I try to grip the wall—anything—but it's impossible. Nothing can help me. I'm already so aroused by life, that his touch is merely taking me over the edge of the precipice I was already balancing on.

I cry out in the street, chest heaving, disappointed when it's over so quickly.

He takes his fill of my essence before regaining his feet.

He pulls me into his arms and holds me close as he tells me forthrightly, "Your cunt is life, Freya. When I taste you, I know life. From the moment we met, I knew one day, I would taste you. I never doubted it. Ever. I knew I would have you, one day, it was just a matter of time." He kisses me tenderly, strokes his hands across my cheeks and smiles. "I saw the look in your eyes when we were dancing and I knew you'd be so wet and so sweet. I can always tell when you're wet and it drives me crazy." He pushes the hair back from my face and whispers, "We're going to go home now and make love all night. Do you have any complaints?"

"Not one."

"I knew you wouldn't. Every day I can read you easier. Every day I'm getting further inside you."

I wrap my arms tight around his neck and kiss him messily. Carefree. Rampant. It's not pretty. We break apart breathless, hoarse.

He pulls my buttocks towards him so I can feel the huge erection inside his trousers.

"Let's get home as quickly as possible," he chuckles, and we run down the alley, finding our car parked on the street as we reach the end of it.

Just like in a movie, I decide—our getaway vehicle ready and waiting, magically just there.

WE POUR IN THROUGH the door in fits of giggles, some of the locals as we drove home making us laugh as they danced, sang, urinated or chased after a partner in the street. It's half past one in the morning and I have no idea where the time went tonight.

Ruben locks the door and pushes me up against the wall, lifting my skirt. He digs his hands into my bum cheeks and growls, "You're so fucking hot, woman."

He only drank a glass and a half of wine, so I'm inclined to believe him.

I tip my head back to give him my throat and he kisses my skin, licks it, thoroughly worshipping my neck and jaw. He lifts me up and I wrap my legs around his waist. He's walking towards the bedroom at the same time as lifting my dress. I help him with it and it pulls off, then I drop it to the floor, wherever it falls.

We arrive in the bedroom and he kicks his shoes off before lowering me to the bed and kissing my mouth, giving me no time to breathe. How can it be that we're endlessly hungry like this? I wrap my hands around his head and kiss him back as passionately as he's kissing me.

He surrounds my breasts with his hands and kisses my nipples softly, the occasional tug making me cry out and shudder. I untuck his shirt from his jeans and sneak my hands up his back, gripping his muscles as he plays with my breasts. My nipples harden and point in his direction, the ache inside them almost painful, but outweighed by the pleasure.

When he comes back to kiss my mouth, I slip my fingers between his buttons and open his shirt, pushing it off him. I spread my legs open and our kisses are fraught and wild as we rock together, his cock still trapped inside his trousers, hard against my belly. I almost come as just the edge of his jeans brushes against my clit.

He takes a moment to breathe and stares down into my eyes, my hands on his shoulders, his on my face.

"Freya, be my wife?"

"Forever."

He starts to fall apart, his face twitching with emotion, but I slide my hands down his stomach until finding his waistband, tugging open the button and sliding down the zipper.

"Commando," I breathe, his hot cock pushing out to meet my waiting hand.

"Just for you."

I kick his jeans down at the same time as wrapping my hand around his length. He pushes his hips in and out of my grip, groaning, precum sticking to my fingers.

"Baby, are you ready for tonight's lesson?" I ask, and he gives me a dark look. "You'll like it, I promise."

"Do I get to come inside you?" He licks his lips. "Because I'd really like to do that soon."

I bite my lip and chuckle. "Maybe. Why don't you lie down, honey?"

He does as I bid him and I lie on top of him, his thick, hard cock lovely and prominent against my belly. I could mount him now and ride us both to the most delirious orgasm... but tonight, I want more.

"Is this the night we're officially engaged?" I ask, pressing my fingers to his cheeks, his hands wandering all over my back as we stare at one another. His green eyes seem to be full of fire... and the room is mostly dark aside from a glow coming in from outside, the curtains and blinds open. The private pool just beyond the window is cut off from any of our neighbours and isn't at all lit, but it is Rio's light pollution casting a haze over everything.

His avid stare sends butterflies careering around my belly and he sounds breathless. "That'll only be once I have that ring on your finger, and we need to go back to France for it. Paris, to be exact."

I groan and brush my nose against his, wriggling my stomach against his cock.

"But we're celebrating something tonight, my love?" I kiss his throat, smelling his gorgeous masculine scent—woody and spicy—driving me wild, to the point where I feel myself clench.

I kiss the pronounced muscles in his neck and lick the dips beneath his clavicle.

"Let's celebrate every day," he tells me.

I tug his nipple between my teeth and he hisses, grabs my hair and pulls.

"We're going to do it differently tonight, my love. Take my lead, okay?" I murmur, seeking his agreement.

"We'll see."

I lift my head and look at him, warning him to behave. "Trust me?"

"I trust you," he says, conceding.

I kiss his body, the muscles of his chest and stomach. I kiss his hips, my hands stroking his sides. I kiss his cock lightly, lick his balls, encourage him to turn over so I can lick the dimples in his back. I bite his bum, kiss him all over his gorgeous back. I lie on top of him, kissing the nape of his neck, my pussy so wet I seep onto his backside.

I get him up on his knees and sit behind him. I rub my hands over his chest, massage his shoulders and soothe my breasts by pushing them into his back.

My hands and mouth never stop. I worship his body and he loses himself, his eyes shut, groaning with every touch. I kiss his neck, his ears, his shoulders, stroking my hands up and down his abdominals and pecs until I can tell he's getting impatient.

When I move and lie on my back, he starts a slow trail of kisses all over my body. Not one inch goes un-kissed and I prickle all over with desire, trembling and almost unable to deal with the emotion he evokes. He's shifting into position, ready to make love to me, when he rests his erection on my stomach instead and looks down into my eyes, his hands surrounding my cheeks.

"I loved you the night we met, I will never stop loving you, Freya," he tells me, emotion thick within his voice. "No man has ever loved another woman more, I promise you. Everything I did was to protect you. It killed me to leave. It wrecked me. It was the single most wretched, most painful... the hardest thing I have ever done." He kisses me gently, finding some relief in being able to, though the memory still hurts... bad. "I couldn't leave you now, even if I tried. We're in too deep this time, my darling. So damn deep. We're one. From tonight, we're one. Say it, Freya. Say it."

I'm shaking all over and bursting with need. My insides ache beyond anything I've ever felt before. I feel entirely hollow and empty. My pelvic bone feels more pronounced somehow, my body deprived of him, gaping and painful.

"We're one," I gasp.

Ruben pushes inside me and I scream, pull at my hair and arch dramatically. I can't help this... whatever it is coming... I can't stop it.

With every lunge inside me, he groans and grunts, unashamed... voicing his delight loudly. Every stroke of his cock inside my swollen belly makes me cry out and I rock with him, taking all of him, never quite getting enough.

"Oh god, Frey, oh god," he moans, "holy fucking god, Frey... FREYA!"

"God, hold on, hold on, Ruben! Fuck, I'm gonna come so hard... so fucking hard!" I grit my teeth and watch as he gets on his knees and holds my legs wide open. We watch his cock fully swallowed into me each time, my body so prepared for his, our extended foreplay making this possible. I can feel the surge of pleasure pushing its way up out of my depths and into my clit and pussy...

Electricity slingshots up and down my back and legs until I gasp, paralysed, when everything that's been slackened suddenly tightens and grips him with a force I've never experienced before... gripping and gripping until there's no more room, the clenching only stopping once I'm sure he's become part of me.

He loses his momentum and I'm drowned, utterly boneless and moaning, over and over, as he spills into me, his cock throbbing with multiple bursts of pleasure. He faceplants in the pillow beside me and we roll over so we're side by side. His breathing is ragged and uneven and I can't even remember my own name.

He shakes his head, trying to get back his vision or something, his legs starting to tremble, his arms seeking me out, pulling me in close, seeking the comfort of my body.

I kiss his mouth gently and he watches my eyes as I stroke my hands over his neck and continue dotting kisses all over his beautiful face.

Ruben slips carefully out of my body and it's horrible and I hate it, even though he looks relieved. We stare at one another for a long time, not sure if that really did just happen or not.

"Nothing means anything without you," he tells me, his lip trembling.

"I hate it when you cry. Don't," I tell him, "unless it's over something very, very sad."

He laughs through tears. "I love you so much, Freya."

"I know, sweetheart. I know."

I roll on my back and he rests his face against my shoulder, little tears rolling across my chest.

"The sun will be up soon," he murmurs.

"I know."

"We should sleep."

I stroke his head and whisper, "Grow this back long, but not the beard. The beard's gone."

"Why?" he asks, chuckling.

"It hides your beautiful face and when you give me oral pleasure, I like the feeling... I can tell when it's your mouth touching me now. It's magical."

"You're magical," he says, still shaking a little. "You're the special one, Freya—"

"Hush, baby."

"No, I really mean it. I knew it the moment you first spoke to me. I knew you were special." He looks at me, pained and anguished. "I was so in love with you within a few weeks and I... I knew you could get hurt. I held off. You held off. You being you, you must've sensed there was something I was holding back." I nod I agree; couldn't agree more, in fact. "I didn't have time to plan once we finally couldn't hold back any longer. What happened, happened, because I didn't have much time. We got together, it was unplanned, I was terrified... Even now we're back together, after all this time, I still don't know how safe we are, Frey. The silence frightens me... I'm not used to it. For all we know, everyone has forgotten about us. I don't know. But I promise, whatever happens, it'll be us, facing it together."

I nod my head and feel the backs of my eyes get hot. "That is all I want."

"You've got it."

Chapter Twenty-Two

A Trap?

Another morning, another delightful surprise... to be waking up next to him. However, this morning when he wakes, he looks hungrier than ever. We start kissing and I'm almost lost... when my body suddenly sends a signal to my brain, telling me I'm too exhausted for this.

"Ruben, stop," I ask, and he pulls up.

"What, baby?" He trembles, concerned.

I push him off me. "I'm sore and achy."

I shift off the bed quickly and waddle towards the bathroom to empty my bladder which feels heavy and wrung out, too.

"I'll just rub it then, shall I?" he shouts through.

"Rub it and see how painful I can make life for you. I get none, you get none. It's the deal, remember?" I'm cursing my frail human body, which can only take so much.

It got so mental last night. I mean, he licked me out in an alleyway! It's not that I haven't done risqué things before... but with Ruben, I can't ever be quiet and anyone could've heard. Plus, it's never been about almost getting caught for us. Prior to last night, our lovemaking has always been in private, aside from him continually trying to grope me in public, that is.

I wander back into the bedroom and see he's plumped up the cushions behind him. He pats the bed and grins as he watches me pull knickers out of the drawer and pull them on.

"No fun," he groans.

I leap onto the bed and into his arms. We're kissing again and he doesn't complain. After I've had enough, I pull the duvet over us both and rest my head on his chest.

"You all right, angel mine?" he asks.

"Never better, honey."

"You look absolutely beautiful this morning."

"Thank you."

He plays with my baby hairs and kisses my forehead.

"What shall we do today?" he asks, drumming his fingers against my back.

"I'm sore and bone-tired. How about you bring the TV in here and we eat breakfast in bed, then watch a film?"

"Hmm, sounds good."

"And eat all the bad stuff later on..."

"Hmm," he whispers.

"And cuddle, all day."

"Sounds awful, let's do it!"

WE JUST WATCHED *Venom* and Ruben keeps trying to get me to admit I fancy Tom Hardy, the same as every other girl.

"I don't. I just don't."

"Yeah, but... come on... a little."

I throw popcorn at him and scoff, "Come on, then? Who's your celebrity crush?"

"Don't have one," he mumbles, "never have time to read the rags or watch TV."

I tip my head back and laugh. "Oh my god."

"Anyway, evidently I fancy strange women... because I found the only woman not attracted to Tom Hardy!"

I slap his shoulder and he shrinks away.

"He's just... I don't know. I've never been into that sort of physicality. I like leaner men. I don't know. Like you."

He taps his lips. "But you wanted me to beef up again?"

"Nah, I never said that," I argue, snickering behind my hand. "I said I wanted the brutish guy. It's a way of being, not a look. The man I fell in love with will do just fine." I reach up and kiss his forehead. "But, I don't know..." I settle back on my side of the bed and eat more popcorn. "I can appreciate his acting. I loved him in *Peaky Blinders*. Total class act. But fancy him?"

"Hmm..." He looks at me, perplexed. "So, you do watch TV and you do read the rags... there must be a celebrity crush of some sort you're not telling me about."

"Why so interested?" I laugh, highly amused. "You can't be jealous of a competitor that doesn't exist?"

He shrugs his shoulders. "It's not that at all, Freya. It's normal for people to have crushes. I don't mind. Would you mind if I had a crush?"

I toss a bit of popcorn into my mouth and give him a look that says, yes, fuck yes, I would mind. I'm a jealous woman and I'm incredibly possessive of him. All other women better beware. And men, too.

"Unless of course, it's a weird crush. I know some women have weird crushes they can't explain sometimes."

Man, he keeps trying to dig, doesn't he?

I have to think hard. A crush. A crush? When did I last have a crush?

"I suppose I've always quite liked Adrien Brody. And weirdly, Clint Eastwood. More his *Bridges of Madison County* turn. And, oh, yeah... Hugh Jackman, a bit of Keanu, I suppose... maybe a little Adam Driver. I don't know what it is, I like men with strong noses. With black hair or dark brown. And the types who are really successful at what they do but also quietly very kind and generous. And the brooding types. I mean, if you'd like me to think a bit harder—"

"Okay, you've made your bloody point!" he laughs, hard. He sits absorbing what I just said. "Isn't Clint a bit old for you?"

I shake my head. "Okay, yeah, *now* he's too old for me... but I'm talking about when he was, you know, young and stuff... I mean..." I start daydreaming a bit and he shakes his head, wishing he'd never asked. I hold in a chuckle.

"Well, I suppose Jessica Chastain is all right," he says, his lip curling, "and maybe, oh well, maybe that other redhead... can't remember her name, though!"

I shoot him daggers. "Are you saying you like redheads? Because I'm not fucking redheaded, here."

He holds his hands up. "I forgot! Scarlett Johansson!"

I throw my head back, pretending to be mortified. "Perfect!"

I fall about laughing and he climbs across the bed, kisses my mouth and murmurs, "What shall we do now?"

"I don't know. Should we make dinner?"

"Or order in?"

"GOD, YES!" I cry. "PIZZA! All the damn pizza. Get everything."

"Okaaaaay," he whispers under his breath, taking up his phone and searching for a pizza place. "I'll get everything."

While he's ordering, I go about looking for my phone and eventually find it in the living room. I'm surprised to discover I have a message from Adam.

Please call when you get this. No biggie x

Ooh, interesting.

I hop back to the bedroom and wait for Ruben to finish ordering before I show him the message and let him know, "Just gonna give him a quick call. It's not that late there."

I dial Adam on WhatsApp and he picks up fairly quickly. Owing to my current state of undress (dressing gown, knickers and nothing else, plus matted hair on top of my head) I'm glad I'm only audio calling him.

"Frey, how's it going? Glad you've called."

"All right, little brother. It's going all right. We were all over Santa Teresa the other day. Then we ate barbecue meat last night. You'd have absolutely loved it!"

"Wow, sounds like you're loving it out there." He seems a little down about that.

"How are the dogs?"

"Oh, fat and happy! Think I've been feeding them too much. I'm knocking down their rations now, don't worry!"

"Ah, they conned you into thinking they were starving..."

Ruben rolls his eyes, scrolling through films on Netflix.

"Something like that," he coughs. "Listen, the reason I got in touch... everything is okay, don't worry... but somehow, I don't know how, word got out about Ruben's debut collection and we've had an offer."

"WHAT?" I explode with confusion and Ruben looks at me, concerned. "An offer?"

"Yep, I mean, I have no idea how it got out. You said I wasn't to sell, at least for the time being. So, I haven't even... I said nothing to nobody, trust me. And, they've been in storage and nobody goes in there but us. And the only other person—"

"Fucking Alexia," I murmur.

"Could be," he says, "I rather think it could be. But listen, do you want to hear the offer?"

"May as well, though we're not going to—"

"Five million euro," he gasps, "for the wood panels, the sculpture, everything. An anonymous buyer. The broker contacted the gallery. I couldn't believe it, either."

"Okay, hang on, Adam..." I put him on hold because Ruben's face has turned white. "You heard that?"

"Umm," he mumbles.

I take it from his expression, he's not pleased by this news.

I take Adam off hold.

"Adam?"

"Still here," he says.

"Are you sure you didn't tell anyone about Ruben's work?"

"I'm positive."

"You didn't get drunk and you didn't spill the beans—"

"Even if I had, how would this person know the details of the pieces? How many panels there are and the carving, too. They listed them individually in their offer... and I swear, I haven't put out a brochure or photographed them. Nada."

I bite my lip and see Ruben, hunched over, shaking his head and thinking how it could have...

"Don't do anything, Adam. It's late where you are. I'll call you tomorrow, okay?"

"Sure, no worries. It'd be helpful to know what to say next time they call. It's currently every day. But I haven't wanted to disturb you on holiday. I thought it was maybe a prankster or something... but then I... I don't know, Frey."

"Don't worry, I'll... we'll... have a think. I'll get back to you. Take care, Adam."

"Speak later."

I ring off and watch Ruben. He appears disturbed, more than anything.

"Get my mother on the phone," he asks, his fury palpable, "now!"

"It's late there... can't we...?"

"Now," he demands.

I dial Alexia next and it's ringing out for ages before she picks up, croakily answering, "Freya?"

"Sorry, Alexia. Sorry. Ruben asked me to call."

"Oh? What's... what time is it?"

"It's not late here. We're in Brazil. Is it late there?"

"Oh, god, I don't know," she says, "probably."

Sounds like we're going to get a lot of sense out of her at this time of night... when she doesn't even seem to recognise time anymore.

"I have to ask, Alexia. Did you tell anyone about Ruben's art? He's had a rather substantial offer for his pieces. It's come anonymously, through a broker."

She cackles, almost. Then, it's a rather flat, "No."

"Are you sure, Alexia? What about... when it was all transported?"

"I didn't tell anyone. Ruben had already crated the pieces before he flew out to you and then I came a little later. I only told a couple of friends in Nice that I thought Ruben might follow in my footsteps, but I didn't confirm anything substantial. It was just a passing comment. Small talk. Nothing more."

So, how could this anonymous buyer know the ins and outs of what it is Ruben has created?

"You're absolutely certain, Alexia? If you're sure, then this potentially means Adam has gone behind my back. And you know I'll have to punish him. After everything we've been through..."

"Freya. Listen. To. Me. I watched my boy suffer. For four long years. So, I know about why he created that art and about the place inside him it came from. I don't care what you think of me. Or what he thinks, for that matter. Because, inside, I know I am not a monster. Nor am I in need of any cash. Nor is Ruben. Nor am I desperate to brag about him. So, maybe you should look closer to home, huh? Maybe you should."

She unceremoniously hangs up and I feel like I've been told.

I wait for Ruben to say something, but when he doesn't, I reach over and touch his hand.

"What do you think, baby?"

He turns to me and smiles sadly. "Let the little fucker sell it."

My immediate reaction is to panic. "No! No! They picture me, Ruben! ME! They're private!"

He shakes his head, eyes narrowed and full of contempt. "We know they're you. Nobody else does. Besides, they're of a person you used to be. Long ago. We're starting out again, and my vision of you has changed... deepened. Let him sell them. Let him prove whether he's loyal. Let them come at us, whoever *they* are, Freya. We can't keep living in the shadows. We won't."

I'm shocked and throw my hands up. "Where the hell has this come from? What about the portrait of Laurent? And the one of your mother? I don't understand how you could part with any of them!"

"We've come halfway around the world to escape everything and it just doesn't go away, does it? We take it with us. All we've done since we got here is talk about the past. Maybe it's time to let go of the past, let it all fall away and start fresh. Enjoy our time here, yes, but then... decide on the life we mean to live and live it. I won't hide anymore, Freya. Whatever may come, let's just try to live, shall we? I'm tired of it."

"I don't understand—"

"What are you afraid of?" he asks, coming closer and taking my hand, then bringing it to his lips.

I look up and into his eyes, holding his cheek. "I'm afraid Adam's like him... and I'm afraid you've set him a trap."

Ruben nods his head, smiling but not happy. "I wish I had, Freya. Oh, I wish I had."

Chapter Twenty-Three

Botanical Secrets

Days pass and I feel that as they do, I understand what Ruben is thinking less and less. I've tried to provoke him into coming clean about his true feelings on the matter of his work being sold, but he's not budging.

We've now done a lot of touristy things like the Museum of Modern Art and the Museum of Tomorrow. We easily spent a day at each when it was raining and the best way to spend our time was indoors. I like how bright everything is in Brazil... how airy... spacious... yet compact.

Today, because the weather is better, we've driven over to the city's Botanical Gardens and I've fallen in love with the place. It's magical, a world of its own. A divine space. Such lush green trees and plants of all varieties. I discovered when I was living in Nice how much of a gardener I am. Here, I can lose myself wandering around, absorbing the elements; the ponds and streams and fountains; the trees and animals the only things making a sound; the city as though non-existent.

It's tranquil and I feel like I need that, more than ever.

Ruben and I find a quiet bench beneath a canopy of trees, taking shade before exploring the orchid house. From where we're sitting, we can see the famous 'Christ the Redeemer' up in the distance. This place couldn't possibly get any more pleasing on the eye.

I take his hand and kiss his cheek. "Are you okay, bubba?"

"I'm okay," he murmurs, guarding himself.

He puts his arm around me and I cuddle into his side. His lips find my temple and I sigh with relief. Moments like this are all that really matter.

"You're bored," I tell him.

"You're happy, so it doesn't matter."

I laugh in his ear and bite his lobe gently. "Fair enough."

Ruben turns on the bench and searches my eyes, places his hands on my cheeks and moves in to kiss me. I close my eyes and let him transport me to an even more otherworldly place while he presses his lips to mine, gently slips his tongue under my top lip and then seals our kiss, taking me until I'm breathless. When he pulls away, he's happier and grinning at the look on my face.

"Fine, it's not bad here," he says, struggling not to look pleased with himself. "I can handle it."

We sit on the bench letting the sounds of nature entertain us, which is in stark contrast to all the loud noise beyond the garden gates, which we've been told all our whole lives is the real entertainment.

I can handle this better than any night on the tiles.

"I forget sometimes you're a city boy."

"I forget you're a country girl."

"I am," I admit, scrunching up my nose. "Which means it might be difficult to find somewhere we both want to settle."

"Can't we settle back in Nice? You like it there, don't you? Up in the hills. Away from it when you're tired. Close enough when you went to get stuck back in."

"True." I wrap my arms around his shoulders. "But do you like Nice?"

"Yes."

"You wouldn't rather live in Paris?"

His nose twitches. That means yes. However, he shrugs it off. "I did survive in the country with Mother for four long years. Trust me, Nice is fine. But a little apartment in Paris, too... I'm not going to say no."

"Oh, okay. That sounds doable. I can deal."

"There's no rush. No rush at all," he whispers, leaning back against the bench and sighing, his eyes closed.

I stare at him while he relaxes. He seems... what's the word? Resolved? Resigned? I'm not sure which. He's also very beautiful, the sunshine having kissed his skin again. His hair is growing back but his face is still smooth. I am even more madly in love with him than I was yesterday.

"About the sale..." I begin, watching as his smile immediately fades.

"I don't want to talk about it."

His bad temper is back, then?

"Not at all?"

"Nope," he says, being short with me.

"But we don't know who the buyer is. Yes, he agreed to your inflated price..." Eight million euro, no less. "What is this person going to do with your pieces? And you're an unknown in the art world. Aren't you scared this is some weirdo? Some wealthy stalker?"

"Freya," he sighs, still with his eyes closed, "all I'm thinking right now is that I can't wait to get you back home later. And that I love you very much. And that when you wear a dress it drives me bananas. Especially when I can see the lace bit of your bra poking out."

I look down at my bit of lace poking out and giggle. "Oh, well, I'm so sorry..."

He chuckles and pulls me close. "Just shut up and listen to the damn birds."

I do as he says and enjoy the moment. When else am I going to be sitting in such a beautiful garden with such a handsome man, so in love and looking forward to spending the rest of my life with him?

"I love you," I murmur.

"I know you do," he whispers, sighing.

THE SALE TAKES PLACE. Of course, neither of us is there to bear witness, but I'm sitting in bed with my laptop the day I know the sale will happen (morning here, but afternoon there). I see the money go into the business account and virtually within seconds, Adam is calling me on FaceTime.

I pick up and he looks in shock.

"Fucking hell," he laughs, sounding nervous.

"I saw."

"I know technically I didn't make this sale because they approached us, but I was wondering..."

"Yes, you can take your commission."

His little face lights up. "God, thank you sis! I can probably put a deposit down on my own place now. Fuck, yeah!"

I choose to believe he's sincere. I do. I pray he's honest... I pray... and I pray.

"Where are you?" I ask.

"Oh, god, I'm in the back," he says, nervous laughing. "I called because I'm shitting my pants. I packed everything the way you said, just the way, with all the paper and covers and stuff, but I'm just shit scared."

"First off, Adam. These are brand-new pieces. Just because we sold them for millions doesn't mean they need the same treatment as the older stuff. Besides, chill out. I'm sure whoever bought them will be inspecting them before they ship. Trust me. I would be."

"Yep, yeah. You're right." He shakes it off, rolling his shoulders. "Just nerves. We've never had such a big sale. Have we? Can you remember?"

"Nope, never. It's mental, Adam. I know how you must be feeling. But just chill."

"Okay, and how is Ruben? What's he think of it all?" He's so eager to find out, but little does he know...

"Ruben?" I laugh, scratching my head. "He's out running this morning. He refuses to talk about it. I don't know."

Ruben doesn't understand how talented he is. He doesn't want to know. However, it's more than that. I don't think he believes it. I don't. I think he's sceptical of someone wanting to pay so much for his work.

"The dogs miss you," he says, pouting, "really bad."

"Still sleeping in your bed with you?"

"Yup. Sooty's farts have me going online to look up hazmat suits. If I have a girl over, I'll have to lock them downstairs in the laundry room or something."

I laugh down the line. "Poor Adam."

"Listen, I'll call you for a more in-depth chat, maybe at the weekend? The broker is waiting outside. I don't want to keep them waiting too long."

"I trust you, Adam. Everything will be fine."

"Awesome, well, catch you later."

He's gone and I chuckle to myself. This is the Ruben Kitchener effect. Sure, my gallery has seen some special sales, now and again, but we've mainly operated as a discoverer of up-and-coming talent—and newbies rarely sell for as much as Ruben's first work. I didn't start a gallery to make money because I don't need any more; I started out because I wanted to help artists have a space in which to exhibit. I've often gone above and beyond to give them space if I've liked their work.

While I'm on the laptop, I put most of the sale money in Ruben's account and leave a bit in the business account for Adam to take his cut and also cover costs to the gallery. I don't know how much money Ruben has in his bank account, but I'm betting a few million more won't make a massive difference. I found out the other night when we visited the *churrascaria* why they were bending over backwards to do everything and anything to keep us waited on, literally hand and foot—Ruben is a big tipper and put the equivalent of 2,000 euros in the tip jar which is a lot of money for the people here.

I'm in the kitchen opening a bottle of champagne to make mimosas when I hear Ruben pull up in the car outside. Funny, I thought he was going for a run.

He enters the house and I shout, "In here."

He comes in bare-chested and sweating, his skin red and glowing, still out of breath. His discarded vest is hanging off his waistband.

"Where have you been?" I chuckle, fanning myself.

"Oh, I went down to the beach."

"And you're still out of breath?"

"I ran down the beach for miles... and back. It's hard-going."

I grin and hand him a mimosa. "Not sure you should be drinking this but you just made eight million this morning, honey. So, cheers!"

He throws back his drink and stamps his empty glass on the counter. "I'm hitting the shower. Fuck, that was good!"

"The run, I assume?"

"Fuck, yeah!"

While he's showering, I throw some eggs in a frying pan and make an omelette with onions, coriander, tomatoes and goat's cheese. Ruben is out of the shower and has a towel wrapped around his waist by the time it's cooked.

"I'm hoping that's for me."

"Yep, want some coffee too?"

"Wouldn't say no."

I continue sipping my mimosa while I serve him, and as he eats, I help myself to yoghurt and fresh fruit, honey and a few chunks of granola.

"What are your plans today?" he asks, because for the past few days—since the Botanical Gardens—I've been gallery hopping while he's wanted me out of the house so that he can paint in peace (his words, not mine).

"I'm going to the mall today," I tell him. "What about you?"

"More painting," he says, not elaborating.

"Okay." I only hope he is painting and not spending his time doing something else.

"What do you need from the mall?"

I purse my lips. "That would be telling."

"Seriously, you have a lot of stuff already."

"So? It's our responsibility when visiting countries like this to put something into their economy. Besides, all my clothes don't suit Rio. They suit charity galas or gallery openings or little trips to Paris to meet new people and do research. Rio is different. So, I need different clothes. My kaftans are only meant for lounging around the house in so I need a few newer looser fitting things that are more suitable for the climate here. You wouldn't understand."

He laughs, then heads to the sink to wash his plate, his food having mysteriously disappeared somewhere when I wasn't looking, it seems. "This isn't the woman I first met. Your wardrobe extended to one or two skirts, remember?"

"I remember."

He kisses my head on his way back to the bedroom to get dressed. "I'd like a new shirt. I can't remember when I last got one. I'll write down my measurements for you. Anything bold, but not wacky. And if they need to alter and deliver it, use a pseudonym and pay in cash."

"All right then, boss." I wink, and he goes into the bedroom to get dressed.

I ENJOY A STARBUCKS before getting started at the Rio Sul shopping mall—feeling almost lame for going with the obvious choice—but sometimes, you just need to taste something familiar. I can't remember how many days we've been in Brazil, but the sight of a Starbucks drew me in and I couldn't escape its tractor beam, feeling as if I've been away from Europe for months. I promise myself not to give in to either of the fast-food restaurant chains in residence here come lunchtime, even knowing I can't a hundred per cent uphold that promise.

It feels great to be out and about without Ruben. I always miss him when we're apart but I'm a nobody on my own. I don't matter. These people passing by don't care who I am. I'm just a woman in cut-off jeans and a t-shirt with my hair wild and a headband holding it back. I'm not wearing any make-up and I'm pulling a roller case around to put my purchases in so I don't have to carry them.

Smelling the air, it's definitely still Rio, with so many different flavours. Still, the fragrance stores remind me of home... assaulting all who pass by within twenty yards.

By home, I mean France. The UK hasn't been my home for quite some time now. I left. My life there spat me out and I only emerged from my chrysalis in the South of France and became who I am now. I'm not sure I'd recognise the people, or who I used to be and the life I used to live, if I went back to Old Windsor now. I think everything would look so different. Possibly smaller. They say that, don't they? That when you go back and face your demons after time away, old ghosts seem so much smaller than they used to—mine being my father, and I guess, the hotel hideout where I languished for so many years.

I take a deep breath and head into a beauty place. I could do with some new cosmetics.

SEVERAL HOURS LATER, my case is full and this is after going back to the car a couple of times to unload it. I had Italian for lunch earlier—a pile of spaghetti and meatballs—but it's almost evening now and I've sat down for a Burger King. I snap a picture and send it to Ruben, who replies: *BRING ME ONE HOME. OR ELSE.*

I'm quite frightened what he might do if I don't, which leaves me wondering... then he sends another message: *Love you. You've been gone hours? xxx*

Retail therapy. Will have this, then order one for you and jump in the car. Might be cold by the time I get back, depends on traffic xx

Don't fucking care. Get home asap. Miss you xxx

I send him a ton of emojis in response letting him know I love him and I've bought a lot of shit.

Feeling wretched after gorging on a fast-food burger, only because I already went to Carb City earlier today, I grab my over-spill of bags and pull my bulging case behind me, ordering an-other burger. The guys behind the counter are laughing and I tell them, "It's for my boyfriend! Any chance you could wrap it in foil?"

They shrug and mutter among themselves, like they don't be-lieve me... but they do indeed wrap it up in foil... and even dou-ble box it. As I'm waiting, I'm wondering if boyfriend is even the right word. Fiancé? Lover? Partner? Boyfriend seems such a ju-venile term, really. There needs to be an alternative once you're dating a man thirty-five or over.

I race back to the car and realise I didn't even think to ask whether he wanted fries. Nah, he can get those anytime. I throw in my bags and case, rounding the vehicle until I'm in the front seat. I remember what Ruben said and put the child lock on right away because a woman on her own is not always safe abroad.

KARMA

I can't wait to show him all the things I bought for him. I just hope he's not one of those people impossible to shop for—never happy with anything anyone else buys him.

LIKE OUR PLACE IN NICE, this rented villa in Rio of ours has a bit of a driveaway, except mine back home is just paved and this one here has an actual circular fountain in the middle, I guess to encourage cars to park in an arc around it, leaving space for others to get in and out. I pull up but reverse back around the fountain and up towards the front door a bit so I can unload easier. Almost as soon as I have the car door open, Ruben is there. I get out of the vehicle in a hurry and he throws his arms around me.

"Uh, missed you." He squeezes me tight in his arms, then kisses my cheek on his way to my mouth, which he assaults for a good long while before giving me my freedom back.

"You did miss me," I gush, wondering why I sound so surprised. "And what about the taste of fast food? Did you miss that?"

I hand him the burger and he grins. "I'd help you bring the shopping in, but fuck that."

He dashes off with the burger to the lounge area and groans after unwrapping the foil.

"Is it still hot?"

"Barely warm... but it tastes so good!" he growls, smashing it into his mouth.

"Did you eat today?" I ask, wondering what he may have been up to.

"I went to the deli down the road and got a footlong. It was amazing."

I take a deep breath, studying him for a second as he gorges on a Burger King, even after already chomping down a footlong today. He's wearing sweats and a t-shirt slightly spattered with paint. I guess he changed his shirt at lunchtime to go out and that's why it's not fully gross. Fingers crossed he has only been painting today... and not getting himself into trouble.

I go back to the car and the boot door opens. I start bringing bags into the reception area and he's watching me with his head poking around the corner.

"Did you leave anything in that mall?"

"Potentially not!" I laugh.

By the time I'm done unloading, the floor in the entrance hall is covered in stuff and I'm having to step around things as I get back indoors, the car locked, then the front door slamming shut.

I take one very important purchase off the floor and head for the fridge with it. "I grabbed this just as I was heading out. It looks divine, right?"

There was this cake shop selling off full cakes at half price towards the end of the day and I couldn't resist a black forest cake, lathered in cream and black cherries and chocolate pieces.

"I'm having some of that next," he says, finishing his burger and swigging water from his sports bottle. I rather hope he's refreshed that since this morning. His tongue works around his mouth to clear bits of burger and salad out of his teeth, then he's on me again, trying to kiss and hug me.

We haven't been having as much sex the past few days because he won't talk about how he feels about the sale. I refuse to put out until he does.

"I booked us a table at this really nice place near the beach tonight," he whispers against my ear, rubbing my bum. "We're likely to be the least recognisable people there. Plus, they serve the best seafood around, so I read. No dodgy bellies tomorrow."

"Great, I can wear one of my new dresses." I'm so excited, giddy even. "Why don't I show you what I bought?"

"Why don't we... umm... you know."

I see from his face, he's suggesting we skip the fashion show and go straight to the sex show, instead.

"No, let me show you what I bought..."

He steps back and folds his arms. "Okay."

"Sit down then."

I start with the stuff he doesn't need to see, placing those bags on the sofa. "Make-up, creams, bath things, new flip flops and a load more sun cream."

"More sunblock. Yay." He chuckles to himself. "Woohoo."

"And these... are... all..." I gather up the stuff I bought for him, puffing and panting. "For you."

He looks scared when I place numerous bags at his feet. "What did you do, Freya?"

"Well, you won't come to the shop, so the shop will come to you. Come on, take a look! I've got all the receipts if you don't like something. Here, look in this one first..."

He opens the largest bag to discover seven new pairs of trunks. They're white. Calvin Klein. Perfect. Each has its own cardboard box, of course. I can tell he's trying not to react, staring down into the bag like he's got to make sure he's not seeing things.

"Okay, I caved, all right? The monks won't get fed this year."

"Oh...kay. You could've got me some more shitty ones," he snickers, unable to contain his amusement.

"Well, I bloody choked, okay? I choked. I had Starbucks as well today. So call me a brand whore, or whatever. But admit it, you do need them for running. I've seen the shorts you go out in. It's pornographic."

He covers his face, laughing his head off; it's so good to see him like this.

"Those poor monks," he exclaims.

"Wasn't going to make that mistake again."

He moves on swiftly, checking out the other things I bought him. A shirt I picked out this morning, one of my first purchases, which is fitted and his exact size. He takes it out of the tissue wrapping and starts unfolding it, pulling out the cardboard and pins. He pulls off his white t-shirt and pulls on his new shirt, which is long-sleeved, black and has a stylish white trim on the collar and cuffs.

"I think I could wear this tonight? What do you think? Just need to put it through a quick wash and iron it."

"You like it?" I wonder, though why he wouldn't—when the damn thing cost almost a thousand real—I don't know.

"I do, it's different, I like it... and it fits."

My, my... does it fit. It hugs his shoulders perfectly, tapers to the waist and gives his chest the chance to show off, being that it's fitted across that part of him.

He sits down and checks out what else I got him. Only jeans... new chino shorts... some polo shirts and a pair of round

320

sunglasses with retro side shields. His other glasses, I noticed the other day, are quite scratched, perhaps from overuse. Ruben tries on the glasses and looks at his own reflection in his phone screen.

"Wow. Couldn't have done better myself. And how did you know my other sizes?"

"I've washed your clothes enough times now, bubba. 34/34 is pretty easy to remember."

"Well, thank you!" he exclaims, actually happy, it would seem. "Why don't you show me what you got yourself now?"

"Nope, I don't think so." I shake my head, gathering up my six bags of clothes, and the other bags of toiletries etcetera. "You'll see one of my purchases at dinner, though... maybe two."

"Can't wait." He grins wildly. "Let me get these things in the wash and I'll join you in the bath... that's if you are bathing before tonight?"

"Sure. Listen, you've got room for dinner, then? Even after a footlong and a burger?"

"Sure, have you, though?" he goads, looking cocky. "We could... dine in."

"I'm sure." How I'm resisting him, I have no flipping clue, but I am.

I dash from the living room and take my bags into the closet. I can't keep this up. My cheeks are burning. My body is screaming for his but other things are more important... like getting to the bottom of his heart.

After stashing my new clothes, I walk into the adjoining bathroom and begin emptying my bags of toiletries. I start the taps on the bath, too and pour in bits of everything. I'll add a bath bomb towards the end. I arrange my new creams on the vanity, then take my new cosmetics and add them to my make-up bag, humming as I amuse myself.

Today I think I purchased the raciest underwear I ever bought. It is the dirtiest, filthiest thing I ever saw... and I will use it to get him to confess, even if it means risking my dignity... I don't care. But, later. Later. I'll deal with that... when the time comes.

Ruben comes wandering into the bathroom butt naked and heads for the toilet around the corner, nonchalant as you like. Damn him. Damn. Him.

I have a thought, and while his back is turned, I drop one of the bombs into the tub and pretend like I didn't do anything when he's strides back into the room.

"Is it ready to dunk myself in?" he asks.

I stare him up and down and decide he would waggle that thing around right in front of me if he thought it would make a blind bit of difference.

"Take the far end, I'll be with you any second."

He lowers himself into the big tub and almost leaps up when he feels something. "What did you put in here?"

"Ah, can you feel the fizzing?"

"It's right up my... up my..." He settles back, eyebrows raised, eventually deciding he's not that averse. "I kinda like it."

I remove my headband and place it on the vanity, then gather up all of my hair and tie it with a big scrunchie on top of my head so it's secure but not tight and heavy. The weight of my hair can give me a chronic headache sometimes.

I shimmy out of my cut-offs and t-shirt, throwing them in the direction of the laundry hamper. Then I wander around, searching for the make-up I'll use later... lining it up... picking out a nail colour. All the while I'm wearing the white lace set he loves. I can almost feel his throbbing cock... because I'm throbbing, too.

"Are you getting in, *fofo*?" he asks, sounding slightly annoyed.

I turn around and stand akimbo. "*Fofo?*"

"You've started calling me bubba all the time. I'm calling you *fofo*." He purses his lips.

"But I don't know what it means," I laugh, shaking my head. "It could mean anything."

"It really could," he says, throwing his head back laughing, "and right now it certainly applies."

I shake my head and take my underwear off, getting in at the other side of the tub. How I would love to know whether he's hard right now... but accidentally touching him with my foot would be much too obvious.

Wouldn't it?

"Does it mean fuck?" I ask, delighted the bubbles are covering my breasts and all he can see is my head. He turns the taps off and we have ourselves a luxurious bath for two. Even he is submerged apart from his head.

"Nope," he says, sniggering, "it's not sexual, at all. And nope, I'm not telling you what it means. But it's on the same level as bubba. So as long as you're calling me bubba, I'll be calling you *fofo*."

I manage to keep a straight face by looking anywhere but at him, but only just. He wants me to crack, I know that, but I won't. I can't.

"I'm glad you had fun today." I look up and he's gazing at me intently, still trying to endear me to his incessant demand, it would seem.

"It was fun."

"What about when we get home later, can we have even more fun, then?"

I wonder if to play the card... should I?

"Remember that time I tied you up?"

He looks up at the ceiling and grins. "Oh yeah."

"If you want me tonight, you'll be tied up."

"Oh, what are you going to do to me?" He tries to sound scared, but we both know not much scares him.

"Oh, it'll be your worst fucking nightmare," I reassure, tapping my lip with my index finger.

He wriggles his eyebrows. "I can't wait."

He hoists himself out of the bath and all I see as he leaves and grabs a towel is that his cock is beautiful, pink and warm from the bath. He licks his lips and saunters off, desperate to iron his new clothes, I bet... that's if I know him at all.

What I wouldn't give to slide my mouth over him when he's like that...

Fuck!

I reach over to the vanity unit, slide my hand into my bag of sanitary products and reach to the back for my vibrator. I have it beneath the water before he comes back in wearing his sexy-as-fuck new boxers. I quickly switch off the vibrator.

"What do you think?" he asks, twirling.

"Amazing." I try not to pant.

Jesus, the shape of him... the utter, utter sexiness of those legs...

"I'll keep them on, then," he says, like butter wouldn't sodding melt.

"Yep. Good. I would."

KARMA

He gives me a funny look, then leaves the room.
I recommence taking my frustrations out on the vibrator.

Chapter Twenty-Four

Beauty and the Beast

J ust along from Copacabana Beach, there's this lovely place called Marius Degustare. As you walk up you can tell they cater to an international clientele as there are flags of several countries hanging above the door. Inside, it's unusual. The décor is really hard to describe. It feels a bit like a witch's cave, or a pirate's lair, with all kinds of random things hanging from the ceiling like pans and nets. There are crystal-encrusted walls and columns that make you feel like you're dining underwater or something—the blue lighting adding to the effect. It's an experience, to say the least. It could be a crazy shipwreck we're eating in, or some very eccentric person's front room, with all sorts of reclaimed bits and pieces stuck to the walls and ceilings. It feels very *Beauty and the Beast* with the beautiful clock, but also *Alice in Wonderland* too with glasses and bottles stuck upside down. It's a mishmash of all sorts.

"Do you like it here?" Ruben asks, as I'm sipping some kind of blue cocktail.

"I do," I giggle, feeling trippy. "I like quirky places like this. It also feels a little more like what I'm used to from a South American restaurant."

We already went to the appetizer bar and filled our plates full of oysters and crab claws and mussels the size of my fist. It's raucous but not manic in here. It doesn't feel like there's any rush and I think each party has their table for the night, so there's nothing to get too excited about... except the fresh, exquisite food... to die for!

"I knew you'd like it here." He looks pleased with himself.

He's wearing the new shirt and his new black jeans and looks ridiculous. He shaved his hair again today, I noticed earlier, but left the top thicker than the sides. He put some product in the thick crop on top and looks sexier than ever now his hair is starting to grow back. And of course, he's utterly clean shaven. Which reminds me, I'm due to receive another clean shave from him myself. The last shave he gave me lasted so well, but I'm eager to be as smooth as silk again.

"You look gorgeous, *fofo*," he says, and a passing waiter grins as they zoom on by carrying a platter full of seafood delicacies.

"Do I?"

"You look stunning."

While I was out today, I bought something a little nice. It's one of those dresses you could imagine being high-end, but also easily coming off some woman's back-room sewing machine. But I love it. It is neither atelier nor dodgy, more middle ground—not cheap but not ridiculous, either. It's a one-shoulder, light-pink dress with ruffle detailing starting at the shoulder and crossing diagonally over the waist, then falling down to the midi skirt. It's not a sexy dress, nor is it stuffy. It's elegant and slightly flirty but not half as revealing as my naked dress, thus, I think, intriguing people more because they can imagine what is beneath. I paired the dress with some rose gold strappy sandals, of course.

And the ridiculous underwear I picked up earlier today is beneath... but Ruben doesn't know that yet.

"You don't look so bad yourself, you know." I can't help but stare at the way his throat looks in that shirt... the way his Adam's apple moves when he swallows.

I've hardly been able to take my eyes off him the entire time we've been in here. If I undressed him with my eyes any more, I'd be lying on the floor in a puddle, foaming from the mouth and needing treatment for overdosing on his masculinity. It's bad, isn't it? Really bad.

"I thought we could walk along the beach after dinner." He has that dreamy look in his eye. "Or maybe sit outside and have a digestif?"

"Whatever you like," I tell him, breezy my middle name. "And maybe we could talk about the fact you made a few million today."

He looks right at me but doesn't react whatsoever, his face frozen. Man, I need to learn how to do that.

"I told you, Freya. I don't have any thoughts on that. It's just a transaction. It's done and dusted with."

He says that, but...

I finish the crustaceans on my plate and give him a warning look. "So, what are you working on in the studio at the minute? And will you sell those? Or are they a pointless exercise, too?"

He takes a deep breath, his broad chest expanding to almost unsettling proportions.

"We could spend another day at the beach tomorrow, if you like? Grumari again, or maybe closer to home, like down here? But if we went somewhere quieter, I'd like to paint you... on the beach."

I shake my head at him. "Is this your attempt to sweet talk me? To play on my weaknesses."

"Yeah," he admits, without a hint of shame. "But, you know, sometimes, the art is just about having it out there. Earning from it or not, sometimes, you just have to have it out. That's all. And I did the job of getting it out onto those wood panels, months ago. The artist should always be moving onto something else, as it is in life. That's just how I am. Always moving forwards. Sure, this week I might be obsessed painting you naked... next week I might want you crying beneath the stars. So sue me if the artistic spirit is capricious."

I roll my eyes. "There are places you will hurt tonight and it'll be even sweeter to take pleasure from your pain."

His cheeks look rosy as he smiles grimly, wriggling his eyebrows.

He thinks he has the upper hand.

I won't allow that.

I lean forward in my seat and whisper, "I came twice just before we came out. Twice. In the bath."

He has a frozen expression again. He's not even a bit shocked or surprised. Damn him! He must've known what I was doing beneath the water. Perhaps it's time to go even dirtier.

I take out my phone and send him a picture, feeling very smarmy and entirely sure this will take him down. Oh, yes. If it doesn't, it'll eat my own hat.

I'm putting my phone back in my handbag just as his beeps. On his lock screen he must see enough to know he should really shield his device from prying eyes.

After he's seen what I've sent him, he takes a drink of water and swallows past whatever shock it is he's experiencing. I took the shot earlier in the closet in front of the mirror, seconds before sheathing myself in this dress.

"You're wearing that now? Right now?" he asks, still speaking as though parched.

"I'm not going to give you what you want until you give me what I want."

He puts his elbows on the table, stares at me and lets his jaw hang loose.

"You're crazy," he grunts.

"That's why you love me."

THE MEAL WAS EXTRAORDINARY and as we walk along the beach afterwards, I'm so grateful of the cool night air and the sand between my toes, my sandals long gone and being swung at my side.

Ruben is quiet, either contemplative or trying not to get himself in even more hot water. It was one of those meals where the food actually became the main topic of conversation—it was that good. Like the other evening, we enjoyed some of the finest cuts of steak (it's all about the meat down here), but to top it off, we enjoyed some of the most delicious lobster, squid and other assorted seafood dishes. I also made the most of the buffet, trying little bits of salad and cheese and fruit, not to mention paella.

Oh, and then the puddings... the puddings.

In truth, I don't know if either of us is up for fucking now. The meal was epic, and on top of all the other stuff we've eaten today, man oh man.

"Come on, let's take a minute," he says, falling on the sand and patting the space between his legs.

I sit down and we watch the waves roll in together, like we once did in Nice. I huddle inside his warmth and feel safe, his breath against my hair, his thighs outside mine, arms wrapped around my shoulders.

"You could never truly punish me, you know?" he whispers, between gusts of air whipping around us. "Except if you left and I never saw you again. The rest... it's just too much fun."

I lean back against his shoulder and twist my neck to look up at him. He twists slightly to look down at me, then cradles my chin in his hand and kisses me softly. Slowly. Until I'm fully enveloped by his embrace, his aura, his strength and his love.

We go back to staring at the sea.

"I could never leave you. To do so would be to cause myself injury."

"I understand that more than you imagine. I know you still can't fully grasp my decisions, but I truly know what you would feel if you had to leave me."

My lip trembles and I press my cheek to his chest. "I forgive you."

"If only I could forgive myself," he whispers, "but I'll settle for spending the rest of my life loving you. Making it up to you."

He wraps his arms tight around me and the waves mesmerize, hypnotize almost—something about the sea and the air and the space around us utterly calming. The smell of the beach is different here, still salty and earthy, but there's something exotic... something about the breeze containing all the different scents of the forests and flowers around here. Something about the cold and the warm often mingling, warring... something about the world feeling upside down but at the same time, the right way up, too. It's bizarre but seems to make perfect sense to me.

"You're really not going to talk about the sale, are you?"

"Nope," he whispers.

"Okay, then. Take me home now, please."

He helps me up and doesn't try to hide his disappointment when he sees the unsettled look in my eyes.

WE WALK THROUGH THE door and half of me wants to jump his bones and lose myself in all his nooks and crannies, wriggle my way into his embrace and never let go, while the other half of me is annoyed he won't talk about something so straightforward as the sale of his art. It baffles me. Aside from telling me to up the price of his work, he's said literally nothing about any of it. Even when I asked him earlier, "Did you check your bank balance yet?" – he shrugged in response and said, "It'll be there if you sent it," – like he didn't need to check. Like those seven figures mean nothing.

I'm wearing the most uncomfortable lingerie known to man. It's a bodysuit with absolutely no material. It's just straps. That's it. Straps. Meaning I'm nearly naked and there's nothing left to the imagination once I do get this dress off. I'm in a harness and everything is practically on show. I have two discreet nipple covers but my crotch has been exposed all night and I've had to keep my legs firmly closed or else. I was thankful my pink dress is lined or else anyone might have seen what I've got beneath.

"We could just... you know," he says, but I don't know what he means.

"I'm tired and lethargic from dinner."

I head to the bathroom and lock myself in. I don't want to waste this... but I don't want to fuck when I feel like he's hiding something from me.

It was one of the most incredible meals I've ever experienced and I really enjoyed tonight, but I can't switch off my instinct that something is wrong.

I take off the dress, wriggle out of the straps and remove the nipple covers, leaving everything piled on the vanity. I use the loo, wash my face, clean my teeth and then pull on my thick towelling robe and head for the bedroom. He's nowhere to be seen so I climb beneath the covers and let my red wine headache take over, pulling me beneath the surface... down and down and down, right to the bottom.

WHEN I WAKE, IT FEELS like I slept for years. Everything is so silent. There's just him, lying beside me, arms thrown over his head. White boxers. Legs slightly bent, head turned to the side and the sheets firmly kicked off. I don't know if he kicked them off or if I did. Maybe the robe was warm enough for me. Ruben rarely gets cold so he's not bothered about sleeping with no covers on.

I watch him for a little while. My lover. My life. He's so sickeningly handsome, with his neat jaw and tight cheekbones, high arched brows and big eyes, broad mouth and dark hair... tanned skin. The smell of his body... sleep and paint, the sea and his pheromones... I sigh. I'm desperate to wake him, for my face to be the first thing he sees, to witness his unadulterated reaction to waking up and seeing only me.

KARMA

God, those white underpants look glorious on his strong body. He's happy in sleep, a little erect and bulging against the crotch. Is he dreaming of me? Does he want the straps?

Or does he just want me? No drama. Just his woman, naked and his.

I look at the clock and see it's eleven a.m., so I slept in big style after getting home at one a.m. last night. But Ruben? I can't remember him coming to bed. So, maybe he painted and then came to bed later... because he never sleeps in like this. Ever. Or maybe this is the meal. It was extravagant and I was so full at one stage, I thought I might throw up. Thank goodness for the sea air.

Is this what it's like for him, usually? Does he sit here and watch me sleep, then get up and attend to his routines... whatever they are. A run, sometimes. A shower, I expect. A cup of coffee. A few minutes staring outside while he thinks about what he'll paint that day.

I slide my hand inside his boxers and he doesn't move. My hand is resting on his pubic hair but when I slide it further to touch his cock, he shifts around slightly, stirring. He feels warm and big in my hand and he isn't even erect yet.

Ruben's eyes are still closed so I use my free hand and untie the belt on my robe, slipping out of it easily being that it's so oversized, then snake down the bed until being level with his groin.

I lift my hand out of his pants and slowly inch down his waistband until his cock is resting on his belly. His eyes are still closed but I'm not stupid... he could easily be pretending to still be asleep, enjoying this little morning wake-up call without letting me know.

Licking his cock, he groans a little. Then I suck the head into my mouth. He wriggles around a bit—still no eye contact. I sink my mouth over him and he begins hardening all of a sudden, his head pushing against the inside of my cheek, then there's a hand in my hair and I look up, but his eyes are STILL closed.

I swirl my tongue around him, sucking, enjoying his natural, musky scent. He grows bigger and harder. Gently fondling his balls, I roll them in my hands and feel those tighten, too.

When I've tasted enough of him and got tired of trying to slacken my jaw, I move back up the bed until I'm level with his head and he whispers, "Why did you stop?"

"I'm just getting started."

I climb over him and rub my breasts all over his face. He slides his hands up and down my back, groaning. When he nips one of my nipples, I yelp, not expecting him to do that. I give him my throat and he kisses me softly, making my insides tighten and contract. Then he brings my face to his and kisses my mouth, plucking my lips with his, opening my mouth and drawing my tongue out.

Everything quickly gets crazy and I'm pulling the small crop of hair on his head. I have his lip between my teeth and he's grabbing my arse, trying to position me over his cock. I lean down and bite his chest, scratch my nails down his upper arms and flick my tongue over his nipple. At some point his strength wins and he positions me just right, holds his cock at my entrance... and we find one another.

I still and moan, sinking over him slowly, then all at once. I stare down into his eyes, shuddering.

"I love you, Freya," he tells me, his eyes so expressive.

"I love you, too."

KARMA

We kiss and I roll my hips over his cock, our arms fastened around one another. Our kisses soften and we find a rhythm, then I'm kissing his throat and he's kissing mine. We're holding one another so tight and it's not the dirtiest, filthiest, hottest sex we've ever had... but it feels like the most honest.

He sits up and I'm propelled backwards, having to shift my knees forward so I'm upright over him. I tuck my feet beneath his thighs to steady myself and he cups my breasts in his hands, burying his face between them one moment, then laving my nipples the next. I take hold of his shoulders and swing over him. Soon my insides gather and pulse around him, a small and tender orgasm gripping me momentarily as we rock together, his face planted in my chest.

"Oh, baby, *fofo*," he groans, making me laugh.

I giggle and tip my head back. He wraps his hands around my buttocks and licks the sweat from between my breasts. I grab the small amount of hair on his head and moan as I move into him, jutting against his strong thighs and groin, his bush chafing me as I fuck him. He's got comfortable with that... because he knows I like it.

It's soon obvious he's lost and somehow hanging on. His kisses have stopped, he's got his face pressed against my arm and he's not as vocal, just panting like crazy. I push him forcefully onto his back but maintain my position, bouncing harder up and down his cock, the juice of my orgasm lubricating my movements so I can go wild. I reach for my clit and play with it like it's an on-off switch. He lies back with his eyes closed, his chest heaving up and down, his hands on my thighs.

I fuck him hard and make the bed groan beneath us, shoving him into the mattress. When I come, he covers his face with his hands and grunts, his heat spewing up into me. I let go and bear down, covering him in my squirt.

He removes his hands from his face and he's grimacing. I would even say he looks pained... thinks I'm evil and a bad woman. He's not unimpressed, but he's decidedly ticked off that he succumbed to me... that easily.

I lower to his body and kiss his nose. "Who's the better fuck-er, bubba?"

He shakes his head, angry and annoyed. "Fuck if it isn't you."

I laugh the filthiest laugh I have, right in his ear, then slip off his cock and slide to his side, wrapping my arms around him.

"I'm mad for you in white pants."

"I'm mad for you entirely naked and not wearing some weird harness."

"I'm mad for you, even stinking of fish."

"I'm mad for you, full stop."

He rolls me onto my back and I'm both excited and terrified when he kisses me so hard, I feel my head sink two inches into the bed. He's back inside me in no time and I'm screaming so loud, anyone would think he's the better fucker.

Chapter Twenty-Five

Dark Truths

Being that it's a warm day, when Ruben and I finally emerge from bed, we jump in the car and head down to one of the local beaches. We pick a spot just back from the crowds and he gets out his easel and paints while I lounge on the sand on a towel, trying to pretend I'm not posing.

"You're pouting," he accuses, peering at me from behind his prescription glasses, which he rarely wears, even though he should, at least for reading, watching TV and things like that. I guess he could be slipping in contacts when I'm not looking, or else he's only put them on today because he really wants to get this right.

In any case, he rocks a pair of glasses, especially thick-rimmed, big frames—he looks like the ultimate hot geek.

So hot!

"I can't see my own face," I retort, sticking out my tongue. "How am I meant to know what I look like?"

"Look natural."

"What *is* natural," I laugh.

He lifts one eyebrow and carries on, painting me allegedly pulling a face. I cannot judge myself without a mirror (which sadly at the moment I don't possess).

He's sitting on one of the fold-up chairs, peering over the top of his canvas at me, occasionally gurning as he works. Sometimes I want to burst out laughing, but I know that will ruin the whole thing because I'll end up rolling about. It's not that he looks serious, just so very unsure and laboured, I suppose. I'm wondering why he can't take a photo and work from that?

"Am I always to be your subject matter?"

"No," he says, quick to correct me. "I've painted other things while we've been here. Scenes we passed on the street. You know. Things imprinted on my mind."

"Aren't I imprinted on your mind?"

That one eyebrow seems to have a life of its own again. "I study some things more keenly, I expect."

Memories stir the desire in my belly and I smile to myself. I'm wearing a white halter-neck bikini and high-leg bottoms. I have my hair piled on my head (his choice) and a pair of sunglasses almost hanging off the edge of my nose. The type of glasses Wilma Flintstone would wear, I expect. Ruben bought them from a beach seller earlier and told me to wear them (only after I thoroughly rubbed them clean).

"You're thinking about sex," he says, sounding arrogant.

"Am not," I return, trying to hide my flush cheeks.

He catches sight of me and smiles, then furiously gets to work doing something with his portrait of me.

I decide to change the subject. "I'm thinking we'll go to Buenos Aires next. What do you think?"

"Wherever you like," he says, sounding indifferent, "just as long as there's you."

"The climate will be slightly better, I think. I want to wander their artistic neighbourhoods and listen to music all day."

"Sounds fine," he whispers absent-mindedly, humming as he works.

I'm not sure he's really in the moment. Where is his mind today?

He's there in his chinos and a thin white vest, not bothered if he gets paint on either. He looks perfect and I'm happier than I've ever been. What am I worrying about?

"Are you distracted over there, or not sure about Buenos Aires?" I ask, trying to pluck something from him... a slight doubt, perhaps.

"Honestly?" he asks, blinking fast.

"Yes..."

"I didn't think we'd stay here the whole month. I thought somehow we'd end up on a plane back to France."

Okay, well... there are a few ways to interpret that. "You thought I'd get too homesick?"

"Nope," he sings, brushing paint against the canvas. "I thought you'd miss the dogs, maybe. If not the dogs, the gallery. Maybe even Adam. I'm surprised you want to go on elsewhere."

I try to maintain my pose but it's difficult because I want to fidget and I want to tell him he's wrong, even though he isn't. The act of being here, thousands of miles away from home, doesn't feel right. However, he's more important. We're more important.

Letting his words sink in for a bit, I get a hold of myself and think on them. He probably does know me better than I know myself.

"Don't you think we should go to Argentina, then?"

All he does is shrug in response, seeming more interested in his painting, his focus on his brushstrokes and not on my quandary.

"What about Mexico? I've always wanted to go there, too." I twirl my toes in the air, trying to help my circulation, but he doesn't even notice. "The food... the art. The art, Ruben!"

He gives a tiny smile. "I suppose."

"Oh, come on," I ask, demanding he show some enthusiasm... for something.

He's staring at the canvas as he speaks. "I guess when you've travelled as much as I have, it's not that much of a novelty anymore. I'd rather get on with the business of starting our real life, wouldn't you?"

I feel slightly scolded by his words because I thought we'd come here for his betterment. Our betterment, even. He turns and catches sight of me, looking disappointed. He shakes his head and cleans his brush.

"Freya, come on."

I pout and look away. "I'm not upset. I just thought..."

"I'm not bothered, that's all I'm saying." He uses grand hand gestures to try and explain himself. "If you want to go to Buenos Aires, I'll come along for the trip because you're there. But I don't need to travel anywhere else for inspiration. I can be right at home in France or Spain—anywhere in the world—because as long as I've got you there, I've got my inspiration."

"Flattery will get you nowhere with me." I give him a dissatisfied look.

"I know, but you asked me to be honest. You've made me this person who finally understands the benefits of being honest." He sighs with annoyance, knowing full well he has upset me, and even though it's a bit silly, he is just being honest. And he's right.

"I suppose next week we'll have been here a month and that would be quite a long holiday for most people..." I roll my eyes and nervously dig my nails in the sand at the edge of the towel. "And we have had a lot of time to talk, we've got a lot out into the open..." It's true we've made a good start at progress and it feels like that is hopefully going to continue, unhindered.

His green eyes widen and he looks like a man desperate not to upset me, but also really not keen on hanging around another continent for longer than he has to. "It's been really good to come here, Frey. I'm not arguing that, whatsoever. I'm easy either way, but I'm just not fussed. If you really, really feel a desire to visit elsewhere, we can... but sleep on it, see how you feel. Okay? I'm good either way. Just not fussed, baby. Okay?"

"I hear you." Loud and clear.

I guess I wish we'd met as students or something, travelled the world with backpacks on our shoulders, seen and done everything together as virgins to every new experience. Up until recently, Ruben had virtually lived all his life without me, a whole thirty-five years. And I'd lived a whole thirty-two years without him. We've done so much apart. What is it that we're destined to do together? That's what I'm always asking myself. Is it a good idea to start out as wanderers, have adventures and be nomadic? Be a little reckless, neglect to put down roots and instead, grow into ourselves, first? Give each other fun memories to look back on, before life gets boring and staid and ordinary.

Or are we beyond that? Isn't it time maybe—and well overdue—for us to settle down, allow something secure and predictable and calm to overtake us?

"It's my birthday next week," he says, shocking me.

He never admitted his birthday before. I've always vaguely known his age, but he never actually told me which month.

"Good lord, someone is taking the honesty a little too seriously now, methinks."

He chuckles and puts down his brush to signal he's finished, suggesting I lift myself off the sand and come and see what he's been working on. I'm on my feet and excitedly chasing over to see what he's done... when I see it.

"You dirtbag," I chastise, shoving him from behind but barely moving him an inch.

He laughs and hands the smallish canvas to me. It's a cartoon and rather exaggerated, it must be said.

"If someone had approached us, I was going to convince them I was just a penniless artist doing this for supper... and not the footballer they're hunting an autograph from."

"You're not going to let me see your real work, then?" I try to hide how impressed I am that he painted this in less than half an hour. Aside from the Jessica Rabbit proportions he's given my body, it's pretty darn good. He's even written my nickname in big cartoon writing at the bottom.

Fofo.

"I know what that means, you know?" I tell him, not impressed.

"Words like that can mean anything, really," he states, folding his arms.

I'm staring at the picture, shaking my head. "It makes me look like a blonde bimbo."

"It's a fantasy, that's all," he says, chuckling. "Art can be anything."

I replace the painting on the easel and he stands up to put his hands on my waist and look into my eyes. I'm very in love with him and it's hard to act serious when he's this close and I'm so lacking in clothes.

"Freya, I don't take myself too seriously, which this cartoon hopefully proves. But my other work... is different. It requires a lot of me. It's not easy and there's no way you'd catch me out in the open painting my serious stuff. I don't like to think about it too much sometimes. My work and me, it has to be the same thing, right?"

I swallow hard and nod that I understand. "Okay."

He tugs me closer and I wrap my arms around his shoulders. He's looking sideways at the canvas when he murmurs, "So, it's my birthday. September third."

I try not to gasp the moment it's out. I take a deep breath and pray he can't feel the thrill running through me. I'm sure I could have found it somewhere online, but I vowed a long time ago never to dig too deeply on the internet... in case I didn't like what I found. Or more specifically, who I saw him pictured with. I know myself too well, therefore I knew once I started looking, I wouldn't be able to stop.

"We'll still be here for your birthday, then?" I gently nudge him.

"Yes," he whispers.

"Want to do something special for it, Ruben?"

He turns his head and shines his green eyes down on me. "Celebrate me becoming thirty-six? Noooooo."

I don't hide my disappointment this time. "Why tell me, then? I'm going to get you a cake at least."

Dark storm clouds seem to overtake the green inside his eyes and I realise there's something about his birthday he finds difficult. Is it Laurent? The guilt of living longer than his brother? What is it? I stroke his hair and wait for him to spill.

"What is it?" I eventually ask, gently coaxing him.

"It was my birthday when I found out she was cheating on me. A few days later, she was dead."

Emotions of all kinds tumult through me, heavy and unwanted and unbearable. I can't hide my reaction. I'm tired of hearing about the past. So is he. We both wanted to draw a line under the past and start fresh, but that didn't work four years ago, so this time we're trying to go straight and get it all out—but it's so fucking hard.

"I would never cheat on you, you know that."

"It's not about that, Freya."

"So, what is it about?"

His neck sinks into his shoulders and he looks out at the rolling waves of the sea, still with his hands on my waist.

"I've not celebrated a single birthday since. It's only a number to me these days."

"But you've mentioned it to me now?"

"I guess I can't keep my trap shut." His mouth tightens at one side, annoyed with himself.

Again, with the honesty crap. He's trying to tell me he feels no compulsion to celebrate it, but he doesn't want to keep anything back, either—and that's the point.

I gesture for us to sit and we take the two foldable chairs, looking out at the beach and the ocean rolling in. I keep hold of his hand and wait for him to say more, but again, it rather feels like he needs prompting.

"I brought us out here because I was sick of the lies, Ruben." It feels so good to get it off my chest.

"I know."

"The lies cannot continue."

"I've realised that," he assures me, and I glance his way, seeing the resolve in his features. "It can't go on. I can't lie to you anymore. It was never right. Ever."

"It wasn't, but I can understand." I squeeze his hand and he squeezes back. "I can see how it'd become so normal for you, being brought up in the house you were."

"Exactly, yes. That still doesn't make it right, though." He rubs his hand over his short hair, frustrated at all the things he let happen—and now can never go back on.

"What made you realise this?" I have to ask.

He turns in his chair and holds my hand between his, seeming so certain of what he has to say. "It's coming here and it being just us. I've realised it's better when we're honest. I can't lie anymore."

I pick up on a flicker of something in his eyes. "What are you feeling so guilty about?"

He's shocked I can read him so succinctly and without judgement. "Freya, I was thinking for my birthday, I was going to organise a threesome for us and see how you'd react."

Shock isn't the word. It's utter paralysis. I don't know what to say or do. It becomes clear after a few minutes that my head has flopped so far forward, my chin is almost touching my chest. I can see from the look in his eyes, he knew I wouldn't react well but he's been having a hard time keeping his insecurities to himself.

"With another man?" I whisper, my throat parched.

"I was going to..." His face twitches with revulsion and self-hate. "I was going to pay someone. I wasn't going to discuss it with you beforehand. I was going to spring it on you to test you. See how you'd react."

I resist the urge to vomit and ask simply, "Why?"

"Because birthdays are really bad for me and I flipped out?"

When he sees from the look on my face that I don't buy that, he tries to come up with something else, rather quickly...

"I was trying to find a distraction from all the bad memories that resurface around my birthday? Or maybe, I thought you'd run off scared and prove that all the women I love see through me eventually, and I don't know..." I notice his lip wobbling. "I don't know, Frey."

He rubs his eyes and I'm floored. I honestly don't know what to say.

I stroke my fingers down his cheek and he turns to look at me, surprised I'm even touching him. "How could I ever want or need another man? You're my beautiful man. I'm mad for you, Ruben. I can't see beyond you."

He turns his chair and faces me, takes my hands and hunches over, his eyes looking up at me, some kind of challenge or something inside his expression.

"I know it sounds odd," he whispers, shaking with nerves, "but I guess I wanted to see you being fucked by another man. Just so I could see if there's any difference in the way you'd react to him. I know that's not right, but I can't help feeling like that."

I stroke my hands over his and stare down at the sand, trying to hold it together as I think of words to resolve this crisis he's going through. "I think I understand why you want to go home now."

"You do?" he asks, sounding so innocent and hopeful, it almost breaks my heart.

"You want to get on with the business of settling down, and feeling secure, because for so long, you haven't?"

"Yes," he cries, "yes!"

"But my belief is that having a few adventures outside the realms of domesticity could also make us stronger. Don't you agree?"

He shrugs and looks away, hiding his feelings again.

"Would you have gone through with it? Put me on the spot like that?"

"I don't know," he says in a croaky tone of voice.

"If you'd brought me another man home and told me it was your pleasure to watch me fuck him, I would've done it, but only to please you... knowing I was doing it for you. If, as my lover, you'd demanded it from me and really wanted it, I would've done it. You'd have seen as I fucked someone else, it's still ultimately you I live and breathe for, and I'd have only been doing it to please you. All these years, you have held my heart, my mind, my soul... even while I've been with other men. You'd have seen that I'm only yours, that even in sharing my body, it's still you who owns me. But deep down, that's not what you want and we both know it." He looks utterly shocked and astounded, hearing these words come out of my mouth. "Similarly, if I told you, maybe, I wanted you to seduce a woman and let me watch you taste her because it would make me wet, you'd do it, if I asked, wouldn't you? If I asked."

"But you wouldn't ask," he snaps, "you wouldn't want me to."

"So why are you asking it of me?" I exclaim.

"Because I'm sick, Freya," he says, reeling off words. "Because I'm nothing. Because I want to torture myself."

"Because you expect me to be like the rest." My words come out sharp and bitter.

"No, because it's easier to be alone," he mumbles, "it's easier. There, I said it. It's goddamn hard to give someone your heart. Some people find it easy. I've found it so goddamn hard, Freya. I thought loving you from afar would be better for us both, that maybe it'd be enough, but it never was. I can't say enough how sorry I am that my mind works in this way, but it does... and I'm sorry."

Part of me wants to run into the sea and start swimming, and keep swimming, until a random boat picks me up and takes me someplace else. Maybe I could take to living in a cave, eating berries off trees and washing my hair in magical lagoons until I'm suffused enough with nature to be absorbed by it and disappear, into a puff of smoke. Don't we all sometimes wish we could be carted off and lose all our responsibilities, worries and cares? Is that why I brought him out here?

I could be mad about this, but how can I be? He's being honest with me. I know it's not pretty, but that's honesty.

I have to remember that, surrounded by Alexia and Fred growing up, he was living a life of perpetual deceit. Dishonesty was his normal. Avoiding the truth was his default setting. Fred no doubt preferred it when his kids were acting up rather than being well-behaved, because he wouldn't have understood that. So, have I done the previously unimaginable and yanked him out of the mindset of lying? Have I? Lying must have been a way of life for the Kitchener's. To have left that behind, perhaps I have to see that him admitting something so bleak is actually a really good thing?

"Do you want to know how I would've punished you if you'd brought a man to our bed?" I stare hard, urging him to nod his head. When he does, I reveal, "I would've made you have your cock sucked by a man for my pleasure. And I would've made him kiss your body, each and every square inch, just so I could see that men adore you, too... and I would've been so aroused watching it. You think you can shock me, Ruben, but you can't. I've heard things over the years that'd make even your toes curl."

"You're really not mad?" he gasps.

"Oh, I'm always mad, Ruben, but in life, you have to pick the things that are worth being mad about." He frowns, trying to predict what I might say next. "Some thoughts and ideas are just manifestations of doubts, fears and stresses, and that's normal. Now, but if you had actually brought a guy home, yep, I absolutely would've forced you to let a man touch you. Or I'd have left your ass."

His face scrunches up. "I'd only do it for you."

"Now you know exactly how I'd feel about it. The same as how you feel now contemplating it. That's exactly how I'd feel. I wouldn't be invested, at all; nor would it appeal, in any way shape or form. It wouldn't be for my own benefit. I'd be doing it just for you. It wouldn't matter how pretty he was, that's how I'd feel, Ruben. Because he wouldn't be you."

"God, I wanna lick you out so bad," he groans, finally understanding my take on it.

"And you really want to go back to Nice where that always gets interrupted?"

"Myeah..."

WHEN WE ARRIVE HOME, I realise I've been without my phone all day and go hunting for it. I've been so relaxed, I didn't think. When I see a missed call from France, plus a text message, I start to think someone must have forgot I said I'd be out of the country. However, the text message leads me to believe this may be more than a client after my opinion.

It's written in French and the colloquialisms are a bit too much for my ill-educated eyes, so I pass the phone to Ruben. "What does this all mean, bubs?"

He scans the text and says, "Oh, it's your maid, Rosi. She says... oh. Oh." His voice drops so low, his expression darkening.

"Please, Ruben. Don't sugar-coat it. Come on."

"She says she got to the house to clean and found the dogs had made a mess and were home alone. She called the dog walker and discovered Adam had told the woman she wasn't needed anymore. So, then she tried your brother but couldn't reach his phone. She thinks they weren't alone for more than a day and a half, but they had made a terrific mess."

My stomach plunges somewhere else... what feels like the other side of the world... maybe Asia. I have the wind knocked out of me and have to take a seat.

Ruben's at my side and tries to speak to me, but I don't hear him. I don't even want him to touch me.

"MY LAPTOP! GET IT! MY LAPTOP!" I scream, shaking and manic.

He comes back and I try to blink through blurry vision... my fingers are trembling as I punch at the keys. When I log on to the business account, I see everything is gone. Not just the commission from yesterday's sale... but all the money I kept in there for emergencies... for expenses, running costs...

In fact, enough to cover running costs for the next six months.

The laptop flies out of my hands and hits a wall in the room. I can't... I can't even breathe.

It's not that...

It's not...

I have money.

That's not it.

It's not *that*.

No.

"You knew he was going to do this," I accuse Ruben. "You fucking knew."

I go to the liquor cabinet, pull out the tequila and pour myself one. Ruben is hovering in the background, frightened, I think. He's never seen this side of me before.

"One of your admirers bought the pieces," he finally admits, and now I understand why he didn't want to talk about the sale—at all. "I knew it was no coincidence. Adam must've let word get out... knowing one of your admirers would take the bait. He sold the whole lot as a series. Said the seller wouldn't part with them individually."

He has a tremble in his voice that wrecks me. How am I meant to empathise with his own anguish over *this*... when he knew my anguish would be ten times bloody worse!

"Why didn't you TELL ME?!" I yell, my throat burning thricely—from the yelling, tequila and my heart trying to budge its way up out of my chest.

"You'd have intervened, tried to stop him, but he was always going to do this, and if I'd forewarned you, you'd have— and it would've only been delaying the inevitable. We can't save everyone, Freya. Some people are who they are. I was trying to protect you, that's all."

"Well, fuck you, Ruben," I slaver, "fuck you!"

I race into the bedroom, slam the door behind me and pour my heart out into the pillows.

Just like Dad.

Fucking just like that prick.

Fuck.

Chapter Twenty-Six

Home Again

I don't know what time I fell asleep or even what day it is. Time seems meaningless as I wake, like everything else. I do know it must be a new day because it's cool and the birds are singing. I remember getting home from the beach and it being early evening... so I must have slept. I lift my head off the pillow and look around the room. Where's Ruben?

My phone is on the side and I check the time. It's 5.30a.m. Where is he?

He must have brought my phone in here because last night I threw myself onto the bed crying and spent the next few hours wrestling with the sheets in response to Adam's utter betrayal—I definitely wasn't thinking about calling him or solving all my problems. I wasn't thinking at all. I was reacting and hurting... deeply.

I shuffle out of the room, still wearing my white bikini and lilac kaftan over the top. I hear noise coming from the studio, so I knock on the door. He opens up and I find him bare-chested and strangely serene. He welcomes me in and I wander around the room, seeing a number of large paintings wrapped and ready for transport.

"What's happening?" I ask, my voice weak.

"I'm packing up, ready for home. Rosi has taken the dogs to the kennels until we get back. I sent her some money and a little extra for her trouble. Our flight is tomorrow morning. We'll either have to not sleep tonight or go to sleep very early and get up very early—"

I burst into tears, sobbing into my hands. "Oh, Ruben."

He comes towards me, wraps his arms around me and envelops me. I cry into his chest, hating myself for how I reacted last night... hating the situation...

"Let's get coffee, shall we?"

He directs me towards the kitchen and sets up the machine while I take a seat at the breakfast bar.

"I take it you're in agreement that we should go home?" he asks, his back to the counter.

"I don't really want to go, but yes." So much for Buenos Aires or Mexico City or wherever. It's all been taken out of our hands. I couldn't enjoy myself now.

Ruben nods his head. "It's the right thing to do, so we can get to the bottom of this."

I shake my head, throw my arms up and exclaim, "Get to the bottom of what? We know what he's done. He's cleared me out."

Ruben purses his lips and stares at the floor, saying nothing.

"What did you really mean, then?" I ask, sensing something. He's not overly worried, I don't think, but...

"Maybe he got himself into debt," he muses, "and just didn't have the balls to admit he needed your help."

"Don't tell me you're making excuses for someone like him."

"No way," he says, folding his arms and lifting his face to mine. "But it would be nice to know the actual details, no? And perhaps... find out where he's gone."

I take a deep breath and read what's really in his expression. "You could find him?"

"I know people who can," he says, giving me his serious expression. "I also know people who could get your money back, every penny. You just say the word. If you want answers—"

"No!"

He's not fraught, but he is firm, using strong hand gestures. "Either way works for me, Freya. Either way, okay? He's the one who's going to suffer more long-term because the only good thing in his life now hates him. Either way. So let him go, if you like. I'll respect your wishes to let him get on with it. But what about when he runs out of money, hmm? Because he will. He doesn't have the skills and talent and business craft you have. He hasn't got a fucking clue. He used you, Freya. He used you."

Tears spring to my eyes and I rub them, still not wanting to believe he could have done this to me. "You told me, you warned me... and I didn't listen! You warned me... said he was pressuring me to let him have the gallery while we were away... and I didn't listen, Ruben! How can I trust my own decision-making again? I left him with the keys to the kingdom and look how he repaid me. Look!"

Ruben worries his lip, shakes his head and turns around to pour the coffee once the machine beeps. He carries the cups to the living area and we sit on the couch. I take a sip of coffee before putting my cup down. Then he pulls me back into his arms.

"I am so sorry, Freya. You trusted him."

"Yes."

"You thought better of him."

"YES!"

"And he's done this."

"Yes," I whisper meekly, pushing my face into his chest. "Yes."

I cry a little, not as violently or as manically as I cried last night, just tiny sobs. The last of it is leaving me... getting out of my system.

"You did all you could, Freya. You tried to show him what a sibling bond could be. You gave it a shot. He betrayed you, yes. But you tried. You can console yourself knowing you tried. And I bet a part of him does feel rotten. He probably justified himself because you've got plenty of money... and I'm back in your life now... maybe he thought it was time to move on."

I look into his eyes. "But he knows I would've given him money, Ruben. He knows that. I paid his tuition fees in Paris. He worked for me in the summer and earnt enough to pay for his lodgings while studying... he wasn't strapped. He had a little bar work in Paris during term-time that got him a bit extra, too. He wasn't poor. I didn't... I never... I don't understand!"

I never gave things to him on a plate, but I wasn't a total miser, either. I looked after him. I wanted to give him a chance to be all the things I should've been... a student. A carefree young-ster. A young person about town, having fun, enjoying experi-ences... living a life. Not rushing into adulthood. Ruben's right... he'll be out there in the big bad world now, alone, not knowing what to do with himself. Was a million euros really worth losing his big sister over? Or did he never really love me? Did Dad do his job properly, after all? Contorting the heart of my brother so that all this time, it wasn't real? Living with me through the summer, taking bike rides together, laughing about the clients to-gether. Sharing stories. Was it all fake? Was he pretending to care about me the entire time? Did Dad send him to live with me and encourage him to squeeze me for all I'm worth? (A bit more than a measly million.)

"I don't get it, Ruben. He must know he's worse off for doing this. In the long-term, he could've had a lot more out of us. He knows that. I don't get it."

Ruben holds my cheeks and stares into my eyes, reassuring me. "Adam always did act defensive around me, don't you think? Perhaps he viewed me as an obstacle or competition. Or someone who'd be watching and catch him out. Think about it. He bided his time and made his move once we were gone. I bet he was hoping you'd leave the sale money in the business account a little longer, but even from thousands of miles away, you moved it quickly... why did you do that, Frey?"

I work the tension out of my jaw, moving it side to side. "Because it's your money, Ruben. Not the gallery's. Not mine. Yours."

"You didn't think it might be... I don't know... prudent to move it so quickly, because deep down, you didn't entirely trust him?"

He's looking at me for an honest answer, but the honest answer is... "I didn't trust the sale, Ruben. Something about it was off, to me. I didn't want to contemplate that Adam fucked us over, trying to sell the pieces when we expressly said for him not to just yet. I didn't trust the sale, but I truly did trust him. I trusted him..." My bottom lip wobbles like crazy. "And he's proven himself to be just like Dad. Just like him. This is something Dad would do. If he was a young man again and had a rich relative and he thought he could benefit, this is something he absolutely would do. I know it. And now I understand what it must be like for Mum. She always, always must have trusted him... and instead of seeing anything like the cold, hard evidence as I have, she's only ever known that his menace bubbles subtly beneath that charm. She's always buried it under the carpet... lying to herself. Hiding from the truth of what he is. She can't face it... like I don't want to face it, even now... here... and I've seen the evidence of Adam's greed in black and white... and I still don't want to believe it... I don't."

I cry for a long time. Ruben holds me throughout. It feels like I opened myself up even knowing I would only get hurt, and the tiny piece of faith I had in us ever being a great brother and sister—even after the childhood we shared—has been trampled on and burnt, a piece of my heart dying with that tiny piece of faith. I always feared he might be just like Dad, especially when he would say to me, "Nah, he was never violent towards me." And I would just think *why?*

Why?

Why was my father never violent towards Adam?

Because he knew he could bend Adam to his will, whereas with me, I would never succumb and that's why he smacked me. Because he couldn't get inside.

And the saddest thing?

I wanted to save Adam. I think if I'm honest with myself, I think I knew he needed saving... but when Ruben came back into my life, something else became more important.

Love.

And even now, a miniscule part of me still believes... that with a little more time, I could've saved Adam.

But Ruben's right.

He was jealous, knew he couldn't get between Ruben and me... as a consequence, threw his metaphorical toys out of the pram. Now here we are.

It makes me wonder what happened with that girl he really liked. Did she see right through him?

Did I see only what I wanted to?

Or was I duped by one of the most skilled dupers out there?

"Let him loose," I tell Ruben, my tone of voice low and unforgiving. "We've got our own lives to lead. But if he ever comes back, make sure you deal with him. I don't want to see him ever again. Are we agreed?"

"I agree. I'll deal with him if he comes sniffing around again. Until then—and that's a big if—he doesn't exist. The Adam you knew... that was all a lie."

I shudder at the thought. "I want to go home, Ruben."

"Don't worry, I'll get you home, girl. I'll get you home."

THREE DAYS LATER, RUBEN arrives home from the kennels carrying the dogs under his arms and I burst into tears. The dogs leap at me and lick furiously at my face, hands, knees... any part of me they can get hold of.

"I'll never leave you again, I'll never leave you... I'm back, babies. Mummy is back." I pet them like crazy and give them big kisses and cuddles. I don't care if it's grossing out Ruben. They remember me and I'm so happy to see they're okay. "Mummy's not going to leave you again. I won't. I won't. No, I won't."

"I'll make a drink," Ruben says, probably feeling left out.

Once they tire and rest on my lap, one chin on each thigh, I try to get up to find Ruben but they're up on their feet and won't rest unless I'm beside them. I pat their heads and remain where I am. Ruben comes around the corner from the kitchen carrying a cup of tea and murmurs, "Just relax, *fofo*." He kisses my cheek and I almost blush at the gesture. He's been so loving, ever since it all happened. I don't know how I would have got through this without him.

When we landed it was night-time here and we came back to the house, got into bed and crashed for almost fourteen hours. The journey home was exhausting. Even more so with a mountain of emotions bubbling up out of my eyes. I didn't want to leave Rio. Not at all. Ruben had to practically carry me to the car because I was crying my eyes out. We were meant to stay at the villa for another week and a part of me wondered why we were flying back when the dogs had been put safely in kennels and the gallery would survive without opening for a couple of weeks. But Ruben was right... I only wanted to take him away because I was avoiding what was at home. In Rio, we had some difficult conversations and came to terms with a lot. Here, I'm not sure any of that would've been possible. We had to go, but we also had to come back... because I needed to see if he'd done any more damage. And it turns out, he has.

My Tesla is gone. Ruben rang the local dealers and found out Adam sold it a week ago. He'd changed the ownership, forging my signature so he could sell it and take the sale money for himself. Granted, I had told him he could take the vehicle... but, it still cut me for some reason.

Yesterday, when the jetlag was still intense, I went by the gallery when I should have left it a few days. Most of the stock had been sold. I don't know how much for. I found no evidence of sale. Just that it was all gone... even the paintings that were really tricky to sell and would have to be put in the back and brought out again when they would seem fresh to our customers. He really took everything I had at the gallery, lock, stock and barrel.

I've been trying to figure it out. Should I despise him? Should I pity him?

Is it Dad's fault he's like this?

But the cunning of it... the planning.

He planned it all.

There was no second thought.

He didn't come to his senses... didn't change his mind. No conscience.

He knew all along what he was going to do... and he did it.

If he were being tried for killing someone, the punishment would be severe because it'd be classed as premeditated and that makes it all so much worse. That it was in no way a random, stupid act makes it brutally hard to take. An impulse he acted on and regretted later I may have forgiven, but he'd planned to diddle me out of money... and he didn't even leave a letter.

On the flight home, I was constantly between nightmares and nothing, staring out of the window into the abyss while Ruben snored on happily next to me. In many of my waking dreams, I imagined Adam having left a goodbye note. Something with a few words. Maybe a sentiment like, "It was fun, but I want to strike out on my own," or even, "I really don't like Ruben, so this is your punishment..." Anything. Just anything. Something I could understand. But I can't understand any of this. Because I'm not dishonest. Never have been.

He didn't leave one word of explanation. Not one. Nor an apology of any kind. I could have forgiven him, if he were genuinely sorry, but he's not. All Adam sees is that I got very rich because I met Ruben... and deep down, all this time, he's secretly hated my wealth. My gallery. My life. He gave in to the green-eyed monster.

I could've forgiven him. But now I can't. And that's worse. Not being able to forgive hurts me most... and I bet he knows that. Oh, I bet he does.

I think if I hadn't taken my clothes and jewellery with us, he would've hocked all my things, too if he could have. I checked the bedroom safe last night... I didn't think I could take even one more disappointment, so I was glad to see it hadn't been broken into... having never told Adam the code.

Inside the safe, some of my most treasured possessions are intact. Some photos of me and my mother. My old phone with hundreds of messages on it, all between me and Ruben. When I was going through really bad times, I would break out the scotch and re-read them, until I thought my eyes were going to bleed.

Then, my most treasured possession of all...

The small ballerina painting I bought years and years ago from a fayre in Kentish town. It was cheap at the time and somebody was selling it because their friend had painted it. I knew as soon as I saw it, there was talent in that picture. I snapped it up. That unknown artist is now very well-known and when the painting became valuable, I decided to keep it in the safe. Not just because it was more valuable, but because if there was a chance I could lose it to treasure hunters, I wasn't going to take it. Me and that painting have been through hell together. I wouldn't sell it for love nor money. It means too much. I take it out now and again to stare at, but I'm happy for it to stay safe.

KARMA

And what hurts the most? I confided in Adam about so many things. About my undying love for Ruben. About my days as an escort. About the horrible times at home. It stings that he's done this, because I thought most of all, we were friends.

I'M HUMMING TO MYSELF as I undertake my bedtime routine in the bathroom. It's hard to describe how nice it is to be home. My own home. Ruben changed the locks yesterday—his first task when we woke from our jetlag coma. It's not just that we have this place all to ourselves now, no. It's also that it's safe. It's comforting. It seems ridiculous for someone who once relied on getting kicks out of fucking strangers to have reached the point now where I enjoy knowing my way around a bathroom or a kitchen, but that is who I have become. Everything in here is where I want it. I can find my cosmetics and my creams and my other various products in this bathroom, because it's mine, because I designed and had it built to my specific requirements... and something as simple as having a drawer for hairbrushes makes me happier than I realised. Because when you have hair like mine, sometimes you need a brush for every eventuality.

Ruben walks up behind me, slings his arms around my waist and stares at me in the mirror as I rub cream on, then wipe it off. He's naked from the waist up, his only clothes a pair of black silk pyjama trousers. I didn't know he had them but I'm thankful nonetheless.

"You were humming, I heard you," he says, grinning, "you're happy to be home."

"I am, I am... so happy, Ruben. I didn't realise how much... how good it feels to have a home. You know?"

He buries his face in my neck and shuts his eyes, sighing, "Me too."

I run my hands over his arms and lean back into him, allowing myself this happiness.

"Betrayal and all that bollocks aside, maybe this is exactly how it was all meant to happen."

He pulls his head out of my neck. "What do you mean?"

"Now we have the house to ourselves and we can carry on as we like, we don't have to feel guilty for expressing ourselves and worrying what he would think. And to think he made us feel uncomfortable in our own home."

Ruben gives me a look of disapproval. "He thought he had his feet under the table here."

"We had to go away, but we had to come back, Rube... and well..." I roll my eyes. "It hurts, but I think, well..." I blow out a deep breath. "In a way, I don't think I could've thrown him out. He did me a favour. Has it cost us? Yes. Less in terms of money than in loss of trust and my heart being broken, but... he showed his true colours... and if I'd had to throw him out because he was getting too bullish about keeping hold of his territory, I think I'd have felt worse for throwing him out into the world with less than he stole from me."

Ruben kisses my cheek and gives a throaty laugh. "Oh, you don't know what I would've done with him. Especially after he had a bunch of girls upstairs and was doing lines."

I see the sadist in him peering out of his eyes and smirk. "Tell me what you'd have done to punish him."

"I'd have stripped him of everything you ever gave him, hog-tied him and driven him right to the door of your parents' house, dumping him on their doorstep naked." He presses his lips together, satisfied that would be how he'd have dealt with it all. "Maybe I'd have actually dumped him at Dover with a tenner. He'd have had to put his intelligence to use for once. Because he doesn't put it to much use in any other way, does he?"

I scratch my head. "I even wonder if he really is into art or if he lied just to build up some rapport with me. If he was so willing to give up his studies in Paris even when thousands would kill to be in that same position... it can't have meant all that much to him."

"Did you ever think he lied? That he wasn't really studying?"

"I visited him in Paris... he was living the student life." I'm almost certain of that. "But maybe he got kicked off the course before the start of summer this year... who knows... and he decided he was going to go through with his plan to steal from me because he'd decided he had nothing to lose."

Ruben has that all-knowing look. "There's no reasoning it, Frey. None at all. He wants an easy life. Thinks money will get him that. I could've told him that the more money you have, the more problems... but it would have fallen on deaf ears. And how he thinks he can just... get away with it... some form of karma will happen upon him, mark my words."

The thought of how I've felt the past few days—absolutely terrible, like my guts got ripped out—being somehow wreaked back on him almost makes me feel sorry for Adam.

He made his choice, though.

"I'll wait for you in bed," Ruben says, gently letting me go. "I've just managed to get the dogs to sleep on their beds in the corner. They each have one of your cardigans and I think we'll avoid having Sooty fart in our faces tonight."

I chuckle and continue my bedtime routine, happy that the mundane stuff of real life feels like a gift again, in a strange way.

I even sit in front of the mirror in my salon chair and brush my hair out, section by section. It normally requires a few handfuls of hair mask before I even contemplate brushing out the knots, but tonight I'm feeling indulgent.

When I arrive in the bedroom, Ruben is lying on the bed in his reading glasses, idly scrolling through his phone and looking like sex on legs. He doesn't look over when I remove my dressing gown and reveal a tiny gold silk camisole and matching shorts with a delicate lace trim.

I shift across the bed and stroke my fingers over his chest but he doesn't respond, and when I catch a look at his phone, I see he's trawling the internet for art supplies... expensive paints you can't get just anywhere.

"Ruben..." I say softly.

"You're vulnerable and fragile. It's not right."

He doesn't even look at me. Maybe if he saw my little night set and my hair brushed out... it wouldn't be so easy for him to say no.

"Is this why you put on the sexy black pyjama trousers... to put me off." I lean over and kiss his chest.

Again, he doesn't look at me, shaking his head. "No, if I thought it was the time for sex, I'd be bloody naked."

Sometimes I forget he's an Englishman, at heart. I often watch him speak different languages and look a certain way—a traveller, an adventurer, a man of the world—not just of one continent, but many. He can be like a chameleon, but deep down, he's a moody Brit and a gentleman and I love that about him.

I snatch his phone and throw it at the chaise longue, giggling when it bounces. The dogs look up from slumber and groan, then fall back to sleep. Ruben looks up at me annoyed, but as I slide my chest on top of his, his eye twitches and he has to suppress a grin.

"There's no better time to love me, than when what I need most is to be loved."

I see the surrender in his eyes and he reaches his hands out to stroke his fingers through my hair. I remove his sexy glasses and place them on the side.

"God damn," he groans, "you get more beautiful every day."

"I haven't had you shave me in a little while. I want to be smooth and silky again."

He bites his lip ever so slightly. "I see."

"What do you think?"

"Let me go and get the stuff."

He leaves the bed and I lie still, waiting patiently for his return from the bathroom to collect supplies. It's the heavy-handled razor he brings out, the same as last time. It gives such a close shave.

"Lift your hips," he says, so I do.

He slides a towel underneath my bottom.

"Take down those shorts," he whispers, a tremor in his voice.

I take them down and spread my legs. He sits on the bed beside me and stares as he spreads shaving cream over my vulva and mound. I can't take my eyes off the way he can't take his off what he's shaving. Last time I was standing up and no way this exposed.

It's utterly erotic as he shaves me. Not to mention as intimate as our encounters have ever been. I love him beyond anything else. He's my special person. My one. I don't need anyone else, so long as I have him.

He concentrates hard, especially as he's working near the most delicate parts. He bites his lip and grins when he shaves within millimetres of my opening.

"Making sure I'm properly done, are you?" I goad, peering down at his face between my legs.

"Why not? I'll be getting all the benefit."

"Are you sure about that?" I titter, then he's wearing a face like thunder. "Don't you think it might be me getting most, if not all, the benefit? Walking around with it like this... all day long."

He arches one eyebrow and gives a cocky smile. "It's a win-win all round, I would argue."

He's soon done and dries me off on the towel, patting my area, his teeth digging back into his bottom lip. He takes away the stuff and comes back, a massive erection tenting all that black silk.

"Fuck me, Ruben." I reach for the hem of my camisole and tug it off. When I look up, I see he's pushed down his trousers and is naked for me, too. Also wearing a fuck-me grin.

He climbs onto the bed and kisses from my ankle to my thigh, rubbing his smooth face against my delicate skin. I rub my hands through his short hair and groan, arching into his touch, my eyes closed as the delirium starts to take hold. He presses his nose to my clit and inhales.

"Fuck me, I need your cunt, Freya. Fucking hell."

He teases my clit with a few strokes of his tongue, laughing when I drape my legs down his back. He kisses my vulva, my delicate folds and around my opening.

"Feel it, Freya," he says, his voice full of desire.

I slide my fingers down and feel just how silken my skin is, the same as last time, like he's made me his, all over again. He slides his tongue inside me and it's almost too much, I feel like I might burst, and when he re-routes his tongue to my clit and slides his fingers gently into me, thrumming my g-spot, I overflow with desire and rock my hips against him, drowning... a lot of emotion catching in my throat as I climb down again, immediately after.

Ruben senses my immediate change of mood and moves up the bed, bands his arms around me and waits for me to open my eyes. Laid on our sides, facing one another, I can just about bear it when I open my eyes and see him.

He kisses my mouth softly, brushes my hair back and kisses my shoulder.

"I told you, Freya."

"I know, but I still want to feel your love, even if it is going to crack open my emotions, all over again."

He holds me against him, kisses my face tenderly, if not my mouth then my cheeks or my hair or my forehead. I stroke my hands over the nape of his neck and try to lose myself in his touch. If my eyes are closed, hopefully my mind will be, too—to everything else.

I gasp when he licks around my nipple in circles. I'm soon grabbing his hair again and sucking in air. He takes hold of my bum with one hand, his other hand grasping my shoulder as he holds my body close. He pulls me into him and I slide my thigh over him, his cock nudging at my entrance as we kiss open-mouthed, our tongues sliding against each other's. He kisses my shoulder again and I don't know why, but there's something terribly arousing about the way he does it—delicate and lingering, worshipful. I use my calf strength to bring him towards me and he pushes past my entrance and into my body, filling me with his love.

"God, Freya. I love you so much. You're my life."

I hear the words—every single syllable, every note of meaning, every breath of emotion—and my heart almost can't take it.

"I love you, Ruben. Make love to me, please. Make love to me."

He does as requested, his kisses never abating as he pulls me to him and pushes inside me. My arms are locked around his shoulders so that I may feel the strength of him surrounding me, taking me into his embrace.

His kisses stray to my breasts and my throat. He slides his hands down my back and squeezes my bottom. Then moves them back up again, to my waist, my breasts, and we become truly lost—this sexy, tender embrace the only thing that matters to me.

I open my eyes even when I know I might not be able to handle it, but when I see him, I see a horny, devilish lover, proud to be plundering my body with his thick, greedy prick... and I respond. I grab his face and kiss him wildly, because we promised one another that even if we don't have decades together, the days we do have will be special.

He growls and holds my thighs open, his hand holding up one of my knees. He wears a look of animal passion as he rocks into me faster, his brick of a cock slipping in and out of my grateful body, his erection so thick and nasty that every time he rubs my clit as he pushes in and out, it feels like I'm being seized by the most awful pain... when in reality, it's just going to be so good.

I feel a shudder and a massive explosion of electricity shoot into my legs, then I'm boneless and barely able to breathe as my body contracts beyond my control... and it aches somewhere inexplicable when he slaps my clit and sucks my nipple so hard, I think I'm going to die. He comes all over my belly and I'm almost disgruntled when he does, aghast.

"Why?" I ask, sounding weak and hurt.

"It's not the right time... and I know from how horny you seem... you must be ovulating."

There he goes again... trying to save me.

He just doesn't know that I don't need saving.

I need to feel him, every day, for the rest of my life.

I don't require anything else to survive.

Just him.

"But I want your baby," I cry, burying my head in his chest.

"After we're married, Freya. Once it's right. You'll be my wife and our baby will know love and stability. Forgive me for being a bit old-fashioned about it. I just want to do what's right."

I break open in his arms and turn into an ugly mess, but he holds me tight and doesn't complain.

"I can't be without you, Ruben. I know you hate him, but Adam kept me going when I didn't think I could go on. That's the truth."

He takes my cheeks in his hands and kisses me on the mouth, hard. "I'm not going anywhere. We're not going to be apart. We decided, remember? I won't leave you. You're my world, Freya. I swear, I would die without you now. I need you just as much if not more. You still don't see it, but you have no idea how much I fucking love you. No idea."

He squishes me against his body and even though I can't see or feel them, I know his tears are there. And there's something consoling about sharing tears... it's the only real exchange that means a damn.

Chapter Twenty-Seven

A Black Pearl

In the morning, I wake up to two wet noses and no sign of Ruben. I suppose that's as normal as could be really. The dogs are tucked in against my legs, breathing heavily. That means they're fed... so Ruben must've got up with them. I sometimes wonder if he's happy to have a lazy over-sleeper for a lover... so he's got time for himself first thing in the morning, before I'm alert.

I hear the clatter of crockery and wonder if I woke up because something in me sensed he was bringing me breakfast. He arrives with a big tray and a grin, plus those sexy pyjama trousers leaving nothing to the imagination. He mustn't have been outdoors then yet, therefore potentially not up for very long.

"Good morning, my love." He places the tray on the bed, shoos the dogs away and urges them to scurry in the direction of their beds. He leans across, kisses my cheek and whispers, "You look very, very beautiful today."

I realise when I see where his eyes are looking, the sheet has fallen and he can see my breasts. I shake my head and he passes me my dressing gown, which I pull straight on.

"What's all this, then?" I ask, grinning as he pulls the tray closer so I can reach my coffee and juice. I partake of both before searching through the other things he's arranged here.

"Just the first day of the rest of our lives, honey. May as well start as we mean to go on."

He's already buttered the toast and I'm salivating at the sight of it, grabbing a slice and biting into it hungrily. He appears to be watching me carefully as I partake.

"What?" I ask, starting to get paranoid.

"Nothing at all," he chuckles, taking a slice for himself.

On the tray there is also fresh fruit and pots of yoghurt, a plate of croissant and a jar of jam. Then, the little serving dish the jam is supposed to go in is all lonesome at the far side of the tray. I'm intrigued by it. It's not like him to use crockery like this. Why bring the jam jar *and* the dish? You bring one or the other.

I pick up the little bowl, ease off the lid and nearly suffer a collapsed lung when I see what's inside.

"Oh! Oh!" I laugh throatily. "Oh!"

"I picked it up yesterday on the way to getting the dogs. It was just waiting for me at my PO Box."

All I can do is stare. Is this real? Am I going to wake up?

"You can take it out, if you like."

I bite my lip and shake my head. "I can't. I can't. You take it out."

I thrust the pot at him and wipe away a tear.

"My mother would have us believe she doesn't approve but when I said I was going to propose, she brought this black pearl over with her from Portugal. It's been in her family for genera-tions. Legend has it the pearl was given to one of my great-grand-mothers when she was visiting Barcelona one summer. The man who gave it to her had set it in a necklace and told her his pirate uncle had stolen it from the vaults of the Spanish Royal fami-ly. It doesn't seem as far-fetched as my great-aunt's version of the pearl's origin... that a mermaid beached on land, only to find a black pearl between her toes that brought her luck during her time as a human, before she had to go back to the sea."

I cover my face, laughing, wondering if these aren't stories *he* made up.

"I wondered about this pearl because my mother always kept it in her jewellery box, a solitary pearl doing nothing, tucked away in a corner. She didn't use it for anything. She said it would become of use, one day, though. And so, I can't help but feel like it might bring us luck, somehow, what do you think?"

I look up and into his eyes and he's wearing the softest countenance. I can hardly bear to look at him, he's so handsome in this light, so gentle and patient.

"Make me the happiest man alive, Freya. What do you say? Will you marry me?"

I respond to his earnest question with an earnest answer: "I don't see why not!"

He laughs so hard his chest shakes and he tips his head back, little tears glistening in the corners of his eyes. He removes the ring from the pot and I hold out my finger, desperate to see all the details.

My god, it's beautiful.

The black pearl is set skilfully at the centre of an infinity band, the two loops—rose gold, my favourite—decorated with black diamonds and hugging the pearl. It's exquisite and so unique and I don't care which story is most accurate, perhaps both contain a shred of truth. I feel that as I rub my finger over the pearl, this has known some adventure and seen some life and so I'm honoured it's come to me.

"It's so different and I love it so much, Ruben. It's perfect."

I lean across and kiss him firmly on the mouth, laughing and smiling.

"Thank fuck for that," he says, catching his breath. "I was going to propose last night but you seemed... and I bottled it... and it was..."

"Shut up and kiss me." He kisses me, and while he's kissing me, I have an impulse I'm absolutely sure of. "This was meant to be, Ruben. Let's not mess around anymore. I want to do this as soon as possible, what do you say?"

He strokes my face and looks as sure as I feel. "We can but dream, my love. But maybe dreams do come true, after all."

WE CELEBRATE OUR ENGAGEMENT with lunch at a little place called Maïnis, where we can get food that is the best of both worlds. I can have an exquisite salad with a bucketload of fries and Ruben can have his bloody burger, a beer and pudding, just around the corner from the Promenade des Anglais. Nice is at its best as we head into autumn because with the arrival of September, there are fewer tourists, the waiters have more time to chat and there's less noise and more a lilting hum as you wander around the city.

While we're waiting for my tuna salad and his blue burger, I fish my phone out of my bag and check the date. I don't believe it. He's drinking an ice-cold Trappist ale and I'm enjoying the crispest Pinot Grigio known to man, when he catches sight of my raised brow and realises I have figured it out. Days haven't been counted recently, not as I've been grappling with Adam absconding, so I'm surprised to discover September the third has crept up on us like this.

KARMA

Our food arrives and my belly growls with approval. Ruben doesn't hang about and cuts his burger in half, tearing into it without further ado. The man can eat like a pig. I love that and can't wait to scoff our way through life together. My tuna is seared perfectly and gorgeously pink in the middle. I notice meat juice dripping between Ruben's fingers as I bite into some tuna and grin, my accompanying balsamic salad just as delightful.

"It's usually an unmarked event, so... something must have changed," I murmur, dabbing my mouth with a napkin.

Just because it's approaching autumn doesn't mean it's freezing yet. We're eating at an outdoor table and people passing by on the street are still in shorts and flip flops. Ruben is in a pair of chino shorts and a navy polo shirt. I've got on a frilly, floral summer dress I picked up in Rio. The material is fluttering in the breeze and the pattern is a little bold. It's now one of my top ten wardrobe favourites.

"It just felt right," he says, still so sure of it. "This morning, I woke up holding you in my arms, and it just felt so right to give you that ring."

I instinctively look down at it and grin, sighing. It's still as beautiful as when I first laid eyes on it. What's even more marvellous is that it fits perfectly. I do have rings I've worn on that finger and perhaps he knew that and sized me up.

"I can't tell you how much I love this ring." I'm still staring at it, rubbing it with my thumb. "It feels like I'm wearing a piece of you. It's so elegant... so artful... so you."

"I wanted you to have something absolutely beautiful, just like you."

I lift my eyes and he's even stopped eating just so we can connect. That's love. He takes my hand and brings it to his lips, kissing the ring. My heart flutters, I swear, and I never believed myself to be this kind of person. I genuinely didn't.

I take my hand back and kiss the ring, too. I know I can reciprocate his love today by letting him eat, enjoy this... and not make a big deal of it being his birthday.

He orders another beer and pours me more wine from the chilled bottle. After his burger is demolished, he begins eating fries with his fingers, intermittently dipping them in mayo.

I eat my salad with a fork and grin after every bite. I'm going to save my fries for later, too.

"So, all that nonsense... is that gone?" I put it out there, wondering if he's given up on his idea of us having a threesome.

He's staring at a fry and contemplating its crispy magnificence, when he admits, "I was mad with jealousy when I discovered it was one of your admirers who'd shelled out eight million for just a couple of pictures of you."

"Ha! You did a bloody good job of holding it all in."

"I know," he remarks, sheepish, perhaps regretting that. "It's just, at first, I wasn't sure it was Adam who'd..."

I inhale deeply and try to shake off my feelings of dread, horror and disappointment. Today, only good things are happening, I try to tell myself.

"You suspected Alexia."

"Not outright, I mean, sometimes... if I'm quiet on things... it's because I'm waiting for the full report to come in. And when the full report arrived—with that phone call from Rosi—it was already too late to stop him. I can't always protect you and that kills me."

I shake my head and scratch my nose, a little annoyed, a little nonplussed.

"I suppose you've got far too used to expecting people to do something bad."

"I suppose so," he admits, turning his head when he hears a woman pushing a crying baby past the restaurant.

Either he does want kids or he's even suspicious of women with crying babies.

"So, the thing you wanted to corner me into, that's definitely off the table, right?"

He turns to stare at me with a jolt. "Why, do you want to try it?"

I laugh my head off. "God, no! I know you've been there and got the t-shirt. I don't want to be lumped into that bracket... become like the others... who just... I don't know... you know?"

It feels like I'm digging my own grave, or something. I'm hopeful he realises what it is I'm getting at.

"Like I said, I was struggling with paranoia and jealousy." His expression turns dark and ugly. "The thought of men out there who pine for you. Who will always carry a torch for you. It makes me feel physically sick. It's just something I'm going to have to deal with."

I suppose it's different for men and women. When women are done with men, we're pretty much done. If the fantasy has worn off, the man can bog off, too. However, for men, I guess a woman can be offish, cruel, indifferent, calculating, even evil towards them, and for some blokes, they're still obsessed and invested. I know that can be true for some women, too but on the whole, out of all the women I've ever known, if a man has shown himself to be less than worthy, usually women are swift to move on. I also know many women prefer to entertain the fantasy even when the reality is much different—some women even prefer the fantasy to the real thing and never saddle themselves with a partner their whole lives long—but generally, my experience, on the whole, has taught me that men and their sexual fantasies are one thing, but when they really love a woman, they really love her. For men, I don't think it's as easy to get over a romance as it can be for women. We women are just stronger, maybe?

"If I'd known you were one day going to come back to me, I wouldn't have entertained any of them." He knows that and accepts that, I can tell. "We're grown up now Ruben and will have to learn to live with these jealousies and not let them turn us into monsters like your mother and father."

He gulps back some beer, eyes wide, hating to admit it but knowing it's absolutely true.

"You're not going to tell me who bought them, are you?"

He shakes his head.

I suppose I could make an educated guess because I only dated a handful of men along the Riviera who had money to burn and who did end up voicing their desire for something long-term—which I absolutely and utterly shot down, obviously. I never loved one of them.

"What about a woman?" I ask, and his ears prick up.

"What?" he whispers, leaning over, terrified.

"If you were to watch me with a woman. You'd know I couldn't fall in love with her. It'd help you get your rocks off that bit extra, no?"

He gives me a dark look and a wink. "Now you're just fucking with me."

I shrug my shoulders and wink back. "Well, it is your birthday."

His eyes tell me he's worried, fearful... but actually can't help thinking about the possibility of it. "You'd do that, for me?"

"I mean, I've never done it before. Wouldn't it be a bit like the whole frogs' legs and chicken, thing? Tastes sort of the same."

He almost spits out his beer laughing and reiterates, "You're fucking with me."

I'm fucking with him, obviously.

I take his hand and squeeze it. "What do I have to do to prove to you it's only you?"

"You really wouldn't ever want another man, ever again?" He's so cute when he's unsure of himself.

I slam my hands on the table, but not too dramatically. "NO!"

"All right, all right," he concedes, looking around, embarrassed.

I snicker and finish the last leaves on my plate.

"I do wonder, though..." I give him a subtle hint, fluttering my lashes. "Maybe there's a way we could get even closer. What do you think?"

"You mean that thing I hate doing and you know I do?"

"No, that thing you love doing but hate admitting you love doing it."

A growl rumbles in his throat and he berates the idea. "I don't like it."

"Why are you denying who you really are?"

"I'm not denying anything," he says, highly defensive. "I'm sure I don't like *hurting* you."

"It's not about hurting me," I tell him straight. "Hurting me would be leaving me to fend for myself for four years, which, oh wait, you did! *And* without any qualms."

He's about to get up from the table and walk away, tired of this same discussion, when I smile and give him a look of reassurance. I'm sure it's like people say: everything happens for a reason. Sometimes, I wonder a lot about that reason, that's all.

When steam stops coming out of his ears, he rubs his chin, worrying his lip. "Is it because you think that you're missing out on something?"

"In a way."

"Because I did *that* with Gia, is that why?"

He's hit the nail on the head and he knows it.

"It's the same as you getting jealous of men who've got some fetish for stashing my picture in their attic, like I'm Dorian fucking Gray or some bollocks." He laughs hard and wipes tears from his eyes. I love that I can make him laugh. "I want to know why you did that with her, but not with me—"

"It's simple," he says, cutting me off. "Very, very simple."

"Don't keep me in suspense, then!"

He does indeed keep me in suspense, chewing something over, before he deigns to tell me.

"She literally couldn't get off without pain." He looks so matter-of-fact and I'm stunned.

I'm actually stunned.

"So, you only did it because she wanted it?"

"I did it because I was getting a bit fucking annoyed with failing at everything, and once when I slapped her, that's when I realised..." He purses his lips like he's not proud of it, but she didn't complain, either.

"Do you think she was a masochist? Or was she in love with that other guy?"

"I'd be guessing." He looks much more relaxed now he's told me.

"So, what'd be your guess?" I ask, perplexed and intrigued.

"She also needed it the back way, do you know what I mean?" His eyebrows are so high, urging me to understand without him having to spell it out in public, although I'm sure most of the time people around here don't understand Ruben when he speaks in that heavy cockney accent, anyway.

"She had... some kind of... physical... I don't know...?" I'm trying to guess, but I really can't put myself in the girl's shoes, having never known her.

He covers his face with a hand and snorts with embarrassment and frustration. Once he's got over his staggering annoyance of me not being able to read his mind, he leans in and I do the same. His voice drops to a whisper and he says, "I thought she'd had a bad experience, in the past. She didn't want it the front way. Only the back. I know we've enjoyed both, you and me, but let's be honest, Frey... the front is more convenient, right?"

He cracks me up and I put my chin to my chest, trying not to squeal with laughter. He picks up his drink and looks at it. "What the fuck is in this stuff?"

I can't help myself and I snort, trying to trap as much of it as I can behind my hands, failing miserably. He passes me a paper napkin from the dispenser and I wipe away my tears.

"I did ask you once if you had done anal. You said no?" I think back to a night, a long time ago, when we first tried it.

"It was all I ever did with her and I didn't want to get into it." He looks regretful, yet again. Another lie uncovered. "It was a section of my life I didn't want to rake over. I was also a bit ashamed. I didn't want to give you the wrong impression or scare you off. I didn't want you to think I was going to be wanting to bugger you until the end of time."

I snigger again, unable to stop myself. "Oh god, Ruben. Maybe she kept one hole for him and one for you, who the fuck knows?"

"I honestly wondered that, after she was gone," he says, his eyes twitching, bad memories assaulting him, maybe. "But over the years, I couldn't get it out of my head that maybe she'd had a traumatic pregnancy at some point and she'd sealed that part of her off. I did also wonder if she'd been in an abusive relationship at some point and maybe he'd only wanted her that way and for her, maybe that was normal. We had tried it the conventional way a handful of times but she didn't enjoy it. She was the one who'd present herself a certain way and we'd... and it just became normal. I always used condoms because she was so tiny and it would've been painful, but sometimes she'd beg for me not to wear one... and I wouldn't. Deep down, I didn't trust her."

"Didn't you ever wonder about having children?"

His shoulders lift and he looks doubtful. "I never wanted kids back then. I proposed because I thought it's what you did and because all my teammates were getting married. That was it."

"She really couldn't get off unless..."

He looks sickened by the memory of it. "I thought we were healing each other, in a strange and eerie way. It felt like we were similar, as I said before." He worries his bottom lip again. "I only know now that what I was doing with her was some kind of vicious cycle of harm she was trapped in and I was dragged into. I swore after she died, I wouldn't get myself into that state, ever again."

"You think she was fucked up?"

"Oh, I know so," he tells me, his eyebrows furrowed. "No doubt. At all. She was fucked up. I was in love with the fucked-up aspect."

It makes me feel terrible that I used to be a little bit like Gia, seeking punishment and some sort of reassurance from the world that I was dirt. Being kept down in the dirt was where I thought I belonged. Elevating yourself above that is damn scary, because it means you might actually find something to care about—and caring about something means you may end up, ultimately, getting your heart broken.

"You can be honest with me, Ruben. Okay?" He nods his head, telling me with his eyes he knows that. "Did you get off on it, too? The brutality, the bestiality. Did you?"

I'm nervous waiting for his response and he knows he should be honest, but maybe he doesn't want to be.

"Can I ask you one question before I answer?" He looks sad, just thinking about it.

"Of course."

"Did you ever have a relationship that involved someone giving you pain so you could get off?"

"No." My answer is swift and honest. "I didn't. Ever. I spanked men sometimes, but it was just a bit of fun, really. A bit of slap and tickle. It wasn't hardcore. It was just fun, for them, of course. A lot more men than women enjoy it. Not with a proper riding crop, just a toy thing and some handcuffs and maybe a butt plug... for them."

Ruben licks his dry lips and leans his elbows on the table, wrapping his hands together and leaning his chin against his knuckles. "I told myself I was enjoying it, but inside I was dying."

That makes me feel sadder than I've ever felt. "Oh, god, Ruben."

"I know we shouldn't speak ill of the dead, but I was glad I didn't have to do it anymore when she was gone. I'd been too scared to tell her how I felt. I'd been terrified of upsetting her." He looks truly remorseful as he stares at me. "I missed her, of course. But I'd got myself into that position because I just didn't want to be alone."

"You loved her, didn't you?" I'm terrified of the answer, but also need it.

"Honestly?" he says, looking serious. I nod I'd prefer honesty. "When she died, I was really very sad. I did mourn her. But there was also relief. She was such an enigma. I thought I saw myself in her, I really did. I thought... I don't know..." He looks up at the heavens, thinking back. "In the beginning, yes, she'd ask for this or that—and well, at the time, I was thrilled and thought I'd found exactly the right woman who wanted to entertain all these dark desires. As time went on, her requests just got darker and darker."

My stomach starts to ache and he sees my change of mood and reaches for my hand. His eyes soften and he tries to reassure me. "With hindsight, and especially after I found out she was cheating, I realised she was messed up. And honestly? Having loving sex with you has just been beautiful. It's different because we're best friends and it means so much more, Freya. I've tried everything there is to try in that department, believe me."

I pull a face like I'm not sure I want to know. He cracks a knowing grin.

"I've never enjoyed it as much as I do with you, and I'm not just saying that." My heart skips a beat just hearing those words.

"What we have, is so much more special than anything else, and I'm not happy that I once did take a belt to you. I'm not happy at all. It still feel sick, thinking about it."

I'm fighting tears suddenly because of the look in his eyes, one of regret and revulsion. "I never knew you felt like that. I never imagined."

"It reminded me of the things I'd done before."

I quickly wipe away a tear before it falls down my cheek. Again, I feel a bit like the teacher, maybe even a healer, when it comes to him and his past.

I take his hands in mine and squeeze them. "You know I love you?"

"Yes," he whispers, with a sad smile.

"When we did it, I felt like it was about achieving a deeper level of connection." He sits up a bit straighter and looks right into my eyes. "It was so beautiful, I thought. It was wonderful. The way you held me and made love to me afterwards, it blew my mind."

"I never realised," he whispers, surprised.

"Well, now you know, don't you, baby?"

He squeezes my hands between his. "Okay."

"When you and I said goodbye that night when you were depraved and like a man on death row, I loved that, too. Every minute."

He bites his lip and tries not to smile. "Me too."

"I don't want either of us to be in pain anymore, either emotionally or mentally or physically. Trust me when I say that."

"I do," he murmurs, "I trust you."

"But there's something about the way it stirs up chemicals inside me. It started out that I wanted to feel pain but it ended up that it hadn't been about that at all." I hold his gaze and am reassured he's mostly in agreement with me. "It was about the next level of connection, it was about getting beneath the layers. Don't you agree?"

He swallows thickly. "I think I understand."

"If you trust me, maybe we can open up the possibility of trying again."

He doesn't look convinced; clearly his past experiences still have him holding up a barrier to that.

"We can discuss it all, thoroughly. People set down hard limits, we could do the same. Even I have hard limits. Don't you?"

"Plenty," he says, growling.

"What do you think, then?"

"About what?" he asks, being facetious.

"About trying to get to that next level of connection?"

"By hurting each other?" He's still trying to worm his way out of making any promise.

"You know I don't mean that."

"Why don't you try it out on me first, so you can demonstrate what you mean?"

The idea doesn't thrill me, but I'm intrigued by his proposal. When I shackled him in Rio, it was because I wanted him to sit still and listen.

"You don't like pain," I remind him.

"Maybe I need to understand what you're going on about. Besides, physical pain isn't as bad as other types of pain, right?"

"I agree."

The waiter arrives to take away our plates and Ruben lets him know we're ready for dessert. Left alone again, I'm praying nobody has been listening in on our conversation. It doesn't seem like it. Ruben pours more wine for me and I drink it down, grateful of the fresh taste, taking the edge off the bitterness.

"How she was with it put me off. But maybe I'll enjoy it in a healthy way, who knows?"

"She didn't enjoy it in a healthy way?"

"She had a black heart, I thought," he muses, "and I'll never be able to describe how she was, but it was this insatiable need for rottenness. I don't ever want to go back there."

I reach over and stroke his cheek, my beautiful ring glinting in the light. He kisses my pinkie finger and smiles coyly.

"You can trust me, Ruben. With anything. I'll always do the right thing by you. I promise."

"Then let's try," he whispers. "Let's try."

I celebrate inside, praying for victory. If I could just get Ruben to see that him being my dominant could bring us even closer together, maybe I can unlock that next level and free him from himself.

Chapter Twenty-Eight

Lingering Questions

After a heavy lunch, we return home and head our separate ways for some time to think and get ready for the evening ahead. He heads off to the spare bedroom to relax and perhaps draw, have a sleep... think. I head to the pool area and sink back on a lounger, drinking strong English tea to clear my mind after our boozy, calorific lunch. I'm hoping it'll stand me in good stead.

As six o'clock nears and the sky turns blue-grey, the dogs press their noses into my sides and I get up from the lounger, grinning.

"Why do I even need a clock? All right, I guess I'd better feed you."

They're patient and happy as I prepare their food and fill their water bowl with fresh, life-giving liquid. I listen to their consistent munching and smile to myself. Perhaps Adam did me a favour, forcing me back home. I might have dragged Ruben around South America against his will, just to prove some kind of point, and it could've ended up driving us apart. Will we ever know how it might have turned out had we continued our adventure? I'm so happy to be home, I can't see myself leaving again for any kind of extended break—especially not anywhere so far away. It was awful thinking about my dogs being left alone for so long and not being able to jump in my car or hop on a quick plane ride to rescue them. They say it's the simple things, right?

I ought to have a plan for tonight, but I don't. I'm going to wing it and try to be creative. We're meant to be spending a little time apart thinking about our hard limits, but I honestly can only think of three, so that won't be hard for me. I have maybe a couple of soft limits, too. We'll see.

These past few weeks, since he came back into my life, I've been feeling dizzy with all the confessions, the recollections, the sharing... the emotional outpourings. It hasn't been just one of us, either. We've leaned on one another equally. It's been exhausting. It's been six weeks of near-constant shagging, tears, joy and sadness—plus everything in between. I'm hoping our engagement is the full stop on the whole reunion period and now we're putting that behind us and looking ahead to better times.

However, whenever I get a moment to myself, like right now as I watch the dogs feed and prepare for them to shoot outside, a couple of poop bags in my hands at the ready—it's in these quiet moments that a particular topic pops back into my mind and I'm left wondering an awful lot about this particular topic.

His family.

Alexia. Fred. Laurent.

Then Freddie, the infiltrator.

This is how I always try to break it down and find logic in the madness...

Ruben, trapped in Portugal with Alexia, found out in retrospect about Fred having had money troubles around the time he was having treatment for cancer. Not just temporary money troubles, either. There were three years between the chemo and Fred's death. Three years he spent trying to claw back whatever was lost, but for some reason didn't manage it, dying with those same debts which Alexia had to pay off posthumously.

Given what I now know about the way in which Alexia brushed a fuck-load of lies and murky dealings under her Axminster and Persian rugs, it seems obvious to me that Fred's debts had something to do with Laurent's death. I don't know if Ruben's put that together, or if he can't because he decided long ago it was drugs and that's that—but to me, it seems rather more than coincidence that Fred's livelihood and his health were at stake at the same time as Laurent was so obviously struggling mentally. The family business was going to shit and then Laurent dies before he's even finished his first year of university? This much bad luck doesn't blow down on one family all at once. It must boil down to a chain of events. It was all connected.

What did Fred do to Laurent to keep him quiet about Freddie's parentage?

I don't think I've ever known anyone more sadistic or fouler than Fred—the way he palmed off Debbie onto Freddie with twins already in her belly. Then continued fucking the young woman after she'd married his son.

Yet, Ruben always blamed Freddie for their brother's death—but was it as simple as sibling rivalry? Freddie told me Laurent was found with a needle hanging out of his arm, an enormous amount left in the syringe... his heart having gave out, like he'd meant to end it. But was he telling the truth? Freddie hadn't even known his wife was in love with someone else, so how the hell did he know how Laurent had died if he'd been ostracised from the Kitchener family by that point? He and Laurent both attended Cambridge, but it's unlikely they went to the same college. Not only was Laurent much cleverer, he was studying a different discipline to Freddie, the economics graduate. Did they socialise? Were Laurent's architectural pals much different to the money men Freddie was hanging around with? I imagine so.

So, I see it like this. Fred, the mob boss, was going through chemo and his enterprise was vulnerable. Freddie took advantage of that, stealing a chunk of the market for himself and cementing himself at Cambridge as the most reliable source of a good time. He was building the foundations of what would become something enormous—the El Chapo of London, the newspapers called him. He wouldn't have had time to concern himself with Laurent, he'd have been so busy. I wonder if the brothers even talked at all after what happened at Laurent's party.

Ruben wasn't around when it was happening. He was out of the country. Look at his relationship with Gia, who he never really knew at all.

It makes me wonder how well he even knew Laurent.

Laurent was seven years younger than Ruben and Ruben left home when he was eighteen. The two of them weren't in each other's lives towards the end. Indeed, young people change a lot as they go from school to university and beyond. Who was Laurent towards the end? Had he even joined the family business to help out an ailing Fred, but Ruben couldn't contemplate such a thing?

Is it regret that fuelled Ruben all those years? Vengeance for his brother? Or pure hatred for Fred and the operation he was running? Did he convince himself it was for the greater good, going after Fred? He was pretending to be doing good by supposedly running a charity in Laurent's honour—Laurent's Legacy—a label that made him look exalted and hid his own murky, underhanded deeds.

Has he ever owned up to the fact that he wasn't there for his brother during the last few months of Laurent's life? Did he never deal with it, at all? Instead, did he do everything in his power to place the blame squarely on someone else—probably Freddie? Because blaming Freddie or Fred made it easier to forgive himself.

Did he ever really forgive himself for not being around for Laurent while he was playing football abroad?

Was Laurent caught in some kind of crossfire between Fred and one of the people he owed money to?

Or did Laurent just tire of their messy lives and decide to end his own?

I don't believe Freddie tried to kill Laurent or that he enabled such a massive overdose. The day I spoke to him at his house, he seemed full of bravado and empty threats—a scared boy playing at being a big man.

Laurent wasn't ever a threat to Freddie. Ruben was. The eldest son stood to take it all. Laurent had always been happy to sit in Ruben's shadow, but Freddie? He might not have been so keen on the idea.

It's too much of a stretch for me to imagine that in the same year Fred had cancer, then overcame it, his youngest son died of an alleged overdose which was completely unrelated.

According to various sources, Laurent's overdose was a direct result of one young man's efforts to get so constantly off his face, he eventually took it too far—but is that oversimplifying a much more complex truth?

If Fred really had banished Freddie from the fold, then Laurent would've been given orders not to have anything to do with him, ever again. Not even to buy drugs from him.

So where was Laurent getting his drugs from after the brawl broke out at the hotel where I used to work? Had some sneaky rival started dealing to him and sold him a botch lot that led to his death? Was Laurent's demise a reprisal of some sort, from one of Fred's enemies?

I'm sure, now more than ever, Alexia holds the missing pieces that would explain everything—but she won't show her hand.

Why not, I constantly wonder?

Either she's trying to preserve her husband's far-from-shiny legacy, by not adding any more sin to the pile, or she's preserving herself—because she knows she'll lose Ruben forever if he finds out what was really happening in the lead up to Laurent's death.

My lingering questions are these:

Did Ruben ever find out what was going on with Laurent towards the end?

Does Ruben even know his own mother?

It was right to get rid of Fred, but what about Alexia? Why isn't she held accountable? Is Ruben blind, or doesn't he want to admit women can be just as manipulative, if not more so, than men?

Why hasn't Ruben put Alexia under the microscope?

Because from where I'm standing on the fringe of the Kitchener drama, she seems just as implicated as anyone else. And isn't it strange? How so many have died, yet she lives? She clings on... while everyone else meets their demise.

After picking up the dog poo, I go back into the house and the dogs follow, heading straight for their beds in the corner of the living room, having happily settled back where they used to sleep, now they're assured we're home for good and they're secure.

I rip a sheet of paper off the fridge notepad and write down my limits.

I head to the en suite and run myself a bath.

Taking a deep breath, I know exactly what role to play tonight.

God, what a thrill to know that man is entirely mine... and I'm going to be able to do whatever I want with him.

Chapter Twenty-Nine

A Breakthrough

He walks into the open-plan living area at seven on the dot, our prearranged time. I have some vol-au-vents in the oven that had been in the freezer for months but are still good. I think they were intended for an event at the gallery but ended up in my freezer somehow. They will be perfect to tide us over for a while.

"Wow, you look gorgeous," he says, striding across the space in just his black silk pyjama bottoms.

"I could say the same about you."

He looks like a veritable puma, his body lean and defined, except for those thick shoulders which he's been working on more and more.

He takes a stool at the breakfast bar and sits staring at me as I work off the foil on a bottle of champagne. I'm standing on the other side of the kitchen island.

I've straightened my hair and put it up in a high ponytail. I'm wearing dark plum lipstick and have darkened my eyes with make-up. I can feel him staring at what I'm wearing, too. Beneath a black silk kimono tied loosely at the waist, I'm wearing a black lace basque, matching thong, suspenders and lace-top stockings. I'm also wearing my killer Louboutin's. Literally... killer. My feet are killing me already.

"Can't we do this every night?" he asks, and I look up and see him stroking his chin, that dirty, dark look in his eyes.

I could stride right over to him as we are and lead him to the bedroom and he could kiss me and fuck me without any foreplay and it'd still be amazing...

...but this is about that extra dimension...

...taking it that one tier higher.

"We could but your knob would probably fall off," I return, winking.

He covers his mouth with a hand and tries not to laugh.

Jesus, how much more could I love that man's hands? And yet every day I look at them, and still wonder how the hell I don't spend all my time begging him to stroke his fingers between my legs because they're so damned elegant and beautiful.

I take a deep breath and pour the champagne. It's lucky I have something to distract me from wanting his hands because the vol-au-vents beep at the same time. I remove them from the oven and place them on a serving tray. Handing him a glass of champagne across the counter, I gesture at the sofas.

"Let's have a little chat, Ruben Kitchener. Shall we?"

I'm trying so hard to uphold an air of propriety and I think that shows because his eyes narrow and he doesn't try to even grab hold of me as I pass by him with the vol-au-vents.

Seating myself on the couch, he sits opposite me on my couch's twin and splays his legs, slouched in the seat... chilled as they come.

I take a salmon puff pastry thingy off the tray and pop it in my mouth. He watches as I eat and throw champagne down my neck.

His glass is quickly empty as is mine.

KARMA

"Would you mind bringing the bucket over, darling?"

"No, my love," he mutters, and gets up to retrieve the champagne.

I'm watching his butt the whole time, fixated on the way the black silk hugs his muscular backside to utter perfection. He turns swiftly and tops us both off.

Reaching into my pocket, I lift my eyes to his and give him a dark, seductive stare as I pull out my list of dos and don'ts. He purses his lips, returning that same look with an even more dark and filthy stare, his hand reaching into his pocket for his own list.

I push mine across the table and he reaches for it, flicking his own closer to me so I can pick it up off the edge of the chrome coffee table sitting between us. Holding his in my hand, I'm eager to read it but don't want to appear like I am. Neither does he, still holding his in front of him in both hands.

I unfold his list carefully and watch as he does the same. My heart is pounding once I've finally unravelled the paper in my hand, but I'm scared to actually lower my eyes and see what he's written. When his eyes veer downwards to view my list, I'm too intrigued to avoid it any longer and don't want to give him the upper hand.

His list is shorter than I thought it would be and only includes two things on the hard limits.

1. I won't rape or be raped
2. I don't enjoy water sports or Hot Karl (either giving or receiving)

I almost burst out laughing but somehow stop myself. I worry my lip incessantly instead.

Then there are his soft limits:

1. Making you bleed
2. Suffocation
3. Battery operated sex toys
4. Being unable to move any part of my body
5. Drowning (including waterboarding)
6. Electric shocks

A part of me is wondering if this is really it. Did he think it through properly?

"There's a lot I could still do to you," I murmur, not looking up at him.

"There's an awful lot missing from your list, you mean," he says, sounding surprised.

My list is rather short but a lot goes without saying. For instance, I think it's always been pretty obvious neither of us would enjoy feculence during sex. What I'm quite surprised by though is that he has mentioned a few more things on his soft list. So, he might be open to some of those, then? If I could persuade him. Is he also saying that he doesn't want to make me bleed but he would if I asked him to? He's basically telling me he's up for anything really, except the extreme stuff.

He reads my list out loud, I think to grab my attention. "No rape, no actual torture..." They're my absolute hard limits. Not ever. No way. "No sex or sex acts during menstruation." I look up and find him with one eyebrow raised. "You blew me once, remember?"

"I meant on myself, of course," I say hotly, and he smirks, knowing that already but wanting a rise out of me, I'm sure.

"And on the soft list no public sex, threesomes, orgies, swinging, girl on girl. Or foot fetishizing."

I burst out laughing and he can't help himself, either. I always found BDSM wildly funny when I used to do it with clients and it has to be said, I think that's what it's all about before you get down to it. You've got to face your own inhibitions and laugh about them. You're forced to scrutinize and it's just funny what we human beings will allow, after all is said and done.

"You've not included humiliation." I point at his list and stare at him with a blank expression. "Is that correct?"

"Correct, but what's wrong with feet?" he asks, throwing his hands up.

"They're feet and they shouldn't be worshipped. End of."

"I see." He has his eyebrows raised.

"So, are we ready to get on with things?" I notice a few vol-au-vents have disappeared while I've been studying his list. He finishes the last of his champagne and nods his head—he's ready.

I lift myself off the sofa and head towards the bedroom. He's following close behind, all fourteen stones of him treading heavily, his body pure energy and heat and masculinity.

Standing by the bed, I point at something I've laid out for him.

"Something for later?" he asks.

"Something for now," I tell him, gesturing it's for him—not me.

He's shocked and moves towards the outfit, handling it carefully. "Freya, you can't mean..."

"Your turn first, you said, and this wasn't on the list." His mouth turns upside down. "You didn't say anything about women's underwear." I knew he wouldn't because he didn't imagine I'd want him to wear my undies.

He takes a deep breath and sighs, knowing I've got him. I knew he wouldn't put cross-dressing on the list and now he knows that I'm one step ahead and have the upper hand. He's too predictable and I know him too well.

He steps out of his black silk trousers and I lick my lips, watching as he bends over and pulls a pair of frilly pink panties up his thick, muscular legs. When he turns, it's literally obscene, the way his cock and balls are squished inside the sheer material.

"Wow, honey. Pink is your colour."

"Freya, do I really—"

"Yes, now come on, you said you would..."

He huffs and pulls the next item of clothing off the bed. I picked this next piece out especially for him... a black suspender belt. He gets that on pretty easily, but when he sees the fishnet stockings, he baulks. He should be glad I couldn't find a bra that would fit. Nothing I own, even my elasticated bralettes, would survive Ruben's broad chest and shoulders.

"Now, now, my love. Fishnets are nice and stretchy."

He rolls his eyes and sits on the edge of the bed, pulling them up his legs with all the elegance of a bull trying to dress itself. I think I last wore those fishnets to a Halloween party when I was dressed as a naughty maid.

He has problems fastening the suspenders to the fishnets but I wait patiently, even though I'd happily get rid of these fucking high heels if I could.

Once he's triumphed over the clips, he stands up and twirls, the look in his eye one of fury and 'I can't believe I'm bloody doing this'.

"A couple of nipple covers and we could surely sell you for a buck or two, baby."

He puts his hands on his hips and I can tell he's never dressed like this before—ever. He never let anyone tell him what to do before he met me. Well, isn't that delightful?

"Nah, there's something missing," I decide, chewing my lip. "There's something..."

I move across the room and our eyes meet at the same level because I'm in skyscraper heels. The heat in his cheeks makes him look shy and endearing, but I know what's really going on underneath.

I gesture for him to sit in front of the dressing table on the stool and find a lovely pink lipstick for him, encouraging him to put it on. He does so with more panache than he pulled on the fishnets. Has he dabbled with lipstick before? Or perhaps it's the artist's touch?

I pick up the blusher and stand behind him, dabbing the brush in the powder and then sweeping a bit over his already flush cheeks, merely adding a little more shine. I offer him the mascara and he goes ahead, though he need not bother. He has longer lashes than any man has the right to possess, especially when he's already so beautiful.

"And how do you feel, my love?" I ask, stroking his shoulders.

"Silly?"

"Silly? Not sexy?"

"Nope."

"Come now, let's have you stand up, shall we?"

He stands up and faces me, looking awfully like a bit of a pantomime dame. His lashes are ridiculous and his cheeks too pink.

"I wasn't joking about the nipple tassels," I tell him, pulling a pair out of my pocket, holding them up in front of him.

I lick the underside of one and attach it to his body, then do the same with the other. He's wearing scarlet tassels and couldn't look any prettier.

"For the finishing touch..." I reach around the dressing table for something I prepared earlier. "Et voilà!"

I hand over a real feather duster and he takes it, lips pressed together, not sure how he should react. I do love an ostrich feather duster and this one I bought some moons ago now and it still hasn't worn out. It's great for getting into all the nooks and crannies.

"Follow me," I tell him, striding from the room.

He clomps along behind me, rather less enthused than he was before, when he thought we'd be getting down to some action instead of some housekeeping.

I stand in the middle of the living space and announce. "Okay, well, I noticed we are getting rather overrun with cobwebs, perhaps because Rosi isn't tall enough to reach, perhaps because we weren't living here for a month and the little critters thought they could move in with Adam and he wouldn't mind. Anyhow, if you'd be a dear and start work, I'd be rather thankful."

I turn on my heel and swan off to the lounge area, lifting my feet to the coffee table and pouring myself more champagne. Sinking back into the sofa without a care in the world, I even take up a magazine and pretend to be reading.

I want him to understand that this is how most men expect women to be. To look pretty. Smell pretty. But still do the cooking, cleaning, the running around—holding up everyone but themselves at the same time. And we gladly do it, because it's in most women's nature to nurture and nest and keep house. And we give not only moral and spiritual, but emotional guidance, as well. But in exchange, do you know what? We just want to be fucked. Hard. We want to be used like a ragdoll and feel appreciated. That's how it goes. After we work hard, we expect them to at least work hard in the bedroom and do something special in there. It's all we want. We'll do everything else... except that.

I look up and see him still standing there, having not moved. His brow is creased and he's not sure where to put himself even though I just gave him instructions.

"You could start with dusting around the lights."

"I'm trying to figure out what the point of this is," he states, his muscular body such a contrast to that feminine underwear.

I catch sight of a slight nip slip and have to stop myself staring and giggling at the same time.

"You think this is funny?" he demands, catching sight of my eyes.

Can't hide what's behind the eyes!

"I think I'd like my ceiling dusted. You've got longer arms."

He shakes his head and frowns even more deeply. "Come on, Freya. What's the point of this? It doesn't get you off, me dressing up in women's underwear."

"On the contrary, I'm highly tantalised by how obscene those underpants look on you."

He looks down at himself and almost chokes on a throaty laugh, displeased with the whole situation. His junk is so squished in there, his knob has had to be tucked dramatically to one side.

"You want to prove you're a man, right? Like all men do. You've passed the test. You're man enough to put on the get-up. Now, are you man enough to wave a duster around, or are you too chicken to dismantle a gender stereotype or two?"

His face changes instantly to dark and deadly. He's not impressed, at all.

I know that I could spank him, make him beg, edge him until he's begging me for release...

I could cover him in cream and make him stand on the doorstep outside looking like a tart in women's underwear as people pass by on the street... but none of that would really faze him.

Throwing him into a dynamic he's not comfortable with, well... that's how we get to the bottom of Ruben Kitchener.

The thing that'll be pissing him off the most is that he knows this is a test and he might not pass it, depending on how he responds. He can't put himself inside my head because he's not a woman. He's a man. What was it Alexia once said to me, the first time we met?

"He knows how to use his body and his mind, but only as part of a game..."

I want to know if among the lies she told, that was the one truth. After all, he made a highly successful career out of knowing how to play a game. At the end of the day, isn't it not just skill and strength, but tactics, too?

When he quit football, did he swap one game for another? Did he decide avenging Laurent would be his new career, or was it a little game for him to pursue, once he got tired of football?

My fear is that without the chase, the pursuit, the game... will Ruben get bored? Is he up to the task of living a normal life? Or will that never, ever be for him?

When I'm sure he's going to throw down that duster and come storming over to assert his authority over me, he grunts a displeased sound and pulls out one of the dining chairs from behind the table, positioning it beneath the ceiling lights. He has to stand on the chair as well as extend his arm quite far so he can reach, but he manages to get the lights and I watch as clumps of dust fall down.

Well, I told him they really needed doing, didn't I?

I doubt Adam was really living here while we were away. The place went to rack and ruin without anyone around. Adam would've been out on the pull every night, wouldn't he? And the poor dogs would've been sat here in the cold, wondering when their next bit of human contact would come.

Ruben attends to the other lights and then moves into the corners of the room, spluttering as cobwebs fall down and into his face. I try not to laugh, but I can't help a sputter or two. He gives me evils and carries on, cursing, "Rosi will be docked for this."

"No she will not, you'll buy her an extending duster, my dear. Blame the equipment."

He chews his mouth and appears highly unsettled.

"Is that me done, then?" he says in a stroppy tone, once he's finished.

I walk around and check the worst offending corners are clear. They are.

"Ten points," I tell him, "and you haven't even put a hole in the fishnets yet, but your nipple cover is looking a little..."

He looks down and sees it's fucking halfway down his stomach. I put my chin to my chest and hold in a laugh, but only just, as he adjusts the tassel to where it's meant to be.

"What's my next task, then?" he asks, looking impatient and annoyed.

He looks a treat, with his make-up, suspenders and bits of cobweb in his hair.

I press my thumb and index finger to my mouth and hold my mouth closed for a second while I wonder what to have him do next. Part of me wants to see how far I can push him before he snaps. I can hardly contain myself thinking about that.

I press the button for the doors to the terrace to open and they slowly fold to the sides. The dogs are still in their beds and look up.

"Stay," I command, and they grunt and bury their heads again.

"Wait on the lawn for me," I tell Ruben, "sans duster, of course."

"I'm not going out there." He looks mortified I'd send him outside.

"Whyever not? I'm going out there. I'll be along shortly."

Now, there's little chance anyone will see us, but there's still a chance. My trees have grown a bit wild and the nearest neighbour isn't home at the moment. However, if someone on the street were to pop their head above the six-foot-tall side gate, they might catch sight of us looking like this.

We engage in a bit of a stand-off of sorts, arms folded, before he harrumphs and heads outdoors. The solar lights are on but once the security light settles down, you can't really see him. While he's out there, looking severely hard done by, I quickly reach into the dog drawer and pull out a slip lead I once used with a dalmatian I was fostering and thinking of adopting. That experience fairly irrevocably put me off that breed for life. That was years ago, before I got my two French bulldogs. The lead is still like new, though.

"Stay," I remind the dogs, and the tone of my voice alerts them I'm serious.

I join Ruben on the lawn and find him in shadow, but obviously with his arms folded, unimpressed.

"Hands and knees, like a dog," I tell him.

As my eyes adjust to the darkness, I see his confliction in the way his face twitches and he chews his lip, not sure he can keep on with this.

Finally, he takes to his hands and knees and I slip the lead around his neck.

"You said no feculence, you didn't say I couldn't walk you, though. Off you trot, lad."

I can't keep a straight face as he trots around the grass. It's lucky for me it's dark and his head is down. I look around and don't see anyone peering over the boundary fences to stare. It's very lucky Adam isn't home anymore, too.

"A lovely evening stroll, how nice, and your knees won't shred on this nice soft grass."

Nobody touches my grass but me and I took great care in mowing it the other day, much to his annoyance. He told me, and I quote, *"That's a man's job."*

Did he think I was going to take his money four years ago and spend it all on salon visits, wardrobe refreshes and a fleet of cars? Not to mention an entire team that would be needed to look after this house if I didn't cook for myself, mow the lawn, tend the flowerpots and the roses... all of the garden, in fact. I even painted most of this house myself and used some very tricky software to take measurements for the new kitchen, bathrooms and built-in furniture. Everything inside it is me. I didn't hire an interior designer. I picked out everything, sans a husband. And it looks good. And I ran a gallery, all by myself. And I was making a profit, year on year.

I mean, what the hell do I really need a man for? I've survived all on my own, all these years, and I would've done quite well even if I hadn't had his hush money to tide me over.

"Isn't this nice?" I ask Ruben, my harsh tone demanding a response.

"Yeah, oh, it's wonderful," he breathes, circling the lawn and being well-behaved.

"You know," I say, failing to hide my amusement, "you could take a shit if you want, being that you are a dog and all. Pretending you hadn't fucked anyone during our time apart." I yank on the leash a little and he growls. "Pretending you were in Portugal to save me." I sound obnoxious and he snaps his teeth. "When you were actually just scared to love me, weren't you? Because it was easier with your silly games, chasing the bad guys and all that fucking nonsense. Making a home with me is what you really fear, isn't it? Admit it. Admit why."

He shakes his head and almost lowers it to the floor, aggravated like hell. He stops moving and threatens to rebel, still shaking his head, side to side.

"Because my home growing up wasn't a happy one," he says in a sharp, condescending way—the big man reduced, and hating every second.

"No, it wasn't," I agree, "but nor was mine. Keep making your excuses, fuckboy."

I lead him around the garden for another turn, but his teeth are gnashing and he feels abused and unfairly treated. He doesn't want me to keep returning to that topic.

"Fine, I don't have any excuses," he exclaims. "I am what you say I am. I'm a coward. I wanted him dead. I wanted them all dead. All the drug dealers and all the bad guys... I wanted them all annihilated. Yes, I couldn't stop myself. I wanted the pain to go away, but it hasn't. They're gone, but it hasn't."

He picks up the pace a bit, his head thrashing around on his shoulders, annoyed and reduced to this broken specimen of a man. I inhale deeply, taking the fresh evening air into my lungs, every ounce of oxygen keeping me upright and alive—strong enough to see this through.

"What you did was wrong. All of it was wrong. We could've escaped, you and I. But you wanted revenge. You wanted blood. You told yourself you were saving me, but you weren't. You were getting what you wanted." We're in deep now, playing this mind game. I'm agitating him and he knows that, but he also wants to spew his bile. He welcomes the chance to tell it like it is.

"He tortured her to find out where we were staying in Florence. He waterboarded her like he had Debbie..."

"Alexia?" I ask, squeaking.

"He threatened to pull her nails off. He made her stand naked as someone constantly hosed her with ice-cold water. He broke two of her ribs stamping on her. He threatened to rape her if she didn't tell him where we were. Of course, I had to take him down, Freya. I would do anything to protect you from a monster like him."

Alexia...

My god, how did she summon the strength to face that man again and put on the show she did at the funeral?

"So, you'd do anything to protect me, but not to love me?"

He stops right where he is in the centre of the lawn and turns his head up to look at me.

"You'd do anything to preserve me, but what's the good of that? If I'm preserved but not living. Why do you refuse to submit to your desire to possess me, when that's what we both want?"

"You know why!" His gaze is almost as fierce as his lashing tongue.

"Because you fear we'll become so utterly entwined, you won't be able to leave me again if it came to it. In fact, we'll be joined so tightly, you'll reveal just how possessive and territorial you can be and you fear it'll push an independent woman like me away."

"I've always feared that," he snarls, lifting slightly so he's not resting weight on his hands anymore. Instead he's up on his knees, hands on his thighs, staring up at me.

"You want to own a woman."

"Yes," he murmurs.

"To own her body, soul and heart."

"Yes."

"You want to unleash on her."

"Yes."

"So why don't you?" I snap, my quickfire round aiming to catch him unawares.

"Because I went there once before and I can't lie anymore. I loved Gia. Losing her was terrible." His chin falls to his chest.

"I've tried to protect you, and although what I had with her doesn't equal what I have with you, I don't want you to feel in pain, knowing I did love someone else." He bows his head and looks down at his hands, remembering what he was once capable of. "Yes, it was dark and we were depraved together. It was like a nightmare you'd wake up from every day, and you'd tell yourself it wouldn't happen again the next night, but it did. I loved her. It still hurts, what happened. I can't deny that. It hurts. I know what it's like to love someone and lose them and I'm terrified of it happening again. My kid brother was once my best friend in the whole world, but the truth is, who was he when he died? I don't know. Because I wasn't there! When Gia and Laurent died within months of one another, that was like someone handing me a gun and saying, 'It's fine, this shit happened to you, so you're off the hook. Whatever you need to do, do it.' That's how it felt."

"I see."

"I don't want you to know who I really am," he insists, spitting feathers, his face contorted with pain. "Not this gnarled corpse beneath the surface. You don't deserve that. So, just take whatever is left of me. Most couples have secrets and love each other despite them. Secrets from the past shouldn't inform the present."

"But that's not what love is," I remind him, putting my hand beneath his chin and lifting it so he has to look up at me. "I recognise all the mistakes you made and all the dumb fucking decisions you took on my behalf. I can imagine the things you haven't told me yet and guess at the stuff you may never admit, but do you know what? Love just is, Ruben. It's there, whether we want it to be or not. But even I have my hard limits. I'm not one of those people who can switch off entirely. I pretended to be for a long time, but I never was. Even I have a pain barrier, which you've tested many times. But sometimes the mistakes can be overcome through love, because it's strong enough, because ultimately, you want to dive in with that person and never let them go. You don't get to choose who you love. My heart chose you. You have to fight this impulse to keep yourself guarded, this notion that you're protecting me is bullshit, utter bullshit. Even when you lie and omit a truth, I still know. Don't you see? I'm stronger than you and more intuitive and more forgiving and I'm asking you to let go, to let me have—even if just for a few minutes in a blue moon—a piece of the real Ruben Kitchener. Don't you trust me to know my own limits? Don't you trust me to hold your heart even if it gets ugly? I never realised before how fucking introverted you are but you are, holding too much inside and never admitting just how much you carry. But you can be who you are and I will still love you. In my arms, can't you just be yourself, once in a while? Without any thought or preparedness or any of that. Once in a while, can't you just let go, for me? Like you did before. Because that's all I want from you."

Within seconds, I'm yanked down to the ground with him and he throws me to the floor.

The wind is knocked out of me and his eyes are wild. He presses his weight on top of me and I'm squashed until almost breathless. After getting rid of the lead, he rubs his palm over his mouth to wipe away the lipstick and brushes his cheeks against his forearms to remove the blusher. He yanks off the nipple tassels and grunts, tossing them away. He tears a hole in the front of his panties and I look down, gasping when I see his rampant erection freed from his underwear. I spread my legs in a hurry and his mouth and nose twitch with evil intent when he sees my knickers are crotchless.

He's inside me in one swift move. Then he pins my arms down, my legs are pushed back together, and I'm trapped as he shifts his legs outside of mine.

"I'm your master," he growls, "and you obey me. Do you agree?"

I nod my head.

"You're mine."

"I'm yours," I repeat.

Ruben uses the strength in his limbs to lever up and down, and within moments, I'm trying not to come as his cock surfs against my very sensitive clit and g-spot, all at the same time.

He slams one hand over my mouth and pins my arms above me with the other one. I scream against his hand as my walls squeeze around him, over and over again, yelling that I want him to stop. My cries go unheard as he presses his palm into my mouth and my tongue meets the thick flesh of the side of his hand.

He's not afraid to keep going even as I'm trying to push him out of me and he's constantly shoving himself inside, creating such a friction I'm sure my orgasms are rolling from one to another until it's just this jagged feeling, like my clit is now a firecracker and it's going to keep igniting itself unless he stops.

Once he's satisfied I'm depleted, that I can give him no more for the time being, he lifts his body off mine and I'm left sprawled on the ground. He shreds the clothes he's wearing as they're torn off and then he's just one naked towering inferno of a man, still exquisitely erect and fully himself again.

He takes the leash and puts it around my neck. "Inside, little princess."

I struggle to get up so he helps me, but as I'm crawling in a daze, he slides the kimono off my back and unclips my basque. In the end, I'm crawling my way inside with my tits swinging free and my arse mostly exposed.

And one of my limits was meant to be outdoor sex.

"You know where I want you," he growls, as I steer myself towards the bedroom.

The dogs look up and appear not to want to get involved. Ruben presses the button for the sliding doors to close, lobbing my kimono and basque onto one of the sofas as we're passing.

My insides are on fire and I don't think I could take any more if I wanted to. That was the roughest sex I've ever had with Ruben and the orgasms matched the style of his fucking, my insides pummelling around his enormous thick cock, which was relentless. It hurts to rub my thighs together and my belly feels like a molten rock, heavy and unnaturally gaping.

"You still love me?" he asks.

"Bastard," I groan.

"That's my girl."

We make it to the bedroom and I climb wearily up onto the bed, curling up into a ball. He takes the leash from around my neck and tosses it to the floor. My shoes got left behind somewhere, I don't know where, and I don't know if my knickers are even still on. When I feel him pulling them down my legs, that's when I realise they are.

"You always want more from me," he growls, "always more."

He tosses me onto my front and I bring my hands into my chest, holding them together, my face also pushed into the bed. I know what's coming next before it's even happened.

He slaps my bum so hard, the crack sounds like thunder. Then... the other cheek... and I'm burning. Salty tears leave the corners of my eyes.

He lifts my bum off the bed and I beg, "No, no!"

He shoves his tongue into my centre and I scream for him to get off.

I get a slap, silencing me.

The pain is so intense, everything has gone numb down there.

"Behave, little girl. Fucking behave."

He's wriggling his tongue into my vagina and I hate it when he does this, right after I've just come and it's beyond sensitive and too much. My clit is still throbbing and I couldn't bear it if he went there, too.

He soon tires of trying to coax anything from my weary pussy and enters my arse with his tongue.

A groan leaves me that makes me sound not myself and when he touches my clit with just the pad of his fingertip, that firecracker is brought instantly back to life and I jolt, screaming, coming, desperate for it to end.

When he gives up, I collapse on the bed and curl up again in the foetal position. I start shivering and shaking immediately. He lies behind me, spooning my body, and pulls the sheets and blankets over us. His arms are amazing as he wraps them around me, his body instantly warming and comforting mine.

Then he's kissing my shoulder and rubbing his erection through my crack.

"I can't Ruben," I cry, snivelling, "I can't!"

"You can."

He pushes inside me and I start crying. I can feel every inch of him and every inch of myself. I'm on fire, throbbing and aching. He moves slowly and tenderly strokes my clit. When I come again, it's the most awfully obliterating thing of my life, and when he squeezes my breasts hard and grunts in my ear, "Mine, Freya. MINE. Say it," I'm alerted to his real need.

"I'm yours. I'm yours," I cry, sobbing against his arm.

He shoots into me, biting into my shoulder and growling as he releases ream after ream of cum. I've never heard him sound so animalistic or forthcoming with how I make him feel.

In the aftermath he doesn't withdraw nor do his arms slacken around me. He keeps me tight inside his embrace and rests his chin against my shoulder, never letting go.

"I love you," he whispers.

I take a deep breath and shudder. "I love you."

"You're my precious girl and I absolutely adore you."

I nod a little and link my fingers through his. "Don't let go."

He leans over me slightly and turns me towards him, dropping a soft kiss against my mouth. The sparks inside me seem to hiss and die away with his kiss and everything melts and eases a bit. He pulls away and searches my eyes, checking I'm okay.

My pain is quite bad right now, but later the post-coital high will kick in and I will want more.

However, he's taken what he needed to and he's happy, so I have to be happy with that. Plus, my desires often cloud my judgement so that I overestimate just how much my body can cope with in one day.

I love that with him I can feel small and I can feel powerful, too. I love that I can taunt him but he will end up holding me, anyway.

He rubs his nose against mine and seems peaceful and serene.

"Freya?"

"Yes, my love."

"I honestly don't know which of us is more sadistic."

"Oh, me of course," I laugh.

He gives a chuckle and lies down behind me, throwing a leg over me to keep me trapped against him.

"Did I hurt you?" he whispers.

"Yes."

"Are you okay?"

"I will be."

"Why do you always try to make me mad?"

"You always try to hide your anger from me, but it's one of the strongest emotions."

"What do you mean?" he says, sounding suspicious.

"Anger is a direct result of something traumatic. Until you let go of anger, it can often prove to be a stopper on a lot of other emotions that need to get out, too. Lots of people turn to meditation or martial arts to work through anger, but we both know sex is your favourite activity."

"You know me so well."

"It's okay to admit you're angry."

"I'm furious," he mumbles.

"At what?"

"Our situation," he growls. "Having to be apart for four years and even now, I'm still not sure we're safe. The world treated me unfairly, even after I got rid of those toerags."

"I know." I kiss his hand. "I know."

"I do feel freed when it's like this."

"And what do you feel now you're freed?"

"I feel grateful. Sometimes I have to remind myself what I've got."

I roll over onto my back and he lies on his side, propping his head up on his elbow. I'm thankful of the cool sheets against my bottom, but I'm even more happy to see the look in his eyes.

He strokes his fingers down my cheek and looks at ease. "I'm grateful because you still want me, still love me. I'm grateful because you're an angel and a devil all wrapped up in one." I grin and so does he. "I'm grateful because you're breath-taking and I can paint because of you. I feel more whole because you understand me. You're deep and loving and smarter than anyone else I've ever known, and I really mean that, Freya. The way you coped... the way you dragged yourself out and held yourself up. That's not luck or anything like that. That's you, being so fucking strong."

Tears pour from my eyes. "I'm tired of being strong, Ruben."

"I know, angel. I know, baby," he whispers, stroking my cheek and placing a kiss on my forehead.

I move in closer and he lies back so I can put my head on his chest and he can wrap his arms around me. I have a little cry and he strokes my arms and my hair, my face and my hands.

"Just let me love you, Freya. Just let's stop, okay? Just let me adore you for the rest of our lives."

KARMA

I rub the tears out of my eyes. "I don't want you to be held back by your past, Ruben. I want you to let go."

"Day by day, bit by bit, I am letting go. It might not seem like it, but I am, Freya. Just stick with me."

"I just love you so very, very much, Ruben. You're my world."

"And you're mine, starshine. You're mine."

Chapter Thirty

The Dreaded Call

Two weeks later, and I'm sitting with my phone open, dreading the call I must make. I've been in the gallery office for half an hour already, having shut for lunch, and I've eaten my salad at my desk but made no headway at all in completing this call. I take a deep breath and press the green button.

"Hello?" she asks, uncertain.

"It's me, Freya."

"Oh... Freya. Hello."

Wow, I'm only her daughter. She could sound a little more enthusiastic to hear from me.

"How are you?" I ask, trying to push past the awkwardness.

"I'm okay."

She sounds tired... weary... not okay, actually.

"Have you heard from Adam?"

"Not in months," she says.

I could tell her and break her heart... or I could just not.

"I'm getting married," I exclaim, "in three weeks. I'd like you to come."

"Oh, that's... oh. I don't know, Freya."

"I see."

"I'm happy for you, though. I take it you're marrying Ruben?"

"How did you know?"

"I know my daughter, you'd have never married anyone else."

"True."

"I'd like to send something. Where should I post it?"

I clear my throat, trying to not sound disappointed. "Umm, send it to the house. Do you have my address?"

"I'll find it."

"Okay."

"How is Adam?" she asks, sounding nervous.

"He left, so... I don't know."

"Left, where?" she gasps. "I thought he spent summers with you."

"He robbed me of a load of money and left, so, your guess is as good as mine."

It sort of slipped out...

"Oh, Freya."

"Just my ego, Mum. The rest was only money. I don't know if he'd got himself into something, I don't know why... I only know it hurt."

"I'm so sorry. He's got too much of your dad in him."

"I was afraid of that," I sigh.

"I have to go, Freya. I've got a student arriving any minute—"

"It's three weeks on Saturday, Mum. If you change your mind, just come."

"You know I can't."

"Because of him?" I bark, trying to get a rise out of her.

She sighs, says nothing.

I'm afraid the fire I possess and which she once did too was long ago extinguished by his verbal and emotional abuse. She's a mouse. Squeaking now and again. Never reacting. Never provoking. Always staying small and calm, diffusing rather than effusing.

"If you change your mind, Mum just get on a plane and be here. Whatever the factors, just be here. But I won't have him—"

"That's exactly why," she says, "that's why. You know if I attend, he will make my life a living hell."

"So you'll miss your only daughter's wedding because of a pratt like him?"

"You'll be fine, you always have been. You're strong, you don't need me."

"No, but I want you there. Ruben's mother will be here. We want you here, too. We're trying for a baby, Mum. You might be a grandmother one day. This is your chance to be a part of that, otherwise..."

"You want children, Freya?" she gasps, shocked. "Is that such a good idea? With him?"

I shake my head, cover the receiver and curse the world. Her words linger and I almost hang up. In the background, I hear her doorbell go—so she is waiting on a student.

"Freya, that's my—"

"Mum, if you don't come, okay, that's fine. I'll understand. But I want you to know that the only way you'll be a part of your grandchild's life is if you show your support for our marriage, first."

"Freya, you're already talking as if—"

"You heard what I said, Mum. Now goodbye, and if you need money, all you have to do is pick up the phone. You know that. Okay?"

"Goodbye, Freya." She puts the phone down and I rest my head back against my chair and let the tears fall.

I cradle my belly even though I'm not yet positive I'm pregnant. While we were in Brazil, I seemed to have a bit of a period but now I'm not sure it was anything at all. I don't think I've bled properly in nearly two months. And something just feels different, but I'm too afraid to take the test. Too many good things are happening and this can't happen, too. You don't get everything you want in life. I know I've had all these bad things happen and maybe it's time good things did instead, but this has me feeling unsettled...

I want to live a life with Ruben, but I'm also scared that the balance of things is precarious and I don't want to rock the rickety old boat.

In what world does your mother refuse to come to your wedding because your idiot father isn't invited and would make life hell for her, just for attending her own daughter's wedding?

A rotten world, that's what.

Chapter Thirty-One

Finally?

M y wedding day. I can't actually believe it's finally arrived, but it has. My wedding... to Ruben, no less. The guest list is small, the ceremony simple and elegant, the reception afterwards intimate... what could possibly go wrong?

The villa is a hive of activity and I have to say, I'm happy to hide out down here in the bedroom until it's time to go. Ruben stayed in a hotel last night with his mother—they wouldn't say which, because they know only too well, I'd turn up pining for him or freaking out about the wedding—and I don't know who besides his mother he's got coming. I've not got many real friends down here, but I have invited who I know well from my work through the gallery.

There's a knock on the door of the bedroom and I bellow, "Yes?"

The wedding planner Carla tells me, "There's someone who wants to see you."

"No, I'm not up to seeing anyone. I'm not dressed," I say, dismissing the notion.

"She says she's your mother," Carla insists.

I turn in my chair, shocked, not willing to believe it. Carla nods.

"Let her in."

Carla backs out and my mother walks in instead. I'm utterly floored when I see her, especially because she's dressed up and misty-eyed.

"Freya," she cries, and I rush from my chair and into her arms.

"No, my make-up," I complain, "I spent hours on it!"

"As if you can't correct it, with your skills," she chuckles, holding me tight.

We pull back and she strokes my cheek. "When it came to it, I couldn't stay away. He's probably packing my things as we speak, but do you know what? Fuck him."

I cover my mouth and exclaim, "Mother! Such a foul mouth."

She shakes her head, her mouth a firm line. "It's not right, is it, Freya?" She takes a seat on the edge of the bed and I sit beside her. "I think when we talked on the phone I was in shock. I never expected you to marry because I didn't think you and Ruben would... Anyway, the more I thought about it... and then, do you know? When I told him you'd called to say you were getting married, do you know what he said?"

"No, but I'm sure—"

"He said he was sure the man must be insane and that marriage wouldn't improve you any, and I just thought to myself, you know? I thought, 'You're a bitter and twisted old pig and what can you do to me if I go?' So, here I am. And fuck him. Honestly, Freya. No. He's not stopping me from seeing my grandchild grow up, is he? No way."

I burst into tears and blub in front of her. She wraps her arms around me. On the one hand, I'm glad she's finally come to that conclusion, on the other I'm just so sad it took this long.

"Does he know yet?" she asks, rubbing my tummy.

"It's very early, I'm scared to mention it. He must know something is strange because I haven't had a period in weeks, but with all the wedding stuff going on, maybe he just hasn't noticed. I don't know."

"You've done a test?" she asks.

"Three."

She nods her head. "If you're like me the morning sickness will kick in soon and you won't be able to hide it."

"He wanted us to go on honeymoon to the Maldives but I suggested a few days in Paris instead. We can do the Maldives next year, once things have calmed down."

She chuckles, shaking her head. "No, my dear. It'll never calm down after this."

I laugh and throw my head back. She squeezes my hand and we find each other's eyes.

"You're happy, I can tell," she says.

"I really am."

"Then run with it, Freya."

"I really want to, Mum. But I'm scared it's all too good to be true."

"When you really care about something, yes, it's scary. The nerves kick in. You feel sick just at the thought of something going wrong. But never be afraid of feeling scared or anxious or worried, that means you have something to care about and hold onto... it means it's real."

I take a deep breath. "Okay."

"Do you want me to go? Shouldn't you be getting into your dress now?"

"Yes, I should be… it's been a nightmare. I kept losing weight! Thought you were meant to put it on."

"Oh, been there," she says, "don't worry, you'll be going in the opposite direction soon enough."

"Come on, then. Help me with my dress."

I bring it out of the closet and lay the dress on the bed. Mum's eyes widen and she gawps.

"Wow, Freya. It's beautiful."

Ivory lace dominates the huge, puffball skirt. I had it sent down from Paris and altered here, much to the atelier's chagrin. The ruched bodice is snug and just about manages to hold my growing bust in place without a bra. The matching veil is short and simple. We're marrying in a church so it's just for tradition more than to complete the look. I'm wearing my hair down because Ruben loves it best this way and I've done my make-up smoky and dramatic because he fell in love with me when I used to enjoy making myself up like this every day.

"If you just turn around while I step into it," I say, so she doesn't see the white knickers, garter and stockings I have beneath this robe.

"Of course," she giggles, the moment slightly awkward.

I arrange the dress in front of me and step into the skirt, pulling it up around me. I push my arms into the straps and have it almost decent, pulling the zip up slightly to cover my underwear.

"If you could just do the zip the rest of the way, and the buttons, Mum."

Once I'm fastened in, I turn and look at her. She steps back and looks me up and down.

"You're a princess," she says, "a fairy-tale princess. And you love him, don't you, Freya? He's the right man for you."

"The only man," I tell her, so sure of that.

She nods her head fast. "We can talk later, okay?"

"How did you find out about everything, anyway?" I ask, because since she knows we're pressed for time, she must have found out what time the wedding is taking place—but I never sent her a formal invite.

"I'm staying in the same hotel as Ruben and his mother. I think Ruben was dying to call and tell you I'd arrived but I asked him not to because I wanted to speak to you today, properly."

"Wow, coincidence!"

"Not really," she says, shrugging, "it's just that it's the best hotel in town... and I thought I may as well splash out if this trip was going to end my marriage."

When my mother wants to be, she can be hilarious and deadpan. I used to think she was this tiny squeaky mouse and I believed for so many years she was weak. But now I actually think she was strong for staying with him. She gave him chance after chance. I expect after a while, the chances run out... and some things like being able to be a grandmother can be deal breakers. My mother isn't an entire pushover. Her silence was often her strength. Remaining who she is beneath despite the damage done to her is a sign of her resilience.

"She's a strange one, that Alexia," she says, as though pondering something.

"Shake her and the medicine cabinet would fall out."

"No, I don't mean like that," she says, shaking her head, lips pursed. "I mean, she's very ill, obviously, but there's something much more than that... something odd."

"You think so?" I ask, intrigued.

I do wonder if, when women get older and acquire their crone status, whether they can see much more than us younger ones—full of hormones and trying to beat the biological clock, blinkered by the need to be fabulous and young and have it all.

"I don't think she's quite all there, Freya."

"You're going to have to be more specific," I demand, still interested in her opinion, but also irritated by her keeping me in suspense. "I've always found her to be a little disconnected and mysterious, but she's bound to be a bit broken having been married to Fred for so long."

Truth be told, I've always admired Alexia in ways I never could express. She's incredibly stylish, artsy and beautiful. She's a strange soul, though, I agree.

"It's more than that, Freya. I'm an artistic type, too. Don't get me wrong, I'm a specialist in my field, too." She scrunches her face up. "It's just that I think she's an utter fantasist. And I can understand why. But you and me, Freya, we were always able to be honest with one another, even when it hurt, weren't we?"

"I agree."

"But Ruben panders to her in that respect, like he can't bear for her to have to face reality."

"She's been through so much, Mum. She lost her youngest son. Her husband was a murderer and a bully. A misogynist, a violent criminal, a serial cheat. She probably knows Fred has a bunch of kids out there fathered out of wedlock, many more than we will ever know. We both know my father would never have done that to you, he's too cowardly, but imagine all the terrible things Fred did stacking up... she's bound to have found ways of coping that don't necessarily make sense to you or me.

She must rather live in ignorance than admit to herself what he was really like. And trust me, Ruben and I talked about this... he knows as well as us she's in denial about who Fred really was. He knows. It's a wedding, though. He'll just be trying to keep her balanced for the day."

"No, it's still more than that," she says, shaking her head. "After years with your father, and now with Adam having done what he did, I just think... she can't be trusted, Freya. There's something about her. Something that isn't balanced. And I don't mean her mental health. I mean, something absolutely fundamental. I think if it came to it, she'd toss Ruben to the wolves if it meant she might get away scot free. You know what I'm saying, don't you?"

I nod my head slowly. "I absolutely have my reservations about her, too. Believe me. I'm on my guard."

"Good, that's all I wanted to hear," she says, before unceremoniously leaving the room so I can get my shoes on and get my bag ready.

I think what my mum didn't want to say out loud is that she suspects Alexia to be a bad person. Maybe even a terrible person masquerading as weak in order to lull people into a false sense of security.

Say one thing for my mum, she's not stupid. I know everything good inside me came from her, including my wits and my instincts.

I take a deep breath, tuck my handkerchief laced with lavender oil into my dress and shake my hair out down my back.

"It's time to do this," I tell myself, grinning into the mirror and deciding just this once, perhaps I will be a fairy-tale princess.

I'm about to go down when there's another knock on the door. "Oh, god, what now." I'm cursing to myself when I open the door and see Carla, holding a package. "This came for you. The delivery man said it needs to be opened urgently. I told him, but—"

"Okay, okay. I guess the bride is expected to be fashionably late. Give me two minutes." I'm about to shut the door when I turn back and ask, "Carla, is my mother still here?"

"No, she left a few minutes ago. Says she will see you there. She doesn't want to draw attention to herself."

"Ah, okay."

I can understand that. I hadn't expected anyone to walk me down the aisle, but at least I would've liked her to come in the car with me.

I sit on the edge of the bed and rip open the small cardboard box Carla just gave me. It seems odd. Two minutes later, and I may have already been on my way to church and missed this delivery... it can't be that important.

Inside the box, there's a lot of bubble wrap. Inside that, after unravelling it all, a USB stick. This isn't getting any better, is it? Written on the stick in black letters are the words **PLAY ME** and as I turn it over, I read **OR ELSE**.

I haven't got time for this. I throw it onto the bed and head for the door.

But something's nagging me.

Has been nagging me for ages, ever since he came back into my life.

Did Freddie's death really eradicate any danger that still lingered?

Or not?

I find my laptop on the nightstand, power it up and stick the USB in the slot. Within seconds, one file pops onto my screen. It's a video.

I don't know if I have the bottle to click on the little thumbnail and find out what's inside this video file. It could be from my admirer, the one who bought the paintings, begging me not to marry Ruben.

Or it could be Adam... trying to wreck my day.

It could be anyone.

Somebody out there doesn't want me to be happy, or else, why send this? Technology is way beyond my father's capability, but...

Best for me to find out.

I open the file and frozen on the screen is an image of someone I find familiar but am unsure of. It could be anyone. I press play instinctively, wanting to figure out who it is.

"Hello, Freya," he says, *a fancy bedroom behind him.* *"Remember me? You ruined my life. Or do you not recall... probably not."*

I feel a chill run down my spine and slam my hand on the keyboard, pausing the video. I know exactly who that is. But why is he contacting me now?

"When we first met, I realised you didn't have any concept of who you were marrying in Ruben. That was four years ago. I would've thought when it didn't work out the first time, you'd have realised it was a bad idea... but you're so stupid, aren't you? He comes running back and you're unable to say no. Four years pass and it's like you learnt nothing."

I pause it again. There are only sixty seconds left... sixty seconds too many. This cannot be good. I press play.

"I thought you'd see sense, but no. He and I were once so alike, you know? We'd fuck the same girls. Man, sometimes we even did it at the same time. We'd do lines off the same girl's tits and put our cum in the same hole. We pissed and shit and fucked in front of one another, shared the same bags of drugs and screwed around, all over London together... and suddenly one day he thinks he's better. But he isn't, let me tell you. I know the real Ruben Kitchener." His neck twitches and he looks like pure hate incarnate. "I'm here to tell you today that if you marry that cunt, you will never see your brother again."

I pause it again, freezing the frame. The bastard is holding up a photograph of Adam. My brother is pictured going about his day, the shot taken from a distance. Like whoever took this was stalking him, noting his routines and things... like a private detective would. I press play.

"I know you want to know what happened. I know you're aching to know. Especially now." He glares at the camera and pouts. "In fact, I know exactly where Adam is. But first thing's first." He holds up a gun in front of him and looks into the camera suggestively. "Get in your car right now, leave him at the altar, and come to me. Be assured, there will be people watching to see what you do. One false move and I go find Adam. But if you do as I say, and drive out towards Cannes, I will ring you with further instructions. And we can solve all of this, like old friends. You know what needs to be done."

Without thinking, I know what needs to be done.

It's time this ended, once and for all.

It's only myself that can end it.

Me.

KARMA

TO BE CONCLUDED . . .

THANK YOU!

If you liked this book, please show it some love with a review!
Turn the page for a snippet from **KILLER** – the conclusion of
the *Legacy Trilogy*.

Excerpt from Killer, Book Three

The next day, we're in Adam's loft room and Della is wearing a gown Adam went out and purchased. It's a formal gown befitting of a concertmaster, the first chair violinist of an orchestra. It's crimson silk, structured, clutching her petite frame, the huge skirt hiding her tiny bottom half, including the little spindly legs she so fondly dresses in tight-fitting jeans or slacks most days. She's a beautiful woman, but nothing like Freya. Freya has thighs that could crush walnuts and she's tall. Della is not even a miniature Freya. She's not Freya. The two, mother and daughter though they are, are not the same. Freya has the appearance of a Boudica or an Amazon, she's light-haired but with some of Delphine's brown streaks peeking out from under the dozens of layers of thick, wavy hair. Della's hair is arrow straight, short, tucked behind her ears. She has sharp features whereas Freya's are rounder, fuller, her mouth plump, eyes wide. Della is a doll, while Freya is a bountiful woman of epic proportions. I wondered when we first met if I would ever be able to satisfy her. Then it became so that I knew I had to satisfy or I'd die. It became that eventually it wasn't about whether I was good enough, but whether we could be together in happiness without other people trying to fuck us up.

Della is in the green velvet wingback which complements the colour of her gown completely. She's sitting beneath the

Velux window with the light pouring through. Resting on her lap is her priceless Stradivarius, which an admirer gave her years ago. Della never mentioned its worth to James, obviously—and especially not that she'd entertained a little flirtation with another man.

"Freya told me the story about your violin," I mutter, as she looks off into the distance.

"He was a wonderful man. I should've married him."

The story goes that Delphine met the man, a German conductor, at the Royal Albert Hall where they were due to work together—intimately. That's how close the relationship is between conductor and concertmaster, so I am told. It would have been the breakout role of her career. She fell so immediately in love with him, she knew if she stayed, things would progress. Freya was ten years old but Adam still a baby and she feared James would seek custody on the grounds of her many stints on a psych ward. She knew she'd be unable to hide an affair, and she knew how James would be if he found out. She didn't work with the conductor, but they would meet in passing now and again, each time the connection unbearable. She eventually took delivery of the Stradivarius... and never saw him again, though she's never let that thing out of her sight since. We heard the conductor died a few years back—natural causes—he was twenty years Della's senior. I wouldn't be surprised if a staunch, Catholic upbringing convinced Della she should stay with her husband, no matter what.

Delphine reminds me of a much younger Harriet Walter. Such expressive features. A class act. Compact and nothing wasted. The artist's soul inside her is unmistakable; the breeding impeccable. She has the most extraordinary hands—long, gnarled fingers, wizened but strong. Often, she wears a wrist brace, but the intent is still there. I'm eager to get her hands right more than anything else. I'll have to stay awake all week to get this done on time.

"I've wanted to ask you about something," I mumble, working on her outline first.

"Go on."

"Have you got a picture of Freya from her ballet days?"

"I'd have to check." Her expression falters slightly, perhaps as she tries to remember. The forehead wrinkles, the brow furrows, the little lines around her mouth pucker.

"She keeps a painting in the safe. It's a ballet dancer. Once when we fell out and she tried to leave me, all she took was a few bits and bobs, including that painting."

Della smiles quietly and looks down at her lap. I wait for her to recompose before I continue with the outline.

"Why do you want a picture of her like that?"

"Honestly?" I chuckle.

"Of course."

"So she has a new favourite ballet dancer picture to come back for..."

Books by the Author

Kismet (Legacy #1)
Karma (Legacy #2)
Killer (Legacy #3)
Bad Friends (Bad #1)
Bad Actor (Bad #2)
Bad Wife (Bad #3)
Bad Girl (Bad #4)
Bad Guys (Bad #5)
Bad Lover (Bad #6)
Bad Exes (Bad #7)
Bad Night (Bad #8)
Bad Endings (Bad #9)
*this series is available to read in 3 box sets
The Contract (Nightlong #1)
The Fix (Nightlong #2)
The Risk (Nightlong #3)
Surviving Him (Crimson #1)
Becoming Me (Crimson #2)
A Fine Profession (Chambermaid #1)
A Fine Pursuit (Chambermaid #2)
Chambermaid's Tales (short stories)
Angel Avenue
Beyond Angel Avenue

Printed in Great Britain
by Amazon